Humble In Victory

A PRESCIENT WAR-AT-SEA NOVEL BY

Rear Admiral Peter B. Booth
U.S. Navy retired

[handwritten inscription] TO ~~[struck out]~~ Reminda: all [ ] ! my absolute favorite novel

D1601053

Dedicated to the seagoing sailors of the U.S. Navy, past, present and future, and to the brave families so often left behind on the home fronts.

"It's all about real Americans doing the tough job 24/7 for Navy and country with honor, patriotism, courage and sacrifice."

ISBN: 0-9713866-0-9
Published by Dockside Publications, Inc.

Printed by Trent's Prints
www.trentsprints.com
Pace, Florida
850.994.1421

Authored by Peter B. Booth
www.peterbbooth.com
pbooth@bellsouth.net
850.456.2400

Title from the NAVY FLIERS' CREED
"I shall be humble in victory."

Cover: A montage of the American flag, the Naval Academy crest, the logo of the Red Ripper fighter squadron, my Dad's well-stained silk flying scarf, a symbolic number-one Blue Angel and the gold wings and helmet of a United States Naval Aviator. Photographed using the author's old Nikon film camera on a sun-dappled morning overlooking Pensacola Bay.

Other books by the author:

True Faith and Allegiance: A Naval Officer's journals spanning three-and-a-half decades (2004).
Sea Buoy Outbound: An all-maritime journals, half USN and half civilian, on and about the seas and oceans of the world (2008).

AUTHOR'S NOTES EIGHT YEARS FOLLOWING PUBLICATION

Humble in Victory is a great read with a covey of powerful and believable characters and a fast-moving plot that grabs the reader at every turn. Published on 9/11/01, it looks ahead to a ten-day period in November of 2010 and a gender-equal U.S. Navy engaged in deadly combat against an unlikely trio of Iraq, Saudi Arabia and Iran seeking control of the Caspian Sea oil riches. The centerpiece is the carrier USS *Ronald Reagan* and one of its embarked fighter squadrons, the Red Rippers. It bounces out to the hometown men and women left behind on and about idyllic Summerset Lane in Virginia Beach, to the interior of a combat-oriented China and to multiple venues within the beltway including a tearful president and the inner sanctums of the Pentagon. But, always, it returns to the complex web of seething human emotions deep within the giant carrier and its brave women and men facing the unknowns of unconstrained mortal combat. Astoundingly, most of the author's assumptions from the years 2000/2001 have come true including women on the front lines of tough combat while many of the men folk guard the home front, China's insatiable quest for oil and true combat readiness, crooked politicos and maybe, even, missing nukes.

Only a few weeks ago, in late 2009, I reread the novel not having opened it for seven years and was blown away, knees shaking on occasion, eyes watering on others. I think that most readers who finish a book and close the last page spend a moment or two giving it a subjective assessment; good, bad, great or so-so. With Humble, I knew it was a one-of-a-kind — <u>an absolute winner</u>! When someone asks me what the book is about, I tell them, **"It's all about real Americans doing the tough job for Navy and country with honor, patriotism, courage and sacrifice."** I don't bother to mention the crooked politicos or greedy arms merchants or a few who were clear cowards in the face of a tough enemy. The one-liner on my business card states simply, **"Humble in Victory — a prescient war-at-sea novel circa 2010."**

SOME READER COMMENTS:

I realize that putting reader comments into the front of a book is a bit presumptuous, but here are a very few: I have kept a loose-leaf notebook some four-inches thick of written reader comments from several hundred readers and about three-dozen full reviews so the abbreviated list below could go on and on. Lots of happy readers—around 4,500. "Could not put it down," is an oft-repeated accolade. More feedback at the web, peterbbooth.com.

- "You have written a great story and I congratulate you. I enjoyed your tale and look forward to the next one." VADM Bob Dunn, retired USN, Naval Aviator and author.
- "I read it over a week or so after we transited the Suez. Nicely done, it was hyper-entertaining. I had to force myself to put it down to get some sleep every night." LCDR George Michaels
- "Not since Richard McKenna's The Sand Pebbles has a former sailor so aptly captured the complexity of life on a warship." Dr. Carlos Diaz, MD; former senior medical officer on a super carrier.
- "Move over Tom Clancy and Clive Cussler. There's a new kid on the block." Dr. Ron Evans, Ph.D
- "I really enjoyed it — most interesting. It was a good and fast read, which I like — you did a fine job of writing. Congratulations." Nancy Ann Chandler, businesswomen, Dallas.
- "... your novel IS a good read." Tom Cutler, U. S. Naval Institute Press. Annapolis.
- "Booth's experiences in the cockpits and deck plates serve him well in the book and his recounting of day to day life on the boat as well as combat in the air are extremely well done; the tales are well told, on a par with the better military adventure writers of to-day." Wayman Dunlap, editor, *Pacific Flyer*.
- "A lively tale . . . you kept your large cast and a complicated plot in good order and, it was a 'fun read'. What an epic film this will make!" Allan N.Hall, retired master, St. Paul's School.
- "I thought it was great! Being an avid reader all my life, if a book doesn't grab me in the first chapter, I don't finish it. It grabbed me from the first page!" Captain Bob Park, Tampa Bay harbor pilot.
- "Pete Booth is a gifted storyteller. His timely, fascinating and plausible stories are masterfully woven into a colorful tapestry,

showing a giant U. S. aircraft carrier at sea in harm's way, is entertaining, educational and enlightening . . . a remarkable novel and glimpse into the near future." Jack (retired cadiologist) and Carolyn Fleming, both authors. Pensacola, Florida.

• "I tend to evaluate novels based on one criterion: after the last page, do I wish for more? After 452 pages, the answer is rarely yes. For 'Humble in Victory' the answer is an unqualified yes. As a military thriller, it achieves greatness." Lance B. Young, West Florida Literary Association. Pensacola.

• "I read and <u>very much enjoyed</u> your book. It is preposterous to suppose that men and women can be put together under close quarters for months at a time and not have all sorts of disruptive activity antithetical to combat readiness inevitably take place . . . Congratulations on a nice piece of work." Lloyd E. Williams, Jr. Attorney, Chicago.

• "Pete: Usually when I take a book to bed, I manage 5/6 pages before the sandman hits. But not the case with "Humble in Victory." Three nights (452 pages later) I was done. Two words; 'BRAVO ZULU'." Lieutenant Commander Hugh McCabe, USN.

• "I <u>thoroughly enjoyed</u> reading Humble in Victory. My wife has True Faith and Allegiance on her Christmas List--looking forward to the read." Joe Webber, author, Pensacola.

• "Humble in Victory is a fast-moving yarn that takes Naval Aviation into a fascinating future." Admiral Jim Holloway writing in the Fall 2001 issue of *Wings of Gold.*

• "I am so glad that idiot female president got what she deserved. I personally would have hung her from the nearest tree. All in all a great book." Tracy Taylor, flight attendant,

• "You have written a most exceptional book! WOW! You have hit close to home as to what might happen. Thank you for a most exhilarating read. Dan Lower, Forrestal shipmate.

• "Just finished your book and enjoyed it immensely. Your writings are far more subtle than mine would have been, but often subliminal suggestions gain more converts that being overtly aggressive in one's writings. The depth of your evaluation of women at war was quite good." Dr. Jack Moore, former flight surgeon.

• Once I started, I could not put the book down. I don't think Humble is futuristic, I think we are there now. And no middle-aged female admiral is EVER going to fall in love with a Chinese general at first sight!" Glenda Anderson, HS English teacher.

SPECIAL DEDICATION

Dedicated to the thousands of brave souls who perished as innocents and in the line of duty on the morning of the eleventh of September, 2001. At the printers that fateful and tragic day, *Humble in Victory* reminds us as well, of the awesome duty of so many of our nation's young warriors in the months and years to come with the hope that America will always remain militarily viable and strong — a total commitment to the toughest, meanest and leanest combat fighting force possible and a will to win second to no organization, nation or person.

Thanks

Though this tale is a product of my sometimes vivid imagination and non-traditional background, it is too, reflective of many folks who offered pragmatic, useful and occasionally, essential insights. In early drafts, there were three who attacked the manuscript with substantial broadsides and to whom, I am grateful. First, a retired Rear Admiral who prefers to remain anonymous. Second, a younger Naval Academy graduate and Pensacola attorney, Richard Jesmonth. Finally, Tom Cutler of the Naval Institute Press who asked me if I wanted "platitudinous rhetoric" or "constructive criticism."

Several major iterations and months later, I found myself indebted to the equally constructive comments of retired English Professor David Betts, who, at one point, looked me square in the eye and said, "Pete, it's not ready for publication." It was back to the drawing board, again assisted by Stacie Toups of nearby Milton, Florida, a person of amazing attention to detail, proper English and punctuation. In later renditions, I am thankful to Roz Fisher of the University of West Florida Diversity Office, John Dotson, my flight training compatriot and Houston attorney, the same anonymous Rear Admiral, Richard Jesmonth again, and to my number-two daughter, Renee Whitley. Rear Admiral Paul Gillcrist was generous in his time and useful insights from the perspective of a most successful author and Navy fighter pilot. Former naval aviators — Mike Wilson, Paul Stevens and Jim Constantine — provided valuable insights and encouragement. Bonnie Glenz, one of the first WAVES, went "above and beyond" in her efforts to smooth the manuscript. The cover design is a product of Viola Jackson-Reese, an unassuming lady of generous talent. Richard Williams crafted the cover's final artistry. I am lucky in the final rendition to have had the benefit of the ultimate proofer and local author, Rebel Lowrey Covan. Energetic Lyn Zittel put it all together under the auspices of Dockside Publications. Finally, I am indebted to my wife Carolyn, who gave me the love, support and understanding to press on.

CHARACTERS IN ORDER
OF APPEARANCE

Δ **Lieutenant Becky "Big Sister" Turner**: Red Ripper fighter pilot, mother of two, married to the lawyer, Rick Turner. Lives in paradise with "Twidget."

Δ **Lieutenant Scott "Twidget" Jacobs**: Back seat wizo and roommate to Becky Turner. Single. Lives in paradise.

Δ **Captain Tommy "Jaws" Boone**: Commanding officer of the nuclear-powered aircraft carrier USS *Ronald Reagan* a n d husband of Beverly Demming Boone.

Δ **Rear Admiral Nancy Chandler**: Pentagon-based boss of the Reagan battle group, assistant to Vice Admiral Stan Sarodsy and confidant of President Virginia Roberts Stallingsworth.

Δ **Ensign Karen Randolph**: Bachelor roommate of Ensign Patty Butts. Lives in paradise and is the top officer of the deck of the Reagan.

Δ **Commander Angela Batori**: Executive officer of the Reagan. Married to Commander Rock Batori, skipper of the Barking Dogs steath fighter squadron aboard the Reagan.

Δ **Beverly Demming Boone**: Wife of the CO of the Reagan and daughter of retired Vice Admiral Bruce Demming. Lives in Virginia Beach with two high school daughters.

Δ **Vice Admiral Stan Sarodsy**: The combat arms director on the Navy Pentagon staff reporting directly to the Navy CEO. Responsible for anything to do with war fighting.

Δ **Lieutenant Commander Stan Miller**: The up-through-the-ranks weapons officer of the Reagan responsible for all ship defenses and weapons. Reports to the ship's XO.

Δ **Lieutenant Evelyn "Bikini" Swagger**: Back-seat wizo in the Red Rippers and the paradise roommate of Lieutenant Sam "Studs" Newman, her pilot.

Δ **Lieutenant Sam "Studs" Newman**: Red Ripper fighter pilot and roommate and pilot for Swagger.

Δ **Commander Wendy "Iron Lady" Montrose**: Red Ripper commanding officer, fighter pilot and former spouse of Bill Montrose back in Virginia Beach. Three children.

Δ **Lieutenant (junior grade) "Pistol" Pete Dawkins**: Lives in paradise. Bachelor. Flies as wizo with the Ripper skipper, Commander Montrose.

Δ **Ensign Patty "Gumshoe" Butts**: The Red Ripper non-flying intelligence officer. A bachelor, she lives in paradise with Ensign Karen Randolph. Mother is the Director of Naval Intelligence in Washington, Rear Admiral Sally Butts.

Δ **Lieutenant Commander Dave "Blues" Anderson**: Acting executive officer of the Red Rippers and former Blue Angel, he rooms and flies with Lieutenant (junior grade) Nancy "Shorts" Flanagan.

Δ **Sandy Anderson**: Wife of Dave Anderson. A teacher, she lives in Virginia Beach with her two preschoolers. Close friend of Beverly Boone. Lives three houses from Rick Turner, husband of Becky Turner on board the Reagan.

Δ **Lieutenant Commander Lori Miller**: Maintenance officer for the Red Rippers and back-seat wizo. Lives in paradise. Marches to a unique drum beat.

Δ **Master Chief Randy McCormick**: Maintenance chief for the Red Rippers and long-time Navy veteran. Recently married for the first time to the swash-buckling Suzette.

Δ **Bill Montrose**: The ex of Commander Wendy Montrose living next door to the Boones. School administrator. Single dad to three kids at home.

Δ **Vice Admiral Bruce Demming**: Father of Beverly Boone and Susan Randolph. Former combat arms director in the Pentagon and expert in stealth technology and China. Works as a consultant for Killington Associates.

Δ **Lieutenant Susan "MA" Anthony**: American Air Lines co-pilot, wife of Lieutenant Mike Anthony, mother of two, sister of Beverly Boone and second daughter of retired Vice Admiral Demming. Recalled to active duty, she becomes a pilot with the Red Rippers.

Δ **Lieutenant Mike Anthony**: Recalled reserve fighter pilot, FedEx pilot and husband of Susan Anthony. He and his wife room together in paradise.

Δ **Rick Turner**: A Virginia Beach lawyer and husband of Lieutenant Becky Turner of the Red Rippers. He lives near Sandy Anderson with his two small kids.

Δ **Lieutenant Panky Pachino**: An instructor wizo in the shore-based training squadron who is called to join the Red Rippers. A bachelor, he is a close friend of Ensign Karen Randolph. Assigned to fly with Lieutenant Susan Randolph as her back-seater.

Δ **Suzette McCormick**: The oft-married spouse of the Red Ripper maintenance chief and long time bachelor, Randy McCormick.

Δ **Master Chief Mitsi Moore**: The command master chief and senior enlisted person on the Reagan.

Δ **Admiral Carolyn Sweeney**: The CEO of the Navy working in the Pentagon. Reports directly to the president.

Δ **President Virginia Roberts Stallingsworth**: President of the U.S. commencing in 2004.

Δ **Major Ying Tsunami**: Chinese fighter pilot. Commands squadron of F-48 stealth Dynasty jets. Bachelor. Graduate of the U.S. Naval Academy and Navy flight training.

Δ **General Wong**: The four star workaholic head of the Chinese Air Force with headquarters in Chunking, China.

Δ **Major General Ching Wu**: Combat arms assistant to General Wong.

Δ **Joe Montgomery**: U.S. senator from Florida.

Δ **Doctor Rose Johnson**: A medical officer on the Reagan. Attends to the needs of the Red Rippers. Unmarried.

Δ **Senator John Cassidy**: Former U.S. senator and presidential aspirant. Perished in aircraft accident under mysterious conditions.

Δ **Ernie Maltman**: Former U.S. Navy F-18 fighter pilot and squadron commander and long-time civilian aid to Senator Joe Montgomery.

Δ **Richard Redman**: Confidant to the rich and powerful and the master wheeler and dealer of influence inside the Washington beltway. Runs the "Redman Institute for Enlightened Awareness."

Δ **Rear Admiral Sally Butts**: The Director of Naval Intelligence in Washington and mother of Ensign Patty Butts on board the aircraft carrier Reagan.

Δ **Dr. Sam Armstrong**: Head of the Federal Aviation Safety Authority.

Δ **Vice Admiral Sharon McCluskey**: One of three senior vice presidents to the Navy CEO responsible for diversity, read anything to do with people. Equal in rank and authority to Vice Admiral Stan Sarodsy.

Δ **Commander Rock Batori**: Husband of Commander Angela Batori, executive officer of the Reagan and skipper of the Red Ripper sister squadron, the Barking Dogs.

Δ **Captain Sam Banaro**: The officer responsible for the Navy's clandestine arsenal of nuclear weapons and other duties.

Δ **Lieutenant Commander Michelle Hopper**: Pilot of the special-mission helo that performs daring rescue mission in the mountains of eastern Iran.

CHAPTER 1

Nice Job, Dash One

Lieutenant Becky "Big Sister" Turner, U.S. Navy, inched her F-27C stealth fighter gingerly onto the number-two catapult. It was dark — pitch black. Her back-seater, Lieutenant Scott "Twidget" Jacobs, U.S. Navy, matter-of-factly said into the intercom, "Dark as the inside of a cow's ass."

As the pilot's eyes peered into the eerie catapult steam, warily searching out the yellow wands of the unknown aircraft director in the gloom, Becky laconically responded, "You don't need to remind me, big guy."

Her aircraft securely into the catapult holdback, she asked for the takeoff checklist:

"Wings spread and locked?"

"Roger that," said the pilot.

"IFF set?"

"Check."

"Fuel OK?"

"Check."

"Controls free?"

"Good."

"Flaps set for takeoff?"

"Yeah."

" Hydraulic pressure?"

"4,000 on all four systems."

"Weapons safe?"

"All safe."

The yellow wands in the gloom pointed to another body,

the familiar pattern changing to a sidewise motion. Becky pushed the two throttles forward, her eyes seeking the comforting glow of the jet's friendly red and blue dials, heads-up display and engine instruments inside her cockpit.

The one yellow wand started an up-and-down motion. Becky went another notch on the twin throttles, the two big ramjet afterburners throwing a one hundred foot-long tongue of spent JP9 fuel. The big fighter strained futilely against the the thin steel holdback assigned the job of temporarily restraining the jet. A quick glance outside revealed a total blackness, the 253 feet to the bow of the giant ship blending into a vacuous nothing.

"You ready, Twidget?" she muttered into the intercom.

"I'm always ready, Big Sister!" offered Scott, resisting the urge to peek outside, much preferring the comfort of his seventy-six dials, gauges, switches and displays in his back-seat womb.

Following the spine-crunching acceleration of the ship's catapult, senses regaining normalcy, Scott said routinely, "Airborne, good climb." The rate-of-climb pegged at 12,000 feet per minute. Though the routine had been repeated some one hundred forty times since departing Norfolk, had they been wired for a pulse-rate check, the combined total would have been near 310.

The cockpits were silent as the two winged northeast of the battle group to a combat air patrol two hundred miles out at 47,000 feet over a restless Indian Ocean. Mission: Intercept any airborne bad guys heading toward home plate, the aircraft carrier USS *Ronald Reagan*, CVN-76.

Becky's call sign was "Big Sister," its origin lost, no doubt, in a long-forgotten Naval Air Station Oceana Officer Club happy hour. Nestled in the suburban community of Virginia Beach, Oceana was the shore-based home to her fighter squadron, the VF-11 Red Rippers. Becky's two kids and long-neglected lawyer husband, Rick, lived nearby.

Scott was totally occupied in the back-seat of the Phantom III, so nicknamed for its zero radar cross-section signature and, not incidentally, as a tribute to its famed predecessor, the Phantom II of forty years prior. His call sign, "Twidget," was a natural extension of his persona.

Trained in stealth technology at the Naval Academy, Class of 2005, he had readily acclimated to the enormous complexity of the Phantom, and become a master at acquiring and exploiting satellites, programming multiple computers and attaining an air sense that only hard work could produce. A determined bachelor, his loves were the U.S. Navy, the Phantom III and flying, in that order.

Big Sister and Twidget had left Norfolk aboard "Dutch" — all carriers had such affectionate nicknames — over eight months prior on what was scheduled to be a six-month deployment. Two-and-a-half months ago, though, the ships of the battle group had emergency sortied from an idyllic two days in Singapore due to the powder keg of greed extant in this unsettled armpit of the world. This time, an unlikely alliance had emerged, with Iran, Iraq and Saudi Arabia, allied in a quest for the enormous riches of the Caspian Sea oil reserves, the largest in the world, eclipsing even the combined total of the Saudis and the North slope. Sabers rattled like a den of rattlesnakes in summer heat.

For seventy-five days, the routine had been the same for the Reagan, the Red Rippers and the 5,000 men and women of the big bird farm. Like an automated factory, the routine went on, twenty-four hours a day, seven days a week, for months on end.

Becky thought to herself as the Phantom winged towards its way-point in the middle of nowhere, good news, bad news. Good because this was her 68th flight in seventy-four days, and bad because she desperately missed family back in tranquil Virginia Beach. "Can't take the heat, get out of the kitchen," she inadvertently said into the intercom, snapping Twidget out of his satellites, computers and data links mind-set.

"What's that?" he broke the silence.

"Oh, nothing," she said into her oxygen mask, her eyes habitually dancing about the myriad of instruments in her high-tech cockpit.

Becky and Scott not only flew together, they shared a stateroom up forward just below the bow catapults and near their squadron ready room. No hanky-panky for sure — more akin to brother and sister. Becky, a graduate of Virginia Tech, Class of 2004, was not a techie, her major having been in political science with a minor in Middle East affairs. She was tired, he was tired. Tired of the treadmill routine, tired of the constant thump of the bow catapults just inches above their heads and tired of a sterile e-mail relationship with her kids and Rick back home.

Her mind wandered. God, it had been an action-packed ten years. Increasingly, Becky had commiserated to herself while airborne on the long, boring combat air patrol flights. The past years had been hectic. She and Rick had married after a whirl-wind romance early in her junior year, their first-born arriving as she started her last year. Upon graduation, despite her hus-band's reservations, she had moved quickly to training as a naval aviator, a dream long in gestation. She had excelled, some of her instructors calling her a "naturally gifted aviator." After winning her wings of gold as a naval aviator, she was assigned to the VF-11 Red Rippers as a stealth, F-27C carrier-based fighter pilot. Becky soon became a top combat aviator, notwithstanding the arrival of her second little one. Fortunately, Rick was a blessed husband, caring father and surrogate mother who managed the homefront with devotion and love. High above the unfriendly Indian Ocean and so far from home, her eyes moistened. As much as she loved her profession, she was becoming increasingly anxious to return to her brood.

"You awake, Big Sister?" Scott said while manipulating his gadgets. He had always wanted Navy air, his dad having flown as a radar intercept officer in the venerable F-14 Tomcat. Twidget was a natural, as comfortable in his complex nest as most mortals asleep in bed. He had no girlfriends, even at his ripened age of twenty-seven, and none on the horizon, though he was known in some distaff circles of the ship as a "studly" sort of young man with buns to match. None of this fazed Scott. Flying was the name of the game.

Becky, back to reality from her ever-increasing fantasies, replied desultorily, "I'm still here."

This was a typical mission: Take off at 0130, fly around in circles for three hours, and land back aboard at 0430. Two hours and fifty-five minutes of comparative monotony preceded by an attention-getting thirty seconds or so on the catapult and sixty seconds of pulse-rate generation landing aboard the blacked-out home base.

What a way to spend an early Sunday morning, sighed Becky as she monitored the automated fighter. Maybe I should be an airline pilot, she thought. At least they come home to roost a few times a month. Her mind soon wandered again to her David and Jennifer and, longingly, to the love of her life, Rick.

Most of the missions since leaving Singapore were similar — brief, launch, bore holes in the sky for three hours, return to the carrier for an automatic landing, debrief and sack out.

"Sure is quiet up here tonight. Wake me if anything comes up," Becky said to her back-seater, somewhat envious of Twidget's swarm of gadgets to monitor and play with.

"Wonder what dash two is up to?" Scott said, knowing full well what his squadron mates in an identical machine 120 miles to the east were doing. Dash two was Lieutenant Sam "Studs" Newman and his back-seat weapons specialist officer —wizo — Lieutenant Evelyn "Bikini" Swagger, both NROTC graduates of Georgia Tech in 2005. The nicknames were appropriate, thought Scott. Sam was a real hunk, the envy of most of the women aboard the Reagan, and Evelyn the same to practically all 2,500 males. Roommates as well, they were inseparable on the beach and on board. Highly respected as professional warriors and good at their adopted trade, a few had noticed of late though, that Bikini had become somewhat subdued, wearing her baggy flight suit most of the time and seen less and less. Sam, too, had seemed more introspective in recent weeks and even more pro-tective of his back-seater.

"Captain on the bridge," squalled the young boatswain's mate of the watch as her captain strode onto the bridge at 0404. Captain Tommy "Jaws" Boone settled into the familiar grooves of his big leather chair, peered into a rain-swept blackness, and said to no one in particular, "I hope the automatic carrier landing sys-tems are up and working — they're going to need them tonight."

The ACLS was mandatory, simply because it could land the jet far better than the pilots, the only concession to reality being a policy dictum from Washington, that once per month, each pilot must land manually for practice.

Though weary of the constant routine, Boone had a tough job. Leader, role model, disciplinarian and father confessor to his 5,000 charges, he set the tone, the sense of professionalism and readiness for combat on his big warship.

"Come into the wind, Captain?" said the diminutive officer of the deck. Even in his chair, the captain towered above Ensign Karen Randolph.

"Yeah, let's do it, Karen," as she simultaneously hit one button on her command console "Recover Aircraft." Unlike the old days, the bridge had only two lookouts, a boatswain's mate and an officer of the deck. Back in his dad's days as skipper of the Forrestal in the late '70s, there would have been sixteen men on the bridge. Now though, computers did it all — select and steer for the optimum course and speed, send the appropriate signals to the ships in company and the Pentagon, and be on course and on speed when the first jet was one mile out on final approach.

Captain Boone was privy, of course, to the latest intelligence data — real time — and there was genuine cause for concern. The far-flung battle group was at the epicenter of a crisis the world had not known since the dark days of World War II, some seventy years prior. Sure, the Chinese had huffed and puffed and the North Koreans were always on the brink of war. And too, Desert Storm had been a three-day, milk-toast mop-up compared to what the U.S. was facing now. Clearly, in only a few short years, the Iranians, Saudis and Iraqis had melded a fighting force that was technically superb and well led.

Boone had much to worry about. His ship was the centerpiece of a three-carrier battle force of some twenty-six ships and submarines, with supporting contract air refuelers from whatever the Air Force could get to this forlorn piece of ocean. Unable to operate from traditional shore bases, only a few contract refuelers could be relied upon to support the ships close to the action. The battle group — a mostly self-sufficient assemblage of at least one aircraft carrier, one or two subs, frigates and supply ships — could theoretically operate indefinitely at sea, the one drawback in 2010 being a reliance on outside fuel tankers for its pride of stealth fighters.

For the past seven years, technology dictated that the battle group had no embarked at-sea-commander, an elaborate, underground Pentagon command center, acting in its stead. Boone's boss, Rear Admiral Nancy Chandler and her staff were, of course, in real time communication with her far-flung fighting groups, and could see the station, speed, armament status, fuel and personing of all her ships and, with one button, could communicate with and direct each of her commanding officers.

If Admiral Chandler had a nickname, it clearly could have been "blue and gold," for she was a demanding, no-nonsense manager who, in her numerous shore-based assignments, always brought forth the greatest equality, diversity and efficiency. Some thought she would be the Navy CEO one day, the job of Indian Ocean battle group commander, one step up the ladder.

The flashing red button on his private console snapped Captain Boone back to reality.

"How's it going, Tommy?" said the familiar voice bouncing from satellite to satellite, halfway around the world.

"Just fine, Admiral — troops a bit frazzled, but hacking it. I do need some grits and gas, though," referring to the need for a food-laden supply ship and fuel for his hungry fighters.

Ignoring his plea, she gratuitously told him what he had known for several hours. "Intelligence has the ISI build-up accelerating, with several anti-ship forces moving to Bander Abas in the Gulf." ISIs, Boone knew, were the Iraqis, Saudis and Iranians and, while the admiral was at a Sunday brunch at Washington's Army-Navy Club, he had already accessed the same info.

"Thanks, Admiral, I'll get my guys hot on the details," Boone said, never forgetting that like most mortals in charge, bosses needed stroking, particularly admirals, he thought. Like boatswain's mates on the bridge, admirals will never go away as long as the Navy has ships. Fact was, though, the tension meter had just ratcheted up one more notch.

7

Like many others in the captain's position, Chandler was tolerated. No matter who the Admiral, she was still the boss, reflected Boone, his loyalty quotient rock solid. His focus was completely on readiness to do his multi-faceted combat tasks, should that be ordered by the Washington crowd. Chandler, though articulate, smart, respected and liked, was focused on diversity and equality, her mother having been an ardent feminist and politico from her home town of Spokane, Washington back in the '80s and '90s.

"Gotta go, Admiral — have a nice rest of the weekend — got airplanes in the groove and the weather's dog — not too good," catching himself on the last syllable.

"Have a good weekend yourself, Tommy," said the shore-based admiral. "I'll work on the grits and gas. Bye."

At the moment, Big Sister and Twidget were three miles out on final to the Reagan, a hot meal and clean sheets. Becky had noted that the the automatic landing circuit breaker would not reset, Twidget's attempts behind her to no avail. "One hundred and a quarter mile in lowering clouds, rain and fog," radioed a pleasantly-warm voice deep within the ship, meaning a ceiling of 100 feet and visibility of 500 yards. At the Phantom's approach speed of 148 knots, 500 yards would be eaten up in three normal heartbeats. Routine with the auto landing, ruefully thought Becky. What a night to lose the system.

"Gear down, hook down, lights on dim and steady?" interrogated Twidget to his pilot, as the big stealth fighter settled closer to the angry sea, the pilot's eyeballs seeking the comfort of the centerline lights and glide-slope indicator on the port side of the carrier's tiny landing area.

"Roger all that, big guy," said the tired pilot. At 200-feet and one-half mile, no carrier. At 125-feet and one-quarter mile, nothing.

"Let's take it around, Big Sister," barked Twidget, his voice authoritative. As the twin throttles snapped forward and the landing gear retracted, he glanced at a positive rate of climb and a dwindling fuel supply.

Captain Boone had ". . . been there and done that" many times in his twenty-two years of front-line duty. The nearest friendly field was tiny Diego Garcia, 1,200 miles to the south. Becky's jet was low fuel! Punching a guarded button on his console, he called up a real time, infrared satellite image of his piece of the ocean. Spotting a hole in the weather, he monotoned, "Captain has the conn," four words that the sea-going trade had respected for centuries. The captain not only had total authority, he was held accountable in the courts of law, public opinion and reputation for all that occurred on his vessel, the Reagan no exception. Placing his cursor on the hole, he told the air boss one story above him, "Tell dash one and two to delta overhead."

"Aye aye, Captain," responded the air officer, directing the two fighters to save fuel, orbit overhead at 1,500 feet and stand by.

Pressing his cursor on the hole, the Reagan went from 5 to 35 knots in ninety seconds, heeled ten degrees to port, sent out all the right signals and sped for the spot fourteen miles distant.

"Big Sister, I hope El Capitaine knows what he's doing, 'cause that water down there is cold and wet."

"No sweat — not to worry," Becky said sweetly, while mentally computing the time to flame out and getting real wet. "Twenty-two minutes sound right, Twidget?"

"Twenty-one point six," responded her guy in the backseat, pleased to be distracted by this piece of simple mental gymnastics.

"Charlie three," said the captain to the carrier control folks deep within the ship as the Reagan found the hole and a break in the abominable weather, slowed and turned into the wind, the cryptic message ordering the fighter to be at the ramp in three minutes.

At one-quarter mile, Becky called the glide-slope meatball with 400 pounds of exotic JP9 fuel on board, not even enough for a go-around. Line up the center line landing lights, glide slope from a centered orange meatball on the lens, speed 147 knots and "— *crunch — screech*," the stealth fighter slammed to the steel flight deck and pulled out two hundred and forty-feet of one and one-quarter inch arresting cable. Instinctively, Becky went to full power, snapped the throttles back to idle, speed brakes in, flaps up, lights out and started the wings to folding while checking her two o'clock position for the yellow homecoming wands and signal for hook-up on the blacked-out flight deck.

"Nice job, dash one," said the captain over the ultra-low powered radio in a rare display of affection for his front-line pilot and wizo.

"Thank you, sir," responded the lieutenant as she taxied her jet within inches of the bow and an angry, unseen ocean seventy-one feet below, while three blue-shirted youngsters strapped the stealth fighter onto the Reagan's flight deck with sixteen heavy chains. Becky and Scott would remember to thank the unknown trio before dragging themselves to the ready room mission debrief.

CHAPTER 2

USS *Ronald Reagan*

It had been a long two years, thought Captain Tommy Boone, long in many ways. He missed his family back in Virginia Beach and being a normal 44-year-old, moderately successful man, able to do little league, PTAs and cook an occasional paella dish. Why do guys like me strap it on twenty-four hours a day for months on end? His dad had told him long ago that being a carrier commanding officer was 99% endurance and 99% judgment. How true it was.

The USS *Ronald Reagan*, CVN-76, was a super-carrier's carrier, a $7 billion national asset. Decade after decade, the carriers had been called upon to show the American flag in the most godforsaken pieces of ocean imaginable. Seventy years after their coming out in the decisive days of World War II in the early 1940s, the carriers were still at it.

"New station, Captain — 270 miles southeast," said the officer of the deck, Ensign Karen Randolph.

"Make it so," said Boone, his mind elsewhere.

The ensign punched a "go to" button on her master console and once again, the 97,000 tons of high-tech machinery and people accelerated to 35 knots while concurrently and automatically sending out the appropriate signals to the battle group ships, airborne aircraft, the Pentagon command center and internally within the ship's complex innards.

Lieutenant Scott Jacobs was on the bridge after a quick debrief with the intelligence guys, a shower and change of uniform as an assistant in training to Karen. Before long, he too would become a fully qualified officer of the deck, thought Boone. He was a comer, reiterating the words of an unknown captain when then Lieutenant (junior grade) Boone would scramble to the bridge in between combat missions to master the intricacies of driving a big carrier.

Tommy Boone was born with navy-blue diapers. His dad had been a naval aviator, as was his grandfather. Both had commanded carrier-based fighter squadrons as had he, and unbelievably, all three squadrons had been the Red Rippers. It was still the nation's longest consecutive combat unit, having been established nearly eighty years ago. Navy tradition dies slowly, thought Boone.

Like his bloodline, Boone was a graduate of the U.S. Naval Academy at Annapolis, Class of 1988. He had gone directly to pilot training in Pensacola, emerging to find himself on board the old USS *Constellation* in an F-18 Hornet fighter-attack squadron going nose-to-nose against the wild man Saddam Hussein in Desert Storm. "Deja vu — here I am, twenty years later in the identical miserable piece of ocean, with the same rotten weather, getting ready to take on the sons of Saddam, along with a few of his unsavory buddies."

"What's that, Captain?" said his officer of the deck.

"Oh, nothing," he said to Karen. It bothered Boone that his number-one daughter, Lori, a junior at Virginia Tech, wanted to go Navy air. Women are right in the trenches these days, he thought — no place for my daughter. Though a student and modest supporter of diversity and all that the word connoted, Boone's warrior ethic was sometimes at odds with the number-one goal of the Navy. Too many problems, he reflected, harking back on the trials and tribulations of the past fifteen years of social course changes. What a deal — the guys stay home and the mamas and daughters fight the wars, he pondered, knowing that if the thought-patrol folks could tune into his brain, he would be in deep kimshee.

Not all that bad, thought the captain, as he settled deeper into his worn chair eighteen stories above the raging sea, his steed pressing forward at a smooth 35 knots. Young Karen, the ship's officer of the deck; Becky Turner, the pilot of the stealth that had just landed in such miserable weather; and his executive officer, Commander Angela Batori, were all fine officers and as good as they come.

Captain Boone was on the last year of a three-year command tour as number one on the Reagan. He did not cater to the ship's nickname, Dutch, as he felt it somewhat disrespectful, but the moniker stuck. All ships had one, the old Forrestal a case in point: named for the nation's first secretary of defense following World War II and being the first of the super-carriers upon its commissioning in 1956, it became first in defense, or FID for short. Others followed: Indy for the Independence, Kitty Maru for the Kitty Hawk, JFK for the Kennedy, Ike for the Eisenhower, and so on.

The Reagan was indeed a masterpiece of American technology and combat power. Home to 5,000 folks, she had two massive nuclear reactors, either one of which could propel her at a loping 37 knots, millions of gallons of JP9 ram-jet fuel, an air wing of 87 stealth fighters, thousands of tons of high-tech smart weaponry and the latest in crew creature comforts.

Problem is, the captain thought, the shore-based commanders and geo-strategists back in the Pentagon puzzle palace have routinely used the Navy as pawns on a chessboard. The machines could go forever — the troops, not quite so adaptive.

Boone had experienced a somewhat anomalous career pattern in the Navy of 2010, mostly all ships and flying. Marked as a real comer for his performance in Desert Storm, he went from flying to carrier navigator, more flying, commanded the first stealth fighter squadron back in 2005, then on to air wing commander aboard the USS *Eisenhower*. His only shore assignment had been in the Pentagon for two years serving as aide to Vice Admiral Sharon McCluskey, the Navy's long-standing executive vice president for diversity.

Soon after the turn of the century, the Navy had forsaken its convoluted front-office hierarchy. The old title for the head guy in the Navy, the Chief of Naval Operations, became the CEO, his number two, the vice chief, the president and COO and so on down the line. There were three primary branches now, each headed by a three star vice admiral: shore support; diversity — encompassing anything to do with people; and combat arms. All were roads to the top, but diversity, in the minds of most, was clearly the fast track.

His two-year shore tour back then had been a dramatic change of pace from the deck plates and cockpits of his previous fifteen years of mostly sea-going service. His family, though, enjoyed the Washington scene — good schools, lots to do and dad home once in a while, albeit late at night and occasional Sunday mornings.

His boss thought highly of Boone, making sure he was selected early for captain and assigning him to the USS *Ronald Reagan* as commanding officer. Though occasionally lax in his enthusiasm for diversity goals, like a good sailor, Tommy Boone saluted, worked his tail off and promoted the goals of the organization and his boss.

The move back to Virginia Beach and more sea duty was an easy one. Same house in a quiet Virginia Beach suburb, good schools and comfortable friends for the kids and Beverly. To the occasional chagrin of his spouse, he would often introduce her as his first wife. Married sixteen years, Beverly was clearly a top businesswoman in her own right, owning several shops specializing in upscale children's clothes. Tommy was lucky. She was a great wife and mother and managed her budding business from home, the girls well in tow. Thirty-seven years old, she was seven years younger than Tommy, took care of herself, and, more often than not, was the recipient of an appreciative glance from both men and women, young and old. This November Sunday night she was planning a spouse get-together for the husbands, wives and friends of her Tommy's ship, so long at sea and so far away.

"Got a minute, Captain?" the ship's exec said into the personal line between her office and the bridge.

"Anytime, XO."

Commander Angela Batori strode authoritatively onto the bridge after being whisked from her quarters deep within the ship

14

by the high-speed command elevator, her arrival announced by an alert boatswain's mate of the watch as, "XO on the bridge." As executive officer to the captain, she was number two on the ship and directed a covey of fellow commanders and lieutenant commanders, each of whom managed a piece of the action: engineers, air wing, docs, weapons, supply and a few others. Her job was to keep them reading from the same sheet of music. As such, there were no secrets between the XO and the captain. Boone knew full well that the combat effectiveness of the big ship was due in large measure to how well Angela orchestrated her job.

Angela's husband of ten years, Commander Danny "Rock" Batori, was skipper of one of the sister squadrons to the Red Rippers, the VF-143 Barking Dogs. It was now routine for married Navy people to be assigned to the same command and, if a ship, live together. The Batoris were no exception. So, in addition to the normal quarters of the ship's executive officer, they had a small apartment next door. The routine for both though, was a mind-numbing, twenty-four hours per day, with Rock gone for many hours at a time, flying and tending to his brood of high-tech stealth fighters and two hundred men and women. Captain Boone thought to himself, with an inward grin, of the old days, when the Barking Dogs were more affectionately referred to as the Pukin' Dogs, a label that fell prey early on to the mores of correctness.

The captain always made time for the XO. They would meet once or twice daily at random times or places to hash out the multitude of endless issues on this complex web of flesh, feelings and machinery.

"XO, for the umpteenth time, you cannot name the ship's paper 'Dutch,' understood?" barked Boone in an unusually raspy tone of voice.

"Roger that, Captain, but the morale committee is getting increasingly snappish on the issue — just passing it on." Fact was, most all of the discussions were mundane and not worth an e-mail to anywhere. Hair too short, not assigned the right roommate, hours too long, numerous male-female related emotions, and

15

the inevitable complaints of scarce fresh fruits and vegetables.

Angela Batori had experienced a more traditional career pattern in her seventeen years of naval service. In the early nineties, she had been among a cadre of sharp women chosen to pilot the old F-18 Hornet fighter. She had been beset by problems, however, most of which were self-generated by virtue of her challenge to authority, mainly that vested in the carrier's landing signal officers. Known for generations of naval aviators as LSOs, the only one who could argue and win was the air wing commander or CAG. At any rate, Angela Batori not only argued, she was dangerous when landing her expensive jet on the moving flight deck. After a great deal of due diligence on the part of her bosses, she was stripped of carrier flight duty and assigned to mundane, comfortable shore billets as a manager and staff person. Along with then-Lieutenant Commander Boone, she had been assigned to a special stress-study group in the immediate office of her mentor, Vice Admiral Sharon McCluskey, the chief of diversity. Long story short, she was early selected for commander, assigned to a carrier for thirty days of on-the-job training as executive officer and then to the Reagan as Boone's executive officer.

She was sharp, opined the captain. Military in appearance, articulate, decisive, not too feminine and clearly in charge of her domain. She might not know one end of the ship from the other, but she sure knew the system and how to handle the crew.

The Reagan's previous XO had left under a cloud six months prior, a victim of roving eyes, following hands and numerous female allegations. Within hours, he was history, the morale officer taking his place for a month pending the arrival of Batori.

"Twenty miles to station, Captain."

"Roger that, Karen. Next launch at 0730, correct?"

"Affirmative, sir," said his OOD. "Mind if I give the conn to Lieutenant Jacobs? He needs some hands-on."

"By all means — make it so," the captain responded, once again, deep in fatigued thought.

Troubling him were a menagerie of problems. He had

been taught by his dad, and others, not to get lost in the minutia. "Keep your eye on the ball, son," his dad had lectured.

Three big-picture issues were vying for top priority in his overloaded brain. First, was the specter of real warfare and the impact on his untried and stressed-out crew. Second, was the lack of logistic support. The Reagan had received only one carrier on-board-delivery aircraft and but one JP9 fuel ship in the past month. Most of the time, the slowpoke supply ships could not keep up with the high-speed, random maneuvering of the Reagan. Results were a backlog of medical cases to be off-loaded and no morale-lifting fresh chow. Finally, and most puzzling to Boone, was the issue of four supposedly missing nuclear weapons, the subject of a top secret "eyes only" message for the captain from the combat arms honcho in the Pentagon, Vice Admiral Stan Sarodsy. Boone was advised not to discuss this with anyone, including his Rear Admiral boss, Nancy Chandler, and his mentor Vice Admiral Sharon McCluskey, still the diversity leader in the five-sided Pentagon wind tunnel.

"XO, what's our light duty count up to now?"

"Five hundred forty-seven, Captain," she responded authoritatively.

Angela always has the facts, mused Boone. There were always a few medical cases, some psychological problems, pregnancies and the inevitable stress cases.

Tommy Boone had never understood the stress-chit syndrome. It had started long ago at the giant Great Lakes recruit training center, commanded then by Rear Admiral Renée Polger, later to become the Navy's first female CEO. The theory went that if a person felt too much stress, they pulled out a colored chit and sat out whatever it was that was causing the stress.

"Shit," said the captain in a rare display of profanity and incorrectness, "no wonder they can't hack it out here. This ship is Stress City, underlined!" His worries were more pragmatic than emotional. He had airplanes to fix, troops to feed and a fast warship that was proceeding rapidly into harm's way. Already down over five hundred persons, no replacements were in store. Simply put, the remaining 90% had to take up the slack.

17

The nuclear weapons bothered Boone. Just before sailing from Norfolk, the ship had been thoroughly inspected by a host of shore-based nuclear weapons experts and given a clean bill of health. He longed to discuss it with his XO and the weapons officer, Lieutenant Commander Stan Miller, but was specifically ordered not to do so as the case ". . . went to the highest levels of the U.S. government."

Talk about tradition, recalled Boone, the damned Navy could not force itself to part with the old, but still lethal, weapons. Outlawed by international treaty, all twenty-four nations possessing the gruesome weapons had agreed to have their stockpiles destroyed, the U.S. included. Ships though, were different, and subject, in the eyes of the Navy, to the laws of the sea, a higher calling than land-locked agreements signed by a host of temporary, white-haired old men.

The Reagan had forty such weapons on board back in the original special weapons storage spaces on the eighth deck, well below the waterline. Guarded constantly by a contingent of marines and SEALs, the only persons allowed access were the captain, XO, weapons officer and two specially-trained civilian technicians.

The weapons officer, Lieutenant Commander Stan Miller, was a hard-nosed, old-school, up-through-the-ranks mustang, who had enlisted in the Navy to escape the hopelessness of the 1988 version of the south side of Chicago. Back then, most all ships had an array of nukes, though the Navy stuck by its policy of, "We will neither confirm nor deny the existence of nuclear weapons on this or any other ship." Miller was a loner, though it was rumored he had a wife somewhere. He and the XO seemed to spend a lot of time together, reflected Boone, his mind trying to tie a bunch of loose ends into a knot that made sense.

Batori was talking: "Captain, we've got to unload the stress and medical cases soon — far too many to handle." The simply-stated stress policy was the result of her diversity tour: three stress chits and back to rest and relaxation. No exceptions. R&R was an old term, but in this case it was mandatory that the person be sent expeditiously to the Central Diversity College in the Memphis area. Like most other ships, a special space on the Reagan had been devoted for stress relief and light duty. On board the carrier, the forward weapons storage spaces had been converted into a comparatively comfortable complex of dining, individual quarters and a hotel-like common area. After a few days of such relative relaxation, experience showed that most were ready to rejoin their divisions and squadrons. Only designed for four hundred, its occupancy had mushroomed due to the inability to get folks off the big carrier, as well as a rash of medical problems in the past few months.

Miller did not "geehaw" with all this. Old school, he was clearly out of step with the Navy of the past fifteen years. The system tolerated him, though, because so few had his breadth of knowledge of weaponry, particularly nuclear weapons. Trouble was, he had effectively lost 40% of his personnel — down some eighty sailors — not due to stress, but rather their unwillingness to keep their zippers zipped.

Miller's domain, deep within the ship, was a catacomb of individual weapons spaces, most of which had to be inspected daily, but all of which were far removed from the populated areas of the ship. More often than not, he would open an armory to a smart-bomb storage space and find two or more of his troops in less-than-military positions. Kind of like a rabbit's den, he thought. When the new XO had reported aboard six months ago, he had brought this up, but got only a knowing smile in response.

"That's about it, Captain. I hope the damned JP9 and supply ships can find us. We need them bad," said the energetic Angela to her pensive captain.

"Thanks for coming up — appreciate the update. And, Angela, remember no Dutch. By the way, please tell Rock when and if you see him, the Barking Dogs did a great job last night on the 0530 recovery. Weather was rotten."

It was 0715, Sunday, November 7th, 2010. An endless perpetual clock, jumbled days and nights, another November day of thirty. The tenth year of the 21st century, and the world is just as screwed up as in millennia past. I should keep a journal — it

19

would make unbelievable reading one day, he commiserated to himself. Other than the damned nukes, he and the XO had no secrets, but somehow he found it hard to really communicate with her. His total focus was on the Reagan's ability to put smart weapons on dumb targets and keep the hell out of harm's way. Hers, rightfully, was to tend the store down below.

It was Sunday night back home in Virginia Beach. His Beverly would have a fire going, the kids and dog at her side. "Funny, the XO never talks about her family," he said half-aloud in the quiet of the darkened bridge high atop the blacked-out warship powering through heavy seas 8,000 miles from homeport in the middle of nowhere. "Strange."

CHAPTER 3

The Red Rippers

Lieutenant Evelyn "Bikini" Swagger, U. S. Navy, huddled in the back-seat of her stealth jet poised on the number-one catapult of the USS *Ronald Reagan*, CVN-76, puking her guts out. "Good news, bad news," she said plaintively in between heaves. "Good news was that the five-minute alert has not been launched in four weeks, and the chances were slim to none this miserable Sunday morning; and bad in that the damned sickness has become more routine in the past few weeks."

The alert five-minute exercise hearkened back to the ancient days of carrier aviation, the big bird farms always having two to four fighter jets ready to launch on a moment's notice, either to reinforce the airborne defensive fighters or, if none was airborne, to blast off to intercept the bad guys. Most of the time though, it was absolutely deadly boring, cold, cramped and demeaning for the pilot, the wizo in the aft cockpit, the plane captains on deck and the catapult crew. On the Reagan, more often than not, the routine called for the crew that just landed to man the alert aircraft, causing them to suffer the discomfort of being tightly strapped in a lifeless hunk of machinery for another two hours.

"**LAUNCH THE ALERT FIVE!**" boomed the flight deck PA bullhorns, as the big ship started a hard turn to port and accelerated, the listless minions surrounding the catapult swinging into instant action. Chains off, the engines of the F-27C stealth Phantom III fighter started turning before the second announcement, as Lieutenant Sam "Studs" Newman, flicked the multitude of knobs and switches necessary to bring his deadly jet to life.

Ninety-seven seconds after the call to action, the stealth eased into the catapult holdback, its nose firmly yoked to the 253 feet of the starboard catapult, the engines already coming up to military power. "Need the takeoff check list, Evelyn," he said as he quickly scanned his familiar front office. Bikini stuffed her latest barf bag into a rear cockpit crevice, gritted her scummy teeth and gave her pilot what he wanted.

The five fingers of the yellow-shirted catapult officer at his ten o'clock position directed Studs to go to afterburner power. "All set, Ev?" he queried his back-seater in a dialogue most mortals would not call routine.

"Go for it, Sam," she responded, once again feeling the adrenalin and anticipation of going from zero to 180 knots in 2.3 seconds, from cold, uncaring machinery, to the world's most formidable fighter accelerating a scant seventy feet above the cold, angry sea.

A remote satellite downlink said with a pleasant voice: "Your vector 017 for 270 miles, angels 47." Sam whipped the jet to the assigned heading as the Phantom scrambled for altitude. "Not bad," muttered the young pilot, "wheels in the well in less than three minutes — old Jaws would be smiling on the bridge." Actually, Sam knew full well the performance had less to do with the flight crew than the exquisite teamwork of the guys on deck. His squadron commanding officer, Commander Wendy "Iron Lady" Montrose, U.S. Navy, would already be getting a one-way call from the ship's captain, a short compliment to follow.

Bikini was getting with it. Though tired from the previous mission and puking session, she was all business and had a local reputation as a hotshot wizo in the back seat. Her horizontal situation indicator, or HSI, a flat-plate display the size of a small TV, glittered with symbology. Though it had been around a while, the technology was mind-boggling in its sophistication. The HSI was like looking down on a piece of real estate or ocean and seeing, in real time, any hostile aircraft, ships or missiles as well as the complete friendly-forces scene. Electronically hooking several targets speeding towards her, the symbols went hostile indicating a covey of SU-37 Flagon missile-carrying Iranian fighters with two airborne Reagan combat air patrol aircraft already close to an intercept behind them.

"This is what it's all about," Bikini hollered enthusiastically into the intercom while her pilot monitored the stealth's automatic profile.

"Like a dummy," Sam responded. He thought this must be another one of the constant feints and probes by the ISIs in order to determine the whereabouts and composition of the heavily armed battle group. One of these days, it's going to go high order. The symbology showed his squadron mates easing nicely into a position two miles astern of the hostiles at 34,000 feet.

The rules of engagement as to when a routine intercept situation became hostile were simple and time tested: Don't shoot unless someone shoots at you first. It was a variant of the old axiom that any combat outfit had the fundamental right of self-defense. This time, like all of the previous ones, thought Sam, no bullets.

Suddenly, Sam's back-seater screeched, her voice incredulous. "Shit house, where'd they come from?" noting two unknown bandits closing in astern of the Ripper aircraft. The hunters became the hunted. The lead Ripper called on the open radio circuit for his deck launched buddies to "Get those bastards off our tails!"

Evelyn hooked the fading third set of aircraft behind her squadron mates while Sam took his machine into manual mode, stroked the afterburners and laid the agile fighter into an 8G hard turn to position himself behind the new intruders. Even for Sam, who was hard as nails and with abs to match, eight times the force of gravity was a bunch. "You still with us, baby?" he grunted a bit worriedly into his mike. No response.

Back on the Reagan, Captain Boone hit the general quarters alarm, sending a garish, unmistakable clanging throughout the 2,267 separate compartments of the ship. No matter the activity, within five minutes the ship was in a total combat mode with 4,500 crewmembers at their combat stations. Pilots to ready rooms, damage control stations manned, all watertight doors shut, the nuclear wash-down system ready and missiles warmed-up and ready to go, the Reagan was ready for combat operations. "The only exception, in the year of our Lord 2010, were the souls in Stress City who were not allowed to alter their rest and relaxation routine," muttered Boone, his voice flat, as the final ready report came from the below decks weapons spaces well within the time standards.

The captain's attention returned to his command console as he selected the HSI display to see for himself how the routine intercepts two hundred miles north were proceeding. The computer generated closest point of approach to the Reagan indicated the hostiles had not located the ship. Startled, he noted two unknowns slipping in behind the Rippers, the symbology fading in and out. "Where the hell did they come from?" he called to his wizards deep in the high-tech ship.

"Beats us, Captain." said a laconic voice far below within the carrier.

"Damn," muttered Boone, "we're all groggy."

The gaggle was still heading on a course that would take them no closer than 117 miles from the Reagan. "Clearly it was another feinting job," Boone said half-aloud. He watched his screen as the just-launched ready fighters rolled hard behind the new intruders. "Way to go, guys. Good thinking to cut out the automatic guidance and go manual," hummed the captain, knowing full well that the techie freaks needed a human-brain, live-pilot reality check once in a while.

Sam rolled his Phantom III a mile astern of the unknown fighters of a type they had never seen before. He kept calling his back-seater. No answer. He jabbed the force transducer fore and aft, jerking the big fighter to plus 5 and minus 2Gs while craning to see into the rear cockpit. The little he could see scared him. His knees began to shake. Evelyn was slumped forward in her straps, her helmeted head bobbing loosely with the gyrations of the jet. "Baby, can you hear me?" screamed Sam, his thoughts only on the occupant of the back seat, his love. "Wake up."

Breaking radio silence, Sam made a momentous command decision to bug out and get his wizo back on deck as fast as possible. Sweating, his knees still gyrating, he punched afterburner, dropped the nose, turned starboard 37 degrees and headed at the speed of heat for home plate, calling an emergency "mayday" on the open frequency. "Baby, what's wrong?" the protective pilot called futilely to the lifeless person behind him. "Shit, I never should have honked those Gs back there. It's my fault."

Boone noted the Red Ripper jet breaking away and heading for the ship, heard the "mayday" and ordered the air boss to make a ready deck with an emergency pull forward of the aircraft readying for the next launch. With a chill, he also saw on his HSI the two late comers whom the Ripper, only moments before, had in their sights, breaking off and following the sick Phantom directly to the Reagan. So much for all the stealth technology baloney, he thought. Admiral Chandler would no doubt disengage from her Sunday evening fireplace at home, a twenty question quiz session to follow, while he tried to pay due homage to his boss and mind his store at the same time.

"Captain, having trouble acquiring the incoming bogies — I can see 'em, but can't lock on." said the unflappable weapons officer, Lieutenant Commander Stan Miller deep below.

"Roger that. Keep trying," said Boone. What a pleasure it was to dialogue with Miller, he commiserated. A real pro from the old school.

"Sam, what happened?" said a groggy sounding Evelyn moments later to her pilot.

"Are you OK, baby?"

"Yeah, I guess I just passed out," her eyes pounding into his through the crevice between the two cockpits.

His knees still in an uncontrollable shake, Sam said assertively, "I'm going to get you on deck fast — you scared the shit out of me."

"Please, honey, no. I'm OK," she said abruptly, her mouth a seething cauldron of dried puke and fear. "Let's do our job."

Clearly, Sam thought, she's confused. Nonetheless, he

made another heavy-duty decision, pushed the mike button on his starboard throttle and told the ship he was canceling the emergency, were OK and would explain later.

"EXPLAIN!" roared the captain to no one in particular on his quiet bridge. "He can bet his sweet ass, he'll explain!" Picking up his handset, he called the errant Ripper and told him he had two unknowns trailing him at sixteen miles and "get with it — NOW! Understood?"

"Aye aye, sir," responded Sam in a less than convincing voice as he rolled his jet at reduced G to an intercept heading. Sam's knees were still shaking.

"OK, big guy, I'm fine — let's make Jaws happy and catch those guys before they overfly the good ship Reagan."

Three minutes later, Sam eased the stealth jet alongside the number-two unknown, his energized wizo already getting the digital video camera ready. "Gumshoe," referring to the squadron's intelligence officer, would be happy. "Never seen this type before" he said to his wizo, once again all Navy-fighter-pilot business. Easing in a little closer like the Blue Angel he one day hoped to be, the unknown pilot angrily motioned Sam to move out in the impersonal language of aviators eternal. Sam moved much closer, while Evelyn snapped the computer images. Clearly angry, the hostile pilot dropped a wing into Sam's machine, causing him to pop the stick sharply forward to avoid a mid-air collision. Regaining position, Sam shook his fist at the errant pilot who promptly removed his oxygen mask, revealing a smiling, mustachioed face framed by a wide, toothy smile.

Sam said to Bikini in a petulant tone, "I guess he won this round of wits." Then, "Do us a big favor, will you, baby? Take off your oxygen mask and give this amateur hour your most glamorous come-on smile."

"Roger that, lover boy," said the obviously fully-recovered Evelyn, and flashed to the unknown pilot her best cover-girl smile, rolling her tongue easily around her full lips, all the while thankful he couldn't smell her breath.

The unknown pilot's grin turned to an almost audible laugh accompanied by an effusive thumbs up and a rapid pull-up and max-power climb to the north. Sam was told to escort the two hostiles for a couple of hundred miles as the two intruders apparently headed to their ultra-secret base somewhere deep inland and prepared for some raucous stories of dumb Navy pilots and good-looking girls in back seats.

Sam and Ev headed for a ready deck on the Reagan, their fuel supply dwindling. "The shit will fly," said Sam. "It always flows downhill."

Following a routine full automatic carrier landing, the commanding officer of the VF-11 Red Rippers, along with her infamous pilot and wizo, was standing at parade rest beside the Reagan's captain, having climbed the eleven stories from ready room one to the bridge with gusto. Commander Wendy Montrose was tough, did not know the meaning of mediocrity, could out-fly the best and was torqued to the nth degree as the captain had her for lunch.

"Do you guys realize you've compromised our position? What was the big emergency you had?" Without waiting for a response, he continued in a full transmit mode. "You not only left your squadron mates to hang in the breeze up there, you enabled the whatevers to follow you to home plate, screwed up the next launch and got my tail in a deep crack with the Admiral. Understood?"

Sam fervently hoped his CO would cover for him. She just glowered, her eyeballs fourteen inches from his. Evelyn piped up, breaking the seven-second silence, "Skipper, Captain. Sam laid on some heavy Gs up there and I just went out like a light."

Iron Lady snapped, "Blacking out is not a problem — happens once in a while — but six minutes? What the — hell," the CO lamented, remembering that she was in the sanctity of the carrier's bridge where proper composure and foul language were mutually exclusive.

"I'll take care of it, Captain," said the cool squadron skipper, as she was interrupted by the OOD asking the captain's permission to proceed to random station 701 some 117 miles distant at 35 knots.

"Make it so — we'll keep our fighters airborne during the transit," he replied curtly, his mind still on the unbelievable Red Ripper antics.

Dismissing the two lieutenants, the captain asked the Ripper skipper to stay behind. "Here's the lecture I know you don't need." Wendy stiffened, knowing full well she was about to get the shaft. "Had this been for real, we could have lost our tail. You, of all people, know the action and the consequences. Find out what went on in that jet and shape up! Dismissed."

Iron Lady had been around the block. A highly respected naval officer and tactical pilot, she believed in the adage, "If you can't take the heat, get out of the kitchen." Back in her stateroom, she told the squadron duty officer to, "Get Studs and Bikini down here, stat," her voice in command, the tone abrupt.

Just like the old *Top Gun* movie that Wendy had watched a record fourteen times as a young girl, Sam and Evelyn stood at attention in her tiny stateroom as their commanding officer lectured in clear, concise language. Wendy's squadron had three pilots and four wizos in Stress City, the temporary R&R palace some ten decks below. Not available by law and Navy tradition of the past few years, the load had been shared by their squadron mates. Sam and Evelyn were good, she thought, as the two vibrant young aviators stood before her. As good as they come.

"Blacking out is the biggest bunch of soggy crap I've been exposed to in a long while." She was standing now. "That's for the movies, boys and girls, understood?"

"Aye aye, Skipper," they managed in unison, voices contrite, Evelyn adding, "It won't happen again, ma'am."

Back in their stateroom in paradise, Sam and Evelyn were holding one another closely, Evelyn sobbing. They both knew of her two missed periods and the uncompromising policy of the captain. Any confirmed pregnancy meant an automatic trip to Stress City and release from all duties, no matter how benign or light. So, Evelyn had not confirmed with the Docs that which she and Sam both knew. It was becoming crystal clear that 8G flights, catapult shots and arrested landings were not for expectant mothers. It wasn't that precautions had been lacking — both had taken the super pill — double protection and almost foolproof. But still, it had happened. Sam struggled to keep the tears to himself.

The policy, a carryover from the dramatic Naval Academy approach to pregnancy in the mid-nineties, was an inflexible rule dictating that both partners must take a one-year leave of absence at the Memphis stress facility before returning to full duty.

"What a load," said Sam softly as he held his roommate, his emotions a mixture of pride as a future father, protection of his love and sadness knowing that they may not be a part of the action for long.

Aside from the captain's quarters, Sam and Evelyn lived in the best officer living area on the ship. Known as paradise, this alcove up forward between the flight deck and hangar deck, had only one way in and out and was home to thirteen of the Rippers and one ship's company officer in seven staterooms. It was extremely private — most on the ship had no idea of its existence.

Ensign Patty "Gumshoe" Butts, U.S. Navy Reserve, knocked hesitantly on the door to Sam and Evelyn's room. No answer, though she could sense they were inside. Patty was the intelligence officer for the squadron and a non-flier. Like most spooks, she was called "gumshoe." Patty walked back to her small cubical as Lieutenant (junior grade) "Pistol" Pete Dawkins, U.S. Navy Reserve, squeezed sideways by her in his bathrobe, headed for the showers. Hearing the commotion, Lieutenant Commander Dave "Blues" Anderson sleepily opened his door and then quietly shut it.

Patty roomed with Ensign Karen Randolph, who was, at the time, sound asleep after her 0400 to 0800 stint as officer of the deck on the ship's bridge. Bachelorettes, they loved the ship, the challenge and, so far, the U.S. Navy. Though not exactly raving beauties, both were smart, vivacious and had no qualms about being relished by the opposite sex. Trouble is, mused Patty to herself in the darkened solitude of their tiny home, the guys are a dime a dozen, but so are the girls.

Back to reality, she pondered the mini-mystery of the last

flight. Launch, intercept, discover a stealth variant never before seen, declare an emergency, return to the ship by breaking the sacrosanct stealth silence, cancel the mayday, get called to the CO's stateroom and won't answer a knock on their door. What's going on?

She and Karen had thought of writing a novel based upon the intrigue and loves of paradise's other twelve occupants. No one would believe it, she guessed. Better than *Peyton Place*, it could be dubbed "Reagan's Paradise."

Patty's mind wandered to Pete Dawkins, the CO's cute back-seater, clad only in his robe. "Pete was shy," she and Karen had agreed, "but not Dave." Dave Anderson was the squadron's operations officer, an ex-Blue Angel demonstration pilot and, since the abrupt departure of the regular squadron executive officer three months after leaving Norfolk, the acting executive officer to the Ripper CO. He absolutely wasn't shy, she thought, crossing her legs tighter. On more and more occasions, the guy would make excuses to borrow something or ask questions that had nothing to do with anything, his attentions increasingly direct to both Karen and her. Without doubt, he was a catch — thirty-three, trim and all-American good looks. "He also has a beautiful wife, Sandy, a schoolteacher back in Virginia Beach, and two young ones," clucked the intel officer, shutting the Daves and Petes out of her mind.

Twidget was another story, Patty thought, trying to get her mind back to being an intelligence officer in the front lines of an evolving global confrontation. Both she and Karen sparkled when Lieutenant Scott Jacobs was around, a fact that Scott sublimely did not realize. Scott lived beside them with his pilot, Lieutenant Becky Turner, and, as best the two "twenty-somethings" could deduce, he was totally devoid of any interest in his female neighbors. Anyway, Patty conceded, life aboard the Reagan is tough enough without the added trials and tribulations of the paradise intrigues.

Commander Wendy Montrose was deep in thought in her tiny one-person stateroom not far away. She flashed back to the short-lived euphoria of departing Norfolk, bands playing and flags flying, on what was to be a standard six-month, portal-to-portal deployment with lots of good port calls and a chance for some great flying. But, first, her executive officer gets cold feet after three months at sea and decides she can't be without her kids. Secretly, the CO thought she may have been with child. Then, a few months ago, she had lost three pilots and four wizos to stress, most of whom had already left the ship with no replacements and were, at this moment, comfortably ensconced at the Memphis stress facility. Then, though no big deal, her maintenance officer, Lieutenant Commander Lori Miller, turns out to be openly lesbian and a lousy maintenance department head to boot, incapable of leading her people. The acting executive officer, Dave Anderson, not only thinks he's the CO, but constantly walks around in his tight flight suit like a bull in heat. And now, one of her top combat capable crews, Studs and Bikini, screw up big-time, endanger the entire ship, and she's at parade rest in front of a totally torqued-off aircraft carrier captain. She smiled to herself and thought, now I know why he's called Jaws. The final nail in her ever-tightening leadership box, was that fourteen person, seven-stateroom rabbit's den known as paradise, where even she was not welcome. "I may have a leadership crisis — God knows how much longer we'll be out here," she said softly to the four walls of her spartan stateroom.

Peering at the Red Ripper plaque, the only adornment in her austere quarters, she knew how lucky she was to have been selected for carrier-based fighter squadron command, VF-11 the icing on the cake. The Navy's oldest fighter squadron, the Red Rippers, were formed way back in 1927 during the years of alcohol prohibition. Its logo was a blend of idiocy and machismo, in the skipper's opinion, and many had tried to eliminate it and start over, including the three star head of diversity on the Navy's Pentagon staff, the four star CEO at the time executing a resounding veto. The top part of the logo, she noted, was the obscene head of a wild boar, identical to that on the Gordon's gin bottle of that era and today. Under it was a roll of bologna. The centerpiece was a backwards lightning bolt between two red balls. The toast of the Red Rippers for all eternity? "Here's to the Red Rippers, a bunch of gin-drinking, pig-headed, baloney-slinging, two-balled, he-men bastards."

Bristling in righteous indignation, Wendy wondered what would ever prompt such crap and forbade the toast to reach her ears. I'm not a pig's head nor a bullshitter, I don't drink gin, I'm clearly not a bastard and don't even have one ball — but, believe you me, this squadron's going to continue to come out on top or I'll kiss the ass of every one of the two-balled bastards, whether or not they drink gin.

Her phone buzzed. "Skipper, got a minute?" It was Master Chief Randy McCormick, U.S. Navy. McCormick was older than most of the crew and the maintenance chief in charge of the squadron's stable of fourteen, hyper-sophisticated F-27C stealth Phantom III jets and the 187 technicians that kept them in the air. Lately, availability was down, three machines being in various stages of disrepair, a fact known to the entire chain of command, including Admiral Nancy Chandler in the five-sided Washington puzzle palace.

Increasingly, Wendy was relying on the reasoned main-tenance sense of the master chief. The upshot was more and more head-to-head time with the chief as they struggled with a lack of parts, people shortages due to a plethora of causes, and just plain fatigue and lack of motivation.

"Come in, Master Chief," she welcomed, opening the door and motioning him to the half-made bunk which served as a day couch. "How's 104 doing?"

"Got our best techs on it, Skipper — I'll let you know soon what the verdict is," said the seasoned veteran of many deck plates, COs and problems.

McCormick was Navy through and through. Enlisting at the age of seventeen, he was in his twenty-sixth year of naval service, most of it at sea on carriers. He had seen it all. Change was a phenomenon that chief petty officers in the Navy had learned in the millennium to deal with and adapt to; but God, it had come fast and furious after 2000, he thought. I don't have a prob-lem with diversity, he reflected, just some of the outcomes. His opinion of the stress chit was severely at odds with accepted Navy policy and when one was thrust in his face, he would usually respond with a, "Shit, son, that's for candy asses." Eyeball-to-eyeball, he would also deny he ever made any such a statement.

Commander Wendy Montrose was divorced, the result of a marriage that got in the way of the U.S. Navy. She loved her three kids back in Virginia Beach and faithfully exchanged a round of e-mail with each of them weekly. They lived with her ex, Bill, who was a good man, a good provider and a good school administrator. Trouble was, thought Wendy, I need more than good.

As the muscular, 6 foot 2 inch master chief left the room, she added one more leadership problem to her growing stack. "God, he smelled good."

CHAPTER 4

The Pentagon

Rear Admiral Nancy Chandler, U.S. Navy, huddled in her windowless command center deep within the bowels of the Pentagon. She reminded herself to petition her boss, the combat arms head, Vice Admiral Stan Sarodsy, U.S. Navy, to schedule supply ships to the Reagan, particularly those carrying the precious JP9 ram-jet fuel for the thirsty fighters. First thing she did at 0700 was to punch up a large flat-screen display of her ships 8,000 miles away and rerun the flyover of her carrier by the unknown stealth duo. The two hostile aircraft were indeed intermittent on her display and went blank some two hundred miles from her forces.

On the adjacent screen were the digital image close-ups of the unknown aircraft taken by Lieutenant Swagger, the wizo of the intercepting Reagan deck-launched combat air patrol. The leering face and toothy grin of the pilot almost jumped out at her. But the airplane was strange— no markings, internal weaponry, twin engines and obvious stealth characteristics, like the anechoic skin coating. It was a type never before seen by the intelligence folks.

Nearby, Vice Admiral Sarodsy had observed the same information, only he had spent most of the night in his command center with his key staff officers. Sarodsy, as the Navy's executive VP for combat operations, was in the hot seat, as the tension meter worked its incremental upward slope. "Five carrier battle groups either in the region or en route and two more sailing shortly from San Diego and Norfolk," he thought out loud. "Thank God for the U.S. Navy." And, as an afterthought with an inward smile, "As usual."

Stan Sarodsy was of staunch Navy stock, his dad having been a four star admiral and highly decorated combat warrior in carrier aviation back in Vietnam. Sarodsy had managed to progress up the line from carrier-based fighter squadrons to aircraft carrier command, to the same job as his deputy, Nancy Chandler, and finally, as the three star head of the Navy's combat arms forces. He had tolerated the socialization of the Navy, correct only to the extent necessary to advance his combat readiness thesis to a sometimes reluctant Navy more intent on other agendas. His nemesis had been his present sidekick, Vice Admiral Sharon McCluskey, U.S. Navy, the executive VP for diversity. Equal in rank, stature, authority and prestige, they often clashed, the catalyst, the stress and medical policies of a gender-normed Navy. Admiral Sarodsy knew full well from his real-time squadron and ship status boards that most were at significantly less-than-100% combat personing, and hence, not nearly as combat ready as desired, the stress policy the chief instigator of the reduced readiness.

Being good sailors and loyal advocates of implementing the civilian-forged strategy and policies of the Navy, Sarodsy and his ilk had, for many years, saluted and marched off smartly when told what to do and how to do it by a succession of well-meaning civilian secretariats. Like all senior military officers, his allegiance was to the Constitution of the United States and the fundamental imperative of civilian control. After all, they were the bosses, he would sometimes privately lament. What they dictated, they got.

He had resisted the temptation in the early Monday morning hours to summon Nancy Chandler. She was obviously destined for bigger and better things, he reflected. He was lucky, too, for Chandler was an expert in the region, having spent the better part of her career serving in a variety of assignments dealing with China, Iran, Iraq, Saudi Arabia and Pakistan.

Sarodsy had many heavy-duty concerns: First, the ISIs were clearly gearing up for a thrust at gaining control, once and for all, of the Caspian Sea oil. Second, as best he could tell, it was apparent China was in on the action, albeit not overtly. Third, the unknown fighters were real cause for concern. Where, he pondered, had whomever obtained the technology to thwart the best the U.S. satellite smarts could throw at them? And finally, were there more missing nuclear weapons than just the four from the carrier Reagan? Whoever possessed these weapons had, excepting the U.S. Navy, the decisive swing military power in the world.

Sarodsy finally summoned his assistant for a strategy session in the briefing theater, along with their collective staffs for an intelligence briefing. "Better more heads than going solo, Nancy," he told her.

Projecting a large-screen display on one of the giant digital-electronic boards, the hyper-secure room three stories beneath the Pentagon shopping mall was somberly quiet. Sarodsy was known as a real operator with a warrior's sixth sense for the use of naval power projection. Chandler was equally respected as a seasoned expert in the enormous complexities of the region, geopolitical, religious and economic.

"Ladies and gentlemen and Admirals," the polished and smooth voice of the svelte intelligence commander broke the silence, "before I address the specifics of this morning's action in the Indian Ocean and the drama of the unknown fighters, allow me to provide a macro-perspective of the region." Her red-tipped laser pointer quivered with anticipation. "First, of course, is the Caspian Sea and its neighbors of Iran, Azerbaijan, Kazakhstan and Turkmenistan," the pointer arcing clockwise around the landlocked sea. "The three oil pipelines in Azerbaijan to the Black Sea, Baku to the Persian Gulf through Iran and, the newest, from Baku through Turkmenistan reaching to northern Pakistan, are the jewels. The region's oil reserves have been determined to be greater than the combined total of the North Sea, North Cape and Saudi Arabia combined. I might add that the Saudi and North Cape fields are reputed to be in decline. It is our assessment, and that of the CIA, that the intent of the ISI consortium is to sever the Black Sea and Pakistan pipelines, ship all the oil south to the Gulf and, hence, control 47% of the proven world's oil reserves."

She continued, pointing to western China. "China and her neighbor Pakistan are the unknowns. We do know for a certainty that China is desperately short of energy. Her foul-burning coal reserves were, each year, becoming an increasingly ponderous burden as the specter of global warming due to a pollution-riddled atmosphere loomed. In addition, as you are aware, the massive Dagling oil fields northwest of Beijing discovered in 1959, are now producing 95% water. The consensus is that China is intent on cooperating with the ISIs to (a) remain in their favor and (b) to continue to meet the bulk of their oil needs by importing through the Gulf by tanker." She concluded. "The U.S. considers the region to be in our vital interests, a policy that has not wavered since the days of President Carter's proclamation four decades earlier in the late 1970s."

She paused, knowing full well that the foregoing had been common knowledge to most in the room. "What we don't know is the Chinese connection. Since the pervasive influence of China in our electoral process in the mid-'90s, China has opened its doors to U.S. big business and technology. The quid, of course, were massive funds provided not only to global business leaders, but also to the inner fabric of American politics." She paused once again. "The bottom line though, is that China and Pakistan, as well as the countries of NATO, Japan and Russia, have far more oil needs than there are world supplies."

Follow the money, thought Admiral Sarodsy, thinking back on several generations of wars, money, greed and politics in the region. For a while it looked like coal would be the globe's long-range panacea; but the international community, led by a proactive U.S. Supreme Court bent on environmental correctness, so influenced the global network of industrialized nations that coal had largely remained in the ground.

Rear Admiral Nancy Chandler had been weaned on the geo-strategic, political and economic influence of oil. Educated at the prestigious School of Asian Studies at the University of Washington, she had matriculated to the officer corps of the U.S.

Navy in the mid-nineties and, after a master's degree in Indian Ocean studies at George Washington University, had served in a succession of key assignments in the political-military spheres of the Navy in and about Washington, including a tour of duty as a personal aide to the president and more recently, a three-year hitch as chief of staff to President Stallingsworth. With only fifteen years of service, she was known as a sharp, incisive, articulate and knowledgeable staff officer and, not incidentally, the youngest person in the history of the Navy to have reached flag rank.

"Commander, can you speculate as to where the unknown fighters were based?" quizzed Chandler.

"No, ma'am. From the pilot reports, though, it would appear somewhere in Afghanistan or Pakistan. We're working on some additional sources now."

"Admiral," Chandler continued, turning toward her combat arms boss, "my carrier groups need to get some fuel and grits. They're getting low, as you know, and the stress and medicals on all my ships — the Reagan's typical — are sky high and much greater than allowed by policy. When do you think we can get a ship alongside to off load the most critical, sir?"

Sarodsy was concerned as he mentally ticked off the ramjet JP9 fuel, the food supplies, smart weapons and stress cases on each of Chandler's three carriers and twenty-seven supporting ships. Fuel, food and weapons were adequate for now, he knew. But, some of his ships were down 15% of an already sparse crewing due to the stress and medical cases. He responded to Chandler's request. "Even if we could off load them, we don't have the trained bodies to replace them. Navy's sucking . . ." he caught himself, "going to the bottom of the barrel as it is now to person up the deployed fighter squadrons with pilots and back-seaters."

Sarodsy turned to his rear admiral deputy for diversity in what he knew was an exercise in futility, the coming question clearly rhetorical. "John, is there any way we can put the stress cases at Memphis and on the ships back to full duty on the deck plates and cockpits?" Nancy Chandler glanced at Rear Admiral John Epperson, the son of a once-prominent political appointee as the Navy secretary back in her mom's Washington heydays, knowing that even suggesting such heresy was cause for a severe course correction on the part of the instigator. "He needs his chain jerked," murmured Chandler. "You just don't even suggest such blasphemy."

Epperson, a tough, no-nonsense Bostonian and product of both the diversity and surface operations ladder in the Navy, walked a fine line with his boss, Sarodsy. Like all of them in the room, he knew the priorities and the rules. "There can be no exceptions, boss," respectfully answered the young flag officer, somewhat laconically.

The briefing officer continued: "Sir, ma'am, we know there are at least eleven potentially hostile submarines in the Indian Ocean, including six from China. As long as we keep up our high-speed, random maneuvering, we'll be OK. But, the weaponry is unknown at this time," her agile brain in a shift mode. "The air order of battle is more specific," she said flashing a comprehensive, real-time set of images onto the far screen. "We have total knowledge of the location of all ISI aircraft," dancing her laser to the ISI air bases in Iran, Saudi Arabia and Iraq.

Sarodsy knew most of this. The reality, though, was the U.S. Navy was the only formidable military force in the entire area of operations ever since U.S. ground-based forces had been kicked out of Saudi Arabia and Kuwait in 2004, and Oman and her neighbors in 2005. The nearest Air Force bases were in Italy and tiny Diego Garcia 1,200 miles to the south. So much for the Air Force quick-reaction propaganda, mused the admiral, wishing they were more potent. It takes ten tankers to get one iron-bomb stealth B2 over the area and a whole carrier air wing to protect it.

Admiral Sarodsy's mind was in high gear as the briefing officer continued to spout forth facts and figures, but no clear course of action. He was one of the few in the uniformed services who was aware of the existence of the old nuclear weapons on the six active carriers and six aged Trident missile submarines. This knowledge was a black, compartmented intelligence code, that only a handful of the most senior naval officers and White House staffers were privy to. Aside from the development of the big bomb during World War II, this had been the most closely held secret in the nation. Despite being outlawed by a hard-nosed international edict some eight years previous, the Navy had managed to hang on to about three hundred of the lethal weapons on each of six carriers and subs.

Sarodsy though, had learned an astounding fact about twelve days ago. Four of the weapons aboard the Reagan were unaccounted for and, just yesterday, he had been informed that two or more might be missing from the Reagan's sister carrier, the USS *John Stennis*. He had ordered a thorough inventory to include opening the storage containers and accessing the innards of the weapons, to be completed ASAP on all ships with the results coming direct to him on the "eyes only" back-channel communications network.

It wasn't that the weapons were particularly high-yield, but that they were capable of being delivered by practically any aircraft. Products of 1970s nuclear weapons technology, they were, nonetheless, capable of enormous destruction to warships at sea or in the mountainous choke-points in and about the oil lines snaking out from the Caspian.

Nancy Chandler was deep in thought as well, while the assembled staff officers parried ideas and thoughts. As the daughter of a prominent politician closely associated with the weapons industry in the U.S. and foreign countries, Nancy was, early on in her life, acclimated to guests in her home well-versed in the international arms trade. Upon leaving public office, Nancy's mother had cashed in the chips of years of influence, eased up to the completely legal trough of weapons-related largess, and become a piece of the action at Killington Associates, the most successful purveyor of arms and technology transfer on the globe. Her forte: China and the related hidden mechanisms and inner workings of a sometimes mysterious U.S. Congress.

As the daughter rose rapidly in the Navy in her Washington staff jobs, she was privy, of course, to the economic fortunes of her mother, the succession of captains of industry and heads-of-states endless. Her studies had reminded her of an earlier era in the late seventies when many thought that Japan was buying

up America. By contrast, in the past decade, the Chinese had literally invaded the U.S., the flow of unconstrained money to the
influential, like bees to honey.

Though a recognized expert in the region, the Chinese
connection was never challenged. "Everyone just took it for
granted, and we all rode the gravy train," she reflected, thinking of
the enormous wealth of many well-ensconced Washington politicians, present and former, and big business leaders, "Killington
Associates, no exception."

"The ground order of battle," intoned a new intel briefer,
"shows the ISI ground forces massing to the north on either side
of the Caspian Sea," the three sinuous oil pipelines like super
highways spoking outward from a big city, about to be swallowed by the giant pincers.

"Admiral Sarodsy, the CEO wants to see you, stat," interrupted an officious aide, neatly clad in her blue service uniform.
Stan Sarodsy knew he was in for a grilling, the CEO being the
Navy's top admiral, Admiral Carolyn Sweeney, seven stories
above them in the subdued, polished "E" ring of the Pentagon.

The CEO was all smiles. Sarodsy knew that she only
smiled when uncomfortable, which was seldom. "Good morning,
Admiral," said the tired vice admiral to his fresh and rested four star
boss. "Been a long night."

Sweeney, like many other senior military persons, was a
product of the revolution in the make up and objectives of the
armed forces in the past fifteen years. Early on, like many others,
she had caught the eye of Virginia Roberts Stallingsworth, now
her commander in chief, and had been accelerated up the promo-
tional ladder. At the age of forty-two, she had served a one-year
tour on board ship, attended the obligatory Naval War College in
Newport and prestigious National War College in Washington,
the rest of her career forged in various staffs and key jobs in and
about the Washington arena. Like most of her contemporaries in
the higher ranks, she was intelligent, witty, confident, tough and a
vocal proponent of the notion that gender equality meant dramatically increased combat readiness. She had spent her two dec-

41

ades of service as a firm believer in the adage, "Happy, relaxed sailors produce the best in combat performance," along with the predictable corollary, "A stressed-out naval person must be rehabilitated in order to remain productive."

"Stan, the President wants a briefing ASAP — this morning if possible. Can you do it?" the CEO was all business, her smile faded, forehead creased.

"No problem, ma'am. You name the time. Best, though, we do it down below in our command center rather than the White House," the porosity of the latter anathema to military security.

As he descended in the command elevator to his secure womb deep below, Sarodsy mulled over the convoluted facts surrounding the missing nukes, uncomfortable that his boss was not privy to this latest bombshell of information and that she probably ought to be cut in. She was, however, conversant with the existence of the weapons at sea, having been a key person in establishing the policy to thwart efforts by the international communities to thoroughly inspect all U.S. warships for the presence of nuclear weapons. The standard and decades-tested response had been, "United States warships ply international waters and are therefore not subject to external inspection. We categorically deny the existence of weapons of mass destruction and have heartily endorsed the elimination of such weapons."

"Attention on deck," barked the Marine captain as the President of the United States strode into the underground command center, all present snapping to attention. First order of business for the President was to provide a warm embrace for her former chief of staff, Nancy Chandler. Even at the age of sixty-four, Virginia Roberts Stallingsworth was a commanding figure, her smile masking deep concerns. President for six years, she had ascended to the presidency in a landslide to become the nation's first female head-of-state. Elected on the basis of her proven ability to lead and motivate, she, along with thousands of her political party, had been coasting to victory after victory in the past six years, enormous amounts of funds the bedrock for success, the airways and high definition TV the fodder for a believing mass. Her party, the ECATS — Enlightened Citizens Against The Status Quo — had been an enormously popular alternative to the traditional, body-politic choices. To some, six years later though, it smacked as more of the same, once the smooth rhetoric subsided and political reality emerged.

As the briefer spieled, Admiral Sarodsy was deeply introspective. Apolitical to the extreme, he recalled the chilling news of the missing nukes in the hyper-classified "eyes only" report from a clandestine group within the Navy's intelligence directorate stating that, "The case appears to involve the highest levels of the U.S. government."

Stan Sarodsy was barely paying attention to the situation brief. Something is rotten in Denmark. The icing on the cake is the damned missing weapons, he thought to himself. His deeply ingrained sense of duty told him he must bring the CEO and President in on this, but his common sense told him to hold off. Sarodsy was well aware of the leading role of the U.S. in the exportation of arms, a policy he found hard to abide simply because he felt altruism was a clear runner-up to greed on the part of a substantial slice of America's leadership, both business and government. Even back in '96, the U.S. led the world in the arms industry, exporting almost twice that of the former USSR, four times Great Britain and five times greater than France. Now it's all coming back to bite us, he correctly recalled, dimly remembering his dad's exhortations about the stupidity of the sale of the latest and deadly-accurate, heat-seeking air-to-air missiles to the Iranians back in the early eighties.

It was clear to Sarodsy China had become the world's second superpower, the ISI consortium of recent years, a clear third. He recalled a dinner with his seventy-four-year old father not long ago who reminded him in no uncertain terms, that six of ten of the world's wealthiest persons were Chinese, the kingpin for the past few years being the venerable Charlie Flee, long an enabler to the well-connected and a prominent board member of Killington Associates. Just three nights ago, there had been a black-tie White House gala, CEO of the Navy Sweeney and his deputy, Nancy Chandler, prominent in their dress blue service uniforms, along with a generous sprinkling of Chinese, notably Flee, who sat to the right of the beaming President.

Sarodsy was snapped out of his musings by a strident President wanting an explanation for the high level of stress cases on his warships. "What's going on out there?" she demanded, obviously agitated. "Why so many medical and stress cases?" Sarodsy fumbled for a moment, his mind trying to readjust from the specter of real war and people dying, to the social problems on his front-line warships.

Taking a deep, measured breath, glancing quickly at his boss who unobtrusively nodded her head sideways, Sarodsy responded. "Madame President," he began respectfully, striding to the podium and taking command of the laser pointer, "we have a crisis the world has not known since World War II. I don't need to remind you that the economy of the U.S. is explicitly linked to the region we are addressing."

The President angrily interrupted, her voice shrill, Sweeney and Chandler cringing deep into their well-worn leather seats. "Admiral, I repeat! Please tell me why the high stress and medical levels! If I wanted a tutorial on the region, I would have asked Nancy." Rear Admiral Nancy Chandler was well-attuned to the tirades of her former boss, but knew as well, that rear admirals did not invoke the ire of vice admirals, particularly if they were one's immediate boss.

Blushing imperceptibly, the tough Sarodsy respectfully decided to take on the President of the United States. Eyeballs locked with hers, he continued, his speech clear. "The facts are, ma'am, that we are in deep trouble militarily and I need to remind you that in real terms we took a 35% reduction in defense spending in the mid-nineties and another 25% real reduction over the past decade." Warming to the issue which had long lingered in his gut, the warrior admiral continued. "Furthermore, in my professional judgment, our nation has implemented war-fighting policies in the past fifteen years relative to social agendas that have seriously eroded our ability to fight and win the war at sea."

Sarodsy felt good. At long last, it was out on the table. His CEO boss was red-faced, the attempted smile a feeble facade. Sarodsy was not finished. "And finally, I must, once again most respectfully, remind you, Madame President, that much of the modern weaponry we face this morning is the result of national policies that have encouraged the exportation of arms and advanced technology throughout the world to clients who, in many cases, do not share our deep sense of human values and democracy." Christ, thought Sarodsy, I'm about to join my dad in the south-forty pasture.

He decided to keep the floor, his audience speechless for the moment. "What we are facing is today, not yesterday. If the diplomacy folks can't mediate this pending disaster, then it's up to the U.S. Navy. We have war plans, and have had for decades, to deal with the situation we are faced. If I may be so bold," — Sweeney blanched — "what needs to be done is to get the Chinese influence with the ISIs on board now. They have the most to lose. And, I might add a reminder, Madame President, our warships have been deployed in some cases approaching nine months. The three carrier battle groups of Rear Admiral Chandler have been consecutively at sea for 74 days. Fatigue is a real factor. We have our most capable captains on these ships and I can assure you, they will do the best with whom and what they have."

Sarodsy resisted the urge to speak further on the stress and medical scenarios, figuring he had stepped on himself enough already.

The President left the secret enclave as she had entered, with a bright smile and trademark hug for her former confidante, Rear Admiral Nancy Chandler.

CHAPTER 5

Chinese Fighter Squadron

Major Ying Tsunami, Imperial Chinese Air Force, was on his third, ice-cold Tsingtao beer, laughing so hard he could barely stand at the bar. "Can you believe it," he shouted to his enthusiastic squadron mates, "What a back-seater! — Let's hear it for the U.S. Navy! A toast to the women at sea and in the air!" A resounding clink of glasses raised high and a, "Here's to the U.S. Navy," followed in unison.

It had indeed, been a good week for the major's 57th stealth fighter squadron. All eighteen of their hot, new fighters were operationally ready and had flown over 127 long missions probing for the U.S. fleet massing in the Indian Ocean and the ISI defenses to the west. While most so-called stealth aircraft were somewhat immune to detection by triple-phased-array radars and down-linked satellites, the F-48 Dynasty was, so far, undetectable. Capable of mach 1.55 in basic engine and cruise altitudes over 60,000 feet, the machine was able to launch the most advanced smart weapons U.S. technology could provide. And, thought Tsunami, we had found at least part of the fleet, thanks to dumb Navy fighter pilots.

"Let's hear it for the 'GIBS' and dumb Navy fighter pilots," toasted the squadron's commanding officer. All knew, of course, that GIBS meant girls in the back seat and that dumb U.S. Navy fighter pilots was a redundant phrase.

Major Tsunami's elite squadron had been ordered to a rare one-day stand-down by virtue of its exceptional performance in the past ten days. Normally alcohol and the Imperial Chinese Air

Force did not mix. Tonight, though, was different. The young skipper's description of the Navy GIBS took on several dimensions past reality as the chaste warriors waxed increasingly vocal and descriptive, raucous song filling the small club at the remote, secret air base.

Major Ying Tsunami was a rising star. Educated at the U.S. Naval Academy in the Class of 1998, he had been a pragmatic beneficiary of an astounding openness between China and the U.S. Trade, banking, big business and politics, had become indelibly commingled, along with liberal doses of exchange students at leading colleges and universities. Following graduation, Tsunami was commissioned a 2nd Lieutenant in the Chinese Air Force and immediately entered Navy flight training as an exchange student in Pensacola, Florida and Kingsville, Texas, where again, he excelled, both academically and in the air. He even big-dealed night carrier qualifications, along with a few others, in the venerable Navy training aircraft, the T-45F Goshawk. "What a kick," he recalled, deep down inside harboring a profound respect for Navy carrier aviation and pilots, "including good looking girls in the back-seats."

Within one week of graduation from pilot training, his Navy wings of gold were replaced by the silver emblem of the Imperial Chinese Air Force, his assignment to the country's top fighter wing only logical. In the ensuing ten years, he had amassed over 3,700 hours of tough tactical flying, totally immersed in the warrior's art of becoming the best combat pilot, period.

Following happy hour, Tsunami cloistered himself in his tiny room, deep in thought. Like most of his nation's war-fighting leaders, he was required to continuously study in one of several disciplines, his being geo-political broadly, and America, specifically. His mind wandered to the vision in the aft cockpit of the carrier-based Phantom III only a few hours before. "God, she was gorgeous," he exclaimed to the four walls of his spartan domain.

China's professional military had one hard-nosed and fundamental focus: A total and unwavering dedication to the mission. Marriage for men was "encouraged" to be delayed to at least age thirty-five. Women were a distraction and alcohol only an occasional luxury. The study of the art of warfare was constant and pervasive. Tsunami's life, since his U.S. days, was dedicated to becoming the best warrior, with no exceptions and no latitude.

"Quite at contrast with that of America," he noted recalling a thesis he had written in his off-duty study on "The Attributes of a Real Warrior." "The U.S." he had written, "was bent on social-norming and opportunity for the lowest common denominator, rather than winning in combat." Secretly, he could not imagine the leadership challenges of a Navy warship at sea for months on end with a complement of 50% women. He had written at the time, "The Naval Academy had gone over the edge with its multiple social agendas — clearly over the line." He had spent a formative two-month deployment as a midshipman on the nuclear-powered aircraft carrier Nimitz, one of the Navy's first warships to have sizable contingents of women in the crew. Even then, the pendulum was swinging effortlessly to a unisex environment. On the deckplates, the ship's unofficial motto had been, "Work together, play together, live together and together we will win." He wasn't sure now or then just what "win" meant. In his judgment, the U.S. military was, in many respects, a paper tiger, the enigmatic back-seater a case in point.

He peered about his monastic room. Kind of like the junior officer staterooms on the Nimitz, he remembered from his short stint at sea. His was a sink, single bunk, small desk, straight chair and a rack for uniforms and flight gear. One overhead, unshaded one-hundred-watt bulb provided adequate, no-frills illumination. On the wall above his desk was the simple creed of the Imperial Chinese Air Force. "The job of the fighter pilot is to shoot the enemy from the sky and anything else is rubbish." It was signed with one word, "Wong."

His ten years deep in the interior of a largely-hidden China were in stark contrast to his six years in the U.S., the focus totally on potential combat, the distractions few and far between. Major Tsunami recalled the visit three years ago in which he was selected to be the escort officer for a recently retired U.S. Navy vice admiral, not only due to his professional reputation, but that he

48

and Admiral Demming were Annapolis alumni and, the admiral's daughter Susan, and he, had trained together as student naval aviators, ten years prior. Chinese intelligence also knew that the admiral's son-in-law was the skipper of one of the aircraft carriers in the region. Finally, and unknown to the major, the Chinese government had laid out the gold carpet for Demming, due to his proven depth of knowledge regarding U.S. stealth technology.

Part of the visit had been a tour of a fighter base deep within China and an orientation flight, in then, China's front-line fighter, the pilot Major Tsunami. Demming was a good stick, he recalled. I just sat there in back and kept my mouth shut while he wrung it out — 8.6Gs included. Admirals, he had thought at the time, ought to be chair-bound and fat. Not Demming, though. I would take him on my wing anytime. Following the flight, he and the admiral had done a sprightly three-mile jog about the base before meeting with the wing's assembled 78 combat pilots.

It had been a briefing to remember, Tsunami recalled, once again deeply introspective in his tiny cubical at the remote base in northern Iran. Mostly it was fighter pilot talk and generalizations about U.S. Navy carrier operations, particularly catapult shots and black-night, arrested landings. Like professional aviators everywhere, most were immensely respectful of tactical carrier-based flying, with the seldom argued caveat that it was indisputably the most demanding in the aviation repertoire.

Fielding a question from a young captain, the admiral had explained the perceived feminization of the United States military as, "Getting the best from 100% of the population, not just 50%. And," he would always emphasize in the public settings, "that it was working extremely well indeed." The admiral had confided to Tsunami in private, "I'll bet you wouldn't mind a 50% ratio out here." The celibate and disciplined major wisely refused the bait.

"How's Susan doing, Admiral?" queried the major, changing the subject.

"Just fine, Ying. I'll be sure and let her know I saw you. What a small world. She's a co-pilot with American Airlines now and married to a former Navy pilot who's doing the same with FedEx. Both still stay current flying the F-27C stealth Phantom III in the reserves. Two kids, in fact."

Another stark contrast, thought the Chinese fighter squadron CO. In our military, those who are selected for the top combat units stay the course. He could not recall any of his contemporaries in the past ten years who had left the air force to fly for the airlines.

Unbeknown to Tsunami, his country's doors had opened wide for the admiral and his group. Killington Associates was as well known in the inner power sanctums of China's movers and shakers as FedEx, McDonalds and Marlboro. Demming's visits to China had become more frequent as he parlayed his in-depth knowledge of stealth technology in exchange for the considerable monetary benefits to his employer and himself. All of this was, of course, totally sanctioned by a U.S. government-endorsed, arms and technology transfer policy.

Tsunami was jerked back to reality this Sunday night. "Major, General Wong wants to see you ASAP. His personal jet will be here at 2230." General Wong was the Chief of Staff of the Imperial Chinese Air Force and known as a classic and total Type-A workaholic. Only forty-four, a prominent sign to his office proclaimed, "If it's got something to do with combat readiness, come in." The corollary was evident, trivia a non-starter in his presence.

Grabbing a small, pre-packed overnight bag, Tsunami remembered his Navy flight training so long ago. Susan Demming had lived in the apartment next door at the Kingsville training base when both were in advanced flight training. Susan was known as a nice girl who worked hard. But, he remembered, she did not like the night work and, when his class had the option to night carrier qualify, she had mysteriously been unavailable. As nice as she was, the squadron CO mused, I could not imagine having her as my wingman.

At 2345 Major Tsunami stood at attention in front of the legendary General Wong, a man of few words, whose total commitment was to meld his country's air force into the most formidable fighting team the world had ever known. Without pleasantries, he snapped, "Tell me about the American fighter, the pilot and the back-seater." The major ticked off what had occurred, including his pilot-to-pilot parry with the Navy front-seater and the female-to-male repartee that followed.

The general smiled, not at the latter, but at the clear message that his F-48 Dynasty fighters had evaded the best U.S. technology could throw at them.

Wong was a warrior. A student of the Ming Dynasty reaching back some 1,200 years, he was a staunch believer in certain fundamental notions of military power. "First, of course," he would lecture, "was economic strength, complemented by an aggressive importation of foreign technology." He would use the Chinese invention and use of gunpowder over seven-hundred-years ago, as a prime example. "Second, while technology may change and economies ebb and flow, the vital ingredient in any military force is the uncompromising warrior ethic, the will to win and the sublimation of personal comfort to self-sacrifice."

General Wong was well aware of the energy crisis his country faced. The international community had gone ballistic over the environment — the mandated closure of China's coal mines in the face of world sanctions, a *fait accompli*. "China must have fair access to oil," he would offer to anyone or group who would listen. Just as Japan had been pushed into an oil crisis in the 1930s by a stubborn outside world, the reality was that China could well repeat the scenario within the next decade.

Several years ago, Wong, then a one star general, had been part of a small cadre of military officers who, following the destruction of the few rudimentary nuclear weapons in China's arsenal in accordance with international decree in 2004, had secretly met, off the record, for the purpose of determining (a) if there were any nuclear weapons or devices in the world left intact and (b) if so, how to obtain them.

Wong and his compatriots understood full-well that if backed into a corner, even the tamest of dogs will bite. They had started, first, with a considerable untraceable bank roll and access to their country's best intelligence, with the former states of the USSR including Russia. They batted zero, the international inspection and destruction teams having apparently done a most thorough job. Iraq, Jordan and Israel took a while longer, but with the same disappointing results.

The U.S. however, yielded clues, hints innocuous on the surface. Three years ago, the offer of a mansion estate on the banks of the Whitewater River and a lottery-sized yearly stipend to some pliant former Navy supplicants, had produced positive evidence that the U.S. Navy had somehow not been a signatory to the total elimination of nuclear weapons. It was determined that dozens of old, but still lethal, air-deliverable nuclear weapons were snuggled securely within the innards of several giant aircraft carriers.

Along with a nucleus of ten specialized technical and weapons experts, as well as one international funds specialist, Wong's team went to work. It had really been quite simple, remembered Wong. Big bucks to a key person stationed aboard an in-port aircraft carrier was all it took to get moving, followed by massive donations to several cleverly disguised shell organizations within the U.S., final recipients unknown. The going rate per weapon was one billion dollars, all of which flowed into a complex web of clandestine, overseas Swiss bank accounts.

Actually, General Wong knew, the precedent had been set in years past by greasing America's political system along the same lines, though not quite as obtuse. Though he did not know the details, the facts were that the most sensitive nuclear data within the U.S. National Laboratory in the New Mexico hills had been compromised regularly over the years, compliments of bureaucratic incompetency and bucks under the right tables.

The meeting with Tsunami's air force boss several rungs removed, terminated curtly at 0130, the same jet returning the major westward towards northern Pakistan and Iran. The general's parting words were, "You will be receiving a shipment of four containers by TU-87 transport at 0400. They will be taken to the new base complex. Only you and four personally selected pilots will be allowed access. You are not to discuss this conversation with anyone. A detailed set of instructions is included with the shipment. Questions?" At that the general regained his seat, on to the next set of war-fighting issues, the late hour of little relevance.

Monday was a day off for his pilots, but not the commanding officer of the 57th fighter squadron. With four of his most trusted aviators, Tsunami reviewed the stack of technical and training manuals deep inside the heavily guarded enclave within the covert base.

Tsunami realized that much of the Chinese smart-weapons achievements, accrued from liberal use of the advanced micro-GPS imported from the giant Consolidated Company. The latest modifications were far more accurate and versatile than the old-style, global positioning system, the blending into the air-to-air and air-to-ground modes of the F-48 and its load of smart weapons, fitting like a glove.

He knew, too, that the key to China's economic success and longevity as a superpower was oil, and the key to the oil, could well be the contents of the four sinister containers in the nearby bunker.

Tsunami's brain was in max overload. How fast events have unfolded, he thought. As a senior at the Naval Academy in late 1997, he had watched with awe the state visit to America of his nation's president, the infamous photo of a bowing then-President Bill Clinton in the White House, to a smiling and assured Jiang, transmitted to a worldwide audience of billions. Confident and assured, the Chinese president had taken on the histrionics of human rights and Tiananmen Square with a somewhat jocular snipe at the five hundred or so obscene, violent deaths within the ten-mile-square U.S. capital each year. "Why," the Chinese president had pronounced, his eyebrows raised questionably, "was his entourage cautioned not to enter most areas of the capitol city, day or night? Yes," he would respectfully continue, the smile unbroken, "we have a ways to go. But, it also seems we all do. Is that not the case, Mr. President?" The applause had been politely muted, the rhetorical question left unanswered.

The squadron commanding officer was still reflective of the tumult of the past fifteen years. At about the same time as his leader's visit to America, there had been a little publicized statement from a U.S. congressman denouncing some arms purveyors as the "whores of Wall Street," apparently due to the perception that these mega corporations would sell anything to anyone. "His rhetoric notwithstanding, however," the major murmured in the solitude of his tiny room, "he was no match for a system within which influence and access went dead-center to the highest bidder."

Drifting off to a troubled sleep, the squadron commander thought of the nice girl Susan and the U.S. Navy back-seater's provocative smile of just a few hours ago. Where were they now?

CHAPTER 6

Relationships

Lieutenant Commander Dave "Blues" Anderson, was huddled deep within the secret war-planning confines of the USS *Ronald Reagan,* brain-storming a series of "what ifs" in response to the enormous ISI buildup. This system is incredible, he mused, calling up various real-time satellite images of the northern Iranian military movements, and the closer displays of the substantial military complex near the mouth of the Persian Gulf known as Bandar Abas, a strategic nucleus of historic import.

The acting executive officer of the Red Rippers called up the order of battle of the big naval base at Bandar on the Iranian coast, now a major node in the consortium of power among Iran, Saudi and Iraq. "Damn," he muttered to his sidekicks in the tiny cubicle, Ensign Patty Butts, Lieutenant Becky "Big Sister" Turner and Lieutenant Scott "Twidget" Jacobs, "I've never seen anything like it — it's awesome."

"It" was indeed a formidable build-up. Over one hundred offensive strike and defensive aircraft, several missile-toting, anti-ship vessels, a few submarines and layers of self-defense missilery. The express purpose? To thwart the offensive power of the U.S. Navy's Indian Ocean fleet. Other similar defenses were in central Saudi Arabia as a buffer for carrier battle groups in the Red Sea, and in and about Baghdad, as a counter to naval forces in the eastern Mediterranean. All of these, of course, thought Anderson, were secondary in importance to the ultimate objective, the alarming confluence of hostile ground and air power poised in northern Iran and Iraq, forming tightening pincers about the

Caspian Sea riches.

In addition to her duties as one of the Red Ripper's highly respected carrier fighter pilots, Becky Turner was the strike planning leader responsible for, "Putting smart weapons on dumb targets." Her gifted back-seater and roommate, Twidget, was her assistant. The four-person team would meet regularly to go over the strike planning for potential targets about once a week, though in the past two months, it had been more like daily for two to three hours at a whack. Their job? To orchestrate the mix of weapons, aircraft, refueling, tactics and timing necessary to neutralize the Bandar Abas complex and thereby enable free strike access to the troubled Caspian Sea region further north.

Twidget and Patty had become adept at manipulating the vast amount of data extant in the intelligence systems aboard the big aircraft carrier, and had spent literally hundreds of hours cloistered in the cramped, secret spaces. Twidget, Dave thought, must never sleep. He's flying, on the bridge as junior officer of the deck with Karen, or down here. Many's the time the two would brainstorm after a long flight, malodorous flights suits no hindrance.

The war-planning center was a masterpiece of intelligence fusion into which flowed massive streams of information from shore-based facilities via satellites and on-board sensors as well as a sophisticated, internally-generated data base. Most remarkably, it was part human in its approach to problem solving, an artificial intelligence capability second to none. Aside from the clandestine nuclear weapons storage far below, the center was the most closely-guarded space on the speeding warship.

Tonight the four team members, crammed shoulder-to-shoulder over the seated Anderson, were totally engrossed in the mental art of warfare in the year 2010. Dave's mind wandered. How many hours since leaving Norfolk have we met in the same cubical? Must be about 300. I even know them with my eyes closed — perfume, flight suits and Twidget's Mennon after shave lotion. Patty leaned over him, her animated breath only inches from his right ear. "Check this," she exclaimed, pointing to a Chinese ship alongside the quay. "They look like the latest anti-ship missiles — the Super Pelican — the same as ours." She pushed harder against Dave's back and shoulder with professional excitement.

The intelligence officer was fired up by the revelation, and knew that the Super Pelican anti-ship missile had been a recent sale to China, a compliant U.S. government granting substantial waivers to the benefit of the giant Consolidated Corporation over the strident objections of the service chiefs. Her mind was in high gear. "The Super Pelican just got to us. There are no defenses against it." Patty was burdened by another feeling, her mind wandering back to the pragmatics of the small room. I'm like a sandwich, she thought, fearing to move one way or the other. Twidget's pressing on me and I'm caught in the middle.

Becky broke the impasse. "Check this area, guys," she said, pointing her laser to an airfield eighteen miles inland to the north. "The same type missile containers are lined up ready to be loaded." The sandwich readjusted, the bodies once again in control. They all knew the implications of the Super Pelican, a missile so versatile and advanced, that there were virtually no defenses against it. Becky said to her compatriots, "How incredibly stupid to sell this weaponry to the Chinese. The stuff got to them and to the ISIs faster than to our Navy's front-line forces."

Big Sister and Twidget had to leave the session to brief and fly this Monday afternoon. The group agreed to reassemble at 2200 that night to plan the details of a preemptive strike, should the high command in the five-sided Pentagon puzzle palace in Washington so dictate. Dave and Patty stayed on to do some preliminary work.

For the next hour, the seasoned pilot and the young intelligence officer huddled closely within the confined space, recalling real-time overhead information and the opinions of the shore-based intel folks back in Suitland, Maryland. Patty was flushed with professional excitement, her longish hair occasionally hiding the master display. Dave, too, was animated, but not professionally. He tried to avert his eyes, eyes that wandered to his fellow warrior's open shirt and a flesh-colored undergarment. The inattention to the deadly task at hand, was bolstered by the scent

57

beside him. I can even smell it with my door closed, he thought, referring to the thirteen-person officer berthing area known as paradise.

Patty leaned across the trim Dave Anderson, he clad in his vintage form-fitting flight suit and she in her normal working khaki uniform, her female defenses alert, her mind wandering to her temporary cellmate in the intelligence spaces.

That she was a workaholic was no secret and, much like Twidget, one of her releases was a daily workout in the ship's well-equipped gym. The accepted attire, like any other in the sea-going Navy, was "comfortable." Patty's outfit was typical. A skin-tight, one-piece ensemble that, more often than not, elicited envious glances from a few in the ship's crew, particularly in the last few months of this long deployment. At twenty-two, she was definitely attractive, a fact of which Dave, ten years her senior, was well aware. Patty, though, was seemingly all-business and had a reputation as "not available."

Dave reacted to the movements of his squadronmate by putting his arm around her waist and nuzzling her ear, the familiar perfume invading his senses. Patty relaxed — she sensed it was coming. "Only a matter of time before he makes a move," she had proffered from the wisdom of her early twenties to her roommate, Karen. She had made up her mind on three points: "One, I'll do my best to discourage any intrusions on his part. Two, if it does happen, I'll just say no. And three, I'll not report it to the diversity control officer." The latter point was well-schooled into all on board in clearly understood language stating that, "Any sexual overtures by either sex or of the same sex, were to be reported immediately — NO EXCEPTIONS." The reality was, that a person found so guilty, no matter how innocuous or slight, was to be relieved of all duties and sent immediately to Stress City far below.

Patty's brain said "no," as her face quarter-turned to meet Dave's lips. A tentative kiss and loose embrace followed. In a few short seconds, the brains focused, the embrace ended, the lips disengaged. "No, Dave," she whimpered, her eyes and his still locked, her heart racing, the pending combat strikes for the moment relegated to a back-burner of the hot stove.

Back in paradise, Bikini and Studs awoke from a troubled sleep to prepare for the 1600 launch, a three-hour combat air patrol. They had tearfully discussed what to do. She could confirm her pregnancy knowing that the results were immediate grounding for her and Studs, assignment to Stress City, transfer off the ship when available, and a one-year mandatory leave of absence. Aside from the emotional aspects, they both knew that the impact on their already decimated squadron's combat readiness would be severe. Iron Lady would, of course, go ballistic, a prospect that almost brought them to a smile.

Prior to briefing for the flight, Bikini made a clandestine call to the squadron's flight surgeon, Dr. Rose Johnson, Lieutenant, Medical Corps, U.S. Naval Reserve, and met with her at 1300 in sick bay. Dr. Johnson's job was to minister to the general medical needs of the Reagan and ships in company, but with a particular focus on the aviators of the Red Rippers and Barking Dogs. Though not a genuine pilot or wizo, she did fly on occasion with Blues and Iron Lady. Unquestionably, Rose Johnson was a crackerjack medical officer and flight surgeon. Dual certified in psychiatry and pediatrics, she hoped one day to combine the two into a practice dedicated to providing an emotionally healthy head-start for inner-city preschoolers. What she had witnessed in the battle group of eleven ships and two subs for the past eight and one-half months was the subject for a detailed medical journal, euphemistically entitled, "The Confluence of Young Men and Women Within the Confines of Warships Deployed for Extended Periods, A Behavioral Study."

Rose Johnson knew little of combat, military readiness or war fighting, but was well into a serious documentation of the twenty-four-hours a day, seven days a week, months on end, shoulder-to-shoulder, inter-personal relationships within warships at sea. No social scientist, she was, however, acutely aware of the pragmatics of the Navy's sweeping gender-diversity policies of the past two decades. Because of the patient-doctor relationship, the tales she documented had increased exponentially in the past few months on board the big carrier. "No one would believe all this," she had penned into her expanding journal.

"Evelyn, you are, my friend, 100% with child. How many have you missed?" the doctor's practiced hands weaving a familiar pattern on and about the young body of her patient. "Been happening more and more," she professed and, with a learned chuckle, "I can't imagine why. I guess the super pills aren't all they're cracked up to be."

Bikini was petrified, her life flashing before her like a condemned criminal. Hesitantly, in a low conspiratorial tone, "Isn't there something you can do — please."

"No, honey. Too late for that I'm afraid. I think you and Studs — it is Studs, right? — have a one-way ticket back to shore duty U.S.A, a normal work week and no more black-assed , midnight catapult shots. Besides, you know the policy. Even if it were earlier, I wouldn't do it." And finally, "I'll have to ground you and Studs." She braced for the torrent she knew would follow.

Sobbing, Evelyn let it all out. "This is exactly what's not supposed to happen. We were extra careful, even with the pill we both took. My Skipper will be all over me and Studs like a wet blanket. Can't you wait until this crisis is over — about a week or so, Doc?" said the scared young wizo while getting back into her flight suit.

The Doc commiserated for only a moment. "OK Evelyn, but please, don't talk to anyone about this. If old Jaws heard about it, he'd offer me to the sharks. Keep it to yourself. Studs included — understood?" her voice no longer accommodating, the easy smile replaced with a grim demeanor.

Nearby, Master Chief Mitsi Moore, U.S. Navy, the captain's right-hand person when it came to the care, feeding and well-being of the warship's 5,000 troops, was busy plying her trade. Rising through the ranks for the past fifteen years as an aviation's boatswain's mate responsible for the ship's catapults and arresting gear, no one knew when or where she would show up. Routinely, at least once or twice a day, she and Captain Boone would discuss a slice of the menagerie of issues always simmering on the big ship.

This Monday morning she was atop a stealth fighter, number 104, on the hangar deck, conversing with a trio of VF-11 Red Ripper maintenance personnel about an avionics problem. By getting about and wandering the ship, she managed a great deal of credibility with the crew. Justifiable complaints or suggestions would be passed on to the executive officer at the nightly department head get-together or even to the captain, provided the person had confided first with their chief or division officer. "Go around the chain of command and it will cease to exist," she would preach repeatedly to the crew on the ship's TV.

Master Chief Randy McCormick was also making his rounds, frustration at the non-combat ready status of the jet his focus for the morning. One of the fourteen Ripper jets in a down status was normal. Two was one too many and an insult to his professional reputation as the best F-27C maintenance chief in the fleet.

"Hi, Master Chief," yelled McCormick to the Reagan's senior enlisted person, "How goes it?" He very highly respected Mitsi. She was a pro and, though younger in age and experience than he, was a real sailor who had paid her dues in the tough world of the sea-going Navy. "With or without diversity, she would have been a winner," he would argue to an occasional male malcontent among his fellow chiefs.

After the ship's command master chief and the Red Ripper maintenance chief had chatted for a while, she asked Randy to stop by her office later in the morning. "Roger that, Master Chief," he replied with sincere respect.

Mitsi Moore retreated to her tiny office dead center in the ship, directly beneath the hangar deck, closed the door and reflected on her two hour tour that morning. Increasingly, she was tired, more mentally than physically. In the sometimes rough vernacular of the aviation boatswain's mate, she said to the four walls, "This shit's getting old. Eight months was tough enough, but the unending twelve-hour days and thirty-day months has resulted in a crew that's strained beyond belief."

Fact was, the Reagan's crew was half women and half

men Like a millennium of warships and sailors that had deployed for extended periods in eras past, she knew the dominant difference in the past fifteen years had been the Navy's headlong rush towards gender equality. The legal gates had opened to clear combat billets back in the early '90s, but the fish had not taken the bait. Even in 2000, the overwhelming majority of combat billets open to women in all of the services, had gone unfilled, the chair-bound, nine-to-five feminists in hometown America in high warble over the "lack of equality." The change in the law in 2004, solved the issue by simply mandating gender and lifestyle equality into the law of the land when it came to the personing of military combat billets, no exceptions permitted.

Master Chief McCormick knocked on the closed door of the ship's master chief petty officer. "Coffee hot?"

"For you, big guy, always," she said, standing in welcome, pleased at the distraction.

Both Mitsi and Randy were highly respectful of one another professionally. "How's Jack doing?" Randy asked, referring to his former mentor and shipmate, Mitsi's husband and retired master chief, residing in the Norfolk area.

"Doing fine," she responded somewhat wistfully. "Said he saw your Suzette at the captain's home last night," thinking of the e-mail she had received earlier and wisely leaving out the specifics. Mitsi harbored substantial disapproval of her friend's first and only bride of less than a year. Not good enough for my Randy, she would opine privately.

She and the Red Ripper chief, like most Navy chief petty officers, were most courteous and respectful of one another in public, but good buddies in private. They were a contrast, he at over six feet and she a sprightly 5 foot 2 inches. "It's not how big you are, but how tight your spring is wound," she would offer to those who might doubt her ability to hack the job. Increasingly, on this long deployment, she and Randy had commiserated with one another. Randy, with his longer service could compare the Navy of 2010 with that of far-off 1982 candidly with Mitsi, herself a comparative youngster. In recent months the two had spent more and more time together, comfortable in their laid back professional relationship.

"You know, Randy, we may be in hard, dirty combat before the week is out, don't you? The Captain's convinced we are definitely in harm's way. Problem is, the sense of urgency among our young crew just isn't there. I stopped by the style salon a while ago and it's business as usual — guys getting the latest style-cut and the girls coiffed and fingernailed to a T."

"My troops are too tired to mess around," he responded, knowing full well it was a bunch of crap and Mitsi knew it too. Just that morning, he had to counsel two of his youngsters who had coveted the same young squadron mate. Fissures and rivalries were epidemic, not only in the VF-11 Red Rippers, but throughout the ship as well. "I guess you're right, Mitsi, our troops are never too tired to tango."

The ship's policy, of course, was crystal clear, indoctrinated since day one at the giant recruit training center at Great Lakes. "You can live together, work together and hold hands, but no sexual overtures of any kind," Mitsi and her cohorts would lecture their charges. "If caught in an overt act or the woman became pregnant, it's an automatic trip home for both parties."

"Randy, except for two days in Singapore, we've been at sea non-stop 133 days with only a handful of no-fly days and steel picnics on the flight deck to show for it."

Randy responded, his words measured, "Did just about the same back in 1990 in Desert Storm. Yeah, it was tough, but nowhere near what it is now." He paused, his emotions on the high side. "You know what the problem is? Face it, my friend, this is no environment for social do-gooders. We're paying the price, big time."

"Damn, damn, damn," squawked the normally unflappable Mitsi, knowing she could confide in her shipmate, "why can't the guys keep their pants on? Hell, I was down in the weapons spaces at 0500 this morning and it's like a bunch of rabbits down there. The pregnancy rate is the highest on the ship and — pardon my language — the weapons officer is going apeshit."

Randy smiled. "It's like shoveling sand against the tide. You and I and the Captain can legislate, preach and bleat all day, but nothing's going to change. The kids are normal humans, except they go for twelve-hour work days, days and weeks on end, no liberty, and hardly any days off. Like it or not, hormones have an agenda all their own. We don't help, though, and you know it. As far as I'm concerned, we foster the hormone race just like the nuclear reactors down below heat up with the selective removal of lead rods."

Randy was on a roll, his friend a willing listener. "Look," he continued, "you said you checked out the off-duty guys and gals in the style salon, right? All gussied up in their civilian duds, hair coiffed and smelling like all get-out? Then they go back to their coed berthing compartments and six-person privacy alcoves. Even if we kept them in segregated berthing and heads like the old days, it wouldn't do much good. Where there's a will, there's a way. We've really got ourselves wrapped around the flagpole, and you know as well as anyone else, what the outcome is." He hesitated, his mind seeking the easy answer. "What's at stake is the ability to effectively fight this ship. We're more like a college campus than a warship, if you ask me!"

Silence. At long last, Master Chief Randy McCormick, the crusty, seasoned maintenance chief of the Navy's top combat fighter squadron, had let it all hang out, his eyes moist, his breathing sharp. After a pensive minute or two, the older sailor started to smile.

"Randy, why the grin — what's so funny?"

"Mitsi, do you remember when they took all the urinals off the carriers? I think it was in the late nineties."

"Sure. It was no big deal as I recall. The idea was to reduce the costs of modifying the heads specifically for the women. The results were that all the heads were exactly the same. It sure helped when we started getting more and more females."

Randy was laughing now. "Do you know what the system called them?" Without waiting for an answer, he said, his smile from ear to ear, "Gender neutral water closets — can you believe it? Urinals replaced by gender neutral water closets! Lord only knows what they cost."

Mitsi knew when to be quiet. Her friend needed an understanding shoulder to lean on. Getting up, she offered a cup of hot, black, Navy coffee, stood behind him and, without fanfare or words, proceeded to knead his tense neck and shoulder muscles, the classical CD wafting a familiar tune. Far from suggestive, it was a comforting manifestation of one friend to another. Unrelenting with her probing fingers and strong hands, Randy returned to normal, pulse rate in the green.

"Your beeper, Randy," said the carrier's master chief breaking the golden silence.

"Can't get away. It's my Skipper. Got to go. Thanks Mitsi, you were a real comfort. I needed that," adding an unnecessary, "above and beyond." As an afterthought, he turned on the way out and said, once again with a grin from ear to ear, "Can you believe it? Gender neutral water closets!"

Then he was gone, loping two steps at a time within the catacombs of the carrier to the stateroom and office of the Red Ripper skipper, Commander Wendy "Iron Lady" Montrose, who had just recovered from a long and uneventful combat air patrol in her F-27C stealth Phantom III fighter.

The room, noted Randy, as usual, smelled feminine, her well-worn flight suit not withstanding. "Welcome home, Skipper, how'd it go?" he said, as he sat on the rumpled bunk bed. Even in her flight suit the leader of the Red Rippers cut a commanding figure, thought the maintenance chief. Shortish brown hair, erect, penetrating gaze, she was brief on small talk, but tall in the saddle when it came to her profession as a top all-weather, carrier, combat fighter pilot. As she quickly brushed her helmet-matted hair in the tiny stateroom, McCormick was reluctantly reminded, that she was, too, definitely female.

"Just fine, Randy. That 103 is sure a nice machine — love it." She sat at the small desk in the room's only chair and took a deep breath. "Things are heating up — the balloon may go up any day — the ISIs are massing all over. Hell, we may have an incoming missile right now." She hesitated for a moment. "I'd like to talk to you privately. Off the record."

"Sure, Skipper," he replied, knowing his CO had only an

acting executive officer in Dave Anderson and, in reality, no one to confide with.

"Randy, what's worrying me is that we may go into full surge operations in a day or so and I'm not comfortable that the troops are up to it. Too many act like we're on a love boat. I know they're tired, but aren't we all? That said, I sense an unraveling of our fabric. Too many of our sailors have drifted. They seem to have lost a sense of purpose. Two pregnancies last week and we are down four more folks. It's got to stop." She paused, her eyes blurring, her voice quavering, and said softly, "What can I do, Randy?"

The maintenance chief knew what was happening. Incredibly, his skipper was asking him for help. In his twenty-eight years of naval service, most all at sea, he had been witness to a bell-shaped curve of good to lousy commanding officers. Iron Lady, though, was one of the best, he thought, not daring to break the silence, his mind racing with alternatives.

What he decided upon was in none of the leadership books or Navy schools. He stood, went behind his commanding officer and proceeded to firmly rub her neck and shoulders. His hands and fingers were tense. Neither dared to speak. In less than a minute, she relaxed and stood, her back to him. His strong arms rested lightly on her shoulders as she turned to face him, her head and hair resting easily on his chest.

It seemed like an eternity, but after a few seconds, they parted. "Thanks Randy, I needed that," once again, in control and all business, the phone ringing on her desk. "Roger that, be right up. Air wing commander wants to talk. Got to run."

High above the mini-human, *tête à tête*, Captain Tommy Boone was in his sea cabin just abaft the bridge. "Command Master Chief wants to see you, Captain," said the officer of the deck from the bridge a few steps forward.

"Send her back, Karen."

Like the executive officer, smart ship's COs always made quality time for the command's senior enlisted person. Master Chief Mitsi Moore was dynamite. Boone knew he was lucky to

66

have her. She was all over the ship and knew what the action was.

"Come in, Master Chief — have a seat. Coffee?"

"No thanks, Captain," the respectful chief said, "Need to chat, though."

"Go ahead, Master Chief," he said, settling deeper into the creases of the well-worn leather lounger in his austere sea cabin.

"Captain, it really does look as if we're on the verge of real combat. Unlike Desert Storm and Vietnam, there seems a real likelihood we may be the target of the best the ISIs can throw at us."

"You're right, Master Chief," said the captain, pleased to be in a receive mode and pleasantly impressed with the insight of Mitsi.

"Troops are scared, Captain. Frightened and tired and more than ready to get out of here and back to a normal lifestyle. But what's happening in addition —" she paused, clearing her mind, "is too much intimacy in the crew."

"You mean our troops are doing more than holding hands?"

"Absolutely, Captain — in spades. It almost seems like a way to relieve the tensions. I mean, it's more than just a few and more than just casual. The pregnancies are just the tip of the iceberg, I'm afraid." She paused, thinking of Randy's strong back of just a few minutes ago, her inner-self tingling for the first time in many months. "Could I make a suggestion, sir?"

"Absolutely."

"Captain, if we could operate for a few days further south, away from the ISIs, knock off flying for a while, maybe have a picnic on the flight deck or a smoker in the hangar deck, it would do wonders for morale."

The captain rose and peered through his tiny porthole at the sullen ocean rushing by far below at 35 knots. The ship's executive officer, Commander Batori, had suggested the same to him just the day before. "Master Chief, let me say what I'll put out to the crew on TV later today. Our nation is as close to major military confrontation with a formidable power as it has been since

World War II. It sounds trite, but the reality on this warship is that when the going gets tough, the SOBs have to come out of the woodwork." The words had been coined during WWII by the then-Chief of Naval Operations, five star Admiral Ernie King. "The going has been tough and, unfortunately, in my judgment, it's going to get more demanding. We've got to be tough, as you well know. We can legislate and dictate all we want, but you know and I know that the natural human tensions and desires won't go away. The Reagan is personed by a representative mix of our nation. The policies set over many years are reflective of the finest leadership, both military and civilian, in our country. It's the law of the land. Whatever happened in the past to get us where we are today, is not relevant. We have a ship and air wing to fight and defend. There will be no timeouts." He had said more than he had intended.

He continued. "Master Chief, you, and everyone wearing khaki, are the leaders of this great combat ship-of-war. My sense is that we'll be tested soon. No, we won't disengage. We cannot. It's not an alternative."

"I understand, Captain. I'll do my best to keep the troops pumped up. Thanks, sir," said one sea-going pro to another.

Prior to going on the ship's TV, the captain decided on a spur to tap the medical brain of Dr. Rose Johnson, whom he knew to have been trained in psychiatry. Stopping by her tiny office in the ship's medical spaces, he asked the doctor for her perspective and to "Please keep it simple."

"Roger that, Captain," said the energetic officer. "Here goes. What we're seeing is really very simple: When fatigue sets in, one's senses are numbed somewhat. When severe stress is added, it gets worse. Fear simply exacerbates the melange. The human response is predictable. Nearly all will seek the comfort of another human in the same emotional state. One catch, though. Most of the time this human interaction are opposites attracting. For men, it is far more comfortable to lean on the female, if she is available, and vice versa. Ergo, the normal male-female attractions are magnified by the almost constant physical togetherness, the fear, the stress and just plain being tired. You may not like it, but on this ship the leaning on one another is rampant. Same with the other ships in the battle group," she said as an afterthought. Pausing, she looked up at Boone and added, "Captain, may I change the subject slightly, please?"

"Sure, Doc," he replied.

"You're tired, too. I sense the troops feel it. You said you were going on TV in about an hour, so you need to be extra positive and upbeat."

"Thanks Doc — point well taken. And your thoughts on the underlying people currents are much appreciated."

"And Captain, if you don't mind, I'd like to give you a quick physical down here in sickbay soon." She quit, knowing she had made her point and realizing too, that Jaws Boone would never submit to a probing physical by Dr. Rose Johnson, smiling to herself at the thought.

In paradise, Patty and Twidget huddled deep in reflection, as they watched their captain discuss the overall situation on TV. "Better than CNN," said Patty.

To make his "ready-to-go-to-war" point, Captain Boone hearkened back over two hundred years ago to England's Admiral Horatio Nelson's simple message to his fleet, transmitted by signal flags: "England expects every man to do his duty."

He began to talk to his crew. "Ladies and gentlemen of the Reagan, we have assembled in the Indian Ocean, the Red Sea and the Mediterranean the most powerful fleet since World War II. We must do our individual and collective best for our country and Navy." The somber words permeated every nook and cranny of the pulsating warship, most finding themselves paying rapt attention. The short message resonated throughout.

Twidget was scheduled for a long combat air patrol mission at 1600, flying wing on their skipper, so the interlude in Patty and Karen's stateroom in paradise was a welcome respite. Patty, in her namesake frilly bathrobe, said softly to Scott, "You be careful, OK?"

"What else? Me and Big Sister are invincible." His voice

was gruff, the tone manly.

Patty recalled the intelligence session of two hours ago, the firm body of Twidget pressed against her backside. She hesitantly extended her hand to his. "Please be careful."

He took hers. It felt good, his emotions an unaccustomed blur. "Hey girl, we've been together over eight months. Don't get maudlin on me now," he said in an equally protective, "I'll-take-care-of-you" tone.

His pilot, Becky, banged on the one-eighth inch steel bulkhead separating the two staterooms. "I'm off to the showers. Don't forget, you're briefing the next flight."

"Roger that, Big Sister," he yelled back, thankful for the momentary diversion.

The old "soap down, rinse off, one-minute showers" of earlier seagoing days were long gone. The advent of a 50% female crew mandated increased capacity, not more limited use. Supply followed demand in this scenario. And, much like the rest of America's 2010 unisex society, the showers were showers for anyone. Becky luxuriously soaped in hot, soft, 100%-distilled, ship's water in her private stall. She heard a familiar voice.

"That you, Blues?" Becky brightly commented to her paradise neighbor, Dave Anderson.

"Yeah, Big Sister, can I come visit?" Dave, still throbbing from the intelligence session with Patty, wasn't entirely kidding, but retorted resignedly to the silence, "Have it your way."

Becky, rinsing off, thought of her far-off husband, Rick. It would take ten Blues to make one Rick.

Karen, off duty from her 1200 to 1600 stint as officer of the deck, was singing her way to the showers as Becky and Dave left. She let the water flow and the soap sink in. A pair of woman's legs appeared in the adjoining stall.

"Karen?" airily said the squadron maintenance officer, Lieutenant Commander Lori Miller.

"Hey, Commander, how's it going?" she said respectfully, wanting only to relax for a few hours and pen an e-mail to Panky Pachino back in Norfolk. Quiet, deep in relaxing thought for a few minutes, Karen, her back to the door, felt her neck being rubbed. Startled, she turned to face Miller.

"Relax Karen, it's OK," the older officer smoothly crooned.

Karen was confused. It was well known that Miller's stateroom at the end of paradise would, on more than an infrequent basis, have enlisted female visitors to the room. Karen naturally thought it had something to do with being the maintenance officer of the Rippers. Then, it dawned on her. She's coming on to me. And almost simultaneously, "Get out of here! Leave me alone! **NOW!**"

CHAPTER 7

Washington Intrigue

Senator Joe Montgomery was reading the latest intelligence reports in his Washington office on the evolving ISI crisis. "It is believed that substantial numbers of the Super Pelican antiship missiles have been documented in the port of Bandar Abas on the Iranian gulf coast. The missiles had been part of a controversial arms sale to China by the Consolidated Company in 2009, with the specific notation that they were to be for China's defensive use only. Further details will be provided ASAP."

The senior senator from Florida, a member of one of the two minority parties, was startled. A year before, Senator John Cassidy, a viable presidential hopeful in the past two national elections and an ardent voice arguing for sanity in arms sales, had been vocally opposed to the transaction. His mysterious death in a small private jet had been a blow to the country and a personal loss to his best friend, Joe Montgomery.

The senator buzzed for his military liaison staffer, a former Navy F-14 fighter pilot, Ernie Maltman. The retired naval officer, thirteen years senior to his still-youthful boss, was an encyclopedia of military knowledge. Following command of his carrier-based squadron in the years after the infamous Las Vegas '91 Tailhook fiasco, he had become disenchanted with a Navy leadership bent on political correctness and social gerrymandering, and went to work for a large airplane company which eventually became the most powerful arms and technology consortium in the world. As assistant to the president of the combined companies, he had been in a perfect position to witness the enormously pervasive influence of a voracious arms clientele, mainly China and the oil-rich nations of the Middle East. He was astounded at the seemingly constant parade of former senior military and administration officials knocking at the front-office doors, Killington Associates, no exception.

"Yes sir, I saw that report. You and John Cassidy both argued against the sale. As usual, we're our own worst enemy," resignedly commented the senior staffer. "Nothing we can do now except hope and pray the balloon doesn't go up."

Montgomery stiffened, recalling the night he had learned of the demise of his friend to unexplained causes in a freak aircraft accident aboard a jet that had the best safety record in the world. "Ernie, do me a favor. Drop everything you're doing. Too much doesn't make sense; the Super Pelican to the ISIs so soon; the phenomenal amounts of endless dollars that somehow have made it into the bottomless political coffers year after year; the sudden confluence of Saudi, Iran and Iraq into an ISI military capability that even our forces would be hard pressed to counter; John Cassidy's loss." He paused, his mind racing, the frown on his brow more pronounced.

"You know this town and the big players — start digging. I want the inside scoop on Cassidy's accident, and, not incidentally, who's paying off who in this damned town. It's become an incestuous cesspool. There's so much wealth around here it makes Bill Gates seem like a piker. Go for it! Give me a preliminary update in forty-eight hours. Got it?"

"Roger that, boss," said the former naval officer, his mind already at warp speed, an initial course of action in motion.

"Admiral Sarodsy, please," he said moments later to the flag writer. "Tell him it's Ernie Maltman."

"He's in conference, Mr. Maltman. May he call you back?"

"Yes, Chief, it's Senator Montgomery's office. I'm his military assistant. Thank you."

Ernie had not talked to Sarodsy since he had been promoted to vice admiral a year before. They were, however, friends and had served in the same squadron as junior officers aboard the old carrier Independence and as sister squadron commanders in the same air wing later on. Stan Sarodsy had a no-BS reputation as a warrior, thought Ernie. Both had spent nearly eighteen consecutive years in the cockpits of carrier-based fighters. Stan Sarodsy, of course, had stayed the course, Ernie opting for a more family-friendly and lucrative job in the private sector associated with selling jet fighters to anyone with the requisite cash or influence.

"Stan, thanks for calling back. Got a hot one from my boss — need to talk." Vice Admiral Sarodsy was a fan of Montgomery, not because of his political blood, but rather his stature as a true public servant, one of the few politicians in town who managed to keep his hands out of the public and corporate till. When Montgomery wanted something, Stan knew that whatever the issue, it was best for the country and the Navy. Ernie continued, "Could you and Sally come over for dinner about six?"

"Sure, Ernie. I need a break anyway. Look forward to seeing you both."

After dinner, the two friends retired to the Maltman study, a rich collection of memorabilia, most of which portrayed Ernie as a real swashbuckling hero, the only person believing it being his four-year-old grandson.

"Stan, I've got a two-part, short-fused dictate from Joe, the gist of which is that there's too much going on around this town that makes little sense," and he proceeded to give his friend the highlights. Thoughtfully, Stan put Ernie's request into his muddled brain. As an aviator, he, too, had been mystified by the loss of John Cassidy, a true friend of the Navy on the hill. "He would have made a great president, despite his straight-arrow character and honesty," said Sarodsy with the flicker of a suppressed grin.

"Ernie, I'll tell you what. The first count is doable. I'm not sure about the money part, though." Knowing his former cohort had security clearances as military aide to Montgomery nearly matching his, he said in a low voice, "I have access to a small group in naval intelligence that is working on some extremely classified projects within the Navy who work directly for me as

74

the combat arms director on the Navy staff. As you know, there was an extensive investigation done at the behest of the White House following Cassidy's accident. I never saw it. It was quite closely held, as I recall. But, if it can be found, my guys can do it. Who knows, it may even lead to more closed doors," echoing precisely the brain waves of Ernie Maltman.

Sarodsy and Maltman had commiserated over the years about the state of the Navy, mainly gender-diversity issues as they related to the Navy's steady decline in combat capability and readiness. Both had been at Tailhook '91 when the recently concluded combat action of Desert Storm had been front and center, along with a host of ancillary issues. The cavalier lack of leadership and guts back then from a "correct" naval leadership, both civilian and military, had driven Ernie to the civilian marketplace and Stan Sarodsy to fill the perceived vacuum. Hundreds of others, guilty only by association, were hammered by a system out for blood, including many warriors and military leaders of great repute.

His vice admiral friend told Ernie of the presidential briefing that morning. "Good on you, Stan, they need it." Maltman recalled with distaste, his final couple of years on active duty jousting with the mandated influx of women into the heretofore sacrosanct arena of a male-dominated shipboard culture. When the law of the land modified the policy to dictate a 50-50 ratio, many of his ilk in the middle-leadership positions, had just shook their heads, the pragmatics of combat-readiness goals relegated to a lower priority. Although many seasoned warriors had argued and commiserated in private, practically none had done anything more than salute and march to the tune of the political leadership.

By 2200 that Monday evening, Sarodsy's special naval intelligence unit with no names, no phone numbers and no charter was in high gear, digging deep into the computer archives of the fatal accident that caused the death of a front-running presidential contender. Concurrently, it also put into action a hyper-secret and highly modified, experimental, parallel-computer program that was capable of tracking the wealth of most any person selected, including senior government officials, most politicians and the top executives of several major arms and technology companies. The code names: "Find Cause" and "Green Trees."

Richard Redman, at the ripening age of 62, continued his massive influence in and about the power centers of the nation's capital. Enormously wealthy, he been a successful attorney in a prestigious Oklahoma law firm specializing in international oil deals, principally with China. Redman was a master in the art of the deal and was intimately conversant with the hot buttons of Washington's power elite. In earlier years, though, he had run afoul of the law, minor greed overcoming his sense of fair play to his associates and a trusting clientele, though past transgressions mattered little in the sophisticated scheme of events in those formative years. The icing on the cake for the midwestern lawyer had been the appointment of the land-lubber as Secretary of the Navy. From there, he had fortuitously launched into a series of forays that led to his positions as a member of the prestigious White House Foreign Technology Transfer Board, a board member of Killington Associates, an influential financial advisor to many political organizations — most notably the massively popular ECATS — and a long-time, valued member of the board of the Consolidated Company, the largest producer and purveyor of arms and technology in the world. Richard Redman was soon to be the target of the computer's "Green Trees" program.

At 0700 Tuesday morning, Rear Admiral Sally Butts, U.S. Navy, the Director of Naval Intelligence, also known as the DNI, strode to Sarodsy's office deep underground, the strain of the past week showing in her slowed gait and subdued demeanor. Butts, of course, was one of the few — in addition to an FBI liaison contact — privy to the spook work of Sarodsy's clandestine group who worked around the clock in the triple-tiered, windowless catacombs deep in the Pentagon's multiple basements, armed Marine guards at every layer. Sarodsy directed her to read-in Maltman on developments into "Find Cause" and "Green Trees." This latter guidance was a pin-prick to Butts, whose primary focus was feeding understandable intelligence to the fleets at sea on the enormous ISI build up, the recently discovered stealth fighter of unknown origin, the Super Pelican missile boondoggle and the missing nukes dilemma with a code name of "Missing Jewels."

"Find Cause" had yielded a bushel of documents and data on the mysterious aircraft accident by 0530 Tuesday. At 0615, Ernie, diverted by car phone call while on his way to his senate office, headed for the Pentagon. There had, indeed, been several investigations of the Cassidy accident, all of which resulted in the same unanimous findings as to the cause: "Structural failure of the starboard outboard wing panel due to undetermined causes." The twin-jet executive aircraft, built by Consolidated, was among the safest in the world, a structural failure having occurred only this one time. The graphic computer simulation, in slow motion, starkly showed the airplane in an immediate and incapacitating 12G maneuver, which resulted in an instantaneous in-flight break-up and total disintegration upon ground contact 49,000 feet and 47 seconds after the initial failure.

The lead investigator, Dr. Sam Armstrong, had been a long-time and prestigious member of the Federal Aviation Safety Authority. Along with his assistants, all had worked as a team for many years as modestly-paid civil servants of the U.S. government.

Ernie was puzzled. There was no speculation as to why or how the wing had failed. In fact, the destroyed carcass had been secretly disposed of only two months following the accident. On a hunch, Ernie asked the lead gumshoe to plug into the sophisticated computer, the financial data of Dr. Armstrong under the "Green Trees" code name.

"Bingo," said the determined staffer to the non-committal computer scientist feeding the giant electronic brain. "He went from rags to riches in less than a year. His net worth went from $240,000 to $4.7 million in three months."

The computer's premise, though still experimental, was relatively straightforward. By inputting such information as a name, address, aliases, social security number, medical records or credit card and bank info, the system would seek out all matching financial transactions anywhere in the world and meld the information into the desired financial profile. Literally, any monies saved, expended, deposited, borrowed or cashed, were trackable. Thus, with the necessary access codes, anyone in the country could be the subject of such a financial inquiry. Of all the intelligence windows within the office of the DNI, this was clearly the most sensitive. No person though, could be targeted without the explicit written approval of the Director of Naval Intelligence and FBI liaison, and even at that, the file had to be hand-pouched personally to the director.

Within reason, the bugs not yet worked out, the source of funds were also available. In Dr. Armstrong's case, the following print-out was provided in one-line-summary format for the years 2009 and 2010 up to November 7:

	2009	2010 thru Nov 7
Employer	U. S. Gov't	U. S. Gov't
Salary	$92,419	$78,319
Investment Income	9,419	7,400
Inheritance	5,000	5,000
The Anderson Group	0	847,000*
Foundation for Excellence	0	2,200,000*
Aviation Pioneers, Inc	0	327,000*
Friends of Democracy	0	1,317,000*
Net Income	106,838	4,781,719
		*Swiss accounts

"We've already checked his lifestyle, his home and cars for any significant changes in the past year. Nothing's changed. His U.S. accounts and spending track very closely with that of the previous few years. The substantial additions to his net worth, of course, resulted from multiple deposits into unnumbered Swiss bank accounts," said the computer guru, in a subdued, laconic manner.

On a hunch, Ernie questioned, "Any way you can tell the source of the various funds that were deposited to Armstrong?"

"Sure, no problem. It'll take about fifteen minutes, though."

"Wow," was all Ernie could manage. The sources for the multiple funds, prior to meandering in and about several pots en route to the final payee, were astounding. Various political funds provided $1,200,000, assorted global arms merchants $3,200,000 and Killington Associates, $291,000. "OK," said Ernie, knowing his straight-shooting boss would not believe it all. "Where did they get it?"

The deferential answer: "The Federal Bank of China."

Ernie was stunned. In one hour he had uncovered what was obviously a manufactured aircraft accident, a mishap which had been investigated by a team apparently paid to generate false results. This assumption was buttressed by similar, though with more modest payouts, to the six other members of the accident investigating board.

Richard Redman was the cray's next victim, the profile spanning twenty years even more revealing. His net worth was flat until it bumped up several hundred thousand dollars in the mid-'90s, the sources of funds, the opulent Asian-based Tung group and the infamous Charlie Flee, now the world's wealthiest person. Shortly thereafter, though, in 2004, Redman's net worth went exponential with principle sources from an assortment of arms vendors, Killington Associates, various political funds and, surprisingly, direct from the Federal Bank of China.

At noon, Montgomery, Maltman, Sarodsy and Butts huddled in the secret enclave, trembling with a blend of fear, anticipation and pending doom.

Nearby, Rear Admiral Nancy Chandler had just completed a call to a lackluster-sounding captain of the aircraft carrier USS *Ronald Reagan*. He was tired, she knew. All three of my carrier battle groups are stretched to the limit, she thought, the revelation of the Super Pelican missiles and unknown stealth fighter cause for her concern. As chief of staff to Virginia Roberts Stallingsworth in her first three years in the White House, she recalled being uncomfortable with the endless succession of high-level Asian visitors and senior industrial tycoons, both on and off the public record. As a student of Asian geo-political history at Georgetown University, she had written her master's thesis titled, "A Chinese, Asian, American Rapproachment, A Study in the Pragmatics of International Influence." This work clearly documented the *quid pro quo* at the highest levels of governments, industries and politics and was one of the principal reasons she and the incumbent president were so comfortable with one another.

Nancy Chandler had been, ex-officio, a member of the president's foreign technology transfer board at the time, which met periodically to consider the export of U.S. technology and arms to other countries. The Super Pelican was a case in point. The sale of this extremely sophisticated and state-of-the art missile to the Chinese was vetoed by an angered senior four star officer. When overridden by a compliant board, he had taken the unprecedented action of angrily and vociferously walking out of the highly-classified meeting. Richard Redman had been the principal proponent of the override. Interestingly, Nancy recalled, the irate general had announced his retirement due to "health problems" one month later.

Her private and secure White House phone rang, the President of the U.S., as usual, on the line. "Nancy, can we meet at the 'farm' at 0930? Need to talk." The "farm" was an ordinary three-story structure in a residential neighborhood off Washington's Dupont Circle. The specter of expensive cars and limos that would randomly appear and disappear into a large garage would have been benign to the casual observer. Nancy drove her Explorer VI to the gate, hit the remote code and drove into the cavernous garage, two attendants greeting her with a smile and a "Hi, Admiral, go right on up."

Hugging, as was her style, the President said, "Nancy, I need some answers off the record, please, and without embellishment. OK?"

Nodding, the younger naval officer said, "Sure, Virginia — anything you need."

"First, and this is strictly between us, right?" Nancy nodded again. "Has the subject of nuclear weapons come up in your circles lately?"

Nancy, of course, was privy to the existence of the lethal weapons on the carriers and subs, but nothing more. "No, just the usual internal inspections."

"OK, second. How in the hell did the ISIs get the Super Pelican? We sold them to the Chinese with the explicit proviso they would remain for Chinese defensive use only. What the hell happened?" she barked in an uncharacteristically sharp tone.

"Beats me. Perhaps you should ask Richard Redman. He's the one that orchestrated the entire multi-billion dollar deal. And, as you well know, Killington and Consolidated were solidly behind it. You're probably going to ask about the unknown stealth that overflew the Reagan yesterday, too? The same cause. We've been selling our best arms and technology to anyone with bucks for decades, particularly the Chinese. Reread my master's thesis. It seems I was right on," thinking somewhat irreverently to herself, follow the money, honey.

"Understood. Now I want to ask you a most sensitive question. I hear that somewhere within the Navy intelligence, a considerable amount of black dollars and work is ongoing for a computer model that can somehow track financial transactions without the knowledge of those involved. Am I correct?"

"If so, I don't know about it," responded the president's former confidant, Stallingsworth noticeably miffed at the response.

Curtly, the President explained that Admiral Carolyn Sweeney, the Navy's CEO, had, just two hours ago, said there was no such program. "But I have cause to feel she is not being totally forthcoming with me on this. I want you to do some snooping, on your own. Get back to me ASAP. Understood?"

This time, it was a respectful, "Yes, ma'am."

Softly, the president hugged her friend with a meaningful, "Thanks, Nancy."

On the short, staff-car return to the Pentagon, Rear Admiral Nancy Chandler reflected on her three-year tour as chief of staff to her president. Selected for the sensitive job based on her intimacy with global issues and remarkable intelligence, she was a good fit for the new president, herself a political product neither Democrat or Republican, but rather a plank owning ECATS — Enlightened Citizens Against The Status Quo. The party line? Reinvent a government for the people.

Back in her fifth-floor Pentagon office overlooking Arlington Cemetery, Chandler was deep in thought. Too much did not make sense, she pondered, her agile brain computing at top speed. In all the years I've been close to Virginia, I've never seen her so agitated. The military crisis notwithstanding, clearly she has a plateful. She asked me what I think she already knew the answers to, including the last one. I could just salute and march stealthily on. After all, she is the commander in chief. But, something's not passing the smell test. There's too many *nouveau riche* in this town, including my mom, thinking of the opulent estate built high on a mountain top in the Oregon ranch land, following her mother's retirement from public service.

"Is the Admiral available? I need to see him as soon as possible," Chandler said to Admiral Sarodsy's aide. Her naval officer core values of "duty, honor and country" had won the internal conflict within her inner persona. She had decided to level totally with her boss, a person she deeply admired simply because he was a warrior interested only in the combat readiness of the U.S. Navy while eschewing personal gain, a sometimes rare commodity in a screwed-up town. Working her way down and through the maze of corridors, elevators, guards and checkpoints en route to Sarodsy's warfare command center, she murmured to herself, "He would never win a popularity contest and is constantly at odds with the Navy's top diversity goals, but when the going gets tough, we need folks like him."

Following the candid one-on-one with Chandler, Sarodsy became even more convinced of massive culpability in a host of issues, at least some of which transcended matters military. He sensed that the commander of his Indian Ocean battle groups, though inexperienced, was, deep down inside, a team player who genuinely held the best interests of the Navy and her country paramount. "She knew the politics, money and influence in this convoluted city," he muttered to himself. "I need to keep her on board and focused."

Chandler had departed, comfortable in the explanations of her boss, knowing full well he had withheld at least some info and pleased that she had let him in on her heretofore clandestine meetings with the president. He knew I had been her top staffer as a newly selected captain, but not the continuing relationship vis à vis her confidant, she mused, hurrying to an around-the-world series of phone calls to her carrier and cruiser commanding officers on the other side of the globe.

Stan Sarodsy returned to "Green Trees" somewhat amazed at the information that Ernie had uncovered in less than sixteen hours. One of the facets of the secret software was the ability to go at wealth generation from the back door. For example, the computer could be queried to produce a listing of individuals, the net worth of whom had increased in specified amounts over a given period. He asked the technician to produce a listing of net worth increases of one million dollars or more for the combined period of 2009 and 2010 to date.

"Will take a while, Admiral. That's a tall order, even for us." It took two hours.

The product, in summary, one-line format was over 80,000 names — a few high-visibility sports figures, more than a few politicians and a host of ordinary appearing folks. Formatted by category of principal occupation such as politician, military, business executives, business ownership and so on, it turned out to be even more revealing. Sarodsy thought to himself, I've been in the wrong business all these years. Under "military," one listing caught his eye, that of retired Vice Admiral Bruce Demming. Odd, he thought, his eyes unbelieving. I knew he worked with Killington Associates, but what the hell?

Just for drill, he decided to ratchet the stakes by inputting a more constrained set of parameters. An increase in personal net worth in the ten months of 2010 of twenty million dollars or more. Once again, a surprisingly large list of 437 appeared. Skimming the names, he ran across one whose net worth had increased from $37,000 on 1 January, 2010 to over $47,000,000 as of 1 November. Her name? Mrs. Dolores Miller, residing in a remote corner of Arkansas on the banks of the Whitewater River.

Sarodsy placed an immediate and urgent call to Senator Joe Montgomery, via Ernie, and said to his old squadron mate, "You won't believe it."

CHAPTER 8

Home Front

Beverly Demming Boone sleepily watched the continuous coverage of the evolving ISI crisis. Iran, Saudi, Iraq and oil, she mused, will it ever go away? The latest spin was the behind-the-scenes involvement of the Chinese, who, in recent years could not satisfy an insatiable appetite for electrical power from their own vast reserves of dirty coal and were therefore desperately seeking access to the petroleum riches of the Middle East and the Caspian Sea, the latter the largest reserves in the world. "Another day, another educated spin, but undeniably a heavy-duty web of seething crisis," she half-muttered to herself, nodding in and out of a worry-filled Sunday.

Beverly was not a born worrier. Married to Captain Tommy Boone for eighteen years, theirs had been a thoroughly non-traditional life, Tommy literally living on board ships and flying airplanes. "Typical Tommy, there he was again, dead-center in the eye of a building storm."

The CNN announcer displayed a large world map in vibrant color. Highlighted in red were the ISI forces, covering a large block of the Middle East countryside, the clear-and-present danger. In magenta was the area to the north and inland in and about the vast Caspian Sea. Yellow areas were presumably those nations on the periphery with a passing interest in the boiling pots of red and magenta, including Pakistan, Kuwait, India and Turkey. Truth be told, she thought, the whole damned region ought to be in red.

The confident newscaster placed the outlines of two aircraft carriers in the Indian Ocean, one of which Beverly knew to be the USS *Ronald Reagan*, home to her husband and 5,000 others. Innocuously, the woman placed the outline of three more aircraft carriers with large arrows indicating the presumable point of intended movement, one pointing to the northern reaches of the Indian Ocean, another a day's sailing from the Red Sea and the last in the western Mediterranean Sea, in the vicinity of Cyprus. Five carriers in the area, all fully armed with an air wing of the most advanced fighters in the world. Beverly knew by the grapevine that the two carriers at the giant Naval Station Norfolk were completing essential repairs, their crews recalled, and would sortie in a few days.

Finally, the CNN reporter said that a confidential source within the White House had leaked that defense officials were in the process of urging the recall of selected U.S. Navy reservists associated with combat fighter squadrons to active duty. The cryptic response from the seat of power was a terse, "We can neither confirm nor deny the report."

Bad news, good news, thought Beverly, knowing full well the ramifications of recalling legions of former Navy pilots to active duty, including her younger sister Susan and Susan's husband, Mike Anthony. Good for the Navy — we need them desperately, she knew, but bad for the airlines for which 90% of the reservists flew. It was common knowledge among those in this close-knit Navy community that every shore-based tactical naval aviator, from recruiters, to graduate schools and shore-based staffs, had been put into the training squadron for minimal refresher training — the F-27C stealth Phantom III folks, first in line.

At 10:45 Sunday night, her phone rang. Conditioned by many years of off-hour phone calls, they were usually bad news, a subtlety to which only Navy spouses could relate. "Hey, Bev, you watching the news?" It was her father, retired Vice Admiral Bruce Demming living nearby in a comparatively palatial mansion.

Half awake, she mumbled, "Yes, Daddy — it's more than scary, isn't it?"

Vice Admiral Bruce Demming, retired from the Navy for the

86

past three years, had been the head of naval aviation in the Pentagon and, like many of his senior contemporaries, had been recruited by a large number of global, arms-related clients. A two-decade steady decline in the size of the arms pie worldwide had forced enormous competition among both the recipients and providers of weaponry. Just as in generations past, the thirst for technology and weapons from third-world start-ups to "wannabe" super powers continued, smart bombs or the latest jet fighters, symbols of national prestige with vestiges of self-defense a distant afterthought. Senior military officers, therefore, were often hot commodities. Their ability to gain the access and speak the language of sophisticated weaponry, was a foot in the door for the goliath arms merchants. As the word spread that a certain senior officer or official was due for retirement, the behind-the-scenes bidding rivaled that of the annual NFL draft; the big bucks going to those who had the potential to produce the biggest bang for their clients. Demming had been ambivalent as his retirement loomed. He remembered back in 1988, as a carrier captain, the departure from office of his only political hero, Ronald Reagan, his head high, only to yield to the temptation of the highest bidder, as an economic consortium in Japan paid him two million dollars in return for waving their corporate flags in the arena of public opinion. "Good guy gone greedy," Demming had argued with his contemporaries at the time. "Not for me."

The admiral was indeed a hot commodity. In his later years of active duty, he had realized that sharply declining defense budgets and, in his opinion, a warrior ethic of questionable quality, had reduced the combat effectiveness of the Navy to the lowest level in a half century. The only way to compensate was by engaging the vastly superior technology of the U.S. to a much greater degree than before.

On the other hand, struggling arms and technology firms needed to export their products to keep the stockholders sated. Demming had signed on the day he retired from the Navy as an "analyst" with a prestigious confluence of retired admirals and generals, as well as a liberal sprinkling of former civilian political appointees. They were known worldwide as Killington Associates. His forte was a body of knowledge and contacts gained in ten years of leading the team that produced the phenomenally successful stealth fighter, the F-27C Phantom III. His terms of reference: China.

Over the years, he had often lectured to his junior officers, "You don't get rich in the Navy, but it sure as hell is interesting, challenging and even a bit altruistic." When he finally left the Navy after thirty-five years of mostly tough duty, the accumulation of creature comforts and needs were modestly adequate for him and his long-time wife, Sally. Nice home, kids through college and a legion of good friends, thought Demming introspectively. The brass ring for Demming, though, had come soon with his employment with Killington, the compensation, bonuses and perks, like a genie's lamp, the rewards almost obscene. "What the hell," he would bellow to his enduring Navy mate, harking back to the economic realities of being closer to poor than rich and being away from home most of his life, "We've earned it."

Beverly woke early as usual in the Boone's modest two-story home in a comfortable Virginia Beach suburb. "Got to get cracking on the party today." Actually, it was more a gathering in the late afternoon — kind of a low-key happy hour — of some of Reagan's shoreside husbands and wives. With all the bad news, the timing for the meeting was perfect. The disparate group looked to her as the fount of answers as to what was going on and when their long overdue spouses and loved ones would return to Norfolk.

Returning from her usual early-morning jog, she noted her answering machine blinking. It was another call from her dad. At 7:15 a.m. she thought, once again with her worry vibes in high gear. Her dad never called this early.

Admiral Demming got right to the point. "Got a call from your sister. Apparently the reserve call-up will happen. She says the Navy can't dig up enough pilots to cover the normal shortages and person-up all the squadrons." Susan was Bruce Demming's number-two daughter, Susan Demming Anthony, a co-pilot for American Airlines and an active reserve fighter pilot in the F-27C community. Her husband, Mike, was also in the same reserve outfit and a pilot hauling boxes for FedEx.

They sure have lived a mixed-up life, thought Beverly. Married eight years, they were among the first stealth fighter squadron husband and wife team. Since they lived nearby, their two preschoolers were well taken care of by a skillful manipulation of their complex flying schedules and, occasionally, leaning on Beverly or the grandparents. Now things would really get complicated. Susan, she knew, was scheduled to fly starting at 9:00 p.m. and be gone for seven days in and about the busy airports of Europe and the Middle East. Hopefully, Mike would arrive from Memphis in time for a quick kiss before Susan departed the home front.

Beverly's intrusive phone rang once again. It was Sandy Anderson, the wife of the acting Red Ripper executive officer. Busy as a third-grade schoolteacher and constantly chasing two little ones of her own, she was calling to see if the get-together was still on at five.

"Have you heard all the news?" Beverly asked, knowing that Sandy seldom kept abreast of much outside kids, home and school.

"Wow, I can't believe it. Any word on when they'll come home?" Sandy spoke brokenly into the phone, one son vying for her attention, knowing that the answer was there was no answer, and the eight-and-a-half months so far, could stretch for a long time.

Born and raised in Pensacola, Florida, Sandy met Dave Anderson while in her senior year at the nearby University of West Florida, her studies in education. Dave was finishing up a three-year tour as a Blue Angel demonstration pilot. A stunning contrast, his love was flying on the edge and adventure; hers was home, stability and family. Within a few months, though, they had been married, the ushers the collected Blue Angel team, handsome and sparkling in their blue service uniforms, pearl-studded swords and all-American smiles. This was Dave's second deployment with the Red Rippers aboard the Reagan, the first being the predictable six months. So here she was, a thousand miles from Pensacola, two sons, commitments to her job, a husband eight thousand miles away, and now, the head spouse of a fighter squadron, the commanding officer and her husband both deployed and far away from the problems of the home front.

Sandy and Beverly had become close friends. Beverly had been there and done it all and could empathize with the younger women. Both looked forward to the evening.

"That phone has a mind of its own," Bev said, talking to herself as it rang again." It was Bill Montrose. The former husband of the Red Rippers' commanding officer, Wendy Montrose and next door neighbor to the Boones, they had become close friends, Beverly cooking an occasional dinner for Bill and his three charges and he, in turn, attacking the balky riding lawn mower Tommy had left her. Often, they would share an after-dinner glass of wine while the kids played until darkness fell. Bill is a good man, she thought, a real family man. How different were he and her Tommy — I wonder if he'll ever settle down, thinking of her far-away husband, who had been at sea more than at home.

"Yeah, Bill, still on — the pot's sure boiling over there. I may need some help tonight. Come on over."

"Got you covered, Bev. By the way, looks like we're losing about seventy of our schoolteachers due to the call-up of the reserves. Going to have some doubling-up on classes in the district, I'm afraid."

"Thanks for the call, Bill. See you later."

Aside from Sandy Anderson and Bill next door, Beverly's friend-in-need was Rick Turner, the lawyer husband of fighter pilot Becky Turner of the Red Rippers. Rick was reasoned, unflappable and had a knack for solving problems. Living in the same middle-class neighborhood, Rick and Becky had produced two adorable offspring, Jennifer in the first grade, and David a "spring-loaded-to-the-go-position" three-year-old. Like Bill next door, Rick was a homebody whose hobbies were fix-up projects, reading and keeping fit with a regular jogging routine in the morning before the kids were up. Rick Turner never let his work interfere with his home life. When Becky had e-mailed three months ago that they would be out indefinitely, he had leaned heavily and emotionally on Beverly, knowing she had been through this many times as a Navy wife. He loved his wife dearly, but deep down inside was resentful of an accepted national ethic that sent young women and mothers off to fight, while he stayed home. "It's just not right," he almost sobbed to Bev one evening.

Beverly called her sister to see if their regular, every-other-week luncheon was still on. Following lunch, Susan would try to sleep for a few hours, greet her kids, hope that Mike was on schedule from FedEx; then at six, drive to the Norfolk International airport and prepare for her overnight flight to Paris as first officer of the big 797 jumbo jet with its cargo of 319 trusting souls.

Beverly knew her sister was tired. "Haven't slept much — I'm worried sick. It looks as if I may not even complete this stint. Damn, damn, damn," she cried, seeking comfort from her older sister, knowing full well the reality. When she and Mike had left the Navy six years prior to become airline pilots, the security, extra income and camaraderie of the reserves flying front-line Navy fighters, was available and they both grabbed at the opportunity. "The reserves have never been called up," she lamented, a glimmer of doubtful hope in her strained voice.

Beverly recalled that, long ago, Susan had confided to her that night carrier flying scared her. Fact was, she had been glad to get out of the Navy. Life since had been hectic and busy, but kind, as she and Mike climbed the airline seniority ladder, a sense of stability beginning to coalesce.

As the reality of black-night catapult shots, long deployments halfway around the world, the real specter of combat and getting shot at by a bunch of women-hating Middle Eastern madmen, the well-being of her kids, a combined paycheck a third as much as the generous airlines and a hefty mortgage began to sink in, the two sisters dabbled at the lunch offering, at a loss for meaningful words.

"Don't worry about the kids, Susan. They're the least of your worries. With me and the folks, they won't miss a beat," Beverly offered, realizing full well that Susan's maternal instincts were playing havoc with the realities. "You've got to get some sleep before you strap that big people-hauler on for your flight across the Atlantic," her sister gratuitously added.

Susan said somewhat plaintively, "At least I've got a decent place to land," her mind wandering to the unforgiving realities of aircraft carriers and thinking of the 12,000 feet of Paris runway and an uninterrupted twenty-four hours of off-duty time.

Five more calls on the blinking machine. One from her folks who said they'd be there at five and could they bring anything? She promptly returned the call from Lieutenant Panky Pachino.

Pachino was an instructor wizo in the VF-101 "Grim Reapers" based nearby at the Naval Air Station, Oceana. Beverly had met Panky at the ship's going-away party over eight-months ago. The undeclared beau of the Reagan's top officer of the deck underway, Ensign Karen Randolph, the two had met while attending a diversity workshop at the big Norfolk Naval Base. Though not engaged, they had fallen in love, and Beverly was confident a wedding was in the offing when the big aircraft carrier returned to home base.

Panky had shared with Beverly some interesting tidbits about the required three-week diversity training that all Navy persons must attend annually. The crux was that the top goal of the Navy for some time had been gender, racial and lifestyle equality as dictated by the law of the land for the past six years, equality being simply defined as very close to the proportions extant in the nation's populace. "Successful diversity meant increased combat readiness," the brass intoned constantly.

"It was tough," he had told Beverly. Part of the training were techniques in suppressing natural urges. "I met Karen in one of these sensitivity sessions," he had related to her. "They put us at opposite ends of a six-foot-long table with electrical leads taped to our arms and we had to stare at one another for five minutes without going too high on the emotion scale. Hell, Karen and I never did pass it. Finally, it got so that we were enjoying it all, at which time I guess the system just gave up on us. They even gave us an experimental pill. That didn't work either."

"Bev, I'll see you at five, but I've got two flights tonight, so can't stay too long. We've been going around the clock training the new pilots and wizos." Beverly thanked the young officer and wondered if the ardor generated at the long-ago workshop was still bubbling.

"Looks like I'm the commanding officer of the Reagan's shore tail," she said, talking to herself. "The men and women on the front lines doing the tough job and the left-at-home contingent doing the best they can to cope. I've got to be strong. We have a lot of balls in the air."

"Mom, I'm home," screamed Lori, her number-one daughter, to anyone within earshot. Lori was fifteen, going on twenty-one, having seriously discovered boys the year before. "Can I go to the mall with Daisy?"

"After you do your homework, your room and the trash — in that order. But be back no later than five. I need your help with our little get-together." Lori, like her mother, was destined to be a real "girl-next-door" beauty with a sparkling personality to match. Beverly's one wish was that Lori would someday find a man like her Tommy, but not in the Navy!

Suzette McCormick struts to a different drumbeat, Beverly observed, as the lithesome forty-year-old made her grand arrival to the party, replete in skin-tight leather pants, a hugging halter and four-inch heels. Divorced three times, no kids that any-one knew about and recently married to the Red Ripper's long-time bachelor maintenance chief, Randy McCormick, Suzette was ex-officio the spokesperson for the enlisted spouses of the squadron. At stark contrast was Jack Moore, a recently retired master chief himself, and the husband of the Reagan's command master chief, Mitsi Moore.

Suzette poured herself a second big glass of chardonnay and loudly announced to no one in particular, "At least my previous ex's were home every night. This sleepless in Virginia Beach is for the birds." No one in the crowd at the Boone household could relate to the "three exes," but all could write the book on lonesome beds.

"The answer to what's going on and when our spouses

will return on the Reagan is a total unknown," Beverly spoke after clinking her glass in a toast to their loved ones far away and laying out the potluck. "We've got to stick together." Each of the Reagan's major departments was represented, as well as the six squadrons of F-27C's. Beverly counted thirteen women and twelve men representing the ship and air wing, as well as a few additional such as Bill Montrose from next door and Rick Turner, Becky's lawyer husband.

At seven, Mike Anthony plus his two little ones showed up, having just kissed his airline wife goodbye, concerned that she would keep her mind on the store and not get side-tracked. She had not slept, he worried to himself. As a FedEx pilot on a similar model big transport jumbo jet, albeit a cargo version, he knew full-well that worries and fatigue were mutually exclusive with the mental stamina and sound judgment required by the profession for long-term success.

Sandy Anderson was not a drinker, but tonight she had already sipped two glasses, the tensions relieved somewhat, while CNN blared incessantly nearby. "If this were a commune, no one would believe it," she confided to Beverly, who, along with her next-door neighbor, were refilling the spaghetti and chili pots. It seemed that everyone was bending over backward to help one another, the exchanging of business cards and phone numbers a necessary part of the support network.

God, thought Beverly, that damned Suzette was going after Mitsi's Jack Moore like a bitch in heat. She vowed to call Suzette tomorrow, invite her to lunch and provide a bit of gratuitous homespun "this is the way it is in the Navy" guidance, thoroughly aware that it would, most likely, be useless.

After the party ended at Beverly's behest shortly before eight, she felt physically and emotionally drained. Finally putting the girls to bed, a bit tipsy from the unaccustomed wine, she sat down to talk with her father, Bruce Demming, as he watched the unfolding drama half-way around the world. He too, was concerned.

"It's none of my business, but do you want my two cents?" asked the skeptical retired admiral.

"Sure, Daddy, but before you get started, I'm not sure I like what I see. Tommy and the ship I can handle. The intrigues of those left behind in Virginia Beach, though, are getting to me, not the least of which are lonesome wives and husbands, displaced kids and a scary future."

"Well, Bev," he said, promising himself not to get political or tutorial, "fact is, all this gender-equality crap is hogwash. Those bunch of ass . . .," he caught himself, "dopes in Washington are out to lunch. It won't work. It's tough enough on the deck plates and cockpits without all the next-door temptations." It was no secret that the admiral had been fascinated by how the group had interacted. "Lots of not-so-subtle motions and chemical reactions from what I saw. It's not healthy."

As her folks left for the short drive home, Bev's phone rang. "Bev, it's Bill. We need to talk," said her long-time friend and next-door neighbor.

CHAPTER 9

Susan

"Capitaine, Madame, I am very sorry to awaken you. I know you left specific instructions not to be disturbed for any reason, whatsoever. But, I have a telex for you — from your government in Washington for immediate delivery. No exceptions. May I send it up?"

Susan Anthony, dead-tired from the worst flight she had experienced since piloting for American Airlines, was uncomprehending. It had been eight hours of incredibly poor weather, turbulence, grumpy flight attendants, several route changes and a new captain who was more macho than aviator. Fortunately, she had been grateful, the auto-land system had worked perfectly, the 12,000 feet of the Orley runway like a welcoming red carpet. From the time she opened the door to her Ritz hotel room until she was asleep had been about four minutes.

"What time is it?" she groggily queried to the voice on the other end, finally realizing that she had been asleep for only an hour. "Yes, please, do send it up," hiding a sense of foreboding, her eyes adjusting to the muted light, her brain clicking off fast-moving answers as to the contents of the message. The knock at the door, a tray thrust forward, a two-franc note in return. Fully awake, she ripped open the envelope, the words stark, uncaring, remote:

"You are directed to return to the U.S. on Delta flight 8971 departing Orley airport at 1200 local Paris time. Upon arrival at JFK you will be met by a Navy flight for immediate return to the Naval Air Station, Oceana with

an expected arrival time of 1600 local. Your connecting flight will depart Oceana at 2345 local for Cubi Point International Airport in the Phillipines. Your ultimate duty station will be as a combat pilot assigned to Fighter Squadron Eleven (VF-11) currently aboard the USS *Ronald Reagan* (CVN 76) now somewhere in the Indian Ocean. I very much regret the extremely short notice; however, the dynamics of the present strategic situation require this drastic action. With best personal regards,
Vice Admiral Sharon T. McCluskey, U.S. Navy
Executive Vice President for Diversity."

Unbelievably, Susan reread the terse directive, her swollen eyeballs weaving a dance about the unadorned words. At once, she placed a call to her husband, Mike Anthony, back home in Virginia Beach, frantic at the astounding disruption in her personal, family and business life. "Busy — damn, damn, damn!" she half-screamed, the phone slamming into its cradle. A quick shower, a call to her useless captain, back into her American Airlines uniform, she headed for the lobby and a sea of unknowns.

Home in Virginia Beach, Mike was on the phone anxiously trying to get Susan, betting that, for sure, she had been the recipient of the identical recall message. If so, they would both be on the same overseas flight later that night. Somewhat forewarned, he had held out slim hope that the system would not deploy both the father and the mother of their two preschoolers.

Mike's seance was interrupted by a jangling doorbell. It was Beverly Boone, Susan's older sister. "Just got the news, Mike. Has Susan been called-up, too?"

"Don't know, Bev. All I do know is that it's fast-moving. I have a connecting flight leaving Oceana in ten hours. I'm trying to get Susan — she just arrived in Paris. I'm packing her flight gear and one other bag for her just in case."

Beverly hearkened back to the confusion and pending dread her sister had experienced just fifteen hours before. "Mike, let me worry about the kids. Which squadron were you assigned?"

"The Red Rippers aboard Dutch — the Reagan," remembering that Captain Boone did not like the unofficial moniker of his giant ship. "Anything real light that I can take out to Tommy?"

Deep inside, Mike was pleased with the reserve call-up, knowing well the severe impact and massive disruption for his family. Though he enjoyed the stability, predictability and substantial dollars of a generous employer, truth be known, he had become totally bored hauling boxes around the country and missed the spice and camaraderie of his squadron days. Also, it looked from all the news accounts that the ISIs, this time, were serious. It would have bothered him immensely to have been sitting at home or monitoring autopilots, while his compatriots, or his wife and the mother of his two kids, were out on the front lines.

The phone rang, Beverly answering. "Susan, where are you? What's happened? I just heard about Mike. You, too? When will you arrive here?" She paused, catching her breath. "But that only gives you enough time to change clothes. OK, we'll have your stuff ready. What squadron? Red Rippers? Mike, too. Don't worry about the kids. OK, have a good flight," knowing the reality was a scared, confused and emotionally strung-out thirty-four-year-old younger sister. "She's already a basket case," she said, handing the phone to Mike and retreating to the relative calmness of her nearby home on Summerset Lane.

Vice Admiral Bruce Demming had already made himself comfortable in the Boone's family room thinking back to his last visit to the giant Chinese arms producer, Flee Conglomerates. In recent months, his task had been to simply check the boxes of his diverse set of clients, primarily Yung Industries, the principle supplier of stealth-associated hardware and technology to the Imperial Chinese Air Force, his point of contact the no-nonsense head guy, General Wong. "Wong was, without question, totally oriented to molding his far-flung empire into the preeminent fighting force in the world," muttered the retired vice admiral. "No subsidiary agendas — just all business." The most recent meeting revealed a Chinese general most pleased at the efforts of Demming to expedite certain advanced components, who, with a wink of an eye and the barest hint of a smile, had indicated a substantial bonus was in the offing at the next periodic payment to Killington Associates.

Demming had repeatedly ensured himself that his business efforts were totally within the law and current policy of the U.S. Government. He had worked for Killington for three years and, notwithstanding the legality issue, had increasingly harbored an inner guilt. Partly, it was the obscenely-easy money which grated on his thirty-five years of Navy work ethic compounded by the transfer of cutting-edge technology to an overly generous China. From the tidbits of information he could glean, it was clear that China had accomplished a remarkable make-over of her formerly second-rate military in just under a decade.

"Hey Beverly, I guess the dam's broken. You know if Susan was part of the recall? Back tonight? And gone so soon?" Only those intimately familiar with the retired admiral, would have noticed a barely discernible crumbling of his crusty demeanor.

His number-one daughter nodded affirmatively three times in response to her father's questions, her body trembling in random spots, her psyche bordering on panic at the reality.

The notion that both husband and wife would deploy together no matter the family situation, had been one of Demming's decrees several years prior as the Navy's top aviator. He had won the argument with the diversity folks on that one, the standard counter being the stereotype, "We must not disrupt the family. The family comes before the requirement of combat needs." His successful counter-argument? "Our job is to be ready to fight twenty-four hours-per-day, anywhere in the world, and win. Combat readiness is our *raison d'être*." He won that battle, but soon thereafter was relegated to the ranks of the unemployed, his service to his country ended, retirement an honorable way out.

For Susan, the ten-hour flight to JFK had been a mix of fear, fitful sleep and a brain competing for anything that made sense. For sure, like all carrier-based naval aviators, she had faced adversity when on active duty, but each time she had gutted it out. As a reserve, though, it had been a comparative piece of cake, an occasional good-weather, cross-country flight and yearly day carrier qualifications in the F-27C stealth Phantom III. Ruefully, she recalled that for most of her eight years as a reservist, she had not night carrier qualified, due to a series of rational and justifiable excuses.

In years past, when the going got tough, Susan had leaned for support on an old Navy pilot homily, corny to the more enlightened, but comforting to her. Alongside her certificate designating her as a naval aviator authorized to wear the Navy wings of gold, was, "*A NAVY FLYER'S CREED*," a World War II circa testament as to what it took to be a naval aviator. Closing her eyes, gritting her teeth and holding the tears in abeyance, she silently mouthed the words:

> "*I am a United States Navy flyer.*
> *My countrymen built the best airplane in the world*
> *and entrusted it to me.*
> *They trained me to fly it.*
> *I will use it to the absolute limit of my power.*
> *I will always remember I am a part of an unbeatable combat team,*
> *The United States Navy.*
> *When the going is fast and rough, I will not falter.*
> *I will be uncompromising in every blow I strike.*
> *I will be humble in victory.*
> *I am a United States Navy flyer*
> *I ask the help of God in making that effort great enough.*"

And she felt better.

Later that evening, Admiral Demming hugged his younger daughter with a false sense of bravado and wished her a trite, "good hunting," accompanied by a firmer than necessary handshake for Mike. His eyes moist, Demming's thoughts went out to the hundreds of young warriors called up for combat duty.

"Excepting the Chinese," he said softly, "no one listens to an old warrior like me." With the pending sinkhole of the Middle East going more out-of-control with each day, he wondered about the combat readiness of a Navy he fought so hard to maintain against an endless mantra of diversity, social engineering and making people feel good. His two daughters close by, one about to go directly into harm's way, the children left to fend in a parentless mode for what could be endless months, he wished he could shed the years and take her place.

"Let's go, folks — got to be at Dulles in 45 minutes," barked the young civilian-contract pilot of the old G4 twin-jet transport. No bands playing, no orations and no waving flags this time for the nine pilots and wizos on the Oceana tarmac. Only a cold, blustery north wind, low-scudding clouds and a sad premonition of what might be. All were reserves except Lieutenant Panky Pachino and all were headed for Phantom III stealth fighter squadrons aboard the Reagan. A few, like Mike Anthony, were secretly pleased at the respite from hauling inanimates and bored minions stuffed in the back ends of dollar-producing autopilots. The challenge and excitement of carrier operations and possible combat, reaffirmed the spice and excitement of the naval aviator. Panky Pachino, of course, could have cared less about the forgoing altruism, the specter of Ensign Karen Randolph, the only occupant of his mind. "Go to war and be on the same ship with your girlfriend! What a deal," said the young wizo to his seat-mate. Susan, though, along with a handful of others, was stoically silent, symbolic of shattered lives, dreams askew, kids left in the lurch and, along with dusty family albums, maternal priorities thrust into a bottom drawer for the present.

Thirty-six hours after being awakened in her Paris hotel room, Susan Anthony and her husband were riding backwards in a spartan, carrier-on-board delivery airplane en route from forlorn Diego Garcia to the USS *Ronald Reagan* some 1,500 miles to the north. The loadmaster cautioned all fifteen passengers to "get your straps as tight as you can," followed thirty seconds later with a telltale turbulence just aft of the big carrier, a slight lifting off the seat as the pilot eased the nose down for a better chance at catching an arresting wire and, finally, a bone-jarring arrival on board the speeding, blacked-out warship somewhere in the far reaches of an endless, wind-swept Indian Ocean.

Commander Wendy Montrose was in a transmit mode, the raspiness of the past eight months of stress and non-stop work peeking through her mantra of stolid professionalism.

"Welcome to the Red Rippers, the best damned fighter squadron in the world," intoned the skipper, speaking to a tired Mike and Susan Anthony and a barely attentive Panky Pachino. "Here are the flight and stateroom assignments: Panky, you'll be flying with Susan Anthony and rooming with Lieutenant Commander Lori Miller in paradise." Panky had no idea where paradise was on the ship. As far as he was concerned, he was close to paradise, his thoughts not entirely professional. Miller, he could worry about later. The skipper continued. "Mike, your back-seater will be Lori Miller and you'll be living with your spouse, also in paradise. Susan," she paused thinking to herself that the new pilot looked like death warmed over, "your back-seater will be Panky Pachino." The assignments would pair up experience with the new guys, particularly in Susan's case, Panky having a reputation as one of the best wizos in the stealth community. Miller, of course, will be miffed at having a roommate, thought Montrose, but that's the breaks of naval air.

She paused while the COD transport aircraft that had just landed twenty minutes before turned up to full power on the number-one bow catapult just inches above their heads. Wendy had noticed a confluence of eight men and a like number of female sailors huddled in flight deck control, waiting to board the infrequent carrier-on-board delivery transport aircraft. "What a deal," she irreverently muttered, peering at the TV image of the forlorn couples clutched together in the red-lighted dimness of the steel compartment, Dr. Rose Johnson in attendance, "We stay forever and they end up in the Memphis stress house for a year or so of rest and relaxation. Doesn't make sense."

Iron Lady continued with her briefing to the new flight

crews. "Susan, you and Mike will be scheduled for a day mission at first light in the morning. Brief time is at 0430. I know it's not much sleep, but no one's gotten much sleep the past few months. After that, it's into the regular routine. You'll have one or two three-hour missions daily and at least one session as the alert five. Mike, I understand you're current both day and night in landings. Had your last night work two months ago, right? And, Susan, I know you are not current in the night carrier landings. I'm sorry, but there's no way the Captain will let you run the deck for practice. It will have to be concurrent with your regular hops. For info, the auto-land systems on the ship and our machines have been working great, which will ease the transition." Susan, her mind a fatigued panorama of blanks, nodded respectfully to her new CO.

Dr. Rose Johnson had been in the rear of the ready room, quietly checking on her two new pilots and one wizo. Iron Lady was all business, as usual. "I think I'll sit in on the 0430 brief and monitor the flight from down below," the Doc said, her duties as mentor to her covey of highly trained aviators, never ending. She had gone directly from the flight deck to the Ripper ready room, relieved at last to have off-loaded at least a few of of the burgeoning rash of expectant mothers congregating in Stress City ten decks below. Her secondary motive was to sit in on the brief in which Studs and Bikini were scheduled, the charged encounter with Lieutenant Evelyn Swagger in sick bay only hours before, creating a backlash of worry. Typically, the night mission was a launch at 0030 and recovery at 0330. The troubled wizo exchanged understanding glances with the discrete Doc, Studs oblivious to the nuance.

As the Ripper skipper guessed, Lori Miller was upset at having to share her stateroom in paradise with Panky. At least we're on different schedules, Miller commiserated, so I'll have some privacy, the subject her occasional off-hour liaisons. Her new roommate, scuttlebutt had it, was keen on Ensign Karen Randolph, just down the corridor, and would pose little threat to her well-ordered status quo.

At 0430 sharp, Mike Anthony, Lori Miller, Susan Anthony

and Panky Pachino were being briefed by Patty Butts on the overall strategic situation. It was to be a simple and relatively short mission, the purpose of which was to acclimate the reserve pilots into open ocean, blue water, carrier operations, with no available divert field. The weather was lousy, albeit acceptable, typical for this time of year — scattered rain showers, low, scudding clouds and tops of the overcast at 20,000 feet.

Susan and Mike had finally settled into their austere stateroom in paradise at 2330 the night before. Susan, used to her familiar digs at home or fancy hotels on the road, peered at bare gray bulkheads, navy-blue blankets on the tiered bunk beds, the stainless-steel single sink, two miniature desks with the standard micro-safes and a spotted-white linoleum floor, while fighting off tears of total frustration. Carefully, she unpacked her one bag and placed the photo of Mike, her and their two little ones on the empty desk, her only solace being her emotionally rock-solid husband, already reviewing emergency carrier procedures for the Phantom III.

At 0600, Panky and his pilot were poised on the number-three waist catapult of the somber warship, flecks of daylight thankfully breaking the gloom of spattered rain drops across the fighter's canopy. Susan's call sign, so long ago affixed between her first and last name as a student naval aviator — "MA" — was short for Miss America, symbolic to her warrior cohorts in training at the time, because she was strikingly good-looking, as well as a quick study.

"MA, you ready for the checklist?" questioned Panky as Susan gingerly eased the big jet onto the number-three waist catapult. Wings, flaps, armament, fuel, harness, IFF, were all a familiar regimen to the long-time stealth pilot, who was, nonetheless, pleased that the Navy's best wizo had been assigned to her. Even in daytime, it was standard operating procedure that every catapult shot was totally on instruments, Susan realizing full well that her next flight could be in the complete blackness of the pulse-rate-generating protocol of a night takeoff. Directing her eyes into a dance from the computer-generated heads-up display to the analog backups and back, she saluted the yellow-shirted catapult officer in her left windscreen, the twin flame-spewing ram-jet engines of the exotic fighter, straining against the thin holdback.

"Airborne," she muttered to herself, "Piece of cake." The 100% oxygen sharpened her fatigue-dulled senses, her inner-self all professional aviator. Her husband, launching only seconds behind from the number-four waist catapult, joined beneath the undercast, his jet a smooth mirror of his flight lead.

Doc Johnson watched the two stealth fighters launch and the recovery of two others within seconds of the angle deck being cleared. The first to land was Blues Anderson, followed thirty-seven seconds later by Studs and Bikini. Both landings were the routine, full auto-land and undeniably perfect, the jets grabbing the number-three arresting wire, stopping the nose tire of the jets forty-seven feet from the end of the angle deck and a formidable ocean below.

While the flight crews were personing-up, Rose Johnson and Patty Butts were in deep discussion in a private and quiet corner of the near-empty ready room, the subject an "absolutely confidential" matter that the intelligence officer needed to discuss with the medical officer. The resultant conversation had added yet more grist to the ever-thickening medical journal of Rose — the subject, Patty's short tryst in the intelligence spaces the afternoon before with her boss and acting executive officer of the Red Rippers, Dave Anderson. Surprisingly, Patty had also added the generalities of her roommate Karen's brief, but unsettling, shower encounter with Lori Miller. Rose had assured the young officer that the conversation was most assuredly that of a doctor-patient relationship and that it would go no further. Rose's thoughtful hand-written assessment: "Everyone on this ship clearly knows the policy of the Navy and of this ship regarding the hard-nosed, sexual zero tolerance. What's happening should come as no surprise to anyone with half a brain."

The recently returned flight crews went directly to the intelligence debriefing with Butts, once again reporting for the record, an uneventful combat air patrol. Dave, Rose noted, even though he had launched at 0330 and was obviously tired, looked like the Blue Angel he had once been, fit and athletic in his clinging flight suit. Studs and Bikini followed, looking as if they had not slept for ages, Bikini flopping down onto the nearest ready room chair. Dave led the debrief with the intelligence officer while Rose watched from the coffee corner, her psychiatric training to the fore, the entries in her journal becoming more intertwined.

"Dave Anderson is the epitome of the priaprismatic male," she wrote, observing the pilot intently scoping the intelligence officer, knowing full well that he had no inkling his few seconds of indiscretion with Patty had gone further than the two of them. Rose's minor in premed had been in psychology, the interest blossoming into a medical degree in psychiatry. The case history of group behavior in the controlled arena of a warship constantly at sea, for months on end, was destined one day to hit the leading medical journals. Observing Blues, thinking of Karen and Lori, her daily visits to Stress City, the many private chats with the young women and men of the crew and the mélange of interpersonal dynamics from the captain on down, she said with a plaintive sigh, "What about me?"

The revelation hit her! Thirty-one-years old, never married, only a few sporadic flings interfering with her chosen profession, she too, had wandering thoughts, her eyes returning once again to the lean backside of the former Blue Angel pilot.

Lieutenant Panky Pachino, the newly-assigned wizo to Susan Randolph and the reluctant roommate to Lori Miller, had slept little following the abrupt welcome aboard by his new skipper. His entire being since the edict he would join the Rippers forty-eight short hours before, had been focused on the persona of Ensign Karen Randolph. Though they had dated reasonably often prior to Karen's departure many months prior, and had exchanged regular e-mail, their relationship was more of a puppy-love romance than long-term obligation, particularly on her part. She had fond thoughts of Panky, of course, but her focus had been dedicated to becoming a total naval officer and mastering the intricacies of the big carrier and her profession.

"Panky, my God, I must be dreaming." She felt faint after opening the passageway door to paradise following her 2000-

2400 watch as officer of the deck on the bridge. Hesitantly, she extended her hand, more like a sister than a long lost love. "I had no idea."

There had followed three hours of animated chatter, both keeping a wary physical distance in the rear of the squadron ready room in the wee hours of the early morning. Dave Anderson had arisen in the interim for his 0330 flight, shook hands with Panky, whom he had known professionally, conversant not only with the skills of the new wizo, but of his interest in Karen.

Meanwhile, in the rotten skies above the Reagan, the two new pilots and wary wizos were wringing out the two jets. Formation practice, high-G air-combat maneuvering, in-flight refueling, weapons systems tests and a little tail chase. Panky was pleased. Susan was a good stick and, although she had forgotten a few procedures relative to blue-water ops, she had it in the bag. With Mike and Lori Miller tucked in close aboard to starboard, the pair descended into the thick cloud, vectoring themselves to a point three-miles astern of the ship at 1,200 feet above an inhospitable sea.

"Hey MA, you gonna do a manual or auto pass?" queried Panky, referring to the type of landing on the moderately pitching flight deck.

"Think I'll go manual — need the practice," said the tired pilot to her back-seater.

"OK Panky, I've got the meatball in sight," she muttered, eyes blazing excitedly, the green horizontal lights flashing on top of the glide slope indicator abeam the carrier's angled landing area, the silent signal she was cleared to land. At a sedate 149 knots, a rate of descent of 610 feet per minute and at one-half mile to go, Susan tweaked the nose, microed the twin throttles and brought herself to a centered meatball, dead on the invisible 3.76 degree glide slope. In close, she felt good, the ball only a bit low, her eyes on the 640 feet of the landing area. Concurrently, her well-ordered discipline dissolving, the flashing red wave-off lights streaked into an unbelieving pair of eyeballs. Twidget's frantic screams of "WAVE OFF — WAVE OFF!" echoed between her ears. Susan jammed the throttles full forward, wisely held her attitude and smashed onto the flight deck, the tailhook 61 feet behind her scrapping the steel deck before arresting the first wire.

Back in the ready room, the red-faced landing signal officer, whose job it was to reinforce the unforgiving preciseness of landing aboard an aircraft carrier and whose word was gospel, was bellowing: "What in the hell were you thinking of, Anthony? That's the worst pass I've seen since leaving Norfolk! You pulled power and dropped the nose close in — stupidest thing I've seen. What happened?" knowing precisely that she had taken her eyes off the glide-slope lens and spotted the deck, an elementary "no-no" in carrier aviation instilled from the very first flights in intermediate pilot training.

"Sorry, Paddles," Susan respectfully replied, correctly realizing that LSOs were always right, that this one had most likely prevented a major accident and that she had flat-out screwed up big time. "I guess I spotted the deck," she said, her knees still shaking.

The humiliation was broken by the squadron duty officer calling for Lieutenant Anthony. "Which one?" someone said.

"Susan. Old man wants to see you on the bridge now," adding with an unnecessary wink, "when you're available."

The old man, of course, was Captain Tommy Boone, the Reagan's captain and, not incidentally, the brother-in-law of the recently arrived younger sister to his long-time wife, Beverly. Lieutenant Susan Anthony made her way the eleven stories to the bridge, her gut a seething mass of crosscurrents, her brain locked into a pulsating set of red lights and a back-seater's plea to wave-off. The jet had started to settle one hundred-yards astern of the ship and, had it not been for the mandatory wave-off calls, the expensive machine would have impaled itself solidly onto the butt end of the flight deck, the loss of the airplane a certainty, the demise of several young lives, a strong probability.

"Sorry, Captain," Susan quickly volunteered to her kin, "More than a bit stressed-out and tired, I think."

"Not to worry, we all are. Did Mike come out with you?"

"Yes, sir, he's getting caught up on the strategic situation.

I'm afraid he's a bit more gung-ho than I am. We've had an unbe-lievable thirty-six hours, for sure," she said, describing the bizarre call-up with the attendant short-fuses. "Bev's really helping out. She's got the kids well in tow, so we don't worry too much on that score."

"How's Bev doing?" he queried, knowing that Susan's answer would be "just great." Tommy Boone knew that Susan and her older sister had always been close and had viewed the Anthony family as a typically busy and involved set of conflicting priorities.

"I had lunch with Bev just before leaving for Paris," she recalled, thinking that Bev's husband looked worse than she had ever seen him. He was dead-tired, she correctly reflected. "Anyway, she sends her love. I think she's got her hands full on the home front. Lots going on among those left behind."

Back in ready room one, Susan glanced at the schedule board. LT S. Anthony/LT Pachino were to fly as wing persons to LCDR Anderson/LT(jg) Flanagan on a photo/recon mission up the Gulf to interrogate the Iranian naval base at Bandar Abas. "Good news, bad news," she muttered. "Good, because it was a day flight, but bad as the recovery would be well after nightfall."

Returning to her austere stateroom, she recited the Navy Flyer's Creed. "I can hack it. I CAN hack it."

A soft knock at her door. It was Patty Butts. "I know you've got a lot on your plate, Lieutenant, but please let me know if there is anything I can do for you and Mike. I do have a special briefing set up in the intel spaces at 1000 for the newly-arrived flight crews. The emphasis is on the Bandar Abas complex, as well as an overview of the region. Might be worthwhile. I think your husband's already cramming."

A few minutes later, the still sweaty Dave Anderson said to the young intelligence officer, "Patty, got a minute?"

Patty thought to herself, what an abjectly stupid thing for a lieutenant commander to request of an ensign, followed by an "Of course, Commander," knowing that contriteness would be the order of the morning. "Really, you don't have to say anything. It was partly my fault. I guess we're all human. I do hope that it won't happen again, at least on my part." It was half statement, half question, her confused eyes seeking his for an instant, the corridor encounter in paradise broken by the arrival of Twidget. Awkwardly, the threesome stood for a moment, Twidget, Blues and Patty, young warriors, far from home, confused by emotions driven by some complex, inner-biological chemistry.

Susan, alone in her austere stateroom, heard the chatter, the arrival of Twidget, the silence, and began a bit of self-commiseration, just as if Mike were listening. Her first carrier landing with the Red Rippers had come perilously close to disaster, her amateurish piloting symbolic of the precise opposite of the discipline explicit in the art of being a productive naval aviator. "I wasn't trained to be stupid," she lectured herself. "The creed — *When the going gets fast and rough, I will not falter.*' Here I sit, feeling sorry for myself. These guys have been out here for almost nine months — no fat paychecks, no family, no nine-day work months, no days off, no plushy hotels." She continued, half-aloud. "Most were normal young people from all walks of life thrown into close quarters for twenty-four hour days and nights, little recreation and no chance for meaningful socialization with one another. My guess is that no matter the zero-tolerance fraternization policy, this ship is a beehive of creative togetherness," recalling the awkward encounter just outside her door a few moments ago.

Another knock on her door. "Welcome aboard Dutch," bellowed her next-door shipmate, Lieutenant Sam "Studs" Newman. "Hey Evelyn, come on over. Meet our new neighbor."

Across the narrow passageway, Becky Turner awoke, the unaccustomed noise atypical in the paradise spaces. Before long, at 0900 on this Wednesday, dead center in the absolute middle of nowhere, paradise was abuzz with fighter talk, back-home news, reserve call ups and the irreverent pluses and minuses of the Ripper skipper, Iron Lady Montrose. The camaraderie and fellowship overcame personal problems, the specter of combat clearly taking center stage.

Patty's situation brief, intended only for a few, ended up with twenty stealth aviators in attendance, all anxious to get the latest intelligence. "Bottom line, folks, is the ISIs are loaded for bear. The Super Pelican missile discovery is only the latest bump. We still have no idea as to the whereabouts or capability of the unknown stealth of yesterday. What really concerns the Captain now is how to counter the advanced pelican. The recon flights later today, to be led by Commander Anderson, are equipped with special sensors which we hope will give us a clue to the adjustments the ISIs have made to the weapons' guidance. Panky Pachino, flying with Lieutenant Susan Anthony, will be the wing person with a special satellite downlink capability. Hopefully, we'll be able to make something out of it."

Following the special briefing, Patty returned to her stateroom where Karen was just awakening to prepare for her 1200-1600 bridge watch. "Sweet dreams, Karen?"

"Better than sweet, incredible! What a surprise. I had no idea Panky was en route. We talked for three hours last night," she giggled girlishly, a quiet smile on her youthful face.

Karen and Patty were not only roommates, they had become close friends and confidants. It was clear to both of the young naval officers that the playing field of social interaction on board the Reagan had changed dramatically in the past few months. Well indoctrinated into the strict frat policies, as was everyone, they had entertained no thoughts of stepping over the line. Lately though, it seemed the entire crew was leaning over the edge, the edicts and strident reminders from the ship's executive officer, Commander Batori, ever more clear and direct. More and more, the two had broached quiet "girl talk," Twidget, Blues, Iron Lady, Lori Miller, Pistol Pete and now, Panky, being oft —and sometimes graphically — discussed topics within the privacy of their tiny cubical.

Both of the junior officers were typical all-American young women. Not perfect, for sure, but neither were they risqué. In a society where anything was OK, no matter how far off the mainstream, they would be categorized as of good character and reasonably close to the center of the bell-shaped curve of accept-able social behavior. They were proud to be naval officers, had worked hard to make it, enjoyed being on the Navy's first team and were unequivocally committed to not doing anything stupid. Stupid in their context had little to do with their chosen profession, but everything to do with the opposite sex.

"What would you have done, Karen?" said Patty, referring to her quick hug and kiss session of late yesterday.

"Don't know. I don't mind being looked at once in a while, but lately it seems to be out of control. I even find myself with wandering thoughts. Yesterday, Pistol," referring to the CO's squared-away back-seater, Pete Dawkins, "squeezed by me in his bathrobe headed for the showers and I thought about it for ten minutes. What's going on?"

"I'm not a mind person, but I do know there's an awesome amount of pent-up stress, even fear, out here. And too, a lot of tired cookies. It's natural to want a shoulder to lean on when the going gets tough," said Patty to her roommate. "How about your troops?" referring to Karen's duties as the ship's second division officer responsible for thirty-three men and women.

"It's tough. You can only clean passageways and chip and paint so often. The ship's exec is all over us division offi-cers. Says there's too much hanky-panky. I'm convinced the only way to prevent the obvious is to physically separate the troops — probably a repugnant notion in our enlightened Navy in the year 2010."

On a roll, Karen continued. "Here's an example. Just last night I had the boatswain's mate of the watch on the bridge check on two of my watch team back in after steering. You ever been back there? It's totally off the beaten path. We assign two peo-ple twenty-four hours a day for four-hour watches, in case the regular ship's steering goes out. Well, when she arrived, two of my darlings were entwined in a totally-compromised position. They'll see the Captain tomorrow, but what the heck?" The young officer was really wound up. "Both were high school grad-uates, both are nineteen-years old, both are totally bored with the constant fifteen-hour routine, both are lonely underlined and both are scared stiff. For a while, these two youngsters forgot the trauma and the possibility they could get blown out of the water at any time."

Karen paused, knowing she had said too much already. "And now it's beginning to affect you and me, of all people. We seem to be constantly sweeping the boy-and-girl issues under the deck plates. It's not going to happen. I started out with 42 troops, 21 men and 21 women, like we're supposed to have. As of today, eight have become pregnant, some are off the ship, along with the other eight halves of the equation, but most are still in Stress City doing Lord knows what. What a joke! We got some replacements early on but not in the past three months. Fact is, and our esteemed high command back in Washington may not wish to acknowledge it, the promiscuity index on this warship is off the scale, particularly among the younger folks. Mark my words," she said gratuitously, "where there's a will, there's a way. Got to go. I'll be on the bridge. Didn't mean to go on so. I had to talk to someone though. Thanks for listening. Love you." She scurried out, duties to attend to.

Less than a minute later, a knock on the wall. It was Twidget, next door. "Can I come over?" he questioned through the thin partition.

Patty, her female defenses in high gear, reluctantly said, "OK — give me a couple of minutes," hurriedly brushing her curly hair, dabbing water on her puffy eyes and adding only a hint of fragrance.

Scott Jacobs burst into the miniature stateroom of Ensign Patty Butts, notebook in hand, still in the well-worn flight suit of his earlier flight. "Hey Patty," he said excitedly to the intelligence officer, "I may have a clue on countering the Super Pelican missile!"

Patty, immediately relieved, let out a girlish whoop, sat down at the tiny desk and laughed 'til the tears came. "Bless you, Twidget . You are an absolute piece of work."

CHAPTER 10

Nukes

Commander Angela Batori barked to her Marine orderly outside her office door, "Get me the Command Master Chief — fast."

"Aye, aye, ma'am," he responded respectfully to the Reagan's executive officer, trotting off to the nearby office of Master Chief Mitsi Moore, the diminutive senior enlisted person on the massive carrier.

"XO wants to see you fast, Master Chief," adding, one enlisted to the other, "She's pissed off, big-time."

"Tell her five minutes, please — head call."

"Roger that, Master Chief."

The trim Marine clicked his polished shoes the one hundred feet back to his job as protector, runner, errand boy and receptionist to the ship's exec. Wherever she went, he followed, at her beck and call. Along with several of his platoon mates, he alternated between his orderly duties, guarding the nuclear weapons storage, and his general quarters station manning one of the depleted-uranium close-in weapons systems. His task, should the general quarters alarm sound, was to feed the generous appetite of the rapid-fire gun capable of discharging 100 one-inch-in-diameter projectiles at an incoming missile per second.

"Have a seat, Master Chief. Coffee?" offered the ship's executive officer.

"No thank you, ma'am," thinking to herself that the XO looked a bit worn — frazzled was more descriptive. Increasingly, the discussions between the two were the ubiquitous hormonal issues. Mitsi had just recently learned of the copulating couple in after steering several hours prior and thought, for sure, this was

114

most likely the subject of the XO's ire.

Angela Batori started off softly, measured, direct. "Master Chief, I want your take on what's going on in the weapons department." The weapons department, of course, was one of the ship's major organizational feifdoms. Its complement of 176 souls was divided into several divisions, including offensive missiles, defensive missiles and guns, the consortium of endless weapons storage spaces for the fighter aircraft's bombs and missiles and a few assigned to protect the sanctum, home to forty of the most powerful nuclear weapons in the world. Headed by the tough, no-nonsense Lieutenant Commander Stan Miller, its affairs were generally "out of sight and out of mind," problems, few and far between. In the past few months though, personal problems among its women and men had gone off the scale, much higher than the rest of the ship. Stress City had been the destination for the majority of the offenders, the realities for Miller and his leaders, a severely reduced manning for the multi-faceted department. Miller, a twenty-seven-year, up-from-the-ranks naval officer, had a reputation for solid leadership and few problems he could not handle.

Mitsi Moore's job, on the other hand, was not policy formulation, but policy implementation. Recalling her recent *tête à tête* with her friend and confidant, Master Chief Randy McCormick of the Red Rippers, she chose her words carefully.

"May I speak candidly, XO?"

"Certainly, Master Chief."

Mitsi took a deep breath. "Much as I would like to shrug off our people problems, you know, I know and the Captain knows, a bunch of facts. One, the troops are scared stiff. This entire piece of ocean could blow up in a heartbeat. Two, everyone from the Captain on down is dead tired — just plain weary. They're tired of the 24-hour routine, tired of over eight months at sea and tired of being scared. Three, is the unconstrained female and male accessibility. Mixed facilities, constant shoulder-to-shoulder at meal times, coed berthing compartments and work places, may work in the sanitized forty-hour work week of Proctor and Gamble or the college campus, but not the constant around-the-clock association out here."

"May I continue, ma'am?"

"Sure," said the hard-working, energetic and team-playing executive officer, knowing well what was coming next.

"At a time when we need to be 100% combat ready, we are, in my opinion, just going through the motions. The playing field has changed, XO. I don't have any magic answers, though I wish I did." Her voice trailed off in frustration.

"Thanks for coming up, Master Chief. Facts are that none of us has any simple answers. We are indeed, in a tough situation. From the looks of it — between us — we may be out here for many more months." Her words were spoken softly, one woman to another. "Don't forget the Captain's mast on the bridge at 1000," referring to the minor disciplinary cases the captain would address at non-judicial punishment later that morning on the bridge, including, she thought grimly, the energetic couple from second division caught in after steering the night before.

Angela and her fighter-pilot husband, Commander Danny "Rock" Batori, the skipper of the VF-143 Barking Dogs, led a strange existence. True, they were assigned a common bed, but hers was a fitful five or six hours, and his a series of four-hour catnaps in between flying and running his around-the-clock fighter squadron. The occasional intimacy was a welcome pacifier to both of them, a temporary respite from reality. Along with some ninety-seven married couples on the ship, they were sometimes the recipients of a glimmer of resentment from those not so fortunate, the cracks in crew bonding a subtle reminder. In public, the ship's XO was all business. In private, when in the arms of her husband — though increasingly sporadic in recent months — she was all female, the tensions replaced with a short-lived, soothing inner-self.

She called Lieutenant Commander Stan Miller in his office far below, "Got a few minutes, Stan?"

"Sure XO, anytime."

"OK, be right down."

The ship's XO and her dutiful Marine escort meandered far

below to the pristine archives of the ship's weapons complex.

"Good morning, XO. I was just off on a short tour of the dungeons. Want to come along?"

"Sure, Stan," adding, "I need the exercise. Mind if the Corporal tags along?"

The mainstays of the Reagan's offensive power for her fighters were the 1,760 Mark 82, 83 and 84 standoff weapons of 500, 1,000 and 2,000 pounds respectively. Though the bombs were tried and true, the guidance systems represented the edge of the technical envelope, compliments of the giant weapons manufacturer, the Consolidated Company. The modular, self-contained guidance packages could be installed in minutes and were selectable in flight to one or a combination of infrared-heat detectors, global-positioning receivers, laser or home-on-jam, all capable of putting the weapon into or on a target of one square meter 97% of the time, day or night, good weather or foul.

The weapons officer spun a series of water-tight dogs revealing a gleaming, almost antiseptic, compartment housing 10% of the iron bombs, identical to nine other similar spaces squirreled away in the catacombs below the waterline of the big carrier. Untouched by human hands, the weapons could be selected and run to the hanger or flight decks within ninety seconds. Room temperatures were a constant 68 degrees, the humidity at 50%, plus or minus 10%. No chairs, no desks. Just gleaming machinery and 176 dull weapons encased in a rough thermal protective barrier. "Not much for us to do here, XO. Once a day, two of our troops check it out. The weapons have a twelve-year shelf life before we have to rotate them, so all we do is make sure the temps and humidity are in the green. Let's head for the acquisition radar room."

Donning protective gowns and headgear, the two entered an air lock to the master control station for the ship's defensive missiles. Several sailors were huddled elbow-to-elbow over the powerful computer.

"Trying to determine why we were unable to lock on to the unknown bogies of yesterday. Captain wasn't too happy. They could have bored right in and we could never have locked on or been able to launch our missiles. Still an enigma. What you see now is a real-time, direct data-link to the Hughes plant in Minneapolis, trying to figure out if it's our system or the stealth characteristics of the unknown fighters."

"Stan, it's been a while since I've been in the sanctum. How about let's do it?" said the XO referring to the nuclear weapons storage spaces not far below.

The weapons officer's demeanor chilled for an instant, transparent to the casual observer. "Sure, XO."

They descended two more decks and entered the first of two checkpoints. Leaving the Marine escort at the first, they showed picture ID's to the two guards, one a Marine private and the other a fully-qualified Navy SEAL petty officer with close-cropped hair, well-developed arms and a persona that left no doubt she was in charge of security for the ship's nuclear weapons.

One more checkpoint and they entered the repository for forty Mark 61C nuclear weapons. This was Angela's second time in the sanctum, the first being a hurried introduction upon her arrival several months prior. She nodded to the two civilian technicians idly playing cards at a small table in the corner of the tennis court-sized facility. Along each side were 5x5-foot sized squares much like the cadaver holders of a city morgue except that each had a double built-in combination lock. In the center of the open compartment were two practice weapons on dollies. Were they the real thing, each was capable of decimating a medium-sized city in a flash of nuclear terror.

Noticing the stares of the XO, Miller said, "These two," referring to the exposed weapons in the room's center, "are training shapes. They are precisely like the real weapons behind the closed doors. In fact, only myself and the two techies are able to ascertain the difference."

On an impulse, she abruptly said, "May I see one of the real ones, please," the tone of the ship's executive officer suggesting an imperative rather than a request.

"Sure, take your pick." She pointed to one of the doors. Miller went to a small safe, consulted a bound booklet, closed the safe and twirled the combination locks to the weapon's temporary home. The door slid open, revealing an exact replica of the two exposed weapons.

Miller was in his element, Angela clearly out of hers. Her only exposure to the lethal weapons had been of an historical variety back at the National War College in Washington. "These are actually safer than the iron bombs we just saw. There are sixty-six precise steps that must be taken prior to loading on the aircraft and another ten by the pilot after that before there can be a nuclear explosion. That's the reason for the practice shapes."

"Didn't you have an SWAI prior to leaving Norfolk?" referring to the special weapons acceptance inspection given each of the carriers and submarines every two years.

"Yes, ma'am, came out just fine. It's really more pro forma than substance. These things have not moved since the ship was commissioned. There's very little maintenance. As you know, the main issue regarding the sanctum is security, particularly in port, where we triple the guards. The only persons allowed in here are the Captain, yourself, myself and the two techies," referring to the card-playing and totally-bored duo.

Angela checked her watch. "Got to go. We have Captain's mast on the bridge at 1000." She paused. "Stan, how about we get together later on today?" her voice lowering. "I want your thoughts on the sky-high pregnancy rate down here. OK?"

"Sure, XO. Give me a growl when you're ready. Got to get back to the acquisition radar problem. See you later." And thoughtfully, with the hint of a grin, he added, " Glad you stopped by. Stand by for an earful."

The XO was relieved to to be out of the dungeons and sanctum. It was indeed another world, devoid of the constant bustle of her domain above, the bang and shudder of the four catapults tossing their jets skyward, and an equal number of screeching arresting gears bringing the brood to rest.

At 0956, she and the command master chief rode the elevator to the bridge, greeted by a tired-looking captain. "Let's see what we have today, Angela." The XO handed him several dossiers of errant sailors. Two disrespect to a superior petty officer, three for missing a watch and two for violating the fraternization policies. The nonjudicial punishment — or NJP — was another of those time-honored Navy traditions cast in stone, going back to the days of sail when the captain would greet the violator before the mast of the vessel. The ultimate authority, the captain stands behind a podium on the starboard wing of the bridge, the choppy ocean 117 feet below, the ship's exec on one side, the command master chief on the other. The sailor steps forward, salutes and removes his hat. His division officer and leading petty officer take positions behind and to his side. After reading the man or woman his or her legal rights, the captain will generally open the dialogue with a "What have you to say for yourself?" The thoughtful captain — prosecutor, defense and judge — will usually seek the recommendations of those around him, notwithstanding that his ultimate decision is unquestioned.

The first two cases — disrespect to a superior petty officer — were straightforward. The two had been given a task and, rather than do the obvious, told the superior to "get lost." Support from those flanking him or the XO and master chief? None. Punishment? "Three days in the brig on bread and water," ordered a dispassionate captain. Though this could be construed as somewhat severe to those external to the environment of a warship, it was almost automatic in such circumstances. The three-day hiatus for the miscreant most always resulted in a more contrite and amenable shipmate, the behavior of whom would, in the future, be focused on teamwork and an abidance to the mores of a naval vessel.

The final case was that of the young lovers caught in after steering the evening before, their division officer, Ensign Karen Randolph directly behind. "Captain, both are good sailors and have done an excellent job in second division since leaving Norfolk," she offered in response to the captain's question.

The two youngsters were both nineteen and aspiring boatswain's mates working in the low-tech deck gang. Remorseful and embarrassed, their response to the master chief's "Were you aware of the ship's policy regarding sexual encounters?" was a clear, "Yes, Master Chief."

The captain paused, reflective. Just like the old days in the early 1970s, many imbibed in drugs, but few were caught. These sailors, of course, were discovered *en flagrant*. He knew too, that the entire ship's crew was aware of the deed and anxiously awaiting the outcome of the captain's decision. He turned, seeking wisdom in the sea, winds and clouds framing the starboard beam of the speeding aircraft carrier.

The Navy's policy of zero tolerance regarding fraternization and harassment was crystal clear to all, from captain on down to the newest recruit. The usual antidote was a separation in the most persistent of cases, separation meaning transfer off the ship for one person and a fine or restriction for both offenders. This time, though, his options were limited: Do nothing; fine — realizing there was nothing to spend money on anyway; restriction to the ship — meaningless of course; or brig time, clearly an overkill. Buying time, the captain asked the two what they thought the punishment should be, a gambit his father had used back in his old carrier days.

The young female sailor spoke first, breaking an awkward silence. "Captain, XO, Master Chief, Ms. Randolph, we know we did wrong and broke the rules." Then, with a maturity past her years, she continued in a soft voice, her head high, standing at attention. "Danny and I are in love. We have been since before leaving Norfolk. On our long watches, when assigned together, we talk the entire four hours. Hometown, friends, aspirations and . . ." she paused, gritted her teeth, looked up to her captain and continued. "Captain, we were planning to get married when the ship returned to Norfolk. We wanted you and the Master Chief to be our special guests of honor. When we were extended out here, we did our best to schedule our watches together, including after steering." Glancing up at her future husband, she lowered her eyes, voice quivering with emotion. "We knew the rules, but it all seemed so normal. We were finally caught last night. I guess we knew it would happen eventually. Trouble is, we would be less than truthful if we said it would not happen again, because if we could find a way to express our love for one another, we would. We're sorry, sir ."

Dr. Rose Johnson had quietly slipped onto the bridge, fascinated by the situation, the honest dialogue and the captain's quandary. The captain's eyes probed those of the assembled ship's leadership for guidance. Nothing. As always, when the going got tough, the ship's captain was alone, the choices his.

"I realize your feelings for one another and thank you for your openness and honesty. When we return home, I hope the opportunity to be with you at your wedding still stands. That said, however, we have a ship steaming on the periphery of danger. The Reagan's sole task is to bring deadly power to an enemy, do it decisively and win. Anything less is rubbish. Like all ships in the proud history of the U.S. Navy, we have rules and regulations. If only one percent of our crew did what they felt like, we would be more like a cruise ship than an instrument of war. I know you understand this. Many of our shipmates, myself included, yearn for our loved ones." He resisted the temptation to exchange glances with his XO, and continued. "By all rights and by ship's policy, one of you ought to be transferred off the ship. Accordingly," looking square at the young female sailor, "at the first opportunity — perhaps as early as this afternoon — you will be transferred by helo to the submarine USS *Skate* to replace one of their crew who has experienced a minor medical problem."

Rose Johnson gulped. The sub's medical problem was nothing more than a pregnant submarine sailor destined for the carrier's Stress City. Given the apparent close intimacy of the two young sailors in the past few months, her medical guess gave odds for a repeat. Silently, she had to give her captain an "attaboy" for his handling of a dicey situation. The word would, of course, be spread throughout the ship within the hour, assignment to an attack submarine to most of the crew, a fate even worse than the brig .

"One last thought, Seamen Barkley and Moranovich." The captain paused, his eyes glistening. "I would be most honored to be with you on the occasion of your marriage."

The master chief said curtly: "About face. Dismissed."

To her captain. "Good call, sir."

Some sixteen decks below, Lieutenant Commander Stan Miller was reflective. The XO's discussion of the long-ago nuclear weapons' inspection in Norfolk reminded him how easy it had all been. As a past member of this august inspection team, he knew that the results were always the same. All they did was count the weapons in storage — open and close the doors. Fact was, the bombs were never moved from their secure resting places. Once aboard, they remained locked in each vault, the combinations known only to Miller and the captain.

The practice shapes were a different story. They were routinely in and out, not often, but enough so that no one paid them much heed. To the unpracticed eye, they looked like a normal Mark 83, 1,000 pound conventional bomb, the accountability for which was generally much less stringent. It had all been so easy. The substitution of the practice shapes for the real nukes would never be noticed until they were needed, which, by any reasonable measure, would never occur.

Along with his two card-playing accomplices, Miller recalled a rainy day at the giant Norfolk Naval Station not so long ago when the four real weapons were off-loaded onto dollies, with a police escort to the base ready ordnance depot. From there, they were loaded onto a commercial truck, the invoice directing transfer to the Craney Point ammunition depot. What had happened after the dollies departed the carrier was of no concern to Miller. He had done his job, the four errant weapons replaced in their tombs by four practice-training devices.

He had never met or been face-to face-with any of the intermediaries. The clandestine arrangements had become more specific between him and his far-off wife and several changing voices at different phones about the city. The culmination, of course, had been confirmation of several separate Swiss bank accounts with the numbers known only to him, written confirmation or records nowhere. The amounts were astoundingly enormous. It was axiomatic that there was no way to trace the source of funds, the phone callers, or for that matter, proof that the weapons had been transferred.

Miller had been married to the same woman for twenty-six years, a marriage that had taken a clear second place to that of the U.S. Navy. The old sailor had much preferred the spice of sea duty to that of a lackluster marriage, a long-ago love affair faded by almost three decades of absence. Both, though, had managed to present an aura of acceptability in the marriage even though she had resided in her home state of Arkansas for most of the passing years. Childless, her forays into his Navy world had been sparse, his visits to her, seldom.

His phone rang. The XO again. "How about we do lunch, Stan? In the wardroom," referring to the officer's mess.

Back to reality, contemplated the old mustang. In a few years I can kick back, thinking of what to do with all the newfound wealth. "Sounds good, XO."

"Hear about the Captain's mast, Stan?" said the XO to the seasoned fleet sailor.

"Sure did. Sounds like a good move on his part."

The more Miller dialogued with the ship's exec, the more he accepted her. Hard-working and smart, she managed to keep the dozen or so ship's departments reasonably well coordinated. Back in her office after lunch in the nearby officer's wardroom, they settled back over coffee, the stark and functional odors of the warship embellished by the hint of a lavender fragrance.

"XO, I'm planning on briefing the Captain on the weapons readiness and the problems with acquiring the unknown yesterday. Bottom line is that we are ready for anything. All the ammo elevators and systems are up. Excepting the reduced personing, we're as ready as we'll ever be."

Miller did not know much about the exec other than what he had experienced on a daily basis the past few months. He knew that she was a naval aviator and had flown as one of the first female carrier pilots in her junior officer years. The two of them seemed to get along well, a sense of mutual respect the glue to a bonding still not quite set.

The XO, on the other hand, knew little of the private affairs of the weapons officer. She was aware, of course, that he was married, although she had never met the wife or talked to Stan about her or a possible family. Her comfort factor was influenced increasingly by his solid sense of professionalism and know-how derived from almost three decades on the deck plates. In recent weeks, she had leaned more heavily on his shoulder for his wise counsel on numerous thorny issues for which her background in Washington had ill-prepared her. Increasingly, the weapons officer's private stateroom nearby became a safe refuge from the realities of her multi-faceted job.

Traditionally, a carrier's executive officer remained somewhat detached from operational matters such as airplanes, weapons, strategy and operations, and focused on people matters like feeding, berthing, coordinating and cleanliness.

The subject after lunch was the inevitable passion problems. "It's a cop-out, Stan," referring to the couple caught in the act in after steering the night before. "Your troops are good examples. Why all the problems in your department?" Stridently, she added, "What the hell is going on down there?"

The weapon's officer smiled easily, staring full at the trim commander seated at her jumbled desk. "You know, I tried to brief you when you first checked aboard, but you weren't interested, or at least that was my impression." He paused. "Our problems are compounded by the remoteness of our many spaces. The opportunity factor is much higher than, for instance, the hangar deck. For example — you're familiar with the daily inspection of each of our dozens of weapons spaces. Well, they require two people for security reasons, who, in half the cases, are one male and one female. After a few months of this routine for twelve hours a day, seven days a week, there is, in each of our brains, a one-cubic-centimeter compartment that eventually goes click, the result of which is a minute electrical reaction that releases a few molecules, the genetic makeup of which are called hormones."

Without thinking, the innately intelligent XO retorted to the now-smiling Miller: "Well, it hasn't affected you, has it?" regretting her foray into his personal psyche, while at the same time crossing her panted legs.

CHAPTER 11

Chinese Connections

Deep within the Pentagon, Rear Admiral Nancy Chandler was engrossed in thought. She had just finished talking with the commanding officer of the fourth carrier battle group about to connect with her ships in the northern Indian Ocean, a total now of forty-one ships and submarines, all armed with the latest weaponry, sensors and F-27C stealth Phantom III fighters. She flicked a button, expanding the large-screen display to cover the troubled region from the eastern Mediterranean Sea to the borders of China 2,000 miles to the east.

Nancy Chandler was not only the youngest naval officer to have been selected for flag rank, she was known as a quick study, intensely patriotic, a hard worker and a recognized international expert in the the trials and tribulations of the Middle East and the emergence of China as a true superpower in the early nineties.

Chandler's masters thesis at Georgetown University in 2001 had as its theme the influence of the international arms trade on the access to and prices of oil. Titled "Cascade of Weaponry: Flow of Oil," the study had germinated from a 1997 *Aviation Week and Space Technology* lead editorial which suggested:

> *"The proliferation of conventional weapons*
> *will be a critical dimension of national order,*
> *regional stability and international security in*
> *the decades ahead. The challenge is to*
> *create an international regime, multifaceted*
> *and varied in its approaches, that will bring*

*some order to the unfettered global arms
trade."*

Her arguments had centered on crafting an arms and technology sale and transfer policy for the U.S. that stabilized our
global business interests while placating an enormously-powerful
national-arms lobby, the motives of which were presumably altruistic, but in the boardroom, translated into earnings per share
and lucrative stock options. She recalled in the same magazine
issue an innocuously short piece on the appointment to the board
of directors of a major aircraft company of a former defense secretary one year to the day after he left public service. The article
added that, though the company's by-laws provided for only
twelve directors, a special exception had been made to add one
more, the inference clear.

She remembered a sobering vignette thirteen years before that she had used in her study, the state visit of a high U.S.
official to China. Ostensibly, the magazine piece had suggested
that the real purpose of the parley, photo ops aside, had been to
seek China's agreement to stop selling nuclear technology to the
nemesis of the U.S., Iran. The quid? The U.S. would then be
permitted to export her nuclear expertise to China for the purpose
of nuclear-power generation. Tagging along for a sub-quid was
an influential builder of helicopters, which won the right to export
the latest vertical-lift weaponry to a nation eager for arms and with
cash on the table.

The ensuing largess of cooperation and open doors had,
of course, broken wide with the flow of funds into the political coffers, particularly so in the 1996 presidential election, tipping the
scales in favor of the presidential incumbent, an uninspiring opponent, only icing on the cake. Indeed, access to the U.S. political and economic power infrastructure had been widening since
the late '80s, culminating in an ebullient Chinese President Jiang's
state visit to the U.S. in 1997.

Chandler's mind wandered. It was 2315, she was dead
tired, more mentally than physically. Following her studies at
Georgetown, she had been appointed as a White House personal aide, the aiguellettes on her right shoulder riding above the

three full stripes of a Navy commander. The presidential center-piece had been on the arcane issue of global warming, the foul sulfur-burning coal of China's burgeoning industrial might, a clear affront. Chandler, in addition to her traditional-aide duties, had been thrust onto a global-warming world stage, the result of which was an international treaty barring the use of coal after a twenty-year transition period. China, with an almost inexhaustible sup-ply of coal, was sent scurrying the world markets for oil.

Dimly, her eyes danced a montage on the big electronic screen, from the tiny dots of complex warships in the Indian Ocean to the inland Caspian Sea some 800 miles northwest-ward. She had learned during her two-year Georgetown sabbat-ical that the enormously rich oil reserves of the region would one day be a catalyst for global confrontation. Discovered almost one hundred years ago, the fundamental problem with the under-ground riches was in how to economically transport it to its hungry suitors. Back in the campaign-funding debacles of '95, a minor *cause célèbre* had ensued when the international entrepreneur, Roger Tamraz, had gained intimate access to the Oval Office and the U.S. government with the paltry donation of $300,000 to the incumbent party. All he had wanted was an inside track for a pro-posed new oil pipeline from the Caspian to the Black Sea. Though clearly there were no laws broken, the notoriety resulted in a general awareness of the strategic importance of the region, a fact already well known to the world's oil barons.

Oil pricing, she knew well, was inversely proportional to standards of living. When prices were low, in general, economic conditions amongst the industrialized nations were sound. In l960, oil had sold for $10 a barrel. "Cheaper than water," com-mented *Newsweek*. By 1990, according to a prestigious Stanford University study, the majority of those in the know were forecast-ing $100 a barrel oil by 1997, a catastrophic omen for a world struggling for post cold-war stability and prosperity. Though that clearly had not occurred, the anti-coal "Clean Air Referendum" of 2004 had launched the most rapid real rise in oil prices in over one hundred years, a barrel of oil in 2010 going on the crude market for $140 in 1996 dollars.

"Thanks for coming over, Nancy. Good to see your fourth carrier on board," said her boss, Vice Admiral Stan Sarodsy.

"Didn't expect to see you here, sir," she retorted, somewhat rested from her catnap, her agile brain in high gear, "what ifs" bouncing from one hemisphere to another. "Just talked to the Captain. She said all was well, and, oh, to give you her best."

Sarodsy smiled. "Between Jaws Boone and her, we could lick the world. Good people."

"Nancy, I've been brainstorming the past few hours about the failed intercept from the Reagan yesterday. Three questions. How in heaven's name were we taken totally by surprise by a sophisticated fighter we've never seen, and how did it evade our best anti-stealth satellite detectors? Third, where did they come from, or alternatively, what nationality?"

"Admiral, I think the answer to all three is kind of obvious," she said abruptly, struggling to be respectful to her three star boss.

"That's OK, Nancy. Please speak candidly. Forget all the fluff. We're about to start shooting and I need straight talk."

She looked him flush in both eyes, the silence in the command center deafening, the war scenarios far more complex than the latest war college dictates, the consequences of ill-considered moves catastrophic.

"The answer to all of the above, is China."

"How so?" responded the thoughtful combat leader of the U.S. Navy.

"The technology aspect is easy. We've been selling the latest and most advanced for decades, particularly in the past fifteen years. The primary beneficiary, certainly, is China. It's no surprise to me that they have capitalized on what is, understandably, a giant step forward in fighter aircraft performance. In fact, as you well know, the bits and pieces we have gleaned of the Chinese military in the past decade indicate a remarkable buildup in numerical forces and combat readiness, perhaps," she added somewhat warily, "the best in the world today. China's come a long way, Admiral."

Sarodsy recalled the extraordinary compromise of U.S. nuclear weapons technology back in 1999 with embarrassment and unconcealed anger. It was a loss without precedent in U.S. history "And who paid the price for such astounding incompetence?" he muttered to himself. "Not a blessed soul. All at the chain of command's top echelons, politicians included, blamed lesser personages in the corrupt food chain, accountability gone awry once again."

Back to reality, Sarodsy questioned, "OK, before we get to the Super Pelican fiasco, where could the fighters have come from, in your opinion?"

"China's out. Too far. Pakistan or India? No way. Saudi Arabia, Kuwait or Iraq? Impossible. We've got them covered by satellite like a glove," she commiserated, her brain weaving a pattern on the big screen, slowly, focusing on one area, her laser pointer quivering. "Up here, boss, is an area of heavy construction — supposedly oil-pipeline related," the red dot oriented to a bleak portion of northeastern Iran. "We know little of this region. It's about 500 miles from our battle groups, a comfortable unrefueled range. Iran and China have been blood brothers for many years, the sale of weapons and nuclear technology lucrative for both countries."

Her boss pondered a moment and said, "It makes sense. You're right on. I want you to get with Sally Butts, the DNI, request operational control of every electronic and KH-17 'eye-in-the-sky' satellite we've got and find that base. Got it?"

Without waiting to return to her command center, Chandler snapped to Sarodsy's duty officer, "Get Admiral Butts on the line for me, please," adding her characteristic "stat," forgetting for the moment the hour was only minutes past 0200.

"Oh, Nancy, before you go. What's your educated take on the Super Pelican missiles your guys found at Bandar Abas? How the hell did they get them?" Rhetorical though the questions, Sarodsy needed another piece of Chandler's brain.

"Same song, Admiral, different verse," she said airily and waltzed purposely out of the secret enclave. Sarodsy's guess was that she would find something before the sun came up.

Stan Sarodsy knew he had to get some shuteye, for the morning would bring a series of meetings, problems and possible action halfway around the world. The results of the Reagan's recon flight over Bandar Abas was risky, but he needed real eyeballs on the action and sensors only the fighters could carry. Then, on an impulse, the late hour notwithstanding, his senses fatigued, he dialed the home phone number of his predecessor, retired Vice Admiral Bruce Demming in Virginia Beach. He needed answers.

"Demming," growled the old sea dog and veteran warrior, more than annoyed at a call he presumed to be superfluous.

"Bruce, it's Stan Sarodsy. I need you up here as quickly as possible. We've got a real brouhaha stewing," he said, noting the time as 0247.

"What the hell for?" the grizzled sailor retorted, his sense of duty overcoming the urge to unceremoniously hang up.

"We've got some big problems. I need answers. My gut tells me you may have the connections we need."

The retired vice admiral, a product of the Cold War, Desert Storm, carrier captaincy, over a thousand carrier-arrested landings and a host of related self-sacrifice for himself and his family, knew only of duty, honor and country. Service and duty came instantly to the forefront. "When?"

"How about 0700 in my command center?"

"Wilco, I'll be there. Have a hot pot burning."

The three-and-a-half hour, lonesome drive from Norfolk to the Pentagon, after a quick shower and necessary ablutions, was time for thought. His three years with Killington Associates and many forays to China on business, were common knowledge in senior military circles and the arms industry. The ready access he enjoyed on both sides of the Pacific had resulted in fat consulting fees for Demming and his influential employer, though, increasingly, he felt a twinge of guilt over the enormously successful remake of the Chinese Imperial Air Force, a force he knew would be tough and unrelenting should the stakes so demand. Also, long accustomed to an adequate lifestyle, he was, deep down inside, a reluctant recipient of the practically obscene wealth that flowed his way. "Perhaps," he mouthed aloud in the solitude of the long night drive, "just maybe, I could be of service once again to the U.S. Navy and not to a bunch of money-grubbing old guys." He wondered if Stan Sarodsy was aware of the amount of money available to senior retired folks on the "outside."

At precisely 0700, Bruce Demming appeared at the familiar underground access point to the Navy's Combat Arms Directorate and bounded into the inner sanctum to be greeted by his freshly-shaved and rested former protege. He and Sarodsy had served together twice and, early on, Sarodsy had been Demming's capable wingman in the VF-143 "Pukin' Dogs." Mutual respect ran deep.

"Thanks, Bruce. Good to see you, as always. Let me give you a ten-minute situation brief," his pointer probing the wall-sized screen. Demming, as a retiree, had some of the security clearances, but clearly Sarodsy had opened a few compartments, his reasoning that bureaucratic protocol and the current dangerous situation were mutually exclusive.

He decided to get to the point and briefed Demming on the unknown stealth fighter. "What say you, good friend?"

"Sure, they're working on advanced stealth technology and aircraft applications. That's been my bag, as you probably know, for the past three years. I know most of the Chinese players, military and civilian. Doesn't surprise me a bit. The dearth of intelligence on our part though, is troublesome. What the hell have the gumshoes been doing?" he grumbled acrimoniously.

The vintage admiral added, somewhat plaintively. "You seem surprised by the results the Chinese have garnered in only a few years. The reasons are, very simply, due to commitment and money, both of which are in abundant supply. From what I can gather, their military combat capability has been truly amazing, while," he added gratuitously with the hint of a grin, "our combat goals seem to have focused on other priorities. The Chinese though, have been on a total war-fighting agenda, much akin to that of the old Soviet Union back in the 1960s. Fact is, we've been selling the store to them for a long while — all legal and sanctioned, of course."

"Bruce, how fast can you get to your contacts in China? We need answers on that fighter: How to counter the stealth, how many, range, weapons and so on. But, we need them now!"

Actually, I had a trip scheduled next week. I could move it up, I suppose."

"Would you, please. And, if you don't mind, I'd like to loan you our latest covered, secure satellite voice phone. Only difference from a standard cell phone is that it only connects right here," pointing to a nearby red console, "and cannot be monitored. We'll give you a special access code to memorize. OK?"

"On my way," responded the senior sailor. "I kind of guessed you might be in a transmit mode, so I took the precaution of packing a bag and bringing my passport. Take care. I'll call when I have something."

Sarodsy checked his morning calendar: 0730, "Jewels;" 0830, Senator Montgomery and Ernie Maltman; 0900, RADM Chandler; 1100, Debrief of Reagan's recon flight over Bandar; 1200, Service Chiefs and so on. "Not even time to think," he complained to no one in particular.

Captain Sam Banaro, U.S. Navy, joined Sarodsy in a special 10x10 foot sound-proofed conference cubicle. The subject? The missing nukes off the USS *Ronald Reagan*, code named "Find Jewels." Banaro was the commanding officer of the SWAI team, or special weapons inspection team. Up from the enlisted ranks, he was a veteran of twenty-eight years of service, including stints as weapons officer on an attack submarine and two aircraft carriers each loaded with a cluster of the forbidden weapons. His present assignment was mainly one of security; to act as the point of contact for each of the twelve ships carrying the weapons; to periodically account for the inventory; and to ensure they remained functional. What he had found on the Reagan had been astounding.

It had been a routine, every two-year look-see, prior to

the big carrier departing on a routine six-month deployment. He and his long-time friend, Lieutenant Commander Stan Miller, the Reagan's weapons officer, had had dinner ashore, the conversation, as always, about a changing Navy venue, the priorities of which in recent years, both had trouble comprehending. The next morning, Captain Banaro decided to use, for the first time, a relatively new device that could detect minuscule quantities of weapons-grade nuclear material, a hand-held spin-off of decades-old Cold War technology.

As Miller had opened each vault deep in the Reagan's secret weapons spaces, Banaro noted the painted serial number and, clandestinely, activated a button on the device that recorded a "go, no go" as to the presence of nuclear material within each of the weapons, the results of which would have to be analyzed back at his office.

Some three weeks later, after the carrier had sailed, urgency clearly not an issue, Banaro thought to check the results. The count? Thirty-six of the forty weapons had the real nuclear materials. Four, according to the device, were almost certainly practice shapes used for training.

Since the international ban on nuclear weapons institutionalized by global treaty back in 2004, the world, remarkably, had unilaterally forsaken the deadly remnants of the Cold War. That is, all except the U.S. Navy, which, at the highest levels of the U.S. government, had made the decision to keep forty of the air-delivered weapons aboard each of six aircraft carriers and a total of sixty obsolete, but still lethal, nuclear-tipped Tomahawk GPS-guided missiles, aboard six venerable Trident submarines. There was no traditional shore-side support or maintenance; just the highly classified and severely limited access spaces on the twelve warships.

Few were privy to Captain Banaro's real assignment that he had held for eight years. That he was one of the few in the country with detailed operational knowledge of nuclear weapons, was well-known to a small cadre of such experts around the world, demand for their expertise, of course, severely curtailed in the past few years. On a few occasions over the years, he had been approached by innocuous intermediaries, their tactics akin to a successful business headhunter. "Would you be interested?" The anonymous voice on the other end of the one-way conversations would invariably and casually mention money, which was always many times his ample Navy salary as a captain. Banaro, not unlike many of his contemporaries, had long ago forsaken the quest for wealth. His sense of duty and country clearly transcended material gain.

"Good morning, Admiral," said one real sailor to another. "Tough times, eh?"

"Morning to you, Sam. Always good to see you."

"Good news, sir. We've completed a quick inspection of the five other carriers and six subs and all is well. So far, all the weapons are safe and sound. Any word on the missing jewels from the Reagan?"

"No, Sam. I've had our best gumshoes on it. Not a hint. Are you sure of the accuracy of your device?"

"Yes, sir. I've checked it out on every actual weapon and a host of practice ones. It hasn't failed yet. One hundred percent accurate."

"Sam, got a question. Is there any way those weapons could have been removed from the Reagan without the knowledge of the weapons officer?"

"Admiral, there is zero chance of that. He and the Captain are the only persons on the ship with access to the code safe. Even I don't have it. Plus, unauthorized tampering with any of the vaults will set off a satellite alarm. I would know within seconds," pointing to his beeper. "Sir," he paused, "given that the weapons are not on the Reagan, there is ample reason to point the finger at my long-time friend, Stan Miller."

Sam Banaro was not aware of the vast increase in the net worth of Miller's wife, Dolores, living on the banks of the Whitewater River in Arkansas. A top-level investigative team was in place, probing the records, lifestyle and personal life of Dolores Miller. Before the day was out, Sarodsy should have a preliminary report. Dryly, he thought, Swiss bank accounts, Banaro's convictions and a rather grandiose mansion far from Washington, added up to no good.

"Admiral, it's Admiral Chandler. She needs to see you, stat."

"Send her in, Chief. Thanks, Sam," shaking hands with his friend and solid sailor. To himself — what an incredible national asset.

"Just got these in, boss," said his agitated battle force commander. Punching in the coordinates, she pulled up on the screen a series of revealing photos of a fighter base in the far reaches of Iran, the runway barely discernible, the outline of two aircraft about to enter what appeared to be a camouflaged underground bunker. The next frame revealed nothing more than a slash in the barren landscape. Zooming in on the fighters, they appeared to be identical to the unknowns that almost overflew the Reagan the day before.

Rear Admiral Sally Butts, the Director of Naval Intelligence, joined the twosome. "Stan, Nancy, there's something anomalous about this base, aside from the aircraft. No roads, nothing above ground, no obvious radar sites or missiles. One aspect, though, is curious. See this," she pointed her laser at the blowup of a barely-discernible compound surrounded by three layers of concertina wire fencing. "The tire tracks are recent. Something was delivered there in the past twelve hours. Also, our electronic satellites picked up the transmissions of a Chinese TU-87 transport just several hours ago. Clearly, something's going on there."

"Sally, I agree with you." Butts, as the DNI, was one of the few privy to the missing nukes, her top sleuths frantically seeking the whereabouts of the weapons. "That said, however," he asked, somewhat piqued, "how is it that our national overhead surveillance systems have not found this before?"

"Somehow, we've just missed it," the DNI responded. The national systems were the modern day eyes-in-the-sky and orders of magnitude more capable than those of only a decade before. Each satellite combined electronic and infrared sensors, radar and the KH-17 visual cameras that could literally read the numbers on a runway or a parked aircraft. "Underground facilities with little or no electronic emissions, like this one, are practically impossible to detect," gratuitously added the Navy's top intelligence officer.

Senator Joe Montgomery and Ernie Maltman were due in Sarodsy's office in ten minutes, the subjects the astounding revelations extant in the "Find Cause" and "Green Trees" initiatives.

Senator John Cassidy had been the presidential poster boy in 2004, but had simply been inundated by massive doses of media overtly impugning his loyalty, motives, personal life and competence. America's electorate had opted overwhelmingly for Virginia Roberts Stallingsworth, the nation's first female head-of-state, the ECATS firmly in control. In 2006 though, Cassidy had launched a highly credible attack on a totally out-of-control campaign spending malaise, his focus on the enormously grotesque amounts flowing from foreign sources and generous corporations, practically all destined for the ECATS's coffers. A lesser-understood aspect of his work was an attempt to answer the quid part of the *quid pro quo*, much of which related to a generous U.S. policy regarding arms sales and technology transfer. His campaign for the presidency had begun to resonate with a population gradually awakening to the bleak umbrella of Chinese permeation into the daily fabric of America.

"Senator Montgomery and his aide, Admiral," announced Sarodsy's flag writer.

"Welcome Senator, Ernie. Coffee?"

Retiring to the tiny conference room, Sarodsy asked the DNI to sit in with the group. "It does appear that Cassidy's death three years ago was no accident," referring to the results of "Find Cause." "Who caused it is irrelevant at this point. What is germane is that it is clear he was hot on the trail of some obscenely putrid political dirt and, had his momentum continued, could well have have been our president today. Senator, Ernie briefed you on the preliminary results of 'Green Trees' yesterday. In my judgment, both 'Find Cause' and 'Green Trees' are mutually inclusive. Allow me another piece of the puzzle, if you would," taking the opportunity to refill the coffee mugs and collect his thoughts.

For the next twenty minutes, Sarodsy cautiously outlined the case of the missing nuclear weapons from the Reagan, the possible correlation of the vast increases in wealth extant in the "Green Trees" program, the death of Cassidy and his principal aides and the literally awesome build-up of the Chinese military, the stealth incident of the day before only the tip of a massive iceberg.

"All of this, please understand, is extremely sensitive. The reason I decided to read you in, Senator, is because we are facing a crisis the U.S. people have never before been exposed to. The obvious is the ISI build-up and threat to the Caspian Sea oil. Less apparent are the intentions of China. Equally threatening is the potential of an internal upheaval within our own country. So many in power and on the near side lines have profited from, and are beholden to, the status quo. The crisis we face today permeates the fabric of our nation and transcends traditional party loyalties.

Montgomery, a constitutional lawyer by training and practice, had entered the congress back in 1994, an idealistic thirty-year-old. Now in his fourth year as a U.S. Senator, he had been devastated by the death of his confidant and close friend, John Cassidy, and, futilely, had questioned the provident accident in the world's safest airplane.

"What convolutions," the senator said, his tone strident. "It seems like the entire country is on the take," and, as an afterthought, "most of which may be all legal. Let's see where we are."

As one of the two minority leaders of the senate, Joe Montgomery outlined the priorities within the relative comfort of the small room. It was clear to him that the country needed unifying. The general euphoria had begun to crumble, much like the ultra-slow motion video of high frequency sound waves weaving fissures onto the fine crystal goblet.

Montgomery thought aloud. "Fact one is China, a superpower in her own right and probably unilaterally more militarily capable than us. Fact two is China again: The key to China's economic viability is oil. Without oil, she is a third-rate power.

China clearly needs access to the Caspian reserves. Three," the senator was on a roll, his mind razor-sharp, "is the rest of the world. Sure we can survive. So too can Russia with her vast Siberian gas reserves. But, already oil is skyrocketing in price, potentially disastrous not only to the industrialized community, but those struggling to break the yoke of economic stagnation and concomitant low standards of living. Fourth is China again. China needs us. Without the U.S. as her main trading partner, the Chinese cannot generate the hard currency so necessary to continue her military growth and provide for an increasingly restive and militant population. The key, gentlemen," and belatedly, "lady, is China. The combination to defusing the situation is to involve China on our behalf and leverage the traditional mistrust of the Chinese and her fomenting neighbors in the Middle East, particularly the ISIs." He paused. "No question."

"Admiral, sorry to break in, but Admiral Chandler needs you one-on-one for a few minutes. Says it's extremely important."

"Be right out." Turning directly to the threesome, Sarodsy said, "Don't forget, the net worth, Cassidy and nukes go no further, understood?" his voice commanding, no room for interpretation. "Not even the President knows of the existence of these three compartments. Be right back."

"Sorry to bother you, Admiral," said an agitated Nancy Chandler, "but I just got off the phone with Virginia, er, the President. She wanted to know what Montgomery was doing on your calendar. I told her it was most likely a courtesy situation brief, same as we are doing for all the congressional leaders."

"Good answer, Nancy. That is, in fact, what we were doing. As one of the minority leaders, we jazzed it up a bit. I knew you were busy."

"There's more, sir," her heart beating. "She wanted to know what I had found out about a super-computer net worth program and if there had been any talk of missing nuclear weapons. Told me not to discuss the conversation with anyone. Pretty much the same as what I reported to you yesterday. I told her I had talked with you and there was no basis for either."

"That's essentially correct, Nancy. After the joint meeting with the service chiefs at noon, let's get together about 1500."

"Oh, and Admiral," she reminded her boss, "Don't forget the Reagan's close-in reconnaissance of the Iranian port of Bandar Abas. We'll launch with four Phantom IIIs in about ten minutes. I'll monitor from next door," referring to her battle force command center. "You should have some vibes before the noon jam session with your Air Force and Army counterparts, sir," smiling at her uncharacteristic attempt at levity.

CHAPTER 12

Tough Flight

Late in the waning day, four Red Ripper Phantom IIIs from the USS *Ronald Reagan,* winged aggressively towards the narrow opening of the Persian Gulf, the immense Iranian naval base of Bandar Abas only one hundred and twenty nautical miles further. Led by Lieutenant Commander Dave Anderson in his muted-gray F-27C stealth ram-jet, his wingperson was the recently arrived Lieutenant Susan "MA" Anthony and her wizo, Lieutenant Panky Pachino. Flying cover were two more Ripper fighters led by Lieutenant Becky "Big Sister" Turner and her back-seater, Lieutenant Scott "Twidget" Jacobs, the technical guru of the Navy's top fighter squadron.

The mission, though not overly complex, did have high-visibility attention within the basement command center of the Pentagon. The Ripper skipper, Commander Wendy "Iron Lady" Montrose, had attended the shipboard briefing, wishing it were her turn in the barrel. It would have been a welcome respite from the routine of boring holes in the stormy Indian Ocean skies on autopilot for three or four hours, the finale of a carrier landing notwithstanding. Thinking of her 2345 combat air patrol flight in about eight hours, she needed the sleep.

Patty Butts had stressed in the intelligence briefing, the importance of being overhead the Iranian Bandar Abas seaport at precisely 1747, some thirty minutes before sunset. The parameters for the two lead jets were to overfly the target at an altitude of one hundred feet plus or minus twenty feet at an indicated mach number of 1.46 or 1050 mph, the logic or purpose unknown to the flight crews. Refueling would be accomplished by contract U.S.

Air Force tankers four hundred nautical miles north of the carrier at 10,000 feet, both in and outbound. As per SOP, there would be no electronic emissions unless on the ultra-low-powered emergency satellite frequency.

Dr. Rose Johnson appeared discretely in the rear of the fighter ready room during the brief, the dynamics of her charges fodder for her expanding medical journal. Out of the corner of her eye, she noted the appearance of Ensign Karen Randolph, her focus on Panky. The flight surgeon motioned her over, the two unobtrusive in a quiet corner.

"Hi Karen, all OK, I hope? What are you doing here?" noting the young officer's eyes locked on the the backside of Panky, realizing it was indeed, a dumb question.

"I had a few moments before going on bridge watch and just wanted to stop by," responded the only honorary member of the venerable Red Ripper fighter squadron.

Fact was, Karen had hardly slept the past thirty hours, noted Rose with some discomfort. Piloting a jet or driving a big carrier demanded the best in mental agility, sluggish brain waves unwelcome. Aside from the captain's mast, attending to her division officer duties and standing a long four-hour watch every twelve hours, she and Panky had pushed the overtime button making up for lost opportunities on the dialogue-front. Bottom line was that for the first time in her life, Karen Randolph was worried — not for herself, but for someone she desperately cared for.

Just prior to manning aircraft, the squadron duty officer flashed a message on the briefing screen while handing a hard copy to her skipper.

FROM: NAVY HEADQUARTERS
TO: ALL F-27C SQUADRONS
SUBJ: USE OF AUTO-LAND SYSTEMS
1. EFFECTIVE UPON RECEIPT, THE USE OF THE MODE 1 AUTOMATIC LANDING SYSTEM OF ALL MODELS OF THE F-27C AIRCRAFT ARE PROHIBITED. REPEAT: PROHIBITED.

2. TECHNICAL SERVICES ARE WORKING
OVERTIME TO FIX KNOWN ANOMALIES IN
THE SYSTEM THAT HAVE CAUSED ONE
RAMP STRIKE (DOUBLE FATALITY) AND
SEVERAL NEAR-MISSES IN THE PAST
THREE WEEKS.
3. REPEAT: USE OF THE AUTO-LAND
SYSTEMS IS PROHIBITED UNTIL FURTHER
NOTICE.
SIGNED: REAR ADMIRAL J. SANDUSKY,
U.S. NAVY

Iron Lady gritted her teeth. Just what we don't need,
thankful that her pilots had routinely practiced manual landings the
old-fashioned way, she mused, parroting the words of the ship's
captain. For a moment, she thought of Susan's near-accident that
morning, dismissing the temptation to remove her from the upcoming flight with a she's got to bite the bullet sometime. Now is as
good as ever. Besides, the reality was that it was too late to
change crews anyway.

Rose Johnson observed the newly-arrived pilot, noting
that Susan was a triple victim of fatigue, worry and jet-lag. As the
message flashed on the big screen, the crews took it in stride —
all, that is, except Susan Anthony. Rose watched her stare at
the screen, imagining the blur of competing emotions in the pilot.
Rose, trained in the clinical psychology of stress, noted her
subdued reaction. Susan's new back-seater, Panky Pachino,
and she, huddled for a few moments, the conversation muted.
Susan nodded her head in the affirmative, resolutely grabbed her
helmet bag and led the way to the rainy, windswept flight deck,
her seven squadron mates following behind.

The launch, rendezvous and first refueling had gone as
planned, each jet taking on 7,500 pounds of JP9 from the big contract tanker orbiting above the undercast at 10,000 feet. Then,
with the two supporting fighters remaining in clear international
waters, the two lead fighters descended to one hundred feet over
the frothy ocean at .9 indicated mach number — just subsonic —

some fifty miles from the entrance to the Persian Gulf. Susan and Panky were slightly offset and trailed their flight lead by 1,000 feet. Lieutenant Commander Anderson's three electronic displays, more akin to a video arcade, flashed real-time satellite images of the surface, air and ground order of battle, as well as the initial way-point dead center in the Strait of Hormuz.

Way-point number-one flashed by, the desolate land masses to the north and south and a lumbering supertanker blurring in his peripheral vision. From there it was a straight 117-mile shot to the target, a staging center contiguous to the formidable Iranian naval base at Bandar Abas. Special sensors had been installed where normally a covey of super-smart weapons had hung, the mission briefers insistent that the overflight of this way-point had to be precisely on speed, time and altitude.

Anderson nudged the big ram-jets another notch. The jets smoothly went supersonic, the mach meters rapidly inching towards 1.46, the speed over the confused ocean only scant feet below, passing at eighteen miles each minute. His screen highlighted the second way-point. A quick glance over his shoulder at his five o'clock confirmed his wing person in position, as his wizo, Nancy "Shorts" Flanagan, intoned, "No aircraft airborne. No missile tones." In the low visibility and gloom of the late afternoon, the only confirmation were the comforting computer-generated symbols of his electronic, flat-plate displays.

At three miles, he spotted the target, flashing over it precisely 9.8 seconds later. Like a 3D movie with great graphics and simulation, he thought, honking the big jet into a gut-wrenching 8G, 110-degree turn to the northeast, heading for way-point number-three seventeen miles distant. "Less than a minute," he grunted to himself. For Anderson, the maneuver was only a logical extension of his Blue Angel lead solo routines of a few years ago, albeit a bit faster. He had specifically briefed his wing person to stay slightly high in the turn and get down to one hundred feet above the ground when steady inbound.

Dead ahead was the third way-point, the port's supporting airfield a few miles inland, the heads-up display once again pointing the way. "Hope the intel weenies know what they're doing," he snapped into the intercom, making small adjustments to the throttles and heading. Within seconds, the airfield appeared, the Ripper jets smoking overhead with an ear-splitting sonic boom and headed for international waters and way-point number-four, 110 miles to the east, all the while maintaining supersonic speed and an "in-the-weeds" altitude. Once over water, though, the fighters remained low but dropped the speed to a more sedate 785 mph, just slightly supersonic, finally slowing and climbing to a leisurely 10,000 feet for the return tanking.

"Piece of cake," Anderson said to Shorts. "No shooting — not even a missile warning or lock-on." Rendezvousing on the airborne tanker, he eased his jet into position for his ration of fuel, the pert, smiling face of the boom operator only fifteen feet distant, his wing person close aboard to starboard. The number-three jet, though, had problems: Becky Turner could not extend her in-flight refueling probe. No probe, of course, meant no fuel, and no fuel was a precursor to a high probability of getting wet vice clean sheets back in paradise.

Big Sister was known fleet-wide as a cool and professional stealth fighter pilot. She loved her work and was clearly not only a top-notch aviator, but a leader as well among her junior officer compatriots. Her back-seater, Twidget, was also the best of the best. It was a given that the combat capability of their jet far exceeded that of the normal crew.

Becky moved close aboard the flight leader's wing, signaled to him that her probe would not move and gave him her critically low fuel state by sign language. Anderson signaled for her to return to the ship immediately. Then, via the emergency low-power satellite relay, he advised the ship of Becky's low-fuel state and that she would be on the ball for recovery with just 300 pounds of fuel. He mentally noted that his wing person, Susan Anthony, had had no trouble refueling, hoping that it would be a harbinger of a smooth night recovery. Already the sun had set, the low clouds thickening while unseen turbulence buffeted the three remaining Ripper fighters.

"Captain, we have an emergency low-fuel-state stealth due in twenty-one minutes. OK to get the ship into the wind a bit early?" asked the officer of the deck of her captain.

"Roger that, Karen. Make it so," pleased to note the emergency pull forward of the jets in the landing area in progress, but not as happy with the typically crummy and lowering cloud deck and interruption of the next launch.

Deep within the vessel, an unseen voice dispassionately briefed the captain: "Ripper three will call the ball with 300 pounds, Captain," adding gratuitously, "Only enough for one pass. And, oh, Captain, you did get the word that the auto-land systems for the F-27C's are verboten until further notice?"

"Thanks, I did," responded the weary captain, noting the comforting clatter of the rescue helicopter's rotors far forward on the darkened bow.

"Big Sister, I figure 350 pounds on the ball," said an energized Twidget to his pilot. They had both searched the book and their brains for what to do about the recalcitrant fuel probe. Normally stowed abeam the pilot's cockpit, it extended when ready for airborne refueling. This time, though, it was clearly stuck. As was the case with all flying in the Indian Ocean, there was only one place to land. After a short pause, Twidget continued. "At 87 miles out, pull the power to idle until three miles astern of the carrier." The Ripper jet would, of course, have priority for landing, the ship already having received the word on the low-fuel state.

On the bridge, the captain noted the big carrier turning smartly into the wind, Ensign Karen Randolph intending to adjust the course and speed so as to have thirty knots of wind across the deck at ten degrees to port, or directly down the angled landing area. "All set, sir. Weather is now two-hundred-feet overcast and one-half mile visibility in gusting wind and light rain."

"Thanks, Karen," he responded politely, while glancing habitually at the anemometer. Quizzically, he noted the relative wind to be ten degrees starboard vice port. "Karen, we need to come right to get the wind down the angle!" he snapped authoritatively.

"Damn! Sorry, Captain. Right twenty degrees rudder, steady up smartly on 135!"

A voice from below: "Bridge, the Ripper low state is four

miles out. Are we turning?"

Since the days of Boone's father and grandfather, carrier captains knew never to turn with a plane in the groove, particularly at night or in inclement weather. In this case, though, the wind parameters were far out of limits. A twenty-five degree turn with an airplane at three miles on final approach meant a drastic and difficult left turn for the descending pilot and then a harder right turn to regain the centerline, all while flying the fast-moving jet without outside cues — all on instruments. "It would be close," grumbled Boone, noting the incoming fighter on his display work itself back onto the critical centerline and errant glide path at less than one mile astern.

Becky had responded like the pro she was. While maintaining airspeed, angle of attack and a descent rate of 680 feet per minute, she banked hard to the left and then to the right rolling out at three-quarters of a mile, precisely where she should be.

"Looks good, Big Sister, 300 pounds of fuel," said Twidget confidently into his oxygen mask, knowing positively that in less than thirty seconds he would be comfortably ensconced on board the Reagan or soaking wet in a hostile sea fighting for his life.

"Got the ball," Becky said, as the gloomy centerline lights broke the total blackness. Disciplining every fiber in her young body, the pilot talked her way through the final few critical seconds. "On speed — on glide slope — line-up good — a tad of power — keep the ball centered — fly it all the way down!"

"Nice job, Ripper three," Captain Boone transmitted, breaking radio silence on his ultra-low-powered communications gear to compliment the unknown crew as the jet crunched to a stop on the slick flight deck.

"Good to be home, sir," responded the pilot. Taxiing to the bow spot, the port engine of the jet coughed and quit, its usefulness temporarily curtailed by a lack of fuel.

Deep within the carrier's command center directly below the flight deck, the Ripper commanding officer was pleased. "That Turner is a winner. Cool as can be," she commented to the air wing commander seated beside her. "She'll definitely be on my list for early promotion to Lieutenant Commander. I hope you'll support her, CAG."

"No problem. You know her better than anyone. By the way, how will the auto-land restriction affect your squadron?"

"No problem. We've been diligent on practicing manual landings. One question mark, though, is our newly arrived reserve pilot, Lieutenant Susan Anthony. She had a tough warmup hop this morning. In fact, she'll be recovering in a few minutes," she said, checking the absolutely lousy weather, with an uncomfortable premonition.

For Susan, the flight had been routine, if one could characterize a catapult shot, double in-flight refueling, a supersonic, low-altitude reconnaissance dash into hostile territory and a dark night, lousy-weather manual landing back at the ship as normal or routine. Fact was that Susan's knees had not stopped shaking since climbing into her jet, the genesis of the stress factor being the eventual night-carrier landing, a factor which had confronted carrier aviators for many decades. Day landings were comparatively routine. Night landings, though, were always a challenge. Though Susan had a good reputation as a pilot, those few who bothered to probe would have noticed a distinct disinclination on her part towards flying after the sun set, a trend that originated in her early flight training in Kingsville, Texas as a student naval aviator.

At three miles astern of the ship, still in the dark and turbulent clouds, she settled into the routine of glide slope, speed and line-up, following her flight lead. At one mile, she willed herself not to screw up, knowing her skipper would no doubt be watching her performance for the second time that day. Panky was doing all he could to loosen his pilot, knowing full well that her spring was wound tight.

All is well, solid as a rock, thought the wizo. "There's the meatball — keep it up — don't let it settle, MA — keep the power up." In close, the ball went a tad high, reflecting the jet's slightly high position on the glide slope. Susan reacted by dropping the nose and chopping a handful of power off the twin ram-jets. Instantaneously, the unseen landing signal officer broke radio silence with a strident command for "POWER! — **POWER!**" The big jet slammed to the flight deck, its arresting hook just missing the last arresting wire. Years of training conditioned the pilot to slam on full power, speed brakes in and nose up, while the brain complained of the re-entry into the hostile, dark gloom of turbulent clouds. The stomach reacted predictably with a secretion of bile, fear a constant companion.

"OK, MA, you looked good until the last second." Gratuitously, Panky offered, "Just a tad slow and coming down in close. We've got lots of fuel — no worry on that score." To himself he thought, that was a hard landing, knowing full well that had the pilot not added full power, the jet would have smashed onto the steel flight deck with such force that all three landing gear would have catastrophically exceeded the design limits.

Susan checked a flashing warning light competing for her attention in the busy cockpit. "Got an unsafe starboard main landing gear indicator. Think I ought to cycle the gear?"

"No, MA. That was a pretty hard landing. Best leave it alone."

Iron Lady shook her head sadly, as the flight surgeon, Rose Johnson, entered the darkened space. Rhetorically, she said, "Looked OK 'til over the ramp. She came down like a ton of bricks, though."

As the Ripper jet settled in for a second pass, the air wing commander called the young landing signal officer on the squawk box far astern and told him to break radio silence if necessary.

"Yes ma'am," responded the LSO. "You know this is the same pilot that had such a close call this morning."

"Help her out, please."

"Aye, aye, CAG."

As the pilot tried to calm her pounding heart-rate, Twidget and Patty Butts were already reviewing the contents of the small pods carried by the flight leader's jet, the payloads removed even before the sixteen chains attaching the stealth to the deck were tight. The film was dispatched to the automatic developing room next door, word from the bridge that the captain wanted the results as soon as possible.

Susan's jet looked much better the second time around. Descending out of the gloom, she had a centered meatball, was on-speed and lined-up on the glaring centerline lights. The LSO said calmly, "Keep it coming, Ripper. Looking good. Keep the power up."

The air wing commander, Iron Lady and the landing signal officer relaxed imperceptibly as the fighter approached the blacked-out, slightly heaving deck, steady as a rock. Two seconds out and one-hundred-yards astern, Susan took her tired eyes off the glide-slope meatball, searched for the tiny, blacked-out flight deck and unconsciously eased power. "POWER, POWER, WAVE OFF, **WAVE OFF!**" screamed the incredulous landing signal officer and Panky together. Thump, rumble. The jet careened down the flight deck, the titanium arresting hook leaving a significant dent dead-center in the extreme aft end of the flight deck and a mass of bent structure in the tail of the fighter. It was a repeat of the morning's recovery, only this time she was left with no hook to catch the ship's arresting wire. The wounded jet climbed reluctantly back into the black clouds.

"RIG THE BARRICADE!" hollered the bullhorn to forty-eight women and men on the flight deck. The barricade was a woven mesh of strong nylon fibers twenty-three feet high and extending the width of the flight deck. Hook or no hook, when a jet hit this barrier, it was stuck on deck like a fly to a spider's web. A last-ditch measure, barricade engagements were few and far between, but, when needed, did the job, with one heavy-duty caveat: The pilot must fly a perfect approach. Too low and he or she will hit the ramp of the ship, as Susan had just done. Too high, and the landing gear could engage the top straps and flip the airplane onto the flight deck or into the turbulent sea seventy-feet below.

Meanwhile, the film from Anderson's jet had been developed. The "target" at Bandar Abas were the Super Pelican crates recently offloaded from a docked merchant ship. Clearly marked on the vertical sides of each seventeen-foot container were the words: "SPECIAL HANDLING AT THE DIRECTION

OF KILLINGTON ASSOCIATES." What the Pentagon needed to know was not only a confirmation of the contents, but from whence they had come. Clearly, the consortium of Iraq, Saudi and Iran — the ISIs — had managed to get the deadliest conventional weaponry in the U.S. even before many of the front-line forces. Now the truth was known. The special sensors on the Ripper jets had managed to catch what the best satellites looking from above could not.

While the squadron intelligence officer activated the secure, direct facsimile to the underground command center of Rear Admiral Nancy Chandler, the crippled Ripper jet, now low on fuel as well, made its unerring way to the looming barricade. Susan and Panky knew that once committed to the landing attempt, there was no turning back for another chance. For a few milliseconds, she thought of her kids back home and of the relative simplicity of driving big civilian jumbo-jets from point A to B. Panky brought her back to reality with a "Bit high, MA," thinking too, for a split second, of his rekindled affections in paradise.

On the bridge, Karen's amateurish miscue of the wind had almost resulted in the loss of the critically low-state F-27C stealth Phantom III. Captain Boone, long a student of human behavior under stress, sensed she had been uncharacteristically distracted, even distraught. The young officer of the deck watched the approach on the heads-up display. For the first time in her young life, she was afraid, not for herself, but for another.

Down came the big fighter, its dimmed and steady lights piercing the black gloom. Over the fantail, the LSO ordered her to "CUT, CUT, CUT," the jet falling heavily to the unyielding steel deck, the web of nylon slowing the 175 mph jet to a crunching stop in 214 feet. On the roll-out, the starboard main landing gear collapsed, skewing the plane to the right side of the landing area, just below the bridge and a thankful captain and officer of the deck. The strident crash alarm broke the sudden silence, crash crews springing into a well-rehearsed choreography.

Susan sat in the stricken jet for a full minute, raised the jet's canopy and then began to slowly unbuckle herself from the uncaring machine she knew and trusted so well. She realized her carrier flying days could well be numbered, thankful that she may have another chance to be with her husband and children and some semblance of a stable home life. Mike, awakened by the duty officer from a cat-nap in paradise, scrambled to the broken fighter and held the mother of his kids, sweaty and contrite among the jumbled mass of straps and equipment in the now quiet cockpit. Rose Johnson was just a step behind.

Deep within the carrier's electronic brain centers, Iron Lady and her boss huddled, the clang of the crash alarm echoing through the six inches of flight deck steel just above their heads. The Ripper skipper was shaking her head, remorsefully ruing the arrival of the unprepared reserve pilot, but comfortable the issue would not arise again. Softly, she told the air wing commander, "She's grounded. No more flying."

As the shaken pilot, her husband and the flight surgeon headed for sick bay deep within the ship, the discovery of the markings on the Super Pelican missiles was already the subject of an around-the-world phone conversation with a weary ship's captain and his Pentagon boss, Rear Admiral Nancy Chandler.

"Tommy, your guys did real good. I'm on my way to brief Admiral Sarodsy," said an energized Chandler to her carrier skipper. "The Admiral will have a field day with this info. Please pass along my compliments to the flight crews involved. And, Tommy," she paused, knowing full well that the ship's flight crews were stretched well beyond human limits, "it looks like we may have tasking for a pre-dawn long-range reccee mission to the far north of Iran. Similar to the Bandar flight, but with an even higher priority. Stand by for further instructions."

"Roger that, Admiral. I'll pass your compliments along to the crews. And, oh, one of our jets had a tough recovery, my newly arrived sister-in-law in fact. She'll be OK, I hope. Most likely be grounded for a while, though. She was one of the recalled reserves who were supposed to be combat-ready. Good news is I think we can get the jet back up in a couple of days or so. Talk to you later, boss."

"Bye, Tommy. You guys take care," responded the electronic voice from the other side of the world.

The Ripper commanding officer joined the somber group in sick bay while Susan Anthony sipped a two-ounce bottle of "medicinal brandy" prescribed by the Doc. Her husband held her firmly, relieving the tight muscles of the airline-pilot-turned-instant-all-weather-carrier-combat-fighter pilot in the absolute middle of nowhere. Iron Lady, uncharacteristically, also put her arm around the still shaking pilot. "Take a few days off, Susan," she said softly. "I should have given you more warm-up time. And, oh, I just got word from the Captain that Admiral Chandler in Washington just passed on an 'attaboy' for a job well done on the mission. Coming from her, that's the ultimate compliment. The results of your flight were apparently a real eye opener for the Pentagon crowd." She shifted her focus. "Mike, you have the midnight combat air patrol with me. You need to get an hour or so of shuteye," knowing full well that sleep would come fitfully, if at all, to the former package hauler.

"Skipper, I'm sorry about what happened," said the thirty-four-year-old fighter pilot, naval officer and mother of two pre-school sons, somewhat contritely. "It's been a tough few days. I'll be OK tomorrow."

"Plan for a week or so," said her skipper curtly, knowing the reality was a lot longer, if ever.

Back in paradise, the comforting voice of the ship's chaplain wafted into every crevice of the big warship, taps to follow, the hour 2200. In fact, the hour meant nothing to the mass of steel, high technology and troubled emotions, the momentum of activity unceasing.

Susan and Mike appeared at the only entrance to the officer berthing, he with his arm protectively over the shoulders of his shaken squadron mate and wife. She had mentally accepted the temporary grounding, pride giving way to relief. One by one, the displaced young warriors appeared in the corridor as if on cue. Ensign Karen Randolph, free from her bridge duties for the next eight hours, was sorrowfully attempting to explain to Big Sister and Twidget why the ship had to turn while they were in the groove and critically low on fuel. Panky Pachino was close at her side. When Panky had stepped out of his crippled jet onto the flight deck, Karen had peered down from the bridge and tearfully thanked a higher authority for his safe arrival.

Soon, Twidget and Pistol Pete Dawkins joined the group, followed by Blues Anderson, still mildly pumped up from the supersonic flight over Bandar. Before long, all of paradise was abuzz, the aviators trying to console Susan with untold screwups of their own, knowing full well they could be next in the barrel of unforgiving carrier operations. Rose Johnson was the last arrival, unobtrusively joining the animated group of young warriors, ever more aware of the complex, stress-induced, interpersonal relationships of her charges.

Slowly, the group dispersed. Pete Dawkins, the skipper's wizo, and Mike Anthony had flights to get ready for. A still confused and emotionally distraught Karen asked her roommate, Ensign Patty Butts, for the first time in almost eight months, for some "privacy," leaving Panky Pachino and the young non-flyer alone for the first time. Big Sister took her back-seater by the hand and motherly advised Twidget to cool it, the obvious object of the wizo's attention, Patty Butts. The last to leave was the flight surgeon who, in her best medical doctor inflection, requested Dave Anderson to meet her in sick bay, "when you are cleaned up," the liaison presumably having to do with research into her expanding medical journal.

At midnight, the Reagan launched another clutch of stealth fighters, recovered a like number and randomly changed course and speed, while the brew of five-thousand human emotions deep within the warship continued to simmer. The next twenty-four hours would bring them closer to the terrifying unknowns of a hostile world smoldering with international intrigue and greed.

CHAPTER 13

Scent of Money

Vice Admiral Bruce Demming, lay wide awake in the Chunking Hilton Hotel after an exhausting twelve hours in the air from Dulles Airport near Washington and fifteen hours from his sunrise meeting with Vice Admiral Stan Sarodsy, the Navy's combat arms director in the Pentagon.

Demming, of course, had made the trip dozens of times as a well-heeled, military-arms consultant and door opener for his employer, Killington Associates, his passport liberally stamped with the officialdom of China. One airborne phone call high over the Arctic Ocean to his professional friend, the leader of the Chinese Imperial Air Force, General Dung Wong, had paved the way for a predawn meeting with the esteemed warrior. "The guy absolutely never sleeps," said the retired Navy vice admiral to no one in particular.

This visit though, had taken on a different hue, the previous ones almost always reflecting the scent of money. The long flight from Dulles to Nanking, though fatiguing, allowed time to think for the seasoned admiral suddenly thrust into the back-room limelight.

Front and center in his overloaded brain was his number-two daughter, Susan, now a frontline warrior in her own right. What a crock, he thought. She ought to be home with the kids, knowing full well that the little ones were well attended to on the home front. Deep inside, he wondered if the young mother and airline pilot had the will and determination to hack it in the unforgiving twenty-four-hour-per-day, seven-days-per-week, months-on-end regimen demanded of an aircraft carrier fighter squadron very close to overt combat operations. While "Give me a fast ship for I intend to sail into harm's way," was the clarion call for John Paul Jones over two centuries ago, so too was the 21st century adaptation, "Give me a fast jet, for I will prevail when the going gets tough." He was proud of Susan. She had done well at the Naval Academy and, by all reports, reasonably well in her active-duty fighter squadron after completing Navy flight training at Kingsville, Texas. The first baby, though, had cut short her first carrier deployment, the policy for female combat pilots being a return to home base ashore at the three month point. Rejoining her squadron, the next routine deployment had been without her as well due to her second young one, her Navy duties fulfilled by tending to administrative matters at the Naval Air Station Oceana.

When she had decided to leave the Navy, American Airlines readily accepted her application. There, the regimen was routine, the objectives clear-cut and the cash flow increasingly lucrative. Demming's muddled brain sought relief from a persistent fear that his daughter was in real danger, a dread focused on his perception that she clearly did not have the will to be a killer.

His first daughter, Beverly, eight years older than Susan, was the opposite. She had stoutly maintained no interest in the military or the Navy while growing up, overtly avoiding potential entanglements with young naval officers. With a smile, he recalled his young aide back then, Lieutenant Tommy Boone, meeting Beverly for the first time. One year later, they were married and Beverly Demming Boone had become the all-American mother, supportive Navy wife and blue and gold all over.

The stewardess on the plush Cathy Pacific Boeing 888 said sunnily, "Admiral, we'll arrive in Nanking in four hours. The Captain sends her compliments and asked that I advise you will be met by General Wong's personal jet upon arrival for the flight to Chunking. You will deplane with the crew up forward, sir. May I get anything for you?"

"No, thanks. And, please, pass my thanks and compliments to the Captain for a gracious and smooth flight."

Wong and Demming had become quite close on a professional level. Aside from issues dealing with legally-transferable technology, which was the latter's forte and for which he was handsomely remunerated by his employer, much of the dialogue between the old warrior and the younger Wong was in the form of questions by the general, questions dealing with tactics, strategy and fine tuning the intangibles of the warrior ethic. It wasn't that Wong was a neophyte; quite the contrary. He had been a distinguished graduate of the Air War College at Maxwell Air Force Base in the late '90s. Even back then, recalled Demming, China had somber credentials as the dominant military power in Asia, including, at the time, the third most powerful nuclear capability in the world. Thank God, there are no more nukes, he thought.

On a spur, Demming decided to check out his diminutive secure phone while airborne. He punched in Sarodsy's command center, followed by his memorized personal identification number.

"Navy," the clear voice on the other end immediately answered.

"This is Admiral Demming. Is Admiral Sarodsy available?"

"One moment, sir." In a twinkling, Sarodsy was on the line.

"Bruce, how goes it? And, oh, feel free to say anything. This circuit is totally secure, the best we have."

"Roger that, Stan. I'm about four-hours out from Nanking. General Wong's jet will meet me. I have a meeting set up with him at first light."

"Good. One more point. Please discretely inquire as to how the Super Pelican missile shipments are coming. We have some intelligence that is a bit disturbing."

"Wilco," said the drowsy elder. "Think I'll get some shuteye."

"Bruce, thanks for everything," the chair-bound admiral said to his former mentor, his eyes uncharacteristically moistening at the dedication of the grizzled sailor, even in retirement.

The 700-mile flight from coastal Nanking to interior Chunking had taken only a bit over an hour, the small Chinese Air Force jet having been airborne only minutes after the big Boeing pulled into its slot. On landing, Demming was whisked to the city's top hotel for a quick clean-up and a few hours of needed sleep.

"General Wong. Good to see you, sir," Demming said, greeting the younger warrior in his comparatively austere office, the sun as yet to make its appearance, marking the start of a new day.

He replied in perfectly-enunciated English, "You too, my esteemed Admiral. I trust you had a comfortable trip."

"I did, indeed, including the last hour and fifteen minutes in your personal jet. Quite a machine. Your pilot permitted me to fly from the right seat. Most impressive. Thank you."

Between the two, there was a genuine and mutual bond of respect. First and foremost, both were warriors, senior military officers and seasoned combat aviators. Although Demming's missions to China had reflected the color of money and business, the inescapable catalyst for the relationship forged in the past few years was the shared esteem one had for the other.

"Please accept my apologies for the short notice, General. My employer needed updates in several areas prior to our global board of directors annual meeting next week. I guess you could say I volunteered," his smile reflecting a tone of business realities, as his gaze wandered about the functional office.

"My main mission is to check on the progress of your F-48 fighter as it relates to the stealth technology we have been providing. You seem to be well ahead of our country, and our U.S. clientele feel a need to know how you are doing. Would it be possible to visit your assembly plant?" Without waiting for the answer, he continued. "And, if I may be rightfully accused of being pushy, I would welcome a flight in the production version. Perhaps," hoping he was still being diplomatically polite, "I could manage an orientation flight with my friend, Major Tsunami riding shotgun in the back seat?"

Wong smiled, thinking that if he were in the admiral's position, he would ask the same. "Permission granted, my compatriot. How soon can you be ready?" Wong was a master at the art of *quid pro quo*, something for something; you scratch my back and I'll scratch yours. Facts were that China was indeed a superpower, her economic and industrial strength principally a function of two decades worth of wide-open lines of communication and access at the highest levels within the U.S.

As the admiral departed, followed by an energetic Chinese aide, himself a graduate of the U.S. Air Force Academy in Colorado Springs, Wong was reflective. It was no secret that China was desperate for oil as the use of her vast coal reserves constricted due to global pressures and international decree. The stop-gap use of Persian Gulf super-tankers was laborious and expensive and, he thought, very fragile. The pipeline from the Caspian Sea reserves, an 800-mile project, was, thankfully, 67% complete. But that too, he knew, was strategically fragile.

The construction of the clandestine air base by the Chinese in northern Iran was a brilliant move. It blended with the pipeline work, but more significant, it was only a straight-line 520-mile flight to the opening of the Strait of Hormuz and the Indian Ocean. Iran had been compliant only to the extent that the outside world was not privy to the base's existence and, more importantly, the promise of future high-tech weaponry from China.

"General," an aide brought him back to reality, "we have an urgent communiqué from Iran. They accuse us of overflying the port of Bandar Abas and the Kleski Airfield at an extremely low altitude and very fast. They could not identify the intruders. What should we tell them, sir?"

The tough, gruff Wong was tempted to tell them to go pound sand, but asked politely that the aide get his Iranian counterpart on the phone ASAP and he would explain that the overflight was not of his doing.

Demming, meanwhile, had been spirited from the headquarters of the Imperial Chinese Air Force in Chunking, directly to an awaiting twin-jet transport for the 1,700 mile flight to the F-48 Dynasty factory in the extreme western part of the huge country. Just on the fringes of the Takla Makan desert in the industrial city of Khotan, the sprawling factory was surrounded by a thick haze of smog, the result of generations of electrical energy production fueled by the nearby substantial fields of high-sulfur coal.

"Good morning and welcome, Admiral Demming," said the athletically-trim uniformed major.

"Ying, how good to see you. I had no idea your boss was to have you meet me this soon. You are looking well indeed."

"And, you too sir," said the respectful young fighter pilot and squadron commander, Major Ying Tsunami.

"General Wong asked that I escort you and open any doors you wish," said one Annapolis graduate and fighter pilot to the other. "In fact, he mentioned you might like an orientation flight in the Dynasty. It's been two years since we last flew together, or, should I say, you piloting and me riding," he said with a pleasant smile.

"Love to, Ying. But first I'd like a tour of the factory. I'm particularly interested in how the anechoic treatments are adhering in severe weather conditions."

Tsunami was pleased to be with the old sea-dog. There was indeed great mutual trust between the two, a trust that transcended nationality or politics. His heritage was deeply Chinese, influenced, of course, by six years of the U.S. Naval Academy and Navy flight training, ties that would remain timeless. Fact was, he was deeply interested in news about the U.S. Navy.

"How's Susan doing, Admiral? Still driving the big ones for American?" Tsunami said, as they drove to the grimy center of the darkened industrial complex.

"Would you believe, Ying, she's now on active duty. In the Indian Ocean somewhere, on the USS *Ronald Reagan*. It was so sudden. She was in Paris just starting a layover and less than forty-eight hours later was on board the carrier."

"She's piloting the F-27C, isn't she, sir?" said the major.

"Yes. She'll do OK, but I know the worry factor on the home front is off the scale. She has two preschoolers, you know. What makes it doubly hard is that her husband, a FedEx pilot, was in the same reserve call up. I think they're assigned to the same squadron, the Red Rippers." The two were silent, deep in troubled thought. Tsunami's warrior mind was trying to grasp the logic of sending young mothers off to a potential war zone while the admiral continued to harbor concern for the welfare of his number-two daughter.

Major Ying Tsunami was hesitant to bring up the subject of yesterday's flight over the Indian Ocean. Aside from the sultry back-seater in the F-27C, he had noted the ugly boar's head and backwards lightening bolt of the Red Ripper logo on the tail. He wondered if Susan had been one of the pilots.

The admiral broke the silence on a philosophic note. "The Iranian, Saudi and Iraqi military consortium has the potential for catastrophic global instability. If the ISIs gain control of the Caspian Sea reserves, your country and ours could well become the energy hostages of the decade."

He continued. "How much more do you have to go on the pipeline to your country?" The pipeline, of course, one of the world's engineering feats rivaling the Panama Canal, was to run 800 miles due east from the Caspian to the western border of China.

The young major was thoughtful, knowing his elder was most conversant with global energy concerns. "It is scheduled for completion in 2012. Already, spokes are being constructed from Kashgan to our inland industrial base. In fact, as you know, this is the principal catalyst for our military renaissance of the past fifteen years. Without oil, Admiral, we would return to a third-world status. Our armed forces are dedicated to the premise of protection of our borders, not from overland predators as much as for ensuring a free flow of oil. It is no secret that if the ISIs threaten our present supplies, we will cut them off at the knees very quickly."

The factory tour was nothing new to Demming excepting the massiveness of the complex. Four lines of F-48 Dynasty stealth fighters were constantly in work with an ultimate production of about twenty aircraft per month, working six days a week, double shifts. "It was close to the American World War II production lines and at stark contrast to the absurdly uneconomical rate of fifteen per year back at the F-27C factory in St. Louis," the admiral muttered, shaking his head.

"If you have the time, Admiral Demming, we can fly to our

base about one hour away. General Wong said you might be interested in a familiarization flight in the two seater. The only minor caveat is that the base is not in our country, and he asked that its precise location not be divulged due to its sensitive location. So, if its OK with you, I'll navigate from the back seat while you fly. Oh, and Admiral, we need to land about one hour after sunset, so we'll plan our takeoff right as the sun goes down. That will allow for a few hours of sleep here at the factory VIP suite."

"Sounds good, Ying. Yes, I would like the flight and a chance to visit your base."

"It's the least we can do, sir. If it were not for the efforts of you and your company, we would still be in the old F-35s. We are grateful for U.S. technology and the expertise you bring us."

While the admiral had napped prior to the flight, Ying had called General Wong to double-check what he was doing. "Major, the Admiral is to know everything except the precise location of the base and the topic of our discussion of two nights ago. One day, I will explain the logic of my actions." And, uncharacteristically, "Have a good flight."

Refreshed, the venerable sea warrior climbed into the star-wars front seat of the F-48, Major Ying Tsunami into the back. Modified twin ram-jets, side-stick controller, no bulky oxygen masks, awesome visibility, almost perfect reliability, it almost felt like his worn-leather armchair at home. The practiced hands and nimble brain danced a familiar pattern on the knobs and gauges, an occasional prompt from Tsunami welcome.

The takeoff and climb were routine, the rate of climb pegging at an initial 27,500 feet per minute. At a comfortable 54,000 feet, the throttles at 66% power, the jet settled out at a leisurely cruise of some 910 knots or 17 miles per minute, the setting sun well below the hazy-mountainous horizon twenty degrees off his starboard nose.

"Admiral, we're headed for our base in northeastern Iran which we have constructed contiguous to the oil pipeline work. General Wong trusts you will understand the extreme sensitivity of the location." The major knew that the old flier could take ground speed and heading and come within ten miles of the destination, as did, he suspected, his boss. "Overflight of Afghanistan and Pakistan will be no problem, sir. We are absolutely invisible to any ground-based or satellite sensors. Only tell-tale sign might be a distant sonic boom deep in a far-off valley."

The airplane was a technical marvel and a joy to fly. Even the navigation was independent of the U.S. galaxy of global positioning satellites, the redundant ring-laser gyros providing the same precise location, thanks again to the largess of the U.S. oiled by the access of Killington Associates. Handling of the stealth to the old pilot was a dream, as were the impressive range and maneuvering characteristics. Clearly, the Chinese had not only capitalized upon state-of-the-art U.S. technology, they had surpassed the best America could produce, including the latest variant of the F-27C Phantom III.

"Admiral, would you care to manually fly the approach or go full automatic?" Tsunami knew the answer without asking. "Roger that, sir. Just fly the needles. A good reference airspeed is 147 knots. When we get to about fifty feet above the ground, the runway lights will illuminate for exactly eight seconds. When we are stopped, the 'follow me' lights of a vehicle will be just at your ten o'clock position and guide us to the underground hangar. And — double-check hook down and external lights off, sir."

"Roger that, Ying. I must say this is a most impressive machine. You all have done well in a short period of time."

The admiral flew toward the unseen ground, the guidance needles precisely centered, the altimeter beeping its warning at fifty feet, the runway edge lights appearing as if on demand, piercing the black nothingness of the night desert. Smoothly touching down with only the hint of a flare, the carrier pilot and his Navy-trained back-seater, bumped to the tarmac, the tailhook grabbing an unseen arresting wire across the runway and gently easing the jet to a stop. Up with the hook, Demming glanced to his left and followed the dim lights.

"About to run into a big mountain?" said the pilot to Ying with only a trace of worry.

"Keep on moving, Admiral," said the voice from the rear seat.

Suddenly, the red glow of several hundred lights broke the blackness, while a dozen minions scurried to secure the airplane in the cavernous hangar, the giant steel doors clanging shut behind them.

"Nice job, Admiral. Better than most of my troops." Soon the muted redness was replaced by the glare of a hundred bright lights, revealing an underground complex of enormous proportion. Twenty-four deadly Dynasty jets were closely parked, as if at home on the hangar deck of an aircraft carrier.

During the flight, General Wong had finally managed to connect with his Iranian counterpart in Isfahan, the conversation over the secure phone line muffled and quietly respectful, one wary warrior to another. "I assure you, General, our aircraft were nowhere near Bandar Abas," said Wong politely, yet forcefully. "And, as we have many times discussed, our forces would never do such without prior notification to you. We have, as you know, transited south to the Indian Ocean several times in the past few weeks, to surveil the U.S. fleet, but we have carefully avoided your military bases. Please call me direct should you have further concerns, sir."

The sophisticated, clandestine complex within the mountain was gold-plated testimony to the Chinese focus on readiness for combat. Not plush, but clearly technologically functional, the centerpiece was an assortment of giant, flat-screen, computer-generated mosaics in the command center.

"Like a quick update, Admiral?" said the young fighter pilot, at which point a duo of officers appeared, flanking each screen. Every airborne aircraft within 2,000 miles was tracked to include nationality, type, altitude, destination and so on. In the Persian Gulf and Indian Ocean, every ship was highlighted with the same information, excepting U.S. warships. "It's not that we can't find them. The problem is they move so erratically from one point to another. And," he added somewhat plaintively, "I guess your daughter's out there somewhere?"

"Sir, we have a two-plane training section going out at 0117," said the squadron commander. "Why not get some sleep? I'll wake you a little after midnight so you can listen to the brief and observe the launch."

The VIP suite was nothing more than a small, spartan cubical with an attached shower, sink and commode. No desk, no chair, no TV. Only a phone connecting to the squadron duty officer. Demming took a quick shower, pulled out his miniature phone, noted the latitude and longitude of his location, committed it to memory and resisted the urge to test his secure phone deep within the mountain. Soon, he was asleep.

The training flight was actually a round-robin reconnaissance mission winding the circumference of the Caspian Sea, a lazy 1,100 miles. The two young pilots, both of whom spoke fluent English, one of whom was U.S. Air Force trained, manned the two lifeless jets, started engines, the white lights turning to red and then out as the massive doors opened to an unsuspecting desert scene of black nothingness. Riding in the guidance vehicle, Demming and Tsunami led the way to the darkened runway. Adding partial power to the big ram-jets, the runway lights pierced the darkness, take-off power was added and the jets lifted into the star-lit sky, the runway lights out.

The flight would only take a bit over an hour, so the squadron CO and the old Navy admiral returned to the "wardroom," a combination dining room and lounge, hot coffee already on the table. "Just like the American Navy," growled the sailor, Tsunami smiling at the comparison. "This is more like an aircraft carrier than not. Arresting gear, black takeoffs and landings, no radio talk, airplanes parked within inches and hot black coffee in abundance. I can see your U.S. Navy influence all over."

"Yes, sir. We have indeed managed to clone the best your Navy could offer," he responded politely, with only the hint of a smile.

The complex was indeed impressive as the major and the Navy admiral toured. Totally functional, it was the home to two-dozen fighters and about one-hundred maintenance, administrative and aviator personnel. Nothing fancy, just all utilitarian, including living quarters and mess areas, field maintenance, ordnance storage and a small command center, a remote node off the main module in General Wong's headquarters. One area, flanked by heavy doors, similar to those of a bank vault, replete with two armed sentries, caught the attention of the senior retired officer. "Sorry Admiral, that's off-limits. Nothing exciting anyway," he prevaricated to his compatriot. The admiral's bushy eyebrows raised only imperceptibly.

Back in the wardroom, with fifteen minutes until the return of the airborne section of F-48's, Demming turned introspective and questioned the sharp major. "Ying, I knew your Air Force had accomplished a remarkable make-over in the past decade, but what I've seen recently is only more impressive. Help me out — off the record. What's behind your success?"

Tsunami collected his thoughts. "You want the long or the short, sir?"

"Short, please."

"First," the major began, taking a deep breath, "our country's top goal for the past fifteen years — since 1995 — has been to field a military that has but one purpose — to win in a multitude of possible war-fighting scenarios. No exceptions. No compromises. Since the Clean Air Referendum of 2004 barring the use of coal, this effort has taken on a survival dimension. We get the best people, adequate funding and the total support of the civilian leadership. Second, copying, importing and plagiarizing, as you have seen, is an art with us. Look at our professional bookshelf — forty or so U.S. publications — *Aviation Week, U. S. News, Naval Institute, Air Force Times* and so on. Third, we have managed nicely to eschew social agendas." He paused. "You know, sir, my studies have focused on the warrior aspects of our military, primarily due to my Naval Academy and Navy flight training perspectives. I had the opportunity in the latter '90s to experience the core bedrock of your country's warrior ethic and development. The U.S. overtly and openly transformed its military from a tough, disciplined Cold War power to one of social equality, mainly on the gender front, wherein the top goals appeared to reflect how good one felt about one's self. We watched the U.S. rush headlong into gender norming in combat units and saw how disruptive it was to the psyche of the warrior ethic. Good example is the Naval Academy. A couple of years ago, midshipmen who became pregnant were allowed to continue their studies and place their infants in the academy nursery. Who knows, maybe one day, you'll have nurseries aboard ships."

He stopped. "Sorry Admiral — just kidding. I guess I started into the long answer. Bottom line is that the technology aspects are easy. Big bucks take care of that, as you know. Far more important to us are the intangibles of the warrior make-up. Women are a distraction, even more so in the front lines."

"Major," the duty officer interrupted, "the recon flight is forty miles out for landing. Your vehicle is ready."

Outside it was pitch dark with the hint of a chill in the still air, the stars obscured by a high cover of cloud. The whine of the unlit jets could be heard, the pilots adjusting to maintain speed and descent rate. It seemed as if the aircraft would land on top of them, when suddenly, the runway lights glared into action, the first jet hooking a cross-deck pendant. The scenario was repeated 38 seconds later, the return to the underground entrance almost routine.

Once inside, the two pilots deplaned, looking almost as if they had just finished a board meeting, smiling and chattering as did all fighter pilots after a good-weather, no-stress milk run. En route back to the operations center, the admiral noted the vault-like doors were now covered by large drapes, the observant guards the same.

"Time for a nap, Ying. My bones aren't as resilient as yours, I'm afraid. We'll head back for Khotan just before first light. Is that right?"

"Yes sir. I think I'll follow your lead and catch a couple of winks myself."

"WHANG, WHANG, WHANG, WHANG," the garish,

clanging alarm brought Demming abruptly awake. Glancing at his watch, he noted the time as 0417, too early for his wake-up. Must be a test, he thought, conditioned to decades of a ship's general quarters alarm. Quickly dressing in his flight suit and boots, he scurried outside into the hangar where four armed jets were being hurriedly manned, led by the squadron commanding officer. Canopies down, engines rolling to life, the four jets moved as if on cue less than three minutes from the initial alarm, the hangar doors opening for 47 seconds. Four minutes and seventeen seconds after the first clang of the alarm, the four stealth fighters were airborne.

The admiral half ran to the command center, thinking that Tsunami was staging a show for his high-priced guest, and noted two unknown jets headed south by southeast, very low and well supersonic, the four Chinese fighters in hot pursuit some one hundred miles behind. "Must be the Iranians in response to something," thought the admiral, wondering, if so, how did they find this super-secret base, his warrior self in high gear.

The young duty officer, a captain, briefed the admiral. "They appeared out of nowhere, flying at less than one hundred feet and very slow, then headed south at extremely high speed. Must be the damned Iranians. They periodically scout the pipeline. Funny though, they're not headed for Bandar. Looks like western Pakistan or the Indian Ocean."

Suddenly, the speed vector of the number two unknown bandit went to practically nothing, the lead jet slowing and turning back. The electronic symbol for the international distress signal surrounded the second jet and then soon disappeared.

"Admiral, for some reason, the number-two intruder seems to have crashed in the mountains and my guess is that the pilot has successfully ejected. That's tough country, just to the west of Afghanistan, over 9,000 feet elevation. Our flight is almost on top now."

The seasoned admiral, suddenly older, was struck with a bolt of raw fear. "Oh, my God. Susan!"

CHAPTER 14

A Light In The Window

Back in the tranquil neighborhood of Virginia Beach and far-removed from the crescendo of events a half-world away, Beverly Demming Boone was halfway through her invigorating morning run, her mind in a recharge mode from the complexities of the prior evening. The unexpected call from her next door neighbor, Bill Montrose, following the ship's spousal gathering of the night before, had not been a surprise. What followed was.

Bill, whose former wife, Wendy, now the commanding officer of the Red Rippers, was a rock-solid, homespun type with two kids. His nearby work as a school administrator was an unbendable Monday through Friday, 8-4-routine, with no homework or overtime. When 4:00 p.m. rolled around, Bill was history. In this predominately Navy neighborhood, where many of the husbands and wives were deployed to the far corners for months on end, Bill was a godsend. Fixing recalcitrant lawn mowers, occasional kid pickups for harried fathers and numerous "honey do's" were his stock-in-trade. Plus, she thought, the crisp morning air filling her inner-soul, he was a good father. And, somewhat plaintively, "Quite at contrast to his upwardly-mobile, high-achieving former wife. What a mismatch."

"Hi Bev, can we join you?" It was Rick Turner and Sandy Anderson, who, increasingly, had joined Beverly partway through her routine. Rick and Sandy had much in common. Both were the parents of two preschoolers, lived three houses apart and had a wife and husband deployed with the Red Rippers on board the USS *Ronald Reagan*. Sandy's Dave, the former Blue Angel, was the acting second in command of the venerable stealth fighter squadron, while Rick's Becky was one of the squadron's leading pilots. Both had been gone from home the better part of nine months, with no discernible end in sight. Much like Beverly's next door neighbor, Rick, an attorney, was laid-back, averse to long hours at work and available for a manly hand around the neighborhood.

The talk, in between deep breaths, was as always, about the deepening crisis 8,000 miles away, punctuated by the latest edict, no more e-mail from any of the ships in the Indian Ocean. "Not looking good," said Rick. "Wish there was something we could do."

Sandy, loping along with a conditioned ease said, "We've doubled-up on a lot of school classes due to the reserve call-up. It's affecting all the schools."

"First time in a long while," said Beverly, breathing hard, grimacing at the thought of her younger sister Susan out on the front lines along with her reservist husband. Their two little ones, though suddenly bereft of parents, were snug in Bev's guest room, her high-school eldest jumping into the fray with a maternal gusto.

"Nice party last night, Beverly, "said Sandy smiling. "Quite an eclectic gathering, particularly Suzette."

"Seemed to me to be severely in heat," grinned the lawyer, wishing he had been more circumspect.

"I'm having lunch with her today. Hope to give her some straight talk about the birds and the bees when dad and mom are away," said the wife of the ship's CO, wishing she could think of a way out of it and ignoring Rick's comment. "See you all later."

The lawyer and schoolteacher disappeared around the corner, homeward bound, worry talk the order of the day. "What a crazy world we live in," Beverly said, already planning breakfast for her expanding brood, now doubled with the addition of Susan and Mike's kids.

Sandy came by a couple of hours later, taking the two children off somewhere with her two. "Sandy," correctly surmised the older woman, "is a winner."

Beverly's thoughts turned reluctantly to the previous evening. She and Bill had been spending more and more time together commiserating and helping one another. Fact was, they got along well, the glue, the menagerie of homemaking ablutions necessary in any home with young ones aboard and no spouse. Beverly seldom harbored risque thoughts. She missed Tommy for sure, as she always had, any wandering of her inner-self snapped back to the centerline of responsibility quickly. Bill's call, though, after all had left the night before, caught her in a desperate need to talk sense with someone she trusted.

On her front porch, the tree-lined Summerset Lane empty, the chill of a damp November drizzle permeated her light sweater. Bill had put his arm around her, more protective than suggestive, their quiet talk uninterrupted. Eyes had met, held for a moment, then focused on the nothingness of the front yard. "Beverly, I know it's hard on you. You've got much more to worry about than yourself. I want to help you," his eyes once again within hers, his arm a bit tighter on her shoulder.

For an instant, she rested her head on his chest and said simply, "No, Bill."

The phone jangled her back to reality. "Hi, Beverly, it's Nancy Chandler. I'm in Norfolk for a one-day meeting and thought we could get together, if you had some spare time. I'd like to bring you up-to-speed on what's going on with your husband's ship." Beverly paused. She had only met Rear Admiral Chandler one time some months ago, shortly after she had put on her stars as a flag officer, the occasion the departure of the USS *Ronald Reagan* on a planned, routine, six-month, peacetime deployment.

"Sure, Nancy. Nice of you to think of us folks left behind. How about five? Perhaps you could stay for an early dinner?"

"That sounds good. I'll have my plane pick me up at Oceana instead of Norfolk for the flight back to Andrews."

She knew Nancy Chandler to be a smart, hard-charging, albeit inexperienced naval officer, whose forté was inside the beltway of Washington. Chandler had been a vice presidential personal aide as a commander and, more recently, as the chief of staff for President Virginia Roberts Stallingsworth. Now, the same age as she, Nancy was her Tommy's boss.

"My God, the phone again. It never stops," sighed the tried-and-true Navy wife, thankful for the distraction from the emotional pressure cooker of the night before.

"Hello. Mrs. Boone?"

"Yes, this is she."

"Mrs. Boone, I'm Dolores Miller, the wife of Lieutenant Commander Stan Miller, the weapons officer on the Reagan. I'm in town for a few days and would like to stop by, perhaps later today, with a proposal. Would you be available?"

"Certainly, and call me Beverly, please. How about four? My husband's boss is stopping by. You could meet her as well."

"Thank you, I will," said the well-spoken woman.

Damn, the day was going to be something else, her mind a blur. She knew Dolores Miller by name and had met her husband briefly. Discreet inquiries as to Stan Miller's marital status or where he lived when ashore, had yielded nothing. Now, abruptly out of the blue, his wife appears. Strange. She was grateful to Sandy for having taken Susan's kids off her plate, if only for a while. Best way to describe Sandy, she thought, was the Mrs. All-American Mom.

The luncheon with Suzette McCormick was to have been at noon at the Naval Air Station Oceana officer's club. Finally, at 12:20, the new wife of the Red Ripper's master chief petty officer made her entrance into the club, most every eye focused on the striking woman. Clad in a skimpy, clinging dress, her ample figure blossomed for all to see, her smile locking briefly onto every male officer while she ostentatiously fingered a cigarette from her tiny purse, a willing flame accelerating the tobacco to its intended use.

"Hi, Bev. Hope I'm not too late. Got tied up."

"No, Suzette, it's OK. But, you're not supposed to smoke in here. Sorry." Beverly knew it would be a long lunch.

Crossing her shapely legs in a manner known only to a few females, Suzette snuffed out her cigarette, and, without a wasted breath, exclaimed, "Who was that adorable young lawyer at your party last night? He was definitely cute. Dick something, right?"

"No Suzette, Rick Turner. And I may as well cut the small talk. You and I need to get on the same frequency."

Suggestively, while scanning the club full of young pilots, the new wife recrossed her legs and leaned forward just far enough to keep certain interest levels perking. "Go ahead. We girls can talk."

Beverly's efforts to explain the facts of life to the overly-agitated lady were fruitless. "My God, Bev, you want me to sit at home for eight months tending to my knitting? You're crazy. Got to make hay while the sun shines."

"Well, if you have to make hay, please do it privately, behind closed doors, not out where everyone can see you making an . . . ," she paused, "being foolish. Oh, and Suzette, stay away from Mitsi Moore's husband, please."

"That old fart. All he wants to do is talk about the Navy and his wife. What a bore. I doubt if he can even get it up," her furtive eyes scoping the contents of the lunch bunch.

Beverly flinched. Suzette McCormick was incorrigible. No hope. Damage control was the only option for her type. The shapely lady left as she had entered, coat casually over her bare shoulders, the neckline equally exposed, the legs hardly encumbered by the mini-skirt, a lighted cigarette obscuring penetrating eyes on the search for some willing action.

On the way home, Beverly stopped by the commissary to get some "kids' food" for Susan's youngsters and met Sandy Anderson, toting her foursome. "Tommy's boss, Rear Admiral Chandler, is coming by for a visit around five. Why not come over and join us?"

"Good. I'll leave my kids with Rick and drop off Susan's with you." Sandy, Beverly noted, was her usual ebullient self, trim in her chambray shirt, jeans and aerobic shoes.

Home again, the answering machine flashed its endless blinks, each one a mini-drama of unknown intrigue or mundane problems. "Not much is good news," groaned Beverly, hitting the phone's memory button for her mother, ten blocks away.

"Bev, have you heard anything from your dad?" knowing full well the answer, but anxious to talk nonetheless. The sudden departure of her husband in the early morning hours and his even more abrupt flight to China were unsettling to the older Navy wife.

If Beatrice Demming knew what her husband was doing at the moment, she would have been surprised, but not overly so. Bruce Demming had never been one to shirk the impossible or dodge the tough task. Demming had a well-grounded reputation as a hands-on admiral, more than willing to get down-and-dirty with the issues or the troops.

"No, Mom. I'm sure he's doing the same as always when he's in China." Deep down she knew, as did her mother, that this was different. Too sudden, too abrupt and too coincidental with the evolving crisis on the other side of the world.

The doorbell announced a well-coiffed, matronly lady somewhat older than Beverly. About 45, she guessed. The warm smile and ready handshake of Dolores Miller put Beverly at ease. "Please come in. I'm afraid I've not had a chance to straighten things out. We're in kind of a turmoil here."

"OK to park in your driveway?" asked Miller.

"Quite all right," Beverly smiled, noting the crisp lines of the shiny new Lexus 4000 with its Arkansas license plates. "Nice car. I've heard a lot about them," ruefully averting her gaze from the eight-year-old Honda leaking finite quantities of oil onto the driveway. "We're overdue, I'm afraid."

"Mrs. Boone . . ."

Beverly interrupted. "Bev, please."

"OK, Bev. I know this is rather unexpected, but it's something I had to do. For years Stan and I have lived apart, he on his ship and me, wherever. His life has always been the U.S. Navy. It's been a comfortable relationship." She paused, reflective. "Recently, I have come into a substantial amount of wealth, compliments of the Arkansas lottery. Allow me to get to the point please: I want to set up some scholarships for the children of the Reagan's enlisted personnel — about ten or so — in order that they may attend any school or college they may be admitted to. I'll need someone to administer the fund, but it must be done covertly. I don't want my name or Stan's to be public. What do you think? Would it be possible?" queried the thoughtful lady, a glimmer of concern in her kindly eyes.

"Why, Dolores, that's marvelous. I'm sure we could help set it up. Some sort of a trust-in-perpetuity, I would guess. In fact, the husband of one of the ship's fighter pilots, an attorney, lives nearby and could work up some proposals. If it's all right with you, I'll call him and ask if he can come over tonight, so you two could chat."

She promptly called Rick Turner, who willingly made himself available. Beverly's oldest daughter could tend to the brood about to descend on the tree-shaded home of the Reagan's commanding officer and Beverly, ex-officio the officer-in-charge of the home front.

By a little after five, the ad hoc group were in animated dialogue, the core ingredient, of course, the aircraft carrier Reagan. Rear Admiral Nancy Chandler was the center of attention.

"I'm here in Norfolk because, frankly, we need to get every warship underway ASAP. The situation in the Indian Ocean is critical. The consortium of Iran, Saudi Arabia and Iraq are not backing down. In fact, the ISIs have moved their combat forces into the highest state of readiness. As it stands now, if the free world does nothing, the Caspian Sea and all its oil will belong to the ISIs."

"How about NATO?" questioned Beverly.

The admiral chuckled. "NATO is totally paper, rhetoric and cocktail parties. Too bad. Long ago, there were many who rightfully argued for a NATO expansion, but never followed through with the dollars to support it. I'm afraid we're in this up to our armpits."

The admiral's aide left the room and reappeared with a message from the car's satellite fax. Chandler grimaced. "Bad news, I'm afraid. Just got word that one of our stealth fighters on the Reagan has gone down. No sign of survivors, as of now."

Rick and Sandy blanched, speechless with fear. Beverly though, had been through this same scenario a few times and took charge. "I think we could all do with some wine. Dolores, would you help me with some glasses, please?"

"None for me thanks, Bev," said the admiral. "I've got to mind the store. I promise to call you as soon as I get any more info, no matter the hour." With that, she and her aide were gone, the satellite-secure phone to her underground Pentagon command center already at her ear.

The two Red Ripper spouses held one another closely, fearful of an unknown over which they had no control. Sandy rested her head on the comforting shoulder of her neighbor and friend, Rick's arms protectively around her.

Beverly broke the emotional quiet. "Sandy, why don't you spend the night here and take a vacation day tomorrow from school. OK?"

"That would be nice, thanks," said the younger woman.

"And Dolores, why don't you talk with Rick about your proposal? It'll help take our minds off the worry," said Beverly to her expanding family.

Rick Turner and Dolores Miller talked excitedly for a few minutes, promising to meet the next day and work out the pragmatics of the scholarships, trusts and legal issues. Dolores made it clear, once again, that the entire transaction was to be confidential, the benefactors known only to one attorney.

After the lawyer and Stan Miller's wife left, Sandy and Beverly settled into the deep cushions of the friendly family room, the first fire of the season maturing to glowing embers, the warmth enticing. Kids asleep, Beverly's girls finishing their homework, the two confidantes relaxed into a comforting silence

Sandy broke the quiet. "Beverly, I'm not worried about Dave," she said softly, referring to her Red Ripper husband. "He can take care of himself." She paused, her mind a string of blurry thoughts. "You know, Bev, I can handle the kids, the home front and the schoolhouse, but it's all I can do to deal with . . . ," she paused again, uncomfortable with her thinking. "It's about my Dave. I've always known he had wandering eyes, more macho than substance, I suppose; and I keep hearing stories about the ship. Who knows what goes on out there? I've never been to sea, but my simplistic brain tells me that living, working and flying with your womanly or manly next-door neighbor for almost nine months in the close confines of a ship is dumb. Doesn't make sense."

"And, Bev, could I lean on you some more? I mean, really lean!" plaintively inquired Sandy Anderson.

"Sure, Sandy. Shoot," responded the older woman.

"This is hard for me, but I've got to let it out. In the past month, two friends of mine have been coming on to me. One, you've probably guessed, is Rick. He wants someone to confide in, which is fine. Lately though, it's too close. It's more than a desire to help out, I'm afraid. And, heaven knows, I don't think I've encouraged him. Ours, at least until a few weeks ago, was the quintessential brother and sister act."

Beverly said warily. "And the other?"

"An old Blue Angel buddy of Dave's now flying for American Airlines. He lives nearby and, on his lucrative times-off, has really put the heat on me. I say 'no' over and over and each time he tries another tack. Wanted me to go off to his vacation hideaway in the mountains for a few days. He seems to think I'm fair game. And though it does not come out directly, he describes the social life aboard the carriers at sea in rather lurid detail." She got up, poured herself another splash of chardonnay and continued. "I don't know what to believe. I do know, though, that between Rick and Mr. 'X,' I get some funny feelings deep within me that very much bother my sense of what's right and wrong. What's a little fling to hurt?"

Unexpectedly, the doorbell rang, the hour late. "At 10:30?" Beverly went frigid, cold waves of fear rushing through her resilient self. She peered onto the lighted porch at a neatly-dressed man and women. Without opening the door, "Who is it, please?"

"Naval Criminal Investigative Service, Mrs. Boone. We need to ask you a quick question, please. Sorry for the late hour, but it's very important. It concerns Dolores Miller."

"Mrs. Boone, we must ask that you both keep this inquiry quiet. We are on an extremely high-level and top-secret investigation that may reach to the highest levels of the U.S. government. Understood?"

"Couldn't it wait until morning?"

"No ma'am, I'm afraid not. We have but one question: What was Mrs. Miller doing here this afternoon?"

The trio stood awkwardly in the foyer of the modest home while Beverly explained, including the mention of Dolores Miller's recent lottery winnings. "Mrs. Boone, we don't want to burst your bubble," said the woman agent, "but Mrs. Miller did not win the Arkansas lottery or any other lottery. Thanks for your time. Our apologies for calling so late."

The door closed, the embers burned lower and the two women tried to decipher a puzzle they could not comprehend.

Beverly broke the silence. "Sandy, we're all human. You have a right to feel confused. I have the same problem, I'm afraid — with Bill next door." Sandy's eyes opened wide, her breath coming in short gasps. Beverly continued. "Same scenario, only it's getting more overt lately, to be frank. And I, too, have wandering thoughts once in a while. I guess it's normal."

"What a day!" they both exclaimed together.

"How about this?" said Beverly brightly. "Suppose, if we get tempted, that we just pick up the phone and talk it through. OK?"

"Sure, Bev. But I still wonder what they do on the ship, and that bothers me something fierce."

The phone jangled again, nerves jumped in consonance. Beverly glanced at the time — 11:25 p.m. "Must be my mom," she rationalized. It was Nancy Chandler.

"Beverly, just talked with Tommy on the Reagan. The jet that went down was from the Red Rippers. No news on the crew. It was overland. The pilot was Lieutenant Sam Newman and his wizo, Lieutenant Evelyn Swagger. As soon as I hear more, I'll let you know. It will be on the morning news, but no names. Got to run. Tommy sends his love. Told him we had a nice visit. Take care."

A sincere, "Thanks for calling, Nancy. We'll take it from here."

Normally, the spouse of the squadron's commanding officer would tend to the details of notifying the home front. The

178

dreadful task this time fell to Sandy. She knew that both Studs and Bikini flew together, were roommates and, though unmarried, scuttlebutt had it that they were inseparable. She did have in her purse, however, a small notebook with the names and addresses of each member of the squadron along with the next-of-kin data. Happy for the distraction, she and Beverly reviewed the list. If it were not in person, both knew that the nearest naval facility would go into notification action as soon as confirmations were obtained.

Beverly sighed. She had been through this several times. Never easy, it was always tough and routinely traumatic. They would wait for confirmation. "How about we give it until morning, Sandy?"

"Good idea. I definitely need some sleep," she said resignedly, the fear factor permeating to the core.

Dousing the bedside light, Beverly lay awake, her mind a mush of competing demands, not the least of which were the surprise visits of Dolores Miller, with her generous offer, followed by the clandestine knock on the door by the Navy investigators and the statement, ". . . at the highest levels of the U.S. government," resonating in her stressed-out mind.

A lone light shown in the window next door. "That I can handle. Truth is, she struggled with her thoughts, there's a lot of unspoken tension and worry about what's going on on-board the Reagan and probably every other ship out there. I guess they worry, too. But at least here, we can lock the door and shut out unwanted entanglements much easier than the men and women out on the high seas. Sandy's right. There, it's twenty-four hours a day for literally months on end. It's got to be tough. She vowed to discuss it with Tommy when he returned with the ship to Norfolk. "Whenever that may be," she said softly, hopefully.

Her eyes felt heavy, the brain finally taking a welcome break. She said sadly, "God, I wish he were home!"

CHAPTER 15

Real Big Bucks

Vice Admiral Stan Sarodsy's direct line buzzed urgently on the secure, red phone deep below the five-sided pristine exterior of an immovable Pentagon. It was his battle-force deputy, Rear Admiral Nancy Chandler. "Admiral, I'm en route to Andrews from Oceana now and should be on board the command center by about 2115. I've talked to Captain Boone on the Reagan. Told him to move to a position two hundred miles south-southeast of the entrance to the Persian Gulf where his V-22 Ospreys can effect the search and rescue. So far we have only one emergency beeper, and that's getting weaker by the hour. Hopefully, one of the crew has survived.

"Good, Nancy," responded her boss, shifting his considerable bulk deeper into the worry creases of his command center chair. "Sounds as if you are on top of it. Oh, by the way, your former boss over at the White House is agitated. She wants to know why we were flying over Iran. You handle her, please. Routine reconnaissance."

"Got it, boss," she exclaimed.

Stan Sarodsy continued to read the "Preliminary Information Regarding Operation Green Trees." "Green Trees" was the result of the still-experimental parallel computer program revealing the sources and whereabouts of significant new wealth. He went back to the executive summary and slowly reread it, the dynamics and repercussions leaping off the pages into his brain, his knees revealing the nucleus of an uncontrollable shake, his brow cool to its new-found moisture:

FINDINGS: IN THE FIRST TEN MONTHS OF 2010, ABOUT $3.4B HAVE FLOWED FROM SOURCES THROUGHOUT THE WORLD TO THE REDMAN INSTITUTE FOR ENLIGHT-ENED AWARENESS AND FROM THERE TO SEVERAL NUMBERED SWISS BANK ACCOUNTS, VARIOUS POLITI-CAL ENTITIES AND TO 47 SPECIFIC POLITICAL INDIVIDU-ALS. THE INITIAL SOURCE APPEARS TO BE PREDOMI-NATELY THE FEDERAL BANK OF CHINA, FLOWING THEN THROUGH A SERIES OF COMPLEX TRANSACTIONS, MOST ALL OF WHICH HAVE ONE COMMON CONDUIT THROUGH THE REDMAN INSTITUTE. SEVERAL SIZABLE PAYMENTS HAVE ACCRUED TO SOME WELL-KNOWN PERSONS AND TO THE ACCOUNT OF ONE DOLORES MILLER, THE WIFE OF THE WEAPONS OFFICER ON THE AIRCRAFT CARRIER REAGAN. THOUGH UNSUBSTAN-TIATED AT THIS TIME, THERE MAY BE A CORRELATION BETWEEN THE MISSING NUCLEAR WEAPONS (FIND JEW-ELS) AND THE THREE AND ONE-HALF BILLION DOLLARS WE HAVE BEEN ABLE TO TRACE SO FAR. WE STRESS THAT THIS REPORT IS MOST PRELIMINARY AND THAT AD-DITIONAL FINDINGS MAY BE EXPECTED TO FOLLOW. AS THE INVESTIGATION PROGRESSES AND THE TIME FRAME EXPANDS TO THE YEARS SUBSEQUENT TO 1996, IT IS EXPECTED THAT SIMILAR LARGE AMOUNTS MAY BE TRACEABLE TO THE SAME SOURCES AND, IN GENERAL, USES."

His direct line lit up again. It was Captain Tommy Boone, on the Reagan, steaming in the Indian Ocean ever closer to harm's way. "Admiral, I know you wanted the results of the recon flight this morning as soon as possible. The Red Ripper skipper, Commander Montrose, just landed with the special sensor. The reading is 4.97. Don't know what that means, but over to you, sir."

"Thanks, Tommy. I don't right now, but soon will. Please pass to the skipper my compliments for a job well done and my condolences over any casualties. I know you guys and Admiral Chandler are working the search and rescue, so I'll stay out of it. And, Tommy, one point — we need the sensor on the downed jet. Its contents are very highly classified."

"Roger that, Admiral."

Sarodsy called his aide, and, in an uncharacteristic clipped tone, "Get Captain Banaro on the secure phone ASAP. It's most urgent."

"Aye, aye, sir."

Sarodsy's brain was in overload. Whom to trust? Who's involved? It clearly looks as if fifteen years of cozying up to the Chinese had reached a crescendo, the cymbals banging a beat longing to be heard. Dollars for politics from foreign sources had long been illegal, the machinations to beat the system never-ending from the barrage of enterprising politicos. All, that is, excepting the Chinese. Somehow, some way, the clandestine money had flowed deep into the central psyche of America. He decided to check in with his friend, Senator Joe Montgomery, at home.

"Joe, sorry to bother you, but I need to see you fast. And Ernie too, if possible. Can we make it at your residence in about thirty minutes?"

"Sure, Admiral. I hope it's not as bad as you sound."

"Worse, my esteemed Senator friend."

On his way out, the chilling report securely in his coat pocket, the aide handed him the secure line. "Captain Banaro, Admiral."

"Sam, how are you? I've got to make it fast. What does a reading of 4.97 on the mod sensor indicate?" Silence.

"Sam, are you there?"

"Yes, sir. I'll cut to the bottom line. A reading of 5 is indicative of a moderate-to-strong possibility of weapons-grade nuclear material."

The silence was deafening. The Navy's premier nuclear weapons expert and the combat seasoned warrior hardly needed to add two plus two. "Sir, I think we know the whereabouts of the missing nukes on the Reagan."

"Thanks Sam. Let's get together in the morning — about

0630? We need to do some brainstorming."

On the short ride to Montgomery's apartment in Washington's Watergate complex, Sarodsy mulled over whether to include Nancy Chandler within the ever-expanding equation. She was indeed bright, energetic and had a deep understanding of both the Asian region and the machinating incumbent of the White House. The only real drawback was the degree to which he felt she could stand up to President Virginia Roberts Stallingsworth. His guess was that her loyalty was to the U.S. Navy and the Constitution of the United States, political considerations a clear and convincing runner-up.

"Come in, Admiral. Let's go to the quiet room," greeted the learned U.S. Senator as they entered a spacious, windowless room in the center of the comfortable eighth-floor apartment. Smiling, he explained that the original owner had been an influential senator who had become paranoid about leaks within a money-hungry Washington body politic. It had its own double-lock door and, to the casual observer, was nothing more than a soundproof room within which to listen to the latest classical rendition.

With a broad grin framed beneath a mane of gray-flecked hair, he announced, "Ernie will be here shortly. How about a cup of good Navy coffee while we wait?"

Without preamble or an answer to Montgomery's offer, the admiral said, "What do you know about Richard Redman, Joe?"

"Wow. Got an hour or so? Bottom line? He's the power behind the White House, half of the Congress and most of the Supreme Court including our incumbent president. There's not a shred of this blessed town over which his influence is not felt. Here's Ernie, now."

As Sarodsy slowly read the one copy of the preliminary report, the silence within the room revealed only the deep breathing of the three men. Ten minutes passed. The admiral stood and spoke slowly. "It looks as if the Chinese have purchased four nuclear weapons, the massive funds having gone to enrich and perpetuate in political office some of the most reputable and prominent persons in our country. In addition, the money sources of the past twelve years, though not as massive in the short run, seem to add up to more of the same."

Joe Montgomery wondered aloud. "How did you confirm this?" After explaining the recon mission and the downed jet, Stan Sarodsy gave a quick recapitulation of the evolving military crisis by the ISIs.

The senator continued. "I knew this town was on the take. This list looks like a who's who of influence. No wonder the ECATS have garnered such a monumental plurality," referring to the astounding success of the Enlightened Citizens Against The Status Quo. "It's just plain money. Trouble is, none of the big bucks filtered down to those who needed it the most."

The threesome discussed the pros and cons of whom to include in this latest damaging information, particularly Rear Admiral Nancy Chandler. In the end, there was a short list of seven names, Chandler included. Noticeably absent was the Navy's CEO, Admiral Carolyn Sweeney.

Chandler was, at the moment, back in her Pentagon command center, setting in motion the search and rescue efforts for the missing crew deep in Iranian territory and about fifteen miles from the western border of Pakistan. She would brief Sarodsy when he returned. Troublesome, was the call from the President while she was en route from Andrews AFB. Virginia was blustery and abrupt in demanding, once again, to know why the jets were over Iran. Nancy's logical military necessity explanation was lost in a barrage of unladylike expletives.

Her mind wandered. The three years as Stallingsworth's chief of staff in the White House had raised eyebrows and hackles in equal dimension. Nancy had come on board in 2006 after her former boss had gone through four predecessors in two years, none able to stand up to her constant withering barrage of criticism, her towering intelligence and clandestine mannerisms. Nancy though, had done well, the bonding between the two like the commingling ingredients of a two-part epoxy glue.

Only thirty-four at the time, it had been a formidable transition. Her upbringing with a demanding matriarch, herself a former career politician, had been focused on a total commitment to excellence. A Type-A+ persona, Nancy's social distractions, including men, had been minimal. The latter had caused tongues to wag in some quarters, particularly as regarded her bachelor boss, the President.

Her private secure line buzzed her back to reality. It was Sarodsy. "Nancy, I know you're stretched, but I need to see you at 0630."

"Yes sir, I'll be there. I'm bird-dogging the search and rescue. The Pakistanis, Iranians and the Chinese stealth are flying over the area. Oh, I did talk with the President. I've never heard her so torqued. She's wound tighter than I've ever seen her. See you in a few hours, boss."

One aspect of her tour with Stallingsworth stuck in her craw, the strident tone of the President ringing in her ears. As chief of staff, she had noted the same irascibility within the inner sanctum of the private chambers. Often the stimuli were the three to four visits per week of Richard Redman in private along with a sprinkling of the nation's leading corporate CEOs, meetings generally closed to all, herself included.

Richard Redman had grown steadily in girth and power since being anointed to the highest levels of the U.S. government. His were the dollars that facilitated the tenure of the majority ECATS party, a tenure overwhelming in its breadth, scope and longevity. Nancy had sought to break the code of silence on the subject of campaign finance reform, with zero success. What was clear, however, was an overwhelming mandate by the political power structure and major business moguls not to disturb the status quo, the bounty of the lobbyists feeding at the trough, content with their sated lot riding the political money train.

Back to reality, she awoke to the aroma of freshly-brewed strong coffee, a foul-tasting mouth and tired bones. "Good morning, Admiral. It's 0600 and I'm reminding you of your meeting with Admiral Sarodsy in thirty minutes," said her aide

"How's the SAR coming? It's close to nightfall over there, right?"

"Still working the details, ma'am. We've lost contact with the crew member. Looks like a pair of Navy special forces V-22

Ospreys from the Reagan will attempt a night recovery."

In Sarodsy's command center, the senior admiral took charge. "Admiral Chandler, meet Captain Sam Banaro of our special weapons shop. Sam is an old friend from way back. I'm going to ask him to brief you on an extremely sensitive subject that you have not been read into. Then, after he leaves, I intend to cut you in on more. Go ahead please, Sam."

Nancy was vaguely familiar with the Navy's nuclear weapons policies. As a commander a few years prior, she had been privy to the global agreement to ban all nuclear weapons. Then, as a flag officer, she was aware of the three hundred weapons the U.S. had managed to shield from prying sources, all of which were securely ensconced in perpetuity within six aircraft carriers and an equal number of old Trident missile submarines. Captain Sam Banaro was well-known and respected in higher Navy circles as the godfather of these weapons, which, literally, never saw the light of day.

The briefing lasted fifteen minutes with Admiral Sarodsy adding, "So you see, it was a fluke that Sam noted the missing weapons from the Reagan. The technology is a carry-over from decades-old Cold War devices which have been highly refined into much more useful variants able to ascertain the existence of weapons-grade plutonium. Are there any questions before Captain Banaro has to leave?"

"No, sir. Thank you, Sam."

"Admiral," she continued a few minutes later in private with her superior, her voice low, "the phone call of two days ago from Virginia about the missing weapons? Do you suppose she was just fishing?"

"Yes, I think so. There are only four people who know of these findings, including Captain Boone on the Reagan."

She brightened, happy to know her boss had confidence in her, but not sure why. Admiral Sarodsy spoke, his voice a notch lower, but clearly commanding: "Now let me drop the other shoe. You need the whole enchilada. That base in northern Iran you uncovered — the Red Ripper jets from the Reagan which

186

flew the mission were equipped with special sensors that were simply extensions of the device that Captain Banaro described. It was only a hunch, but the hunch proved fruitful. The reading on the device indicated that, indeed, there were most likely nuclear weapons on board that base."

"My God — from the Reagan!" It was a statement of fact, no doubt. "But how did they get there? Who authorized the transfer?"

"Nancy, they were not transferred. They were stolen and, more than likely, sold to the highest bidder. In this case, China."

Chandler blanched and slowly pronounced, "Where did the money go? To whom? How much?" Each question was articulated more slowly than the previous, the dawn of realization seeking comfort in the obvious. "Oh, NO!"

"Nancy," he said deliberately, "you are being read into what looks to be the most blatantly, felonious conspiracy to subvert the Constitution of the United States in the history of our country. There are forces that appear to be bent on destroying our nation in exchange for the almighty dollar and quest for eternal power. It's orders of magnitude more egregious and damaging than the Los Alamos losses of nuclear secrets ten years ago."

The heart of the youngest flag officer in the U.S. Navy beat wildly, her eyes locked onto Sarodsy's. "My God, it's all coming together." Quickly she hit the high points of her innermost thoughts about her years in the White House.

She continued out loud. "Clearly, there were big bucks from sources unknown flowing into and out of the political coffers. Never could figure it out. One aspect, though, seems clear. Richard Redman was the linchpin and the facilitator. The high command loved him."

There it is, thought Sarodsy. A sideways confirmation of our analysis. That notwithstanding, he had already decided to withhold the "Green Trees" info from Chandler, at least for the present.

They were intercepted by an aide. "Admiral, it's Admiral Demming — says he does not have much time."

"Roger that. Tell him I'll be right there." He got Nancy aside. "I want you to listen to this conversation. There's a lot happening you need to know about. This involves much more than your job as the Indian Ocean battle force commander. Having said that, however, I need your assurance that all of this goes no further than you and me. No aides, no notes and no Madame President. Do I make myself absolutely clear, Admiral?"

"No question, sir." And, with great conviction, her eyes locked with his, "I'm with you 100%."

"That's what I thought and why you are now in this up to your eyebrows," he articulated with a smile and a firm pat on her back.

"Bruce, good to hear from you. Where are you?" The retired naval officer, so recently jerked from his well-creased leather chair back in Virginia Beach and his chief avocation as the leading offerer of gratuitous advice to anyone who cared to listen, spoke into the secure phone.

"I'm at a Chinese base somewhere in Iran. Was supposed to fly back to Chunking a several hours ago with Major Tsunami, but the flyover at first light this morning has the place in an uproar. They've gone to general quarters. The skipper is airborne now with four jets circling the crash scene about 350 miles south of here. I know one of the flyover jets has gone down, so I may be stuck here for a while. Any instructions? Whose aircraft did the overflight?"

Sarodsy responded, happy the old warrior and friend was OK. "It was one of ours. A Red Ripper jet from the Reagan."

"That's what I was afraid of. You know my number-two daughter is a pilot with that squadron. Please let me know if she is OK. And, Stan, I see two of the Chinese's modified helos coming in. They're obviously getting ready for the search and rescue from here."

Sarodsy was thinking quickly. "Bruce, those jets had special sensors on them, a device the size of a cigarette pack in the starboard wing tip. Very highly classified. I need to ask you a big one." Without waiting for an answer, he commanded: "Big deal your way onto that helo, and find out what's going on. It looks as if our SAR effort won't materialize for a few hours — after dark at the earliest. Can you do it?"

"I'll do my best, boss. Got to run." Demming noted the four Dynasty F-48s returning to base, the sun already climbing in the early morning sky. Within four minutes of landing, the cavernous hangar doors had opened, swallowed the jets, and the airfield once again became nothing more than an innocuous desert scene. The vintage admiral tucked his tiny satellite cell phone into its protective cover and followed the last jet inside.

Before Tsunami could unstrap, an aide said urgently, "Major, General Wong wants you on the phone, NOW!"

Ying Tsunami strode to a nearby office and, for several minutes, simply nodded his head, nary a word said on his part. Spying his mentor, Ying walked over to Demming. "Sorry Admiral, I guess we'll be delayed until further notice. The flyover was clearly unsettling to General Wong. He's dispatched me to the scene of the crash to take personal charge."

"How about survivors, Ying?"

"Maybe one, although the beeper stopped about two hours ago. It's very rugged terrain, you know — about 3,100 meters elevation with high winds and snow. The Americans are orbiting overhead trying to establish contact with the pilot. She was talking for a while, then stopped suddenly."

Tsunami continued. "As soon as the helos are ready for flight, I'm going to lead the rescue attempt. Not sure what the Americans are doing or even if they have the capability to effect a rescue at that high an altitude. General Wong sends his best to you, apologizes for the change in plans and is, at this moment, talking with Vice Admiral Sarodsy in your Pentagon about how to coordinate the rescue attempts. He will also, I'm sure, query him about the reason for the overflight of our base."

Demming, usually cool and level-headed, was in a state of agitated turmoil, the persistent thought of his Susan foremost in his brain. Without preamble or fanfare, the seasoned admiral said to Tsunami in a commanding voice, "Ying, I'll go with you."

The young major, doing some fast thinking of his own and

recalling the words of his commanding general to open all doors to Demming, had no option. "OK with me sir, though, you know it may be very rough going."

General Wong knew Vice Admiral Stan Sarodsy by his combat-oriented reputation, his toughness under stress, as Bruce Demming's replacement in the Pentagon and as a possible source for future technology, the latter, an arena in which the Chinese had become exceptionally skillful. Recruiting recently-retired senior flag and general officers of the U.S. military with lucrative consulting contracts, all legal and above board, was one of Wong's strong points.

After exchanging pleasantries, Wong assured his fellow warrior that Demming was enjoying a productive visit. Sarodsy then put Nancy Chandler on the line and the threesome worked out the details of the search-and-rescue coordination. All agreed that the objective was to protect the stealth fighter from prying eyes and to safely rescue any survivors. Discussion as to why the fighters had overflown the super-secret base was discretely tabled for future dialogue.

Nancy explained to the general that the U.S. carriers would move closer to the mainland in order to launch two special-mission V-22 Osprey super-helos, but that it would be well after nightfall before the exotic machines could arrive overhead. Wong, in turn, explained the severe limitations of his rescue craft, particularly at night. That said, however, all agreed that the dual-rescue approach would offer the best probability of success.

Tsunami was uncomfortable in the helo, the clouds darkening, the turbulence confirming his long-held distrust of any flying machine he did not personally pilot, and of helicopters in general. A quick call from General Wong's office confirmed the plan of attack and that the first elements on scene would take charge of the operation. Tsunami was pleased by the notion that the two military leaders had seen fit to converse, the sensitivities notwithstanding.

Back within her command center, Chandler watched the

190

progress of the Chinese helos laboriously tracking to the crash site, a sidebar of the display citing the weather as lousy, even for that part of the world. She had talked with Captain Boone on the Reagan about the rotten weather and possible delays, but was assured by the special forces team that the mission was a go.

The two Chinese helos had separated for safety in the thick weather, both tracking to the precise three-dimensional GPS site in the mountains at 9,760 feet above mean sea level. In the back of the heavily-laden lead machine, Demming and Tsunami were silent, stoically enduring the unknowns. The young pilot in the right front seat called on the intercom to the major. "No telling what the weather is, sir. My guess is we'll be totally on instruments all the way to touchdown. Visibility is probably less than a couple hundred meters. My intention is to press on, sir."

Bruce Demming, listening in on the intercom, muttered to Tsunami over the din, "He's not asking permission or guidance. Just doing it. Impressive."

"About a mile out, Major. We'll execute the zero-visibility option off the GPS position which is basically a zero-airspeed, vertical descent for 500 meters above the highest surrounding elevation," said the energized helo commander.

As the lumbering helo descended, Tsunami was clearly stressed, the source of his churning guts a universal one of aviators turned into lead-weight passengers, no longer in control and trusting their lives to the anonymous stranger up front.

"Fifty meters to go, sir. Visibility zero," said the co-pilot in the left seat.

Suddenly, the big machine lurched violently to the left, the crack of rotor blades impacting an unyielding substance. The pilot screamed a common expletive known to pilots who were about to become helpless in the face of overpowering forces. For a moment, it appeared to continue in controlled flight, but then rolled dreadfully and viciously to the left. Silence. Blackness. Nothing.

Tsunami was the first to awaken, cold and afraid. Wreckage was everywhere. Hanging in his straps, he gingerly felt himself. Seemed OK. Crawling to the cockpit of the smashed helo, he saw the crushed and lifeless bodies of the two pilots hanging inverted, arms dangling, still securely strapped to their seats, blood dripping from one gloved hand. Hearing the hum of an electric motor, he spotted an unfamiliar, large red switch, and turned it off, hoping it was indeed the craft's master electrical switch. The unmistakable odor of fuel was everywhere, particularly the large bladder fuel cell strapped to the former floorboards.

"Admiral, are you all right, sir?"

The naval officer groggily responded, "I think so. Can you unstrap me, please, Ying?"

The two appeared to be the sole survivors, bruises and sore limbs the only manifestation of the fatal crash. Outside the weather was dismal — blowing snow and high winds with a visibility measured in yards. Breaking out his emergency hand-held radio, Tsunami contacted the second helo, now well into its vertical approach, and ordered it to return to base pending improved weather conditions.

The two busily set out to construct a temporary shelter from the biting cold and penetrating wind, salvaging what they could from the fuel-soddened wreckage. Once protected from the elements, Demming pulled out his cell phone. It was still operational.

Sarodsy and Chandler had watched the icon for the Chinese helo on a large-scale electronic screen, the horizontal speed vector working its way to zero. "Looks like a vertical-GPS approach," muttered Sarodsy. "Tough." Then the blip unexpectedly disappeared.

"Nancy, it looks as if they may be in big trouble. I'm going to bird-dog this if you don't mind. We may have a double rescue on our hands. I want you to huddle with Senator Montgomery and Ernie Maltman and figure out where we go from here. In the interim, I'll call General Wong."

"Roger that, sir," said the tireless flag officer, happy to be free of the operations for which she had little background or training.

At this precise moment, the two grounded warriors, high in the mountains of eastern Iran, heard over the howling wind what seemed like a whimper, a muffled cry for help, a woman's strained and muted voice. Marking the exact coordinates of their shelter, Tsunami entered the position of the downed aviator and slowly, cautiously edged his way down the mountain, Demming close behind. The barely audible voice, though only yards away, sounded faint.

With heart in mouth and adrenalin flowing, the old admiral and the young Chinese fighter pilot moved closer to the source of the voice. There, huddled forlornly in the folds of a parachute, was the crumpled form of the young American aviator, her helmet still in place, the oxygen mask hanging loosely to one side.

It was not Susan. "Thank God," said a relieved father.

Gingerly removing the mask from the moaning woman, Tsunami looked full into the bloodstained, ashen face of the U.S. Navy back-seater who had so seductively smiled at him thirty-six hours before. He held her softly. Tears formed in the eyes of the hardened Chinese warrior.

CHAPTER 16

The Rescue

At 1600 in the afternoon, Master Chief Mitsi Moore, the top enlisted person on the USS *Ronald Reagan*, was halfway through a typically busy day aboard the giant warship, her diminutive frame still riding tall in the saddle. The news of the doomed Red Ripper jet had swept like a wind-driven fire in a tinder-dry forest throughout the ship, excited scuttlebutt adding grist to the danger facing the temporary home to the 5,000 young men and women of the crew. Rumor had it that one of the aviators may have survived the crash. Within an hour, most of the crew knew that the hapless flyers were Bikini and Studs — not Lieutenants Swagger and Newman — just Bikini and Studs.

In the comfort and privacy of her tiny office, the squared-away master chief for the complicated aircraft carrier was troubled. Evelyn Swagger was known throughout the male half of the crew as a real beauty, the moniker "Bikini" having taken root in a traditional Navy smoker some seven months prior. Smokers, routine events on U.S. Navy ships since the days of sail, consisted of boxing matches, talent contests, competing divisional bands and, in more enlightened years, quasi-body contests replete with high heels and skimpy attire for the females and just plain skimpy for their male counterparts.

In a rare stand-down two months into what was planned to be a six-month, Norfolk-to-Norfolk deployment, the Reagan's captain had acquiesced to the smoker on a non-flying Sunday far out on a lonely sea. Mitsi recalled the obvious adoration of a screaming crew as the contestants sang, gyrated and performed musically, the body contest the icing on the cake. Both Sam Newman and Evelyn Swagger had won handily to the swooning approval of an aroused crew, "Studs" and "Bikini" becoming instant call-signs within the Red Ripper ready room and about the ship. Evelyn was indeed strikingly beautiful, her generous smile penetrating the facade of even the most hardened, macho male, her pilot reciprocating for the 2,398 women swaying to the disco tunes reverberating among the stealth fighters on the warship's cavernous hangar deck.

Mitsi's visit that afternoon to the ship's style salon had been another eye opener, the young off-duty men and women in cut-off jeans and various casual attire, in a state of animated chatter, the impressionable males clinging to their chosen shipmates, literally as well as figuratively.

A knock on her door. "Got a few minutes, Mitsi?" It was Master Chief Randy McCormick, her friend, and, increasingly, her confidant on a vessel that seemed, at times, like a brakeless train hurtling down the mountain, its occupants oblivious to an uncertain fate.

"Hi, Randy. Please, come in. What's the word?"

"Looks like one of the crew is alive, at least as of an hour ago. The SAR mission will launch in about two hours using the special operations V-22 Osprey. We still have two jets overhead." Rubbing his neck, he paused, "I need to take a break."

Increasingly the two had confided in one another — the tall, veteran McCormick and the winsome, straight-shooting Mitsi Moore. Both had become close friends in a venue that demanded the nicest sense of leadership and propriety in a sea of vastly competing human emotions.

"You know, Randy, that Studs and Bikini were symbolic of a higher order to our crew than even the Captain or you and me. Not only that, but their recognition-factor was sky high. The fact that they flew together in the nation's top combat fighter was not nearly as important to our brethren as the well-accepted rumor that they lived in the same stateroom. That they were obviously in love and inseparable was a given. To most of our youngsters, they represented what life was all about." Randy nodded his head in agreement, his brow furrowed.

"Hey, Mitsi, face it," his deep voice articulating what was, to him, the obvious, "every guy on this ship empathizes with Studs and every female with Bikini. Get real, my friend. We've had this dialogue a few times before. Those two aviators were not only symbolic, they were heroes. They walk about, hand-in-hand, the loving all-American-couple-to-be, flinging themselves fearlessly at a foul enemy, danger only a heartbeat or two away. Maybe this crash will sober up a few of our amorous brethren?" The Red Ripper master chief knew he had overstepped the bounds with his friend, knowing full well that the kinder, gentler Navy of the year 2010 would not approve of his callousness.

The ship's master chief seemed tired, her normally effusive persona muted. Randy wondered what he could do to lift her spirits. It did no good to the stressed-out crew to see their leaders down in the mouth, myself included, he thought.

"Tell you what, Mitsi. How about we get together here about 2300 tonight for a meritorious movie. I've got a good oldie that my skipper loaned me."

"OK, Randy. Maybe it'll give me something to look forward to."

At the same moment, while the formidable warship smoothly motivated to the northwest at over a mile every two minutes, the strike-planning cadre in the ship's intelligence spaces were organizing the rescue mission. Huddled close were the combined brains of the V-22 Osprey detachment headed by Lieutenant Commander Michelle Hopper, Ensign Patty Butts, Lieutenant Becky Turner, representing the covering fighters from the Red Rippers and Dr. Rose Johnson, attending physician. Time was critical, particularly so in view of the presumed crash of the Chinese rescue helicopter high in the rugged mountains. Of real concern to the planners was the range. At the planned launch time of 1940, the distance was 570 miles. With refueling en route and on return, the mission was a go. Without either, it was get-wet time in a wind-driven, stormy sea.

The V-22 pilot and combat SAR detachment commander, Michelle Hopper, was a pro, having been weaned in the tough discipline of special operations. Capable of flying anywhere in the world, the high-tech machines and razor-sharp crews could accomplish a multitude of missions, from routine rescue and search, to SEAL extraction, to covert operations. Hopper, though somewhat under the weather, laid out the mission parameters, Dr. Johnson paying close heed to her pilot-to-be.

The Osprey was a remarkable machine, capable of hovering motionless with its big twin rotors like a conventional helo, or cruising at the speeds of a fast prop jet. Long in development, it had become the mainstay of conventional troop warfare, as well as its uniquely suited covey of spook missions.

"Attention on deck," hollered an intelligence specialist. It was the Reagan's commanding officer, Captain Tommy Boone, in a rare foray off his perch eleven stories above them. Since the ship's operational tempo had accelerated, Boone had forsaken his usual self-discipline of at least two hours in every twenty-four, off-the-bridge-and-about-the-ship style of leadership by wandering about. He huddled with the air wing commander while the brief continued, the eyes of Rose Johnson framing her captain as a playful cat stalking its trustful buddy.

Conspicuous by his absence was the Red Ripper high-cover flight lead who was, at the moment, standing at parade rest in front of his thoroughly pissed-off skipper. Iron Lady, hands on hips, was in full bloom, a living testament to her call sign. "NO, Commander Anderson, you WILL fly with Lori Miller. You and that young back-seater of yours have been getting too friendly of late. Lori will be good for you. And, I need not add, she needs some discipline as well. Understood?"

"But Skipper," the acting executive officer exclaimed, "she's not worth the powder to blow her to hell in the back seat or anywhere else and you know it. Cut me some slack, please," the latter somewhat plaintively.

"NO WAY! I've already told Miller. She needs a strong pilot like you. Make it happen!" her eyes penetrating deeply into the uncomplicated persona of the former Blue Angel pilot. "You need to be at the SAR brief. You're late now."

With a dejected, but respectful, "Yes, ma'am," Anderson left his skipper's stateroom for the combat briefing, his gait a bit more stiff-legged than when his one-way meeting with the Red Ripper commanding officer had begun.

Below the hangar deck, dead in the center of the carrier, the Reagan's executive officer, Commander Angela Batori, was head-to-head with the ship's master chief and the weapons officer, Lieutenant Commander Stan Miller, hashing out the conflicts of feeding the crew and assembling weapons, both of which took place in the main mess areas of the ship. Batori, increasingly convinced that active combat was in the near future, was in a high state of paranoia, worrying about the psychological ability of her crew to handle the stress, fatigue and discipline of being taken under attack by an unforgiving enemy.

"You know, Stan," offered the ship's executive officer, "the cutoff of e-mail two days ago has markedly raised the tensions. I can feel it in the crew. And, Master Chief, I had no idea of the symbolism of Lieutenants Newman and Swagger. That's an astounding observation," said the XO with a quick sideways glance at the stoic ship's weapons officer.

Mitsi Moore, who spent more time with the XO than anyone, could not help but notice the subtle chemistry between Miller and Batori. The latter's husband, Commander Rock Batori, the skipper of the Red Rippers' sister stealth squadron, the Barking Dogs, seldom slept in the same bed with his busy wife, preferring a solitary stateroom up forward near his ready room. Though clearly not her business, Mitsi recalled two private observations concerning the two over the past few months. One, she had never seen Batori or her husband together; and, second, and more troublesome, was her notion that the executive officer had been spending disproportionate attention on the affairs of the weapons department. Though both could be easily rationalized in the press of doing their respective jobs, to Mitsi, the interactions of the two seemed totally in concert with the behavior of the rest of the ship's impressionable crew.

The knock on the door was authoritative, demanding. Her Marine orderly announced crisply, "The Captain, ma'am."

"Captain, please come in. We were just working out the weapons generation plan. Coffee, sir?"

In the early evening quiet, it seemed anomalous that the warship was steaming to a launch point just ninety-six minutes away at 36 knots, the smooth nuclear-powered machinery below them cranking the four giant screws at 241 RPMs. "Angela, Master Chief, I need to chat a bit — with both of you," nodding to the weapons officer. "Stan, if you don't mind."

"Not at all, Captain. XO, I'll brief you later on the details. About 2300?"

"Sounds good, Stan. Thank you."

The Reagan's captain looked weary, the small, functional office reflecting the mood. "The issue on the table is combat. As we speak, we could be the target of a Super Pelican or AS-17C Greta anti-ship missile. My hunch is that within forty-eight hours, the Reagan will join our other carriers and strike assets in a preemptive conventional strike against the ISIs. Not to act, and to do so decisively, would be a tragic error on the part of the national command authority in Washington. The blatant ISI aggression must be countered."

He paused, collecting his thoughts, knowing that what he had to say would smack of outright heresy in the hallowed halls of a gender-driven Pentagon, his career in the balance. The words of his father long ago, himself a flag officer, fighter pilot and carrier captain, had etched in his brain each time the going got tough: "When your back is to the wall, do what you think is right and not what some shore-based expert might think is right."

"As soon as the rescue Ospreys and supporting cover launch, I'm going to get on the ship's TV and announce the following without fanfare or extraneous rhetoric. First, e-mail will remain shut down. Second, the style salon will be closed until further notice, the two dozen stylists distributed to the damage control teams. Third, no incoming satellite HDTV. I want all hands on the job 100% of the time. Fourth, no manifestations of endearment amongst males and females. That means exactly what it says, even to the extent of hand-holding. Fifth, no communal facilities. XO, assign shower times for women and men or however you want to handle it. Understood so far?" He paced the sparse office, the executive officer and master chief busy scribbling notes.

"Yes, sir," they responded in unison.

"Sixth, I want all stress cases in Stress City out of there within two hours, excepting advanced pregnancies or severe medical cases. Assign them back to their respective divisions and squadrons. And, no more stress chits," hitting on his number-one pet peeve of a war-fighting Navy sometimes committed to competing social priorities. Both Mitsi and Angela blanched, the writing on hold until a commanding, "DO IT!"

"Seventh, close the ship's store until further notice. Eighth, effective immediately, all announcements, prayers or other housekeeping on the ship's 1MC public address system will cease. It will be used for emergency uses only. I want all hands not actually on watch to get the maximum amount of sleep and rest possible. Ninth," he paused, on a road to professional oblivion, he knew, but it felt good, "no more civilian clothes, sandals or long fingernails. This is a fighting ship. Combat readiness and short shorts are mutually exclusive. And last," he was interrupted by the orderly announcing an obviously annoyed young sailor who wanted to report to the XO. ". . . an outrageous act of blatant sexual harassment in the berthing compartment housing the ship's third division personnel, and could I see the XO?"

"Not now," stridently ordered Commander Batori.

"But, ma'am . . ."

"NOT NOW! CLOSE THE DOOR, MARINE!"

"Aye, aye, ma'am," said the burly orderly, still in his teens, gently but firmly grabbing the arm of the distraught sailor.

Threateningly, she glared at the command master chief on the way out the door, " I'm going to report this to the diversity control officer — fast."

The captain continued, oblivious to the distraction, his mind clearly on fighting his ship. "Last, and most importantly, I want all khaki leadership on this ship to set the proper professional example. From now on there is only one mandate on this warship — we will not fight the way we have trained. We will fight the way we must in order to win."

Knowing he was on a roll to the south forty, but feeling better than he had in years, the warrior captain added, "As forthrightly as you can, tell the diversity control folks that these calls are mine and mine alone and that I am fully aware of what I have done. Shortly, I intend to let my boss, Rear Admiral Nancy Chandler, know what I have mandated. Any questions?"

On the secure satellite to his boss, Boone explained to Chandler the actions he had taken and for her to please inform her boss, Vice Admiral Stan Sarodsy. Nancy Chandler was no neophyte and was conversant with the enormous prerogatives extant in the authority of a ship's commanding officer. For over two hundred years, Navy regulations made it crystal clear that the captain was totally responsible for the combat readiness of his vessel:

> "THE COMMANDING OFFICER OF A U.S. NAVAL WARSHIP SHALL, WHILE BALANCING THE MYRIAD OF PRIORITIES AND POLICIES OF THE DEPARTMENT OF THE NAVY, ABOVE ALL ELSE, ATTEND TO THE TOTAL WAR-FIGHTING READINESS OF HIS COMMAND TO PREVAIL IN ARMED CONFLICT AND TAKE SUCH ACTIONS AS ARE NECESSARY IN HIS OR HER JUDGMENT TO ASSURE THE OVERWHELMING DESTRUCTION OF AN ENEMY FORCE — WITHOUT WAITING FOR EXTERNAL GUIDANCE."

"Tommy, I understand and support you without reservation. I will relay the gist to the boss. And, Tommy," she paused, thinking fast, "the Admiral wanted me to pass along to you that Senator Montgomery's military aide, a former F-14 Tomcat squadron commander, Ernie Maltman, is en route to you. Should arrive in a few hours. He is cleared for all intelligence compartments. I'll explain later."

Boone knew Maltman. They had been compatriots. Had Maltman stayed in the Navy, he could well have been a carrier skipper himself. Tommy Boone looked forward to seeing him.

A soft knock on the door. "Captain, do you have a minute?" said Dr. Rose Johnson.

"Sure, Doc. Come in." Increasingly, Boone had looked forward to the daily visits of the ship's flight surgeon, Dr. Rose Johnson. Her invitation for a complete physical, he knew, was prudent, but not now. Perhaps later. He knew that, just as with his daily dialogues with the ship's master chief, air wing commander and executive officer, Rose brought a valuable human dimension to his perspective.

"Captain," Rose said as she settled onto the bed-made-into-a-seat couch in his tiny sea cabin abaft the bridge, "I've only got a few minutes before the search and rescue launch — I need to cut you in on something you'll find out anyway."

"Shoot," said a captain who wanted the straight word the first time.

When she had finished the somber tale, the bushed captain asked warily, "How far along was she?"

Rose paused. "I hate to say it, sir. Close to five months. I confirmed it three days ago. My fault. I should have been more aware. The warning signs were there. She had all the manifestations of being pregnant. She wanted me to hold off for a week or so due to the probability of combat. Mistake number two — I agreed."

Boone thought to himself. Of all the convoluted gender controversies of the past fifteen years, none was more sensitive than those associated with pregnancy. Reality was, though, that all the mandatory and preventative super pills and medications did little to curb the appetite of the young men and women forced into such prolonged and stressful close quarters. He knew the Navy's CEO, Admiral Sweeney would be stiff-legged when she heard of it. "That's about strike ten in the past few days," he smiled to himself.

"Thanks for the heads up, Rose. You've got to person-up shortly. It'll be a tough flight, you know?"

"Yes, sir," she looked deep into his eyes and, in a clear and convincing voice, said brightly, with just the hint of a smile, "Perhaps we can do that physical when things cool down a bit?"

Captain Boone's machismo mellowed for a moment, the will to protect the younger women almost irresistible, her pending flight fraught with the specter of real danger. "You take care, Rose," he said softly.

"You too, sir. Got to go."

Rose clambered into the V-22 poised on the bow of the speeding ship. The wind, a combination of 34 knots of ship's speed plus a gusty north wind of 24 knots, added up to almost hurricane force on the darkening flight deck. Inside were the two pilots, a crew chief and five highly-trained special forces troops capable of parachuting, rappelling 300 feet or taking on a hostile force, multiple weapons strapped to the side bulkheads of the unconventional machine.

"Welcome aboard, Doc. Ready for some action?" cried the smiling mission commander and pilot, Lieutenant Commander Michelle Hopper. Above the howling wind, Rose responded with a partially enthusiastic thumbs-up and totally fake smile, careful not to step on the bloated fuel bladder strapped to the craft's floorboards.

The rescue plan dictated that the two V-22s launch at 1940 with a time-on-target of 2152. The two cover fighters from the Red Rippers would catapult at 2014, given the slower ground speed of the Ospreys. Total electronic silence was the order of the night, excepting very low-powered transmissions between the mission aircraft and short, burst-voice satellite with the ship. En route altitude would be 300 feet until over the Iranian coast, then a terrain-following profile to about 11,000 feet mean sea level over the target coordinates.

At precisely 1940, the ship's air boss boomed over the flight deck bullhorns, "Launch the Ospreys." Hopper gave the signal for the removal of all chains, added power to the two big rotors and eased into a hover in the turbulent air near the bow. Co-pilot — "Looks good to go, Commander." Within moments the big machine was swallowed by the low-scudding clouds and settled into a fast cruise of 340 knots just above the hostile sea, the second flying machine in one-mile trail.

Rose Johnson was reflective. Just after her short, but troubling, disclosure to the captain, the former wizo for the acting executive officer of the Red Rippers, Dave Anderson, had asked to meet with her off the record. Tearfully, Lieutenant (junior grade) Nancy Flanagan, U.S. Naval Reserve, wanted to know why she had been removed as Anderson's back-seater and replaced by ". . . that worthless Lori Miller?" Rose, of course, had no idea of the reason for the change. As the squadron flight surgeon, though, she was well aware of the infatuation of the young naval flight officer with Anderson. Both roomed together in paradise and it was no secret that the younger officer had the blatant hots for the svelte former Blue Angel pilot. Interestingly, Rose was aware of the origin of her call sign, "Shorts," a manifestation of Nancy's proclivity to prance about the ship in her off-hours in tightly-revealing attire. Serves her right, thought the Doc. Let her stew for a while.

About the time the Ospreys were approaching feet-dry over the coast, Dave Anderson and his new back-seater, Lori Miller, had launched into the sullen clag along with his wing person, Becky Turner, and her wizo, Scott Jacobs. The two leveled off at an uncomfortable 300 feet and 540 knots, swallowed by an uncaring cloud, Becky in a close starboard-wing position. Dave took his eyes off his instruments for a moment to check his wing-person, Becky's eyes locked onto the inanimates of his F-27C stealth Phantom III, her jet a smooth mirror of her leader. Back on his instruments, the pilot, who had chosen Big Sister for this mission, thought to himself, she was a good stick, with an attitude and brain to match — a winner.

Lieutenant Commander Lori Miller had been like a clam since her skipper had abruptly ordered the shift in crew duties. Fact was, she was livid. She felt, perhaps rightfully, that there was more to it than the transparent attentions of Anderson and the young Flanagan. All were, of course, housed in paradise, within which there were few real secrets, the clear-cut sexual preferences of Miller included. That Iron Lady was not enamored of her acting exec or her maintenance officer, though not general knowledge, was clear to the two lieutenant commanders and squadron department heads. The two were clearly at opposite ends of the naval aviator spectrum in terms of capability, motivation and the will to win.

Dave Anderson was the quintessential professional naval aviator. He knew his stuff and, when airborne, was all business. That said, however, the Ripper fighter was designed, and had to be flown, as a two-person weapons system. The coordination and trust so necessary between pilot and wizo to become a truly effective fighter platform, took many flights to perfect. Deep inside, Anderson felt his skipper had put spite ahead of common sense in this case, to the potential detriment of the mission at hand.

"Come on Lori, you've got to get with it. Swallow your pride and get that satellite," referring to one of the myriad of steps needed from the back seat to make the weapon's system a go.

"Screw you, you macho piece of crap. Iron Lady put us together — that's her problem. Well, let her stew in her own juices." Dave was silent, the battle lines drawn. He busily went to a front seat back-up mode for the complex system, noting out of his peripheral vision, Big Sister close aboard.

Some forty-three miles ahead, he acquired the two rescue craft climbing to the target way-point 290 miles inland. "Lori, you keep up this bullshit and your worthless ass is history. This is a tough mission."

"Get screwed again," her matter-of-fact response.

In a flash, Anderson knew what he had to do. Looking at his wingperson, he tersely pointed to his head and then to hers. Without hesitation, Becky Turner pointed to herself, took her eyes off Anderson's jet and became the flight lead, the simple exercise grounded in eight decades of naval aviation tactical discipline, words superfluous.

"Looks like we've got the lead, Twidget. You got the friendlies up ahead?"

"Sure do, Big Sister, piece of cake. Wonder what the problem with lead was?" noting Miller slouching in the back seat of the former lead fighter, her oxygen mask off and giving a silent finger to her pilot in his rear view mirror. "Uh, oh," he said, " looks like trouble in Dodge City," while concentrating on the satellite intelligence link and the horizontal-situation display in a 490-mile area for airborne activity.

Back in the Pentagon, Nancy Chandler watched the progress of the rescue mission, knowing that the best the U.S. Navy could put forward was at the tip of the spear. It had only been a few minutes since she had briefed Vice Admiral Sarodsy, revealing the contents of her talk with the Reagan's skipper, the old warrior's response a barely concealed smile. What followed though, was a blockbuster.

With Ernie Maltman already airborne headed for a rendezvous with the USS *Ronald Reagan*, Sarodsy had simply stated to Chandler: "I want you to go to Chunking and find out what we can do to get the Chinese energized over the Caspian dilemma." It was not a "What do you think?" or "How about it?" It was an outright edict.

"But Admiral, what about the State Department? How about Virginia?"

"Nancy, I've discussed the ramifications of this with Senator Montgomery. We have reason to distrust anyone associated with some of our nation's leading politicians. The Senator is organizing a cadre of folks he can totally trust on the political front. Our mandate is to get the Chinese focused. As you well know, they have the most to lose. Montgomery is convinced there has been in motion, for many months now, a pattern of appeasement on the part of the Stallingsworth administration toward the ISIs, a policy to allow them what they want in order to obviate armed conflict on our part. I'm afraid our CEO, Admiral Sweeney, feels the same. She does not want our forces engaged in combat, no matter the circumstances or provocation, and has so stated to the service chiefs and the President." He studied the large electronic display covering one wall of his command center, then continued.

"You know more about the region than all of the simulated intellectuals in this town. Your point of contact will be General Wong in Chunking, the head of the Imperial Chinese Air Force, titular leader of the country's military and, not incidentally, a close confidant with the aging President Jiang. Your mission is to engage the Chinese in concert with the U.S. to convince the ISIs to cease and desist in their military encroachment into the Caspian Sea. You may inform him, that, in my judgment, the use of unconstrained U.S. military force is a strong probability."

"When do I leave, sir?"

"As soon as you can, get a bag packed and board a special mission Grumman Gulfstream G-VII which is awaiting your arrival at Andrews. Have a good trip and don't forget the secure cell phone," handing her the tiny, red personal-communications device.

Over the rescue site 8,000 miles away, Hopper transitioned her craft into a motionless hover 11,400 feet above mean sea level, some 600 feet above the highest mountain peak within three miles. To her crew, she announced crisply, "The plan is to descend in a vertical hover to 270 feet above the target area and rappel the remaining distance. Doc, you stay aboard. Team leader, once on deck, give me the weather conditions. If OK, we'll continue to a landing. If not, Doc you go via the rope, we'll go feet-wet and refuel and return ASAP. Understood?" All this while the V-22 descended at a steady seventeen feet per second into the turbulent night clouds.

On the ground at the crash site, Demming and Tsunami had managed to carry the inert aviator about seventy five yards to the improvised shelter. Tsunami had not let go, holding her limp body close to his, her breathing barely audible, her color waning.

Demming watched the chemical reaction between the two young warriors, Tsunami's description of their chance meeting in the air almost unbelievable to the old sailor. It was clear to him that the Chinese fighter squadron commander had been deeply affected by the discovery of the near-lifeless body. For five hours, he had not moved, his lithe body willing life into the stricken Lieutenant Evelyn Swagger.

Suddenly, the wind-driven snow was pierced by an exotic sounding "whop, whop, whop." "Someone's on the way, Ying." The noise increased, then stabilized. For a minute, nothing happened. Then, out of the dark gloom, one figure emerged, then another, until finally, all five SEALs were on deck, having been deposited twenty-yards away in the blowing sleet and biting cold.

The camouflaged leader scurried over to the threesome and, without preamble, pulled out his hand-held transceiver and barked to his unseen mission leader whopping overhead, "Straight down, Commander. Keep it slow. I'll direct you to a small clearing suitable for landing. Recommend you send the second machine back to the initial point."

"Roger that, team leader. Coming down slowly."

"Crew chief, let me know when you see the LZ," Hopper quietly spoke into the intercom, hoping the landing zone to be free of boulders.

"Roger that, ma'am. I think I see it. Looking good. Keep it coming."

"OK, I've got it," said the pilot as she settled the unconventional machine smoothly onto the tiny landing zone.

"Crew chief, get 'em aboard fast. Not much gas."

As the Osprey lifted back into the sodden cloud mass in a vertical ascent, Rose Johnson was attending to Swagger, prying her away from the protective arms of Major Ying Tsunami. Her breathing was shallow, pulse weak and blue-eyes dilated. "Shock." She broke out her IV, elevated the legs of the young woman, then noticed the extensive bleeding in the folds of the parachute.

"Spontaneous abort," Rose muttered to herself while busily tending to the task at hand.

Within twenty-three minutes, Swagger pierced the veil of consciousness, her parched lips only inches from a fearful Major

Ying Tsunami.

Over the intercom, the Doc reported to Hopper, "She'll be OK, I think. Needs more blood badly. Need to get back to the carrier as fast as possible." As an afterthought, she added, "Lost the baby, though."

"The baby?"

"Yeah, I'm afraid she was pretty far along."

"Doc, how's Studs?" weakly mouthed Swagger, still in a state of confused animation.

"I'm afraid we don't know, as of now," responded the doctor. "Do you know if he ejected?"

"No, it's all a big blur." Then to the bedraggled Chinese pilot, she said, "Who are you?" and noticing Demming, "and you? What's going on?" The weakened back-seater started an uncontrollable shake.

Rose took a syringe from her pack, grabbed the arm of her patient and jabbed the needle home. The sedative took effect within seconds.

Forty-seven minutes later, Michelle Hopper quietly said into the intercom, "Hey folks, looks like our ticket home may be in limbo. No tanker. We're going emergency direct home plate."

Captain Boone heard the signal for the critically low-state Ospreys, and ordered his officer of the deck to close the range at flank speed. "Dammed tankers! Those guys can think of fifty reasons why they can't hack the job," referring to the converted, civilian-manned, contract Boeing 888 tanker assigned to rendezvous with the homebound V-22s and fighters. "All four machines would be extremely low state," he mumbled aloud to to his OOD, the ubiquitous Ensign Karen Randolph.

Commander Hopper figured she would have seven minutes of fuel left if the carrier continued to close the range. The tail winds, plus the closure of the ship, added up to a plus and welcome sixty knots.

The big carrier was close to the optimum wind, so all that was needed was to slow the ship for manageable landing winds. Out of the glue, the lead Osprey broke out at 200 feet and one-half mile, gently easing to a landing abeam the island.

The young aviator was placed in a stretcher, her commanding officer at her side, followed closely by Rose Johnson, holding the IV, and a concerned Tsunami who barely flinched when the first low-state Phantom III slammed to the flight deck not seventy-feet away. A tired Bruce Demming was last out of the Osprey, the ship's XO snapping a jaunty salute to the old sailor.

On the bridge several stories above the flight deck, Captain Tommy Boone watched the never-ending panorama of competing human emotions play out. Before calling it a day, he would welcome the unexpected arrival of the retired vice admiral, visit the rescued aviator in sick bay, stop by the XO's office, compliment the Osprey commander in person and meet briefly with the Chinese major. By then, it would be midnight, time for a quick nap before the 0215 rendezvous with the heavily-laden JP9 fuel tanker.

As he left the bridge, he said, with a broad smile and a thumbs-up to his officer of the deck, "Nice job, Karen," and, as an afterthought, "as usual."

CHAPTER 17

Diversity and Reality

News of the Red Ripper crash spread fast through the close-knit Navy community of Virginia Beach, Virginia, the local ABC affiliate squeezing the story for all it was worth. Accidents and death in far-off oceans were never far from the front pages in the Navy town, the loss of an F-27C stealth fighter and its two-person crew from another squadron and carrier in the local news section only three days prior. "Due to operational causes," stated the sterile article.

The curtailment of e-mail from the Reagan only two days before had been a tough hit among the home team. The fragile electronic link had been a thin umbilical to the sprawl of distant emotions and danger. Daily, the news reports iterated stories of dismay, futility and increasing reality of a Middle East region only too used to such rhetoric.

The President had been on national TV only hours before, her well-rehearsed speech an attempt to placate a strident Middle East consortium bent on domination of the strategic Caspian Sea oil reserves. Her message reeked of, ". . . please, let us be reasonable." She knew, and the world knew, of course, that the Chinese had the most to lose, their only alternative to rapproachment, a unilateral rejection of the Clean Air Referendum of 2004 and a reliance on her dirty-burning coal reserves.

Beverly Demming Boone sat with her mother, quietly lamenting the tone of the president's message. To both, it smacked of old-style appeasement. "I wish Bruce were here. He'd be apoplectic," said the obviously annoyed mother, grandmother and long-time wife of retired Vice Admiral Bruce Demming.

She had no way of knowing that, at the moment, her husband of forty-six years was a tired and bruised warrior, having just survived a harrowing crash and daring rescue and was presently a temporary guest in the flag quarters of the USS *Ronald Reagan*.

The raspy ring of the strident phone startled them. "Mrs. Demming, this is Stan Sarodsy in the Pentagon. Is Beverly Boone there by chance?"

With some trepidation formed over many years of tough news, she responded quietly, "She is. Just a moment, please."

"Beverly, I want you to know that we recovered the wizo of the Red Rippers, but not the pilot. The back-seater is Lieutenant Evelyn Swagger. She's OK, but won't fly for a while, I'm afraid. Also, and you won't believe this. As we speak, your dad is onboard the Reagan. I can't provide details other than he is fine. I'll talk to him shortly and tell him I talked with you and Mrs. Demming. By the way, the prognosis for the pilot, Lieutenant Newman, is not good. We think he went in with the plane." He paused, reluctant to continue, the silence penetrating.

"I hear that Dolores Miller visited last night. As you may have guessed by the late-night follow-up visit of the investigators, there is more to her than meets the eye. Please treat her just as you would the spouse of any department head. OK?"

"Sure. Thanks for calling. I'll pass this on to my mother," her voice disciplined with a false bravado.

As Sandy Anderson had her sister's little ones parading about the nearby malls, she decided on some impromptu "girl talk" following Stan Sarodsy's call.

"Mom, I need to talk. You would not believe the vibes bursting out all over our little town."

"Vibes? What kind of vibes, Beverly?"

She went on to explain, in some detail, the confusing feelings triggered by her next-door neighbor, Bill Montrose. Her mother's non-plussed reaction, "I suppose he's just lonely. Wants someone to lean on, I would guess."

"No, Mom, it's more than that. It's me, too." And she went

212

on a roll, telling her of the incorrigible Suzette McCormick and her futile lunch, Sandy Anderson and her two determined suitors and a few other such tales that had yet to reach the light of ordinary day.

Her mom was reflective, introspective, and went into the kitchen to brew a fresh pot of coffee. Cup in hand, time to think, she took a deep breath. "Beverly, in my day it was different. The men went to sea and the women tended the home front. By and large, we took care of one another and the kids. We all stuck together. Lots of mutual support. Hanky-panky was always a temptation, but the mores of the group helped shape a sensible pattern of behavior. Same at sea. There were no distractions. The few women that were around were all on support vessels. Sure, I suppose, there were a few that managed to stray the coop. Happens anywhere."

She took a measured sip, cradled her mug and walked to the window overlooking the stately, well-manicured yard, "I don't want to sound like your father, but I suppose he's been right all along. The genderization seems to have gone overboard. Sea duty is tough enough, but you know, I know, and most every skirt-hiking feminist knows precisely what happens when young men and women are thrust into forced, long-term and pervasive interaction on board ship. Throw in an increased stress level and the chemistry is a given, no matter the high command dictates to the contrary."

Beverly nodded in quiet acquiescence, her usually withdrawn mother's proclamation surprising and insightful.

Her mother continued. "I've watched the socialization on the home front, too. Why, right down the block from us, we have the Michaels. She's at sea on a Navy frigate in the Indian Ocean for months on end, and he's a high-powered salesman for a pharmaceutical company. Two kids with a twenty-two-year-old live-in nanny from England. It's just not right. Not normal. Too much temptation, if you ask me."

"Mom, a good example is my dearest friend, Sandy Anderson. She hears tales of her husband's voyeurisms right in his own stateroom area from an amorous ex-Blue Angel and current airline pilot who calls her incessantly when off duty. Two houses away is the lawyer-husband of a pilot in her husband's squadron who increasingly wants to 'talk.' He's over at her house with his two kids, takes care of her lawn and calls her several times a day. His intentions, from Sandy's perspective, are suspect. She'll handle it OK, I think, but it's hard."

The older woman spoke with the wisdom of years. "Your Dad has struggled with this, as you know, and has stepped onto his soapbox many a time to argue against the Navy's strident socialization agenda. I'm afraid though, that it's too little and too late. He feels that no one really listens anyway — or cares. His bottom-line argument that few, it seems, want to hear, is the adverse impact all this has on the readiness of the combat outfit to fight and win the war at sea."

At this point, the CNN announcer flashed the breaking news of the daring rescue of the Reagan's downed aviator, with the footnote that presumably because of the ejection, the aviator had suffered a miscarriage and had nearly lost her life. Beverly and her mother looked at one another with looks of abject dismay, words unnecessary.

One hundred forty-two miles away in the Pentagon, the door to Vice Admiral Stan Sarodsy's private office slammed open, the unannounced visitor the vice admiral head of the Navy's diversity directorate towering over her seated compatriot and equal on the Navy staff. Sharon McCluskey, impeccable in her sharp, blue service uniform and bunned hairdo, proclaimed in a high-pitched voice resonating with disdain and anger, "What in hell is going on aboard that miserable Reagan?" Without waiting for a reply, Sarodsy settling deeper into his amply-cushioned chair, she went on. "In my entire twenty-one years of service, I have never heard of anything as dumb as flying in a combat aircraft five months pregnant. She should have been in Stress City long ago." Sarodsy opened his mouth to respond, only to be cut off by his distraught contemporary.

She was yelling now. "And, have you heard what's happening aboard that out-of-control aircraft carrier? That dumb-ass

214

Captain has set the top goals of the U.S. Navy back fifteen years. Sweeney," referring to the Navy's CEO, "will go absolutely bonkers. What in hell is all this 'commanding officer prerogative' baloney anyway?"

"Cup of coffee, Admiral?" he finally stood, his ample frame dwarfing the 5-foot-3 inch McCluskey.

"Coffee, my ass, Sarodsy. I want answers."

"Sharon," he said deliberately, his words measured, "I will try to be civil and gentlemanly, but I want you to sit down and take a deep breath. OK?"

He walked to the wall-sized map in his office and placed the laser pointer in an oval 2,000 miles on one axis and 1,000 on the other. "It just so happens that the U.S. Navy is within hours of active combat operations at sea for the first time in twenty years." He let the message sink in. "Do you comprehend what I'm saying or are you so busy listening to all your well-placed diversity folks that you can't see the forest for the trees?"

She stood, moved close, and in a barely-controlled whisper, looked up at the older Sarodsy and proclaimed, "That fact of life does not allow the Reagan's Captain to wipe out fifteen years of diversity efforts based upon some arcane notion of 'commanding officer's prerogative.' "

Sarodsy, in turn, peered down into the creased and angry eyes of the woman and, in a soft and measured voice, exclaimed to McCluskey, "Ill-conceived though they may have been, the top goals of the Navy have indeed been diversity, most of which has been on the gender front. Although no captain in recent history has exercised his or her legal authority to do what he or she thinks prudent and appropriate under the prevailing circumstances, Captain Tommy Boone has done so. Without talking to him, I can assure you flat-out," he paused, his face only fifteen inches from hers, his voice low, eyeballs locked, "that I agree with him and will back him to the hilt. So too, I might add, does his boss, Nancy Chandler."

"Nancy? Don't kid me. The President would have her for lunch and you know it. And, why was an obviously-pregnant woman flying a fighter aircraft on a dangerous mission? How did she get pregnant?" wishing she could withdraw the last question and becoming even more enraged when Sarodsy broke into a broad grin.

"Pregnancy occurs when a willing male places his private parts into the private parts of a compliant female." McCluskey hung her head, speechless. "Chances are, ma'am, her progenitor was not only her pilot, but her roommate as well. What do you expect?"

Sharon, in a barely audible voice, whispered, "What about the super pills?" Sarodsy chose not to respond, the question clearly rhetorical.

"Sharon," Sarodsy continued, his voice measured, "for the better part of twenty years, the Navy has been on a slippery slope. Your job is, and has been, primarily gender equality. Mine is fighting a war at sea, if need be, and to win. The two are not necessarily mutually exclusive. Diversity has been good for the Navy in many respects. That said, however, and don't forget we've had this same conversation for many years, it's gone too far. The Reagan's captain has done what I would have ordered three weeks ago." He paused and said softly, "Sharon, we have about 24,000 young men and women in our Indian Ocean battle groups that have a high probability of coming under hostile fire. No time-outs allowed and no points for second place."

McCluskey was torn. Smart and totally committed, she sensed a rational logic in Sarodsy's point. Her perspective, though, was at stark contrast with his. Never having served on the deck plates or cockpits, hers was a narrow focus, a focus that, like it or not, was diversity and making sure the troops felt good about themselves.

When Stan Sarodsy was called to an urgent phone call, Sharon's mind drifted a few years back when, as a commander serving on a special diversity task force, the initial issue on the agenda had been race. The president had promised to provide more racial diversity in the nation, starting with the military. Problem was though, Sharon recalled, Blacks, Asians and Hispanics were far more over-represented in the armed forces than the population as a whole. If the pending congressional legislation were to dictate racial parity in the military as a function of the nation's population, the services would have had to drastically curtail the input of minorities and actively shift to recruiting non-minorities. McCluskey was the one who chanced on the pragmatics, the 2000 census, the catalyst.

For the first time in the every-ten-year people count, in addition to the standard racial categories, there was a block for "mixed." Though a bit controversial at the time, the shift in policy reflected the realities of America's demographics. Fact was that mixed-racial marriages were increasing exponentially. America's melting pot was boiling. McCluskey had suggested that the issue of racial diversity was a non-issue, under the proviso that in only a generation or two, there would be no easily-defined races in America. "We would all be Americans," she had successfully argued.

The life-style arguments back then before the task force had been far more difficult and acrimonious, the roots of dissent founded in deep-seated religious beliefs. The bottom-line result of the deliberations was that the pendulum of life-style acceptance continued to swing. The Navy, prior to 1990, had been hard-over anti-homosexual, the genesis founded in centuries of the Judeo-Christian ethic and, in later years, the ill-founded notion that blackmail could be leveraged against the "deviant." "Don't ask don't tell" emerged in the '90s, a failed policy that simply offered the option of looking the other way. Sharon's group had taken the policy several steps beyond such that the sexual preferences of a Navy person were a non-issue, so long as his or her shipmates were not offended. "What a person does in private is none of the Navy's business," wrote McCluskey in the internal point paper, much to the delight of the political elite.

Sarodsy was off the phone, the respite welcome, the dust settled somewhat. He said formally and with conviction, "Sharon, does Sweeney realize the severity of this crisis? I just don't think the sense of urgency is getting through to her. Here's her daily calendar. She's visiting the President this morning and speaking to a military women's group at the Sheraton. She seems totally oblivious to the tinderbox in the Middle East and the danger to our forces."

"Well," she argued, "the White House chief of staff is asking questions about the status of weapons of some sort and I'm sure Virginia is walking the overhead at the news of the backseater. You know, too, that our CEO misses no opportunity to argue and advise against military action, no matter the provocation. It's a message that the President wants to hear. She'll talk to her on all three, I'm sure."

"Sir, ma'am, it's Admiral Sweeney on the line. She wants to talk to you, sir," said the aide, handing the phone to Sarodsy, her face grimacing.

Gender diversity had been the most complex and acrimonious issue confronting the task force. The mouthpiece for women's issues in the military had long been DACOWITS, the acronym not as important as the fact that to its prestigious membership, both military and civilian, the organization's *cause célèbre* was the promotion of total gender equality within the military. To its strident members, total equality was not an option, it was a mandate. The vice president, of course, was supportive, his personal aide at the time, Commander Nancy Chandler, a constant and vocal proponent at his side. Several prestigious male-dominated organizations had tried to torpedo the sweeping equality mandate which had at its centerpiece, strict numerical parity within all military units, including combat outfits. "The Retired Officers Association," the "Navy League of the United States," the "Association of Naval Aviation," and the "American Legion," all argued against a policy they felt inimical to the combat capability of the U.S. Based upon the National Security Act of 1948, several of the organizations filed a class-action lawsuit, which had, with great publicity and energy, elevated the contentious debate all the way to the Supreme Court. McCluskey, then a commander and one of the few non-lawyers ever to argue before the high court, caught the discerning eye of then-Congresswoman and gender activist, Virginia Roberts Stallingsworth, the affirmation into the law of the land, clear sailing within the year.

The diversity task force membership, along with the prestigious DACOWITS membership, were a homogeneous assemblage. Overwhelmingly female, few had ever served a meaningful tour aboard ship or in combat other than support forces in long ago Desert Storm. Essentially all had spent the vast majority of their careers in and about the beltway of Washington's power brokers. As a result of the visibility McCluskey had achieved, she had been early promoted to full captain only fifteen years out of the Naval Academy and had taken but one year longer than her protégé, Nancy Chandler, to be advanced to flag rank as a rear admiral. She was, of course, on a personal, first-name basis with the incumbent President.

Sarodsy returned, the phone call completed. "Sweeny's hyper-torqued. She says the President is all over her about the injured Red Ripper lieutenant. Funny, she didn't mention the pilot. You know it's all on the news. CNN has even staked out her parent's home in Milton, Florida. Everyone wants to know why she was pregnant and flying." He strolled to the giant electronic situation display, deep in troubled thought.

"Sharon, I've got to press on. Stick with me a few days, OK? We've got some tough seas ahead. Now — I want to ask you a big one."

He stopped, staring squarely at the Caspian Sea region with the hostile symbols of the combined ISI might moving inexorably as pincers seizing a block of ice. "Sharon," he articulated slowly, "I want you to recommend to Sweeny the release of all Stress City cases, both on-board ship and Memphis, excepting, of course, obvious medical cases. Can you do it?" Without waiting for a reply, he continued. "If we go on the offensive . . . ," he stopped knowing this was not a viable option. "If we are attacked in the near future, it will make no difference. If, however, the tensions are protracted, we'll need those people. No question."

She stood, her three stars matching those of her ample contemporary. "Wow. I can't believe this. You're actually going to feed me to the alligators. What a guy," for the first time in the tense meeting, hinting at a smile. She continued, gathering her thoughts. "There's something you ought to know about the call up of the reserves. Al Fossinger, the CEO of Western Airlines, has asked the President to forgo the recall of any more of his reserve pilots," adding, "WA was a heavy contributor to the last presidential election. Apparently, they are canceling flights right and left due to a lack of pilots, and losing a ton of money in the process. Also, some of their pilots feel the order is prejudicial to their livelihood, disrupts the families and only serves a political end to a potential military conflict they perceive as unnecessary, unjust and wasteful. About 830 pilots are boycotting the call up and are threatening legal action. It's a double whammy, unfortunately." She sat down, crossed her legs, buttoned her blue service blouse, adjusted her tie and waited for the onslaught.

"Thanks for the input, unbelievable though it may be. Sharon, you know my position. It's total crap. What the hell is the point of having reserves to begin with?" Sarodsy stopped, knowing the gesture was fruitless. "You handle it. I've got a big-time potential war on my hands." The two shook hands, eyes interlocking for a brief moment of mutual understanding and respect, a first for the two senior naval officers.

Following the departure of his counterpart on the Navy staff, Sarodsy engaged in a bit of self-commiseration. The one-way conversation with Sweeney was only about the hapless Lieutenant Swagger and how embarrassing it would be for her and the Navy. Sarodsy knew she had been outraged over his unpolitic diatribe in front of the president the day before. He had been out of line. No question. But had he to do it over again, he would have done the same. "It's time that the national command authority realized the world had more than its share of rogues, not all of whom marched to the same rational, feel-good drumbeat," he grumbled through clenched teeth, the strain perceptible.

He reviewed a hastily-crafted, short point-paper Nancy Chandler had given him prior to her abrupt departure for interior China. It read:

"TOP SECRET FOR VICE ADMIRAL SARODSY:
In view of the recent information you have provided me

relative to 'Green Trees,' it is clear that many highly influential people have profited from a corrupt system of political payola. Arms and technology purveyors in our country have been the principal recipients of the (mostly) Chinese largess, the trade routes liberally greased by a one-way flow of massive dollars to the U.S. body politic, which, in turn, has implemented policy to support such trade. The 27% (or so) of the U.S. economy that so benefits, in turn, contributes heavily to a continuation of the process. As a result, the Chinese have accomplished a remarkable make-over of their military that is structured principally to ensure adequate sources of energy. If China is forced into unilateral military action to obtain oil, it will adversely affect the economies of all Asia which will, in turn, impact on the global economy of the U.S. In its simplest terms, China has used hard currency earned in its exports, mainly to the U.S., to purchase influence, policy, arms and technology favorable for her military. <u>It is imperative that China have fair access to the Caspian Sea oil reserves</u>. The vital interests of the U.S. are best enhanced by assisting China, including militarily, if necessary, to assure such reasonable access. That said, it is my sense that the administration is overtly doing its best to disengage and distance itself from China and is not willing to risk one American life, even if our carrier battle groups are taken under attack. It goes without saying, that should the ISIs prevail, the next victims will be Turkey, Jordan and Israel, in that order. Best to take decisive action now and do so in concert militarily with China. Afterthought: Thankfully, nuclear weapons are not part of the Chinese strategic mix.

Very respectfully submitted,
Nancy Chandler, RADM U.S.N"

Sarodsy's aide broke the spell by announcing, "Senator Montgomery, Admiral."

"Good morning, Joe. Come in. Coffee?" he said, shaking hands with the still youthful senator.

"Morning, Stan. You think it's crazy down here, you ought to see my side. I've got 37 Senators and 41 Congressmen lined up, ready to take action against the President and the ECATS leadership, including a covey of disenchanted folks chomping on the minority sidelines. But I need more and better analysis and facts regarding 'Green Trees' and the flow of dollars, particularly in the past few years. Can do?"

"Roger that. Should have more detail by 1400 this afternoon. You'll be the first on the access list. Glad I'm not in your shoes." He stood, went to the wall-mounted situation map, turned to face the senior senator and said, "Joe, the military is charged with providing the best strategic advice to the President possible. Options, risks, pros and cons. Problem is, she's getting none of that. It's all one-way pap, most of which supports what the service chiefs know she wants to hear. Use of force is a non-option replete with all the rhetoric about risking America's young men and women, impacting the balance of trade and our peaceful image among the nations of the world."

"Let me interrupt, if I may, Stan," said the senator, standing. "It's the same song, different verse on the political front. Stallingsworth wants to maintain the status quo, and she's put the word out through Richard Redman that any argument against her policies will result in immediate cut-off of campaign and 'other' funding. In fact," he smiled thinly, "she's addressing the DACOWITS group — you know, the Defense Advisory Committee on Women in the Services — at noon today downtown. It's become a major policy speech in which she will reaffirm her policy of no U.S. involvement in the Caspian issues. The by-line decided upon by the press? 'No young women in body bags.' She will too, I'm sure, have a few choice words for the ineptness of the Navy in allowing an expectant woman to fly in fighter aircraft."

Sarodsy interrupted. "I thought Sweeney was to speak before the DACOWITS?"

"No, sir. She's been preempted by the President. She's got the ball now and will seize the moment. According to my sources, she will espouse, a firm, no-military-action policy, even if attacked. Incidentally, she has wind of whatever one of your captains did on her now least favorite ship, the Reagan, and will make that an issue as well. Oh, and the speech will be live on the leading networks and CNN, her second significant address in a few hours." The minority party lawmaker leaned back in his chair, ran his hand through a generous mat of thick, dark hair and proceeded to read the Chandler report with a profound sense of interest.

"Sir, it's Admiral Demming on the red line," the aide said, gently interrupting.

"Bruce, I was going to give you a chance for some shut-eye. My guess is that you have another great sea story to tell your grandkids that will need little embellishment."

"If they'll listen, which I doubt," said the revitalized vice admiral. Demming proceeded to tell Sarodsy about Tsunami, Wong, the secret air base, the aborted rescue attempt and that he was unable to locate the special sensor in the crashed U.S. Navy fighter. He dwelt at some length on the subjective issue of Chinese combat capability which the venerable admiral categorized as "totally committed to winning in combat."

Sarodsy asked. "Could the Chinese handle the ISIs unilaterally?"

A short pause, Demming's confident response: "No way, simply because of the vast distances involved in projecting air power, even with a considerable in-house refueling capability."

Sarodsy asked, "Would they?"

The pause was greater this time. "I think so, but they wouldn't like the results."

Demming shifted the subject to personal matters. Tommy Boone was his son-in-law and his number-two daughter, Susan and her husband had reported to the ship only shortly before to join the Red Rippers. "I'm looking forward to a family reunion out here in the middle of nowhere."

"Bruce," Sarodsy responded officially, "don't get too settled. Senator Montgomery's aide, Ernie Maltman, is en route to you all now. Should arrive shortly. Rear Admiral Nancy Chandler is airborne as we speak, headed for Chunking to to meet with General Wong." He measured his next step. "You won't like what's coming next, my friend. Sitting down?"

"Go ahead. Nothing will surprise me. I'm hunched over in a defensive crouch," said Demming.

"I want you, Ernie Maltman and the Chinese major to fly direct to Chunking and meet with Wong within the next twenty-four hours. You'll get marching orders sooner, rather than later. Can do?"

The retired vice admiral, suddenly thrust into the boiling pot, replied. "Yeah. Well, I'm off to the showers and then a surprise call on Susan. Hope she's not flying. Then to Tommy and, finally, Susan's husband. Oh, I almost forgot, the plot thickens. Major Ying Tsunami and my Susan went through Navy advanced flight training in Kingsville. My God, I can't believe all this. Used to be an old saying long ago that if you're not having fun, you're not doing it right. I must be doing a lot of right things. Talk to you later."

"Good job, Bruce. If you would, keep the phone with you. And, for your info, the news of the crash, rescue and the loss of the unborn baby is all over the news. The President will be on network TV in a couple of hours on that and a few other salient strategy issues. Take care. I've already called your bride and given her a thumbs-up on her indestructible husband."

The speech by the President was vintage Virginia. No notes, broad smile, sparkling-blonde hair and all the right words. Sweeney was on the dais as an honored guest and was stunningly pleased with the unambiguous message of the commander in chief. The "no combat" and "no women's body bags" portion of her speech to the august women's group met with a thunderous applause, a standing ovation and unladylike stomping of feet in the packed, grand ballroom of Washington's Downtown Sheraton.

Admiral Sweeney's demeanor turned turtle though when Virginia began her castigating comments about the ineptness of the Navy in allowing ". . . the lieutenant to fly in her condition. No longer will our nation condone the mistakes that led to the tragic loss of an unborn and the near-death of a fine young woman and expectant mother," all the while zeroing in on the now thoroughly embarrassed Navy CEO. The receptive audience loved it. The President departed to yet another tumultuous ovation lasting well past her sprightly exit from the hall.

Vice Admiral Stan Sarodsy clicked the monitor to mute, as he and Senator Montgomery pondered their next strategic move. Abruptly, the giant situation board lit up in the vicinity of the Iranian port of Bandar Abas. Within seconds, a breathless intelligence officer burst into the inner sanctum.

The red flashing symbol was unusual in that it indicated an immediate execute precedence message of great import that needed instant attention. Clicking on the icon initiated a scrolling message on a monitor to the side of the map display:

"FLASH: The Super Pelican missiles discovered 28 hours ago on the docks of Bandar Abas have been uncrated and observed loading onto four Whiskey class diesel submarines and onto a squadron of SU-45 Iranian fighters at the nearby Kleski Air Base. In the judgment of this analyst, these are not training-related actions."

Sarodsy's command center deep within the bowels of the Pentagon, came alive, setting into motion a series of preplanned actions. To Sarodsy, the movements of the Iranians were not unexpected. He explained the logic to Montgomery, the massive electronic image his backdrop to a troubled world.

"Joe, it's not complicated. We have three carrier battle groups in the Indian Ocean, about thirty-one ships altogether, plus six submarines and two more battle groups a day out in the Red Sea and Eastern Mediterranean. Their job, in this scenario, is to counter ISI excursions into the approaches to the Caspian. They know, full well, that the mountainous terrain in the area works to our advantage. Using smart weaponry, five carrier battle groups can most effectively block the lines of communications and supply," pointing his laser to the rugged landscape to the west and south of the relatively flat Caspian Sea basin. "The task of the Bandar region is simply to neutralize our offensive sea power."

"How about the Red Sea and Mediterranean naval forces," asked the senator, whose military experience was limited to an occasional Blue Angel air show.

"Both groups are postured to keep the pressure on the rear and flanks of the ISIs. Because of the carriers and the land-based strategic air of our Air Force, the ISIs must allocate substantial forces for protection. Problem now is the Super Pelican missiles. We have no counter for them. In its anti-ship mode, it's incredibly deadly and, while it can't sink a carrier, it can damage it enough to compromise combat operations. It's hard to tell if the weapons are being loaded for drill or rather to test the questionable resolve of a frightened U.S. leadership." Summoning an aide, he ordered her to, "Please ensure that Admiral Sweeny sees this information as well as triple check that each of our combatant ships is in the highest state of offensive and defensive readiness."

Montgomery grinned, once again ruffling his tousled hair. "Looks like the ISIs got an advanced copy of Virginia's speech."

CHAPTER 18

Paradise Visited

Lieutenant Susan "MA" Anthony, U.S. Naval Reserve, was sobbing uncontrollably in the stately flag quarters of the USS *Ronald Reagan*. Her itinerant father, retired Vice Admiral Bruce Demming, still sore and tired from his escapades of several hours before high in the desolate mountains of Iran, had no inkling that the surprise call to his number-two daughter would have been so traumatic.

Susan had tearfully recounted to her dad the high points of her two flights in the F-27C stealth Phantom III with the Red Rippers, both extraordinarily unsatisfactory by any naval aviation standard. Her father's arms, meant to soothe his distraught daughter, were ineffectual, as were his futile words of wisdom.

Suddenly Susan let it all hang out, blurting, "Daddy, I want to go home. I want to be with Jennifer and Joanne. I want the routine of American Airlines." She paused, the sobbing in check for the moment. "Mike's OK. I think he actually likes all this. FedEx is fine with him and the pay is clearly good, but deep down, he resents the title of assistant to the assistant package hauler."

"I'm different," she continued, never having opened up like this to her dad before. "You may not have known this, Daddy, but I have always been terrified of night carrier landings — catapults, too. I've done them many times, but each time, it's an ordeal."

Demming squeezed her shoulder. "I know the feeling, honey."

227

Gathering her composure, she said slowly, "I think the Doc is going to keep me in a grounded status. Fact is, when I look in the mirror, I don't see a tough U.S. Navy fighter pilot ready to launch into a black night and shoot down the enemy. I see a scared mother of two and," hesitantly, "maybe another." She gulped. "Sounds like a good excuse, but I think it may be true."

A knock on the door by the Marine orderly. "Admiral, it's the Captain, sir."

"Tommy, it's good to see you," said the old warrior to his number-one son-in-law, "even under the circumstances."

Tommy Boone noted the reddened face of his sister-in-law. "You OK, Susan?"

"Not really Tommy — er, Captain. I think my Navy flying days may be history," adding plaintively, "Sorry about the botched landings."

"Not to worry, Susan. No one's hurt and we can fix the machine," referring to her very hard landing earlier that evening and the busted stealth jet down below on the hangar deck. "You need to get some rest."

Susan tried mightily to suppress the emotions welling deep within her to no avail, the tears and heaves front and center once again. The two sailors tried their best to comfort her, shoulders to lean on as useful as shoveling sand against a rising tide.

Tommy said to Demming. "Glad to see you up and kicking, sir. How's Major Tsunami?"

Susan, suddenly alert and perky, "Not Ying Tsunami? How in the world? Is he on board?" rattled the confused young woman. "Not my Chinese flight training compatriot of ten years ago?"

"Yes. He asked about you several times, but, of course, we had no idea that you would wind up on the Reagan. He's fine. Anxious to get back to his squadron though."

"Oh, I would love to see him," she said brightly, thinking back to their advanced flight training days at Kingsville, Texas and the genesis of her call sign, "MA," short for Miss America.

"At the moment, he's with Lieutenant Swagger in sick bay. Hardly left her side," said the stoic captain.

The phone, in the hushed, carpeted and wood-paneled opulence of the carrier's flag quarters, rang. It was the ship's XO, touching base with her captain on a number of subjects, including her meeting with Stan Miller and that Major Tsunami would be hosted by the Red Rippers during his stay on board. The Ripper commanding officer had directed the grounded Susan Anthony to be his escort officer and suggested he be temporarily berthed with the Rippers in paradise, specifically to the stateroom of the presumed lost Lieutenant Sam Newman.

"Thanks for the call, Angela. See you in the morning. No need to be on the bridge for the 0200 refueling," said Boone to his hardworking executive officer.

Tsunami was, at the moment, still in the ship's sick bay where Dr. Rose Johnson was busily attending to the weakened Evelyn Swagger. "Be a while before she's wearing a bikini," irreverently opined the Doc, adding a tension-reducing smile for the pensive major.

The flight surgeon had given the Chinese fighter pilot a quick physical and found him bruised, but fit, albeit untalkative. Since the initial meeting with him high in the mountains, Tsunami had not taken his eyes off the heavily-sedated woman. "You OK, Ying?" Rose asked.

"OK, Doc. How's the Admiral?"

"He's a tough one. He'll hack it fine, too. So will Evelyn, though it'll be a while before she flies again, I'm afraid. She was pregnant, you know, but lost the baby in the ejection."

A soft-spoken, tremulous response. "The baby? When will she awaken?"

"May I come in?" It was Susan Anthony, freshened up somewhat since the emotional meeting with her dad. "Ying, what a surprise! I won't dare ask what you are doing here."

"MA," Ying's face brightened for the first time in twenty-eight hours, the sight of a friendly face in a sea of strangers, a welcome respite from his rock-bottom emotional state.

Susan too, momentarily forgot her travails and joyfully hugged the blushing major. "Hey, we've got some catching up to do, Ying," she said, her shimmering voice straining the bounds of her own psyche.

She's really strung-out, noted Rose Johnson to herself. I'd best talk to her in the morning. Rose continued, out loud this time. "Look, you all. It's late. Evelyn will be fine. She just needs quiet and rest. You folks need to get some shuteye too. Ying, that means you."

"Ying," Susan broke in excitedly, "I've been assigned as your escort. You'll be staying in Evelyn's room next door to Mike and me. Come on and I'll get you tucked in," Susan's maternal instincts rising to the fore. "I've got lots of time."

Rose noted she sounded matter-of-fact. I think it's sunk in, she correctly surmised.

Ying and Susan made their way forward and up in the darkened ship, the sounds and smells of the red-hued hangar deck reminiscent of his short carrier qualification training so long ago as a student naval aviator. In the dimness, they paused at a damaged F-27C, a team of maintenance personnel working on the crushed and disfigured after fuselage and starboard main landing gear of the fighter, the tail hook smashed firmly into the structure. "My airplane," said Susan resignedly. "I'll explain later."

Entering paradise, Susan was about to open the door to the stateroom of Studs and Bikini when Shorts Flanagan appeared in her bathrobe — apparently headed for the officer showers — and squeezed by the incredulous visitor with a friendly wink and wholesomely welcome smile.

Susan and Ying stood in the narrow passageway, talking quietly, making up for ten years of varied backgrounds and experiences. Lieutenant Commander Dave Anderson eased by, clad only in a short bathrobe as well. Susan, in her seventy-two hours on board as a temporary resident in paradise, had found many changes in the social milieu of a deployed Navy aircraft carrier since her active duty days a few years before.

"Dave. Meet Major Ying Tsunami. Ying was in the Chinese helo that crashed trying to rescue Bikini."

"Ying, Dave was lead for the fighter cover for your rescue."

"Nice to meet you, Dave," said the Chinese fighter pilot in perfectly-enunciated English. "What's your job?"

"I'm chief pilot, operations officer and acting XO of the world famous VF-11 Red Rippers. Just landed, as you know. Hardly 400 pounds of fuel left. Damned contract tankers. Got to get cleaned up. Talk to you later," he said, scurrying to the showers.

"Dave is one of our top pilots. You'll like him," commented Susan. "My husband Mike is flying now. Will recover at 0340. You'll meet him tomorrow. I've put some of Mike's stuff out for you. You're about the same size. Just bang on the bulkhead if you need something. I'll get you up at 0600."

The quiet in paradise was shaken by the strident roar of twin, after-burning ram-jets, followed by a reverberating thump as the number-two catapult did its job . Susan smiled. "That's my Mike just launching." Thirty seconds later, a repeat, as another fighter blasted into the blackness of a cloud-soddened night. The thought set Susan's knees into an uncontrollable shake.

In the privacy of the tiny stateroom, door closed, Ying's emotions ran deep and confused. The room reeked of female, the lower bunk bed festooned with a collection of furry-stuffed animals strategically placed on a baby-blue bedspread. The aroma and panorama stimulated him, the monastic life of a Chinese pilot, for the time being, swept into the background.

Contrasting, were the tiny room's pair of flight suits in need of washing, bag of dirty laundry, bra on a hook and remnants of the latest teeth-brushing in the functional stainless sink. A picture on the desk of two smiling aviators, the backdrop a Red Ripper F-27C stealth Phantom III, revealed an astonishingly beautiful young woman and an equally handsome pilot. His mind wandered, his loins pulsing, not of the picture, but the gorgeous female who had pressed by him in the narrow corridor only moments before attired in the barest of covering. Back to reality, he shook his head. "This is supposed to be a combatant vessel? I knew the U.S. Navy had gone off the deep end, but not to the extent of my first hours on board."

Susan too, was wide awake next door. "Where to start?"

she muttered, her mind a blur. "Too much and way too fast." The emotional visit with her dad had been a totally unexpected event, but surprisingly, had calmed her nerves. "And Ying Tsunami. What a week it's been. Totally unbelievable."

The comparative quiet of paradise was broken by the animated conversation of Anderson and his roommate returning from the showers. Flanagan, Anderson's former back-seater, was clearly annoyed with the change in crew assignments dictated by the squadron commander only hours before.

Susan, though, had a different take, her female perspectives germane. When she and Ying had entered the one door to paradise at 0015 in the morning, her guess was that Flanagan and Anderson had probably been engaged in activity transcending a discussion of fighter tactics. "Life has really changed out here. If what I've seen in the first three days is any indicator, the folks on the home front have every reason to worry."

Thinking of her Mike, her knees began an uncommanded, self-motivated chatter, her brain thankful it was he and not her, airborne in the unfriendly skies over the stormy ocean.

Dr. Rose Johnson was about to douse the lights in sick bay at 0032 when Captain Tommy Boone walked in, oblivious to the hour and his fatigued physical state. "How's the Lieutenant, Doc?"

Rose countered with her own instant assessment. "You look tired, sir. You need some rest."

"Can't sleep. Anyway, we've got refueling in a couple of hours," thinking of the two-hour alongside evolution with an oiler carrying millions of gallons of JP9 fuel for his thirsty fighters, a task not without its own high-stress level.

"Rose, I'm glad to see you're in one piece. I was worried about you. It was a tough mission, for sure," he said, resisting the urge to protectively put his arms about her sagging shoulders.

"Rose," he said softly, eyes locked with hers, "have you heard about the series of anti-social measures I've taken?"

"Yes, sir. I don't know much about Navy regulations, but it seemed the logical way to go under the circumstances. That said, though, you want my real thoughts — medically speaking?"

"Absolutely," he responded, thankful for the distraction, settling deeper into the padded chair, the sick bay lights low, the quiet relaxing.

With a broad smile, she said, "You know Captain, I'm keeping a medical journal. You're part of it under the rubric of 'Managing Diversity, The Perspective From The Deck Plates.' As the CO, you're in an impossible no-win situation. Positive and enlightened leadership can change the course of history, but not fundamental human nature. What you did was right, but only a finger in the dike," once again with a grin that belied her thinly-veneered physical and emotional state.

The two were quiet, reflective. Boone, torn between his growing dependence on the younger doctor and the worry of impending combat ops, was awash in a complex sea of unbridled emotions flitting about within his job description.

Rose, too, was pensive, the astounding adventure of the past few hours, indeed months, penetrating to every fiber of her being. Thirty-one years of age, never married, no kids, she was aware of the persistent ticking of her maternal clock. Four years out of residency, hers had been an adult life of total commitment to the priorities at hand, with little left over for herself. "Kind of like Tommy Boone," she thought, observing the resting ship's captain, twelve years her senior.

Suddenly alert, the captain, back in command, said in his most manly tone, "Got to go, Rose. I'll stop by the XO's cabin, then on to the bridge. And Rose," he put his arm over her shoulder and held her firmly, his move far more protective than suggestive, "thanks for all you have done and are doing. In Navy jargon, you're a strong anchor to windward. I'm grateful for having you aboard." Softly, he looked into her eyes, her arm ready for a push-off, "I think the going in the next twenty-four hours or so will be tough. We need to be tough." Abruptly disengaging, he left the sick bay, the Marine orderly falling into step alongside and slightly behind his captain.

En route to the amidships office of the ship's executive officer, headed aft, the two were met by a hand-holding young couple, she in tight shorts, clinging tank top and he in low-slung pants, no shirt and flip flops, animatedly engaged in two-way talk, oblivious to the impending confrontation only several steps in front. Glancing up at the Reagan's commanding officer, the two disengaged and came to an abrupt, embarrassed attention.

Boone sighed and said quietly to the two youngsters. "Where are you two from?"

She: "Atlanta, sir."

And he: "Weapons Division, sir."

"And what, may I ask, are you doing at this hour?"

"We're inspecting the weapons magazines, sir."

"And why are dressed like you are? You're clearly not in the working uniform."

"Oh, sir. We always do our night rounds like this."

"Much cooler," added the skimpily-clad young woman, the two once again holding hands and standing at a rough approximation of attention.

The captain looked at his Marine orderly, who was overtly wishing he were somewhere else. "Sailors," he continued, "did you hear or see me on the ship's TV four hours ago?"

"Yes, sir. Sorry, sir," their eyes contrite, the obvious humiliation flooding the narrow passageway.

Boone kept at it, again in a measured, almost fatherly tone. "Why are you dressed this way then and why are you still holding hands? I must not have made myself clear to you two."

The question was rhetorical, the answer obvious. The young male sailor said honestly, "Because, sir, this is the way we've always done it. We thought there would be a grace period," the concurring nod of his attractive partner signaling the realistic end to the fruitless conversation.

"Get into the proper uniform now. Understood?"

"Aye, aye, sir," they said in unison scampering off to their berthing compartment at top speed, hands no longer together.

The repartee had lasted less than two minutes, but the content revealed an abundance of the facts of life on the warship in November of the year 2010. Resolutely, the captain continued aft to the XO's stateroom.

The Marine orderly outside the combination office and living quarters for the exec snapped to instant attention, her surprise transparent. In over eight months, the captain had never visited at this late hour.

"Sir, the Commander gave me strict orders that she not be disturbed," articulated the diminutive private, her uniform creased, her resolve to carry out orders paramount.

"Is she in?"

"No, sir."

"Where is she, please?" The young woman was flustered, at a loss for words.

"Sir, if I may," his orderly said, speaking conspiratorially. The two men, father and son in age, retreated out of sight to another corridor. "The XO is predisposed, Captain. Most likely," his voice lowering, "she's in conference with Commander Miller."

"At this late hour?" The Marine said nothing, the die cast, the conversation ended.

The awkward impasse was interrupted by the ringing of the captain's command phone. It was the war room, the intelligence watch officer announcing an urgent intelligence flash and to "Please come to the integrated operations intelligence center ASAP!"

The super-secret spaces just below the flight deck were abuzz with activity, the time of one hour after midnight of little relevance.

"Good morning, Captain. Got some hot news," said an energized Ensign Patty Butts, the intelligence officer on duty, leading the way to the large flat-screen situation board. In 8x13-foot format, the close-in, real-time blowups of the Super Pelican weapons in the process of loading, flashed to reality, both on the submarine piers and the nearby air base. "No one knows the intent of the Iranians," she offered.

"What's your opinion, Patty?"

"No question, Captain. This smacks of preemptive preparations to neutralize the Indian Ocean battle groups."

Without hesitation, the captain called the officer of the deck on the bridge and ordered the ship to a way-point selected by his laser pointer. To his OOD, "Head 242 degrees and make turns for 36 knots. Inform the oiler we'll delay the refueling until further notice." Within seconds, the carrier heeled her 97,000 tons eight degrees to port, the pulsing power of the four huge propellers pounding the dark sea to a frothy white turbulence.

Noticing the Ripper skipper hunched over in the strike-planning enclaves, Boone put his hand on her shoulder. "Wendy, I'm not surprised to see you here. Can you give me a quick brief as to what you all have in mind, please?"

"Morning, Captain. Yes, sir. We are in the final planning stage for two primary strike options. First of course, is the Bandar complex. The plan is to attack with sixteen fighters and four electronic jammers in one raid from the Reagan followed ten minutes later by the Ike's air wing," referring to the USS *Eisenhower*. "Each fighter will carry the standard load of four 2,000-pound, mark 84, laser-guided-GPS-assisted standoff weapons. Incidentally, sir, these are the latest upgrades with an accuracy of less than one meter, no matter the target or weather."

"How about the Stennis?" asked Boone. It was clearly a redundant question as his reputation as a fighter attack pilot would have him earning a doctorate in advanced tactics were he in the arcane world of academia.

"The Stennis air wing will be ready as a contingency back-up. Don't forget, sir," said Iron Lady, "we must ensure an attack package for the Caspian area at all times," gratuitously offering, "That's our primary area of interest."

The Reagan, awesome though it may have been in the pecking order of power projection from the sea, was only a piece of the giant strategic puzzle. The several submarines and surface combatants of the combined battle groups were assigned pin-point targets of their own including air defenses, command and control nodes and power-generating grids. The complex plan originated deep in the bowels of the Pentagon, the staff of Rear Admiral Nancy Chandler using high-end computers linked to real-time intelligence to produce a near-optimum plan of attack. On the deck plates at sea, the option to alter or refine was always the prerogative of the commanding officer.

A submarine officer, her gold dolphins at contrast to the plethora of equally gold naval aviator wings in the room, assertively added to the input of Montrose. "Captain, we've got the four Iranian Whiskey class subs covered. The moment they exit the Strait of Hormuz for the Indian Ocean, they'll be picked up and trailed by an equal number of our Seawolf class subs. You know, sir, those diesel boats are tough — real quiet. But they have one principal drawback — they must come to periscope depth to obtain targeting information."

"What's the ROE for the subs?" snapped Boone, knowing the answer, but preferring the reaffirmation.

"Sir, the rules of engagement state that if the hostile subs are within the Super Pelican effective surface launched range of 73 miles and our trail assets hear the sound of the weapon's doors opening, our subs shoot. It's unambiguous. The Seawolf class can practically tell when they flush the john," she said brightly. "I know, sir. I've served six years on the submarine USS *Rickover*. It's an amazing weapons system."

"Captain," proudly offered the Red Ripper commanding officer, "have you met Lieutenants Becky Turner and Scott Jacobs?"

"Don't think so, but heard good things about you both," shaking the hands of the young warriors. "That was a nice low-state recovery earlier this evening, Becky. Well done."

The face of the young pilot brightened. "Thanks, sir. Scott was half the success. He's my surrogate brain. Want to see what we're doing, Captain?"

"Shoot," said Boone, no matter the hour, pleased to be in the company of so many real naval aviators and professional sailors.

"Twidget, that's Scott's call sign, sir, is convinced he can find a counter to the Super Pelican using the ASQ-407A electronic counter-measures gear we have in our jets. We've been hitting the classified internet access to Honeywell and the CIA for clues. The missile, as you know, is frequency agile and relies on random algorithms involving constantly changing infrared and target radar characteristics. Land targets are easy, but ships at sea are a tough problem. We think that with a combination of two fighters in conjunction with the ship's suite of jamming gear, we may have a partial solution."

"Good job, guys," said the captain. Then, to himself, where do we get such incredible dedication?

The carrier, of course, had a multitude of decoys, electronic spookers, flares and the like of mind-numbing capability. In the present configuration, though, they were useless against the highly-refined Super Pelican.

The captain went about the intelligence center, shook each person's hand and, in a positive tone, his head high and shoulders squared said, "You all are doing a magnificent job. I am grateful for your dedication, hard work and spirit. Keep it up." With his thumb held high, he departed, the collateral duty of head cheerleader a constant companion to the busy captain of a warship on the high seas.

Iron Lady, pleased with the captain's attaboy, spoke. "Good job. Let's call it a night. Thanks. You all have done well."

"Skipper," Becky Turner said, "Twidget and I want to work the counter-measures bit for a while longer. See you in the morning, ma'am."

Wendy Montrose, tired and stressed, retired to her stateroom about one hundred and twenty feet aft on the same level, changed into a robe and dialed the beeper of her maintenance chief, Randy McCormick, her thoughts on the readiness of the eight jets required of her squadron for the potential strikes. Dashing on a spray of persona-enhancing cologne, she asked if he could give her a status report, "In person please, Master Chief."

Meanwhile, the skipper's back-seater, Lieutenant (junior grade) "Pistol" Pete Dawkins, walked with Patty to the Ripper officer berthing in paradise. "Could we talk a while, Patty?"

"Sure, Pete, but you need some rest. You have the 0500 brief."

"I know," he murmured, his face confused. The door to the stateroom of the intelligence officer and Karen Randolph, who was on watch until 0345, swung quietly shut, the corridor in paradise empty.

Pete Dawkins had never been alone with Patty, or with any of the other 2,450 females on the ship, for that matter. A fun-loving, gregarious graduate of Virginia Tech four years earlier, he thrived in the competitive world of carrier fighter aviation. As the skipper's wizo, he knew a great deal about the skills of his pilot, most all of which were complimentary. When it came to the opposite sex, though, he was a neophyte.

Patty was tired, but sensed the need of her squadron-mate to let off some steam. "It's Shorts," he finally stammered. "She won't give me the time of day. She just flashes me one of those gorgeous smiles and flick of her rear end and eggs me on. Nothing happens, though, Patty, and that's my problem." He stopped, uncomfortable with divulging an innermost male concern to the slightly younger, but more worldly, woman.

"What do you want to happen, Pete?" she responded softly, directly engaging the eyeballs of the likable young officer. Silence permeated the small room.

"You know where I'm coming from, Patty. What everyone else is doing. Sometimes," he paused, embarrassed, "you know my bunk is one thin bulkhead from hers next door. Now and then, I can hear them — you know what I mean," his face reddening at the thought, his pelvic area suddenly alive. Patty, too, flushed with the thought. She suspected some hanky-panky, but not to that extent.

The two were interrupted by a gentle knock on the side wall of the tiny room. "You there, Patty?" asked Twidget, who had just returned from the intelligence spaces. Warily, Dawkins observed the repartee, Patty's cheeks even more rosy. Anxious to depart the confusing menagerie of emotions bouncing about paradise, Pistol Pete Dawkins opened the door,

"Pistol, what are you doing here?" Twidget's crestfallen gaze at Patty revealing volumes. Patty Butts offered a contrite, "We were just talking, Scott."

Without further word, Patty closed her door, Twidget slammed his and Pete followed suit with just a hint more authority, slim vestiges of machismo, the tranquility of paradise found once again behind the locked doors. It would be a good while before the three young warriors would drift off to a troubled sleep, the vibrant emotions awash in a sea of confusing sentiments, competing with the deadly task at hand.

Patty lay awake, her body arguing for needed sleep, her brain waves muddled — mind over body. The strained confrontation between the three was an unnecessary addendum to the realities of what lay ahead. In her trademark nightie, she struggled with the not-so-subtle overtones of the short confrontation with Pete and Twidget.

A somber Karen Randolph, just off a stressful four-hour watch, quietly opened the door, knowing that Patty was most likely asleep. As the door eased open, she was startled by the strange apparition in the doorway to the stateroom of Studs and Bikini across the hallway. Grumbling to the lithe, strange young man dressed only in shorts, "Who the hell are you?" Patty, alone in the darkened room, stood, her young body unprepared for any more male visitors.

"You must be Major Tsunami," Patty said, followed by an awkward silence as she tried to cover herself.

Karen, gathering her composure, managed a contrite, "Oh, I'm sorry, Major. Guess I'm kind of tired. Welcome to paradise."

The two ensigns offered hands of welcome, Tsunami greeting each in turn with a slight bow, marveling at the softness and clean smell of the young naval officers. Patty added with a blushing smile, "Greetings from our humble abode, sir."

"Susan Anthony is my escort and put me in this room. We went through flight training together. Her father is also aboard — in flag quarters," said the alert but markedly uncomfortable Tsunami attempting unsuccessfully to avert his gaze from Patty, the scents in the narrow passageway attacking the focus of his brain. "Could you point me to the showers," he asked, adding unnecessarily, "I need one."

"Men and women?" said the totally confused Chinese fighter pilot a few minutes later as they entered the showers.

"I'm afraid so, Major," said the now bathrobe-clad Patty,

amused at the reticence of their new neighbor. "Don't worry. We'll stand guard outside your stall."

Back in paradise, Patty and Karen, despite the late hour and need for precious sleep, decided on some "girl talk." Once again, the unabashed subject was men.

"The Major was funny in the showers. Did you notice, Patty?"

"Did I ever. He did get nervous when he heard us talking to Nancy Donovan in her stall. Funny. Men are so different."

Without skipping a beat, Karen spoke up. "Different, but so alike. Bashful on the outside, but seething on the inside. Seriously though, Panky and I are having problems."

"Oh, really?"

"Yes. He says I'm not paying enough attention to him. He's only been aboard seventy-two hours and already he wants to go full-bore, read 'roll in the hay.' I'm not ready. Besides, it's against all the rules. He's upset too, about Pete. Says I'm being too nice to him. What the heck, I've been close friends with Pete for almost nine months now. What's the big deal?"

Patty recounted her mini-confrontation of an hour ago, Pete's intentions obviously platonic from her perspective, but threatening to Twidget. "I just hope all this social venue doesn't take people's minds off the ball," added the perceptive intelligence officer to her roommate.

Karen jumped into the animated dialogue. "Fact is, Patty, I'm starved for some tender male attention and not afraid to admit it. Panky's surprise arrival reminded me that I like a lot of what I see around here," and, with a wide-open smile, "including our Chinese neighbor across the hall."

"Karen, how unlike you. By the way, did you catch the Captain on TV a few hours ago? He's really wound up. If he only knew half the shenanigans on his big boat, he'd be 'Double Jaws.'"

"Yeah, but it won't do much good," Karen groaned. "Boys will be boys and girls are always girls." Shifting gears, she commented sadly. "It's too bad about Studs. He was a winner."

"That he was, my friend. Thank God Evelyn's OK," offered Patty, brushing an errant tear from her stoic facade.

Karen opened up a bit more. "Patty, you know that Pete and Panky aren't speaking?"

"No. I had no idea. What's going on?" questioned her roommate, female antenna alert.

Karen sighed. "We're too old for all this."

"What's 'this,' " again from an alert Patty.

"Well," Karen began somewhat warily, "Panky thinks he owns me and Pete wants to be with me for some reason," slipping her well-conditioned body into a uniform of ruffled pink pajamas. "They've got more than a little pissing contest going, I'm afraid." Patty, thinking to herself, decided to forgo comment on Pete's interest in Shorts Flanagan, nineteen-short feet down the darkened and now quiet passageway of paradise.

Patty's mind shifted. Pete had indeed been giving her more than friendly attention of late and she had noticed a coolness between Twidget and him. Softly, she said, "Well, my dear roommate, I also have man feelings. Don't we all? That said, however, who are they to dictate whom I talk to and see behind closed doors? It's none of their damned business."

"Going on all over," sighed Karen. "I've got another intimate liaison case in my division. If I lose anymore troops, my second division will be in name only. I can't even person-up my assigned damage-control stations now and the ship's exec is all over me."

Recalling the hairy legs of a distraught Ying Tsunami in his borrowed bathrobe as he headed to the showers, the two young women ended their talk with squeals of laughter. Oblivious to those in paradise, were the movements of the huge ship motivating at maximum speed to safer waters.

Major Ying Tsunami, by all rights, ought to be a basket case of fatigue. Having scarcely slept in the past thirty-six hours, he felt trapped in a catacomb of human emotions, not the least of which concerned Evelyn Swagger, with whom he had hardly spoken. He dialed the direct line to his mentor, Vice Admiral Bruce

Demming.

      Groggily, "Yes?"

      "Sir, it's Ying. I need to see you, Admiral."

      "Ying, my God, it's 0415."

      "I know, sir. Can I come up, please?"

      "Come on up, my friend."

      "Thank you, sir."

      Ying , still smarting from a few bruises and aches, dressed in the borrowed khaki shirt and pants of Mike Anthony, his scuffed and worn flight boots his only link to reality. Walking towards the entrance to paradise, he realized he had not the slightest notion of where to go. Sheepishly, hearing the chatter and girlish laughter across the way, he knocked softly. The door eased open, revealing the amazed and pleased looks in the faces of Karen and Patty.

      Hastily slipping on a robe once again, Patty led the way up six flights and aft about four hundred feet to the alert Marine orderly outside the flag quarters. "Your destination, sir," Patty exclaimed with an engaging smile, white teeth, pleasant aroma, head tilted and a firm, but still feminine, handshake. "See you later, Major."

      "Admiral, I must be in Disneyland. I cannot believe what I'm seeing." For the next twenty minutes, Ying was in a transmit mode telling the old admiral about the inner workings and hidden mechanisms extant in the warship USS *Ronald Reagan*, at sea. "In only a few hours, I've seen and heard more than I care to know about the American Navy."

      Demming was philosophical. The short, but tearful meeting with his daughter was an eye-opener, the tales of Tsunami, icing on the cake. He vowed to talk one-on-one with his son-in-law at the first opportunity while offering his friend the security and comfort of the living-quarters couch for a few hours of needed rest. The two warriors, young and old, had much to discuss, Ying taking mental notes for his expanding war college thesis on the combat capability of the U.S. Navy.

"CLANG, CLANG, CLANG, CLANG, CLANG,

CLANG. ALL HANDS PERSON YOUR BATTLE STATIONS. REPEAT. ALL HANDS PERSON YOUR BATTLE STATIONS. THIS IS NOT A DRILL. ALL HANDS PERSON YOUR BATTLE STATIONS. **CLANG, CLANG, CLANG, CLANG, CLANG, CLANG, CLANG**."

The huge warship sprang into action. Entanglements of warmth and understanding throughout the carrier, now heeling at ten degrees to starboard in a hard turn, came to jarring cessations, the total focus of 5,000 men and women on personing the battle stations and readying the ship for combat. The weapons officer and ship's executive officer parted in haste. The Red Ripper skipper and her maintenance chief headed for the ready room on a dead run. Blues and Shorts hurriedly donned flight suits. The young couple inspecting the number-six bomb storage magazine deep below, cuddled closer, afraid of the clanging reality-check, their hearts beating wildly.

On the windswept, darkened flight deck, four stealth fighters strained against the unyielding hold backs, anxious to join the fray. Within minutes, the giant aircraft carrier had transformed itself from a hotbed of competing human emotions into a fighting instrument of national resolve.

"ON THE REAGAN. NOW HEAR THIS. THIS IS YOUR CAPTAIN. WE HAVE REASON TO BELIEVE AN ATTACK AGAINST OUR SHIP MAY BE IMMINENT. I ASK THAT EVERY MAN AND WOMAN DO YOUR DUTY FOR YOUR COUNTRY AND FOR THE UNITED STATES NAVY. MAY GOD BLESS YOU ALL AND OUR BRAVE WARSHIP. CARRY ON."

CHAPTER 19

The Thickening Morass

SENATOR: CASSIDY'S DEATH NO ACCIDENT

(AP) In a speech before the National Press Club, Senator Joe Montgomery rocked the influential assemblage by indicating he had strong reason to believe the reported accidental death of Senator John Cassidy two years ago in a mysterious air crash was "not an accident." Citing "recent information from multiple reliable sources," Montgomery, one of the minority leaders in the Senate, indicated the death of his friend and presidential hopeful, was ". . . due to a hard over autopilot command triggered deliberately while the private twin-engined jet cruised at 49,000 feet and near the speed of sound." He further advanced the notion that those close to the accident investigation ". . . could have profited from the findings and that he was having difficulty obtaining the source documents pertaining to the after-accident report." The death of Cassidy who, in most national polls, was running ahead of Virginia Roberts Stallingsworth in her quest for a second presidential term, aborted what would have been the greatest political upset in the nation's history. Further, Montgomery repeatedly alluded to the enormous wealth accumulated by some seasoned politicians in the past decade, citing life-styles clearly at odds with the modest pay of the nation's lawmakers, but declined to offer any clues pending a more thorough review of his sources. *Washington Progress,* November 10, 2010.

Within hours of the startling revelations, Richard Redman, secure in his palatial mansion on the banks of the Cimmaron River in the heart of the Oklahoma vista, was on the phone to Dr. Sam Armstrong. "What in the hell is that crazy Senator talking about? There is no way he could have come to such a conclusion," shifting his corpulent bulk to an attack position.

Redman, at 62, was the nation's quintessential power broker to whom most in the political power structure owed their livelihood. The source of the vast bounty distributed by the "Redman Institute for Enlightened Awareness," was of no interest, the considerable amounts unaccountable. Three years prior, when the reality of a Cassidy bid for president took serious root, unknown persons had engineered the fastest, cleanest and most credible aviation accident in history. The subsequent investigation and cover-up was willingly accepted by the public.

The successful election of the Republican John Cassidy to the 2008 presidency would have, of course, been disastrous to an incumbent ECATS party comfortable in the accumulation of enormous personal wealth with its promise of substantial presidential inquiry into such sources. Cassidy's platform had, as its centerpiece, the unconstrained flow of foreign and large corporate dollars into the coffers of compliant politicians anxious to maintain, in perpetuity, the lucrative status quo.

The rise of the ECATS political party in 2004 had been decidedly amazing, the former congresswomen, Virginia Roberts Stallingsworth, an enormously popular standard-bearer. The Enlightened Citizens Against The Status Quo had become overwhelmingly acceptable to an electorate uncomfortable with the constant parade of charlatan politicians on the take, along with their compliant benefactors in the big monies of unions and corporate America. ECATS, of course, when exposed to the realities of political greed was, in fact, no different than previous decades of political plunder, shifty eyes and outstretched hands.

In Cassidy's case, figuring how to cause a jet flying at 49,000 feet and close to the speed of sound to catastrophically destroy itself and leave no clues, was easy. A "cause undetermined" finding, though, was tough simply because the extremely thorough investigations of the Federal Aviation Safety Authority resulted in some probable findings of cause 99% of the time.

Redman had known Dr. Sam Armstrong, the politically appointed head of the prestigious FASA for many years, and, through him, concocted the perfect accident, the keys to which were an expedited investigation, use of a small team of specialists and removal of the charred and mangled remains from any outside scrutiny.

"Sam, I don't give a rat's ass what you think. That SOB is on to something. Is there any way he can dig up the remains of the aircraft?" boomed a clearly irate Redman.

Sam Armstrong had seen the headlines in his local San Diego newspaper. The call from Redman was not unexpected. There had been only seven people connected with the inquiry, including one structural engineer from Consolidated who not only caused the autopilot to command full nose-up with a resultant instantaneous and total structural failure, but did the post-accident computer simulation as well. All seven members of the investigating team had agreed to maintain their present life styles for five years and to leave untouched, for the same period, the secret Swiss bank accounts with the rather grotesque amount of dollars within them.

Armstrong had complied with the spirit, albeit not the letter of the agreement, having recently moved into an oceanfront La Jolla property with a conservative value of two million dollars, his next-door neighbor in the ultra-affluent neighborhood, the hard-working congressman representing a portion of prosperous San Diego county. As he listened to his agitated mentor, he idly noticed two parked cars across the street and a trimly-clad women walking sprightly up his winding driveway.

"Got someone at the door, Richard. I'll get back to you. You in Oklahoma?"

"I am. Call me back later."

"Are you Dr. Armstrong?" said the perky young lady handing him a small manila envelope.

"Yes. How may I help you?"

"Sir, I have an urgent subpoena for you from Senator Montgomery's office in Washington. He respectfully requests that you appear before his committee on internal affairs the day after tomorrow."

Pleasantly, Armstrong offered a polite, "Thank you, miss."

The return call to Redman from Armstrong was not a happy one. "Virginia's all over me. Just heard about Montgomery's hearings and she's livid. In my life, I've heard some tough cussing and swearing, but hers beats all. She's got my ass in a severe defensive crouch," said Redman.

The old master of the deal and influence, back to reality, was not concerned as much about Cassidy's death as he was of Montgomery's "Oh, by the way" comments at the Press Club about uncovering the sources of the political money trail. His secretary interrupted the transient solitude. "Sir, it's Virginia again."

President Stallingsworth, a recognized quick study, had taken some heavy broadsides of her own in the past few days. First was the intransigence of her "girl Friday," Rear Admiral Nancy Chandler. A call to her former chief of staff's mother, a bell-ringing politico of yesteryear, yielded no clues as to the daughter's aloof behavior. Second, was the mysterious appearance of the Super Pelican missiles at the Iranian port of Bandar Abas, clearly at odds with her specific guidance that they be employed only for Chinese defensive uses. Lately, the alarming news of hostile intent on the part of the ISIs to move against the U.S. fleet in the Indian Ocean, put her back to the wall, her proclamation of "no reaction to an attack," practically a written invitation to those who would choose to tickle the soft underbelly of a neatly-neutered military. And too, that "puppy dog politico" Joe Montgomery's world-wide accusation at the National Press Club, caused every talk-show host and pundit in the nation to launch into a full rhetorical huff and puff. Her ace in the hole, though, for decades, had been the ubiquitous Redman, himself the recipient of a few incoming black balls of his own.

Montgomery's strategy was simple. Given that he could not divulge the "Green Trees" findings relative to the somewhat grotesque wealth of the well-connected, four interrelated aspects of the grime within the beltway provided the significant clues to the expanding puzzle of intrigue and complicity: Cassidy's death, of course, was the master key that had the potential to unlock the enigmas of the Super Pelican missiles to Iran; finding those connected with the sale of the missing nuclear weapons; and the broader issue of the accumulation of vast wealth among the nation's ruling class. Because "Find Cause" and "Green Trees" had, as common denominators, the Redman Institute acting as cash control, the antics of the devious insider were paramount.

The consortium of a dozen senators and congresspersons organized by Montgomery had been provided specific unsettling evidence of the complicity of hundreds of politicians who, in exchange for grossly profitable business arrangements with China and the U.S. arms and technology industries, had accumulated massive personal wealth, the gold flowing mainly into a complicated mix of secret Swiss bank accounts. The "Montgomery troops" consisted of a representative mix of the three political parties, none of whom had apparently so profited.

At the suggestion of Vice Admiral Stan Sarodsy, the senator had holed up following his blockbuster speech in Sarodsy's underground command center, a bunk-room- sized cubicle in stark contrast to his opulent digs at the Watergate. Sarodsy had successfully argued to the senator that he could well be in personal danger. No one on the senator's staff knew his whereabouts, excepting his top aide, Ernie Maltman, now en route to the U.S. aircraft carrier Reagan, a fact of supreme irritation to the President.

The Pentagon command center was focused on the evolving drama of imminent hostilities, the fusion of multiple intelligence sources onto the giant situation screen with its complex web of pulsing lights, graphic symbology and sidebar access to an array of supplementary information. The four Whiskey class submarines were seen underway, working their way in trail, periscopes breaking the surface, toward the opening of the gulf to the Indian Ocean. Four of the Iranian fighters from the nearby Kleski Air Field loaded with two Super Pelican missiles each, had launched, their track and speed vectors to the vast Indian Ocean in full view, status boards at sea and the Pentagon dutifully reflecting their deadly progress.

As the Super Pelican's air-launched range was a nominal 110 nautical miles, the U.S. Navy combat rules of engagement dictated ". . . that if hostile missile carrying aircraft were headed in the general direction of a U.S. ship and penetrated a 125 mile arc, whatever measures deemed necessary by the on-scene commander to protect his forces, shall be taken." Navy battle group F-27C stealth Phantom III fighters were and had been on continuous airborne alert ranging from 200 to 300 miles from the capital ships. Should any hostile forces trespass inside the defensive circle, U.S. fighters would be expected to exercise the ROE, buttressed by the centuries-old general prudential rule of engagement stating ". . . the inherent right of a unit to defend itself."

Sarodsy noted that most all of the thirty-three ships in the Indian Ocean fleet had gone to general quarters, the flashing symbols indicating that the ship's captain had moved their vessel to a maximum state of combat readiness.

Montgomery watched in fascination as the Iranian fighters headed for the USS *Ronald Reagan,* six hundred miles to the southeast, while his host Sarodsy assimilated the displayed data, the hungry bear eyeing the covey of unsuspecting salmon. "Admiral, what's the action? Why the smile?"

"Joe, I need to give you a lecture on fleet defense," he said laconically as the Navy fighters converged to covertly trail the unwelcome intruders.

"Point number one, and most important, is that those four hotshot Iranians have not the slightest notion of the whereabouts of our ships other than somewhere inside a box 1,000 miles on a side. In addition to our forces in the same piece of ocean, there are about seventy-four merchant ships. Without specific targeting parameters, the chances of locking on to one of our carriers is slim." He paused, noting the hostile fighters splitting, one group headed for a Liberian-flagged oil tanker apparently bound for the Orient via the Straits of Malaca, the other towards a Navy frigate, the range to both about 270 miles.

"Second," the admiral continued, " all four are covered by

our fighters in five-mile trail, as you can see. I doubt if the Iranians even know they are being trailed. If they break the 125-mile exclusion zone, the hostiles might just as well start their prayers."

The audio portion of the airborne drama 8,000 miles distant interrupted the tutorial by Sarodsy. "Iranian fighters headed 146 degrees true at 38,000 feet, this is an immediate warning." The satellite link had captured the transmission from the lead U.S. fighter transmitting on frequency 243.0 megahertz, the internationally accepted ultra-high-frequency distress channel. "You are approaching a forbidden area due to missile exercises in progress. If you do not reverse your course within one minute, you will be destroyed. Please acknowledge by an immediate turn or explanation as to your intentions on frequency 243.0 megahertz."

The two Iranians fighters approaching the U.S. warship maintained their heading, not electing to explain their intentions.

At that moment, Stan Sarodsy received an urgent summons deep within his submerged enclave from the leader of his sensitive intelligence unit regarding additional information about "Find Cause." With a casual wave to Montgomery and a, "Be back in few minutes, Joe," he started for the door, only to be interrupted by the flabbergasted senior senator who questioned the judgment of the old warrior in departing the command center at such a critical time.

"Nothing we can do from here. Our Captains know the action," the admiral said, disappearing through a succession of armed guards and locked doors beyond.

"Sir," muttered the dispassionate, bifocal-eyed computer technician and intelligence analyst to Sarodsy, "I think we may have found the *corpus delecti*."

"You mean the wreckage of Cassidy's plane?"

"Yes, sir. You know the final report stated 'cause undetermined' and that the remains were '. . . disposed of to a site where idle curiosity-seekers would not be welcome.' "

"Well," he continued, "one of the Redman Seven was accountable for the wreckage which, following the accident, was transported to a heavily-guarded hangar at Minot Air Force Base in North Dakota for examination. Then, via a containerized truck, it was transported to an abandoned Minuteman missile silo some ninety miles north of Minot. How we obtained this information is of no import. There is no doubt that one of the Redman Seven did, in fact, cause the autopilot G limiter to fail while concurrently commanding an abrupt full nose-up signal to the aircraft flight surfaces. The result was, of course," he continued, still in a tutorial mode, "catastrophic and instant destruction of the aircraft. We have in our possession the black box which will clearly indicate the cause of the crash and point the finger at Mr. 'X.' "

Thoughtfully, the admiral swallowed, his mind sifting the elusive alternatives. This could be the smoking gun that could implicate Richard Redman and perhaps others higher in the food chain. He wished Nancy Chandler was with him, her agile brain, more often than not, a welcome addition to problem solving.

Just as Sarodsy reentered the bustling command center, an agitated Navy CEO, Admiral Carolyn Sweeny, charged the premises. "What's going on? You know we can't shoot, even if provoked, don't you, Stan?" The latter was more a plea than an edict from the Navy's top ranking officer.

"Fox 2. Fox 2," the dispassionate UHF radio transmission from 8,000 miles away drifted into the command center. A moment later, the speed symbols for the two hostile missile-carrying jets, 122 miles from the American frigate, went from 800 knots to zero, the altitude readout decreasing rapidly. "Splash two bandits." The message from the two carrier-based U.S. fighters was without emotion, the job done, time to return to home base.

"What have they done?" screamed Sweeny. "You know they were not supposed to fire! I want their incompetent asses on the chopping block the instant they land!"

Sarodsy kept his cool, his response matter-of-fact. "What are they supposed to do, Admiral? Wait until we lose a frigate with 120 young men and an equal number of young women? They had absolutely no alternatives. To have done anything less would have been a direct disobedience of an order and a clear dereliction of duty."

Noting Senator Montgomery, Sweeny yelled again.

"What are you doing here, Senator? The whole world is looking for you."

Montgomery smiled somewhat sheepishly, the trio interrupted by the sudden arrival of Vice Admiral Sharon McCluskey, the Diversity Chief of the U.S. Navy.

"Hi, Stan. Hi, boss. May I join you?" Sarodsy took his eyes off the situation board.

"Sure, Sharon. Have you met Senator Montgomery?"

The remote radio transmissions from the American fighters broke the impasse. "No chutes and no apparent survivors. Both bandits have hit the ocean and exploded on impact," intoned the anonymous voice, still detached and unemotional, the necessary job done with dispatch.

Concurrently, the four shifted their attention to the remaining two Iranian jets still headed for a hapless Liberian-flagged oil tanker, its name, side-barred on the large screen, the attention-getting "Exxon Valdez II." The symbology switched to an alert mode, signifying that missiles had been fired from both jets.

Sweeny blanched, barely able to talk. "Why didn't you stop that?" she shot at Sarodsy.

"That's not an American-flagged ship, boss. They saw a large target and guessed that it was one of our carriers. Bad move."

Carolyn Sweeny, although a brilliant naval officer, was a product of a Navy weaned on social correctness and feel-good policies. Discounting the relatively benign seventy-eight days on the Kosovo bombing range eleven years ago, in her entire eighteen years of service, her Navy had never fired a shot in anger. Dialogue, stress chits and soft talk had been the main batteries. She had just witnessed an overt hostile act that probably resulted in the death of up to two-dozen seaman. Her woeful response, in a small voice, "What can we do, Stan?"

Joe Montgomery watched with fascination as the drama played out, the naval officers at stark contrast. Sarodsy strode to the situation board. "So far we're OK. I think the ISIs know we mean business by now. Our contingency plan calls for a measured response against one or more Bandar Abas military targets.

We can launch within three hours, given the order."

Sweeny sank lower in her executive chair, her words plaintive. "But Virginia has specifically ordered no military action. She's still the commander in chief, don't forget. We must have her concurrence."

Sensing a need for reality, Sarodsy broke in. "The dominant unknowns are the Chinese. They are the enigma. My guess is that they will side with us. After all, 90% of their strategic national objective is reasonable access to the Caspian oil." He paused, unsure of how to present his next bombshell to the Navy's CEO. "Admiral, Nancy Chandler is en route to meet with General Wong of the Imperial Chinese Air Force as we speak."

Sarodsy knew he had just taken strike two with his designated leader. "Boss, this is fast-moving. I don't have time for conferences or stroking a bunch of staff weenies. We're in this up to our armpits. If we don't have the overt cooperation of the Chinese, we cannot handle the ISIs unilaterally. So far, all the senior State Department folks have managed is a bunch of Monday through Friday hot air. They've gotten nowhere. Sending Nancy was my call. I'll take the hits. But please, let me assure you, we have no choice. General Wong is the top military person in China and wields enormous influence." He waited for the onslaught.

The four were silent, the multi-colored symbols sending a muted message of danger, intrigue and drama. Vice Admiral Sharon McCluskey broke the silence.

"Admiral," she said to the Navy CEO, "I heard, via my White House source, that the President will not only rescind the reserve activation of Western Airline's pilots, but all airline pilots as well. And," she chose her words carefully, "she may return those already called up. My source is convinced she will turn our backs on any military provocation and not respond. She is desperate to avoid actions on our part that could result in any loss of life or injury to our young men and women."

Sarodsy was speechless, McCluskey resigned and Sweeny guarded. It was crunch time and all three knew it. "Time to cut bait," Sarodsy said to himself, glancing at the seasoned senior senator. Joe Montgomery returned a barely perceptible nod. Facing the two women, Sarodsy positioned his ample girth in front of the giant mosaic. "Admiral, I want you to read an 'eyes only' memo written by Nancy Chandler shortly before she left," his aide handing her the only copy of the top secret paper.

Sweeny's eyes scanned the memo, then settled for a repeat, the comprehension level complete. Quietly, in a measured voice, her demeanor braced, she asked, "What's 'Green Trees?' "

For the next hour the three leaders listened to Sarodsy's description of "Green Trees." When finished, Admiral Carolyn Sweeny locked onto the eyes of Sarodsy and articulated the only question she could: "Why did Nancy mention nuclear weapons?"

Montgomery and Sarodsy winced; the rest of the story had to come out. Sarodsy mentally prepared himself for a possible strike three.

Stan Sarodsy zipped open yet another compartment of incredibly sensitive information, the recent findings of "Missing Jewels." "Nancy Chandler had no knowledge of the missing nuclear weapons from the Reagan. I think it was just an honest assessment on her part that, should China possess any such weapons, the balance of power in the world would clearly shift in their favor."

Sweeny, still quietly and deeply introspective, brought the logic trail to the light of day. "So, the recent wealth in the past ten months revealed by your 'Green Trees' program probably came as a result of the sale of the nuclear weapons and the weapons, most likely were destined for China. Correct?"

"Yes, ma'am," said the Navy's combat arms head. Stan Sarodsy then went on to explain the recent mission over the secret Chinese air base in northern Iran. "We know there is at least one of the missing weapons at this base," his laser pointer quivering over the desolate region. As an afterthought, he added, "Probably more."

In the spirit of openness, Joe Montgomery revealed to the two women the political ramifications of the fast-moving events of the past week, McCluskey inquiring as to his recent charges regarding Senator John Cassidy's death. The "Find Cause" conclusions were laid on the command center table. "There is zero doubt as to the cause of Cassidy's premature death nor of the persons who orchestrated it all." The finality of the statement transcended the body politic.

Carolyn Sweeny suddenly realized she was in a hot seat, a seat that was begging for a rational solution. Fact was, the chain of command went directly from the Navy CEO to the president, the result of a 2004 presidential proclamation eliminating all civilian service secretaries, the Joint Staff as well as the Secretary of Defense. Virginia Roberts Stallingsworth had reasoned that as long as she was the commander in chief, why bother with all the intermediaries? Certainly, she could deal with three generals and one admiral, each of whom led their respective service. That she had given scant attention to issues military, excepting a strident and accelerating socialization agenda, had indeed streamlined the decision making, but at a cost of severely limiting the presentation of viable options to America's commander in chief.

At the moment, Richard Redman was in a hot seat of his own, a thoroughly angry Virginia railing at him in a most unladylike vernacular. "What do you mean, you don't know what happened? I thought you knew everything worth knowing in this town."

Redman interrupted, anxious to change the subject. "Have you heard the news about the shoot down?"

"What shoot down?" said the President of the United States, hitting her Oval Office buzzer to summon her chief of staff.

"Madame President," the staffer announced, preempting his boss, "we just got word that the Reagan's fighters have shot down two Iranian fighters over the Indian Ocean."

"GET SWEENY, NOW!" she ordered the casual official, once again in a transmit mode to Redman.

"Richard," she said quietly to her long time confidant, "you know what you have to do." She replaced the phone with trembling anticipation. How many conversations had the two had over the past few years? How many clandestine issues? How

256

many damaged persons the result? Her inner voice was tired and stretched. Richard Redman, she could tell, was worried, notwithstanding his stature, according to Forbes Magazine, as the world's 11th wealthiest person.

To Redman, the "you know what you have to do" did not take a rocket scientist to solve. The practiced art of the cover-up had become a Washington imperative. Begun many years prior, the two, along with a few others, had become the unblemished masters of obfuscation and spin.

Sarodsy's aide burst into the quiet command center, her face flushed. "Ma'am," she gushed at Sweeny, "it's the President." And, in a lower voice, "She chewed me out before I could answer. She's extremely upset."

Sweeny made an instantaneous command decision. "Tell her I'll be there in two minutes. No more or less. Understood?"

Confused and apprehensive, the young aide muttered a thin, "Aye, aye, ma'am."

Sweeny took command. "Here's what I'll tell her," looking squarely at her two top assistants and the senator. "First, we had no choice but to shoot down the enemy. You just don't ask permission when an overtly hostile action is about to take place. Second," she thought for a moment, "we need to execute a punitive strike, most likely at the Bandar Abas complex, and do it fast. Third," she smiled, rising to the fore, "I will strongly recommend that she not rescind the reserve call up, particularly the airline pilots. Lastly, I will, as forcefully as possible, urge that she personally engage Chinese President Jiang on the phone as soon as possible. How's that sound, Stan? Senator?"

Without waiting for a reply, she checked her watch, grabbed the phone from the winsome aide and, in a pleasant voice reeking with assertiveness, said respectfully, "Madame President, please accept my apologies for keeping you waiting. I was just about to call you about the Indian Ocean actions. Do you have a few minutes?"

CHAPTER 20

Barking Dogs Visited

Oh, there are no fighter pilots down in hell
There are no fighter pilots down in hell
The place is full of dears and air force bombardiers
Oh, there are no fighter pilots down in hell

The raucous party down the darkened, tree-lined Virginia Beach street was in full force, the news of the Iranian shoot down only hours before covered practically live by CNN. In the naval aviation game plan, there could hardly be a better excuse for an impromptu bash. The hometown spouses were basking in the full blush of every fighter pilot's dream, the long past epic words of the World War One German ace of aces, Baron Von Richtofen, echoing throughout the tranquil neighborhood: "The duty of the fighter pilot is to shoot down the enemy and anything else is rubbish."

Sandy Anderson and Rick Turner had arrived at the gathering late, their evening having started two hours earlier at the behest of a pleading phone call from her neighbor, the lawyer husband of Lieutenant Becky Turner of the Red Rippers. It was late Friday afternoon, the weekend a welcome respite to Sandy's teaching chores. Rick had really sounded down on the phone, so Sandy, the good neighbor, maternally invited him over so the two could "talk." Much to Sandy's surprise, Rick had arranged for the eighth-grader down the street to take care of his two young ones as well as Sandy's two preschoolers. "What's the harm?" Sandy had rationalized, the recent "girl talk" with Beverly Demming

Boone ringing a siren into the inner sanctum of her psyche. "It has been a long nine months. We need to take care of one another."

The evening had begun innocuously enough, Rick having brought with him a slightly cooled bottle of red wine and two marinating filet mignons, both favorites of Sandy. The talk was, of course, all about the shoot down and how this might affect the return of the Reagan to Norfolk. Soon, though, the excellent wine taking its inevitable course, the conversation eased into the subtleties of the hidden mechanisms and interpersonal relationships of the shipboard-based Red Rippers. Sandy confided to Rick her reservations about the rumors of her husband's roving eyes, a reputation well-known to most, Sandy excepted. Rick, in turn, let loose with the antics of the wife of the Red Ripper maintenance chief, the incorrigible, leather-panted Suzette McCormick.

Sandy and Rick were not only neighbors, they had much in common with one another. Both had been left alone for over eight months, both had two preschoolers and both were quiet, homebody types at heart. Rick had indeed been the surrogate man about the Anderson house, taking care of yards, balky lawnmowers, car problems and occasionally, minding Sandy's kids while she taught school. Of concern to Sandy in the past month or so, though, were the increasingly strident overtures of her friend Rick, advances that transcended their heretofore platonic relationship.

"Sandy," Rick offered, sipping his charged goblet, while the steaks simmered on the gas grill, "that damned Suzette is hounding the hell out of me."

"What do you mean by 'hounding,' Rick?" she asked, holding aloft her glass for a modest refill of the soothing cabernet, the soft gas-log fire permeating the cozy room with a silent ballet of flickering warmth.

"Well, originally she came to me for some legal advice — divorce stuff relating to one of her previous husbands. But then, she kept calling wanting to party. You know," he added gratuitously, with the hint of a smile, "she's really a good-looking woman," the smile turning to a pronounced blush. "The other night, she came by after the kids were in bed and I was very much turned on by her. Hell, Sandy, she practically attacked me in the kitchen. I was OK, but it was hard. I mean — really hard," his demeanor contrite, brow furrowed, the worry obvious.

"What I most wanted to talk about," he continued, the twilight emerging, the sun's rays piercing a last gasp through the autumn leaves, "and I'm embarrassed Sandy, so bear with me — please. OK?"

"Sure, Rick. That's what I'm here for," said the young mother wishing she had dressed more conservatively. She crossed her legs in a futile attempt to eradicate a tingling feeling.

"I know I'm preaching to the choir," said the athletically-conditioned lawyer, "but I'm here to tell you, it's tough. All day, every day, I'm around the opposite sex in my office, half of them made up to a 'T,' most smelling like the latest fragrance mill and, at least a few, who give me the eye like I'm a piece of merchandise." He paused, turning the steaks, the aroma mixing pleasantly with the wine. Softly, emotionally, his back to her, he said, "I love Becky. She's all I ever wanted in life — and my kids — and my home. But," he turned to face the seated Sandy, "she's been gone more in the six years we've been married than she's been home. And," his eyes locked onto hers, "you and Becky are so much alike, it's scary. Except," he whispered, his eyes unmoving, "you are here and she is there."

The quiet interlude, almost intimate, reminded Sandy of her early inquisitive years as the new wife of the swashbuckling Dave Anderson, the aura of her former Blue Angel husband and life away from small-town Pensacola heady reminders of the good life. But, she thought, her eyes breaking the lock of those of her neighbor, life without a husband was tough, too.

Out loud, she asked her friend, the warm glow of the vintage cabernet sauvignon lowering her inner defenses by the barest hint, "Rick, what do you suppose is going on on the ship — in the squadron, I mean," she paused, gathering control, "sexual-wise? Oh, I'm sorry. I should have kept that to myself. Now I'm the one who's embarrassed. Sorry, Rick."

"I wonder too, Sandy. But, fact is, I trust Becky completely. I have no doubt she's a total straight-arrow. That's one reason I'm having such a hard time with my wandering libido," adding gratuitously, "self-control only goes so far, you know."

She sipped the pleasant wine, the searing filets reminders of the kinder and gentler years gone by with her husband. "How about Dave?" she said in a weak voice, the question almost rhetorical.

"Well, Sandy, he lives right near Becky. She's never said anything one way or another, excepting .... ," he stopped, wishing he could retract the last word.

"Excepting what, Rick?" her female antenna striving for the smallest nuance.

"Well, I think she was kidding. It really was no big deal. She simply said that Dave had come on to her one time in the showers. Obviously, nothing happened. She just mentioned it in an e-mail in a fun sort of way just before they were cut off."

The two were quiet, the silent evening broken by the sounds of laughter and loud music emanating from down the street. Rick, breaking the impasse of emotions said, "You know, Sandy," his legally-trained mind in high gear, "there's a hard legal maxim that obviates a dastardly deed in the eyes of the law if the person was unnecessarily provoked. How incredibly stupid to make the berthing and facilities communal. It boggles my mind!"

Sandy smiled. "Rick, you went to UPA, correct? As I recall, the living arrangements only a few years ago were coed — men and women on the same floor and next door to one another — even sharing bathrooms?"

"Sure, no big deal. Same at most all colleges these days."

Sandy laughed. "So what's the problem, hot shot?"

Rick took a break from the increasingly open conversation, leaving the steaks to warm, refilling his glass. "One major difference, my friend," his charismatic grin infectious, "we're not on a warship at sea for nine months with the very real probability of getting blown out of the water at any moment."

Following the steaks and baked potatoes, Sandy suggested a short walk about the comfortable neighborhood. Unconsciously, their hands came together, the glow of the red wine countering the brisk evening. They were both just a bit tipsy, but only pleasantly so. Silently they walked toward the party noises not far down the street.

The couple lingered in front of the modest home in the Kings Grant suburb, the booming music, swaying bodies and the large banner strung between two trees in the front yard proclaiming, "WELCOME TO THE BARKING DOGS, WHERE THE BITE EQUALS THE BARK!"

"Hey Rick, Sandy," said the well-juiced husband of the squadron's executive officer, "come on in. We're celebrating the shoot down. Did you hear?" The voice was the macho husband of the exec of the sister squadron to the Red Rippers aboard the Reagan, his wife the counterpart to Sandy's husband. Sandy knew him by reputation, a notoriety that clearly argued to any female unwilling to take the heat, to stay away from the kitchen.

"The President's going on TV in ten minutes. What are you drinking?" all the while eyeing the well-proportioned Sandy Anderson.

The crisp, night air notwithstanding, the piercing boom boxes surrounding the pool blasted a crescendo of inspirational sounds, the fourteen men and an equal number of women swaying suggestively to one another.

"Come on, honey," squealed the fun-loving, leather-clad, high-heeled, shapely blond to her mustachioed host, "time to wiggle," her hips tracing a random pattern of come-hither enticement, Suzette once again solidly in her environment.

Off in a corner, a trio belted out off-key choruses of long-past naval aviator drinking songs, lyrics that somehow managed to survive the test of time, no matter how ridiculous or specious the content:

> "Hallelujah, hallelujah
>> Throw a nickel on the grass
>>> Save a fighter pilot's ass"

And, equally ludicrous and meaningless, but nonetheless, a tiny piece of the naval aviation mosaic:

"Oh give me operations
    Far out on some lonely atoll
For, I, am, too young to die
    I just want to grow old"

Rick and Sandy stood close, the scene surrealistic. "Just letting off steam, Sandy," he said, sensing her need for some comprehension of the mad scene.

"Yeah, sure. And I'm the Virgin Mary. Would you look at Suzette?"

Rick was indeed eyeballing her, needing no reminder. "She can smell a celebration ten miles away," he said over the pulsating tunes, his arm loosely about her shoulders, her warmth competing with the November chill. "Dance?"

The two eased together, fitting like well-worn gloves, his hand in the small of her back, more protective than suggestive, her head lightly on his shoulder. For both, the stirrings were mutual, senses so long dulled, emerging to a natural state. Her hand crept to the top of his neck, his tighter about her slender waist, the music an afterthought.

"Hey, all you guys, it's Virginia," shouted the macho host, Suzette close aboard, the booming music usurped by the President of the United States striding confidently to the podium. Rick and Sandy, frustrated by the untimely interruption, but thankful nonetheless, moved inside, the mood confused.

"Ladies and gentlemen. We interrupt our regular broadcast to bring to you an important address to the country by our President."

Arranged on the podium in the Map Room of the White House at 9:45 p.m. was an august group representing the nation's leadership. To the President's immediate right, was the Navy's CEO, Admiral Carolyn Sweeney; to her left were the senate majority leader and Senator Joe Montgomery, one of the minority leaders. Arrayed behind and around were the other service chiefs, the leadership of the executive branch and the chief justice of the United States.

Purposefully, solemnly, she walked slowly to each of the twenty or so leaders and shook the hand of each. For a full minute, she peered directly into the CNN world-wide HDTV camera, radiating a confident smile, a persona that reached directly into the living rooms and state capitals throughout the world. She began, characteristically, with no notes, written speech or teleprompters:

"Good evening, my fellow countrypersons and those of you throughout the world. As most of you are aware, our carrier-based fighters in the Indian Ocean have destroyed two Iranian aircraft that demonstrated clear hostile intent to mortally harm one of our frigates engaged in peaceful operations in international waters. I need not remind you that this vessel had on board 120 women — and an equal number of men. If the missiles carried aboard the jets had hit our frigate, I might well have been here at this podium tonight reporting the untimely combat deaths of a large number of vibrant young women and men in the prime of their young lives. Admiral Carolyn Sweeney, the Navy's senior naval officer, has just finished briefing me on the situation in the Indian Ocean and the Caspian Sea areas. It is her reasoned judgment, one with which I agree totally, that we have no choice but to prove our steadfast resolve to the Iranians, indeed the ISIs, that we, as a nation, will not tolerate hostile intent by any nation. Thank you for the applause. Accordingly, as your commander in chief, I have ordered Admiral Sweeney to take appropriate and measured retaliatory measures as she may see fit, at the earliest opportunity, with the proviso that there be no American casualties."

This time the applause in the somber room, the scene of many memorable national emergencies, erupted with even more vigor, the cameras panning to the obvious exuberance of the politicos. The President continued, her head high.

"Additionally, I have asked the Admiral to provide

264

appropriate recognition to the aviators involved in this extraordinary act of courage in the face of immense danger. The 'Barking Dogs' of U.S. Navy Fighter Squadron 143 have added yet another cluster to their already superb combat reputation."

Immediately, the temporary respite at the shore-side home of the Barking Dogs erupted with a crescendo of "Ruffs" and "Grrrrs," the ridiculous sounds understood only by those of similar ilk. Suzette McCormick did not understand, but took the opportunity to plant a lip-lock on her hapless, albeit willing partner in Fun City.

Virginia, as was her style, asked with an effusive smile, if any of the press corps had questions. The first: "Madame President, how many carrier battle groups have we in the region as of today?"

Without hesitation, she answered, "Five and one more on the way."

"What, ma'am, is our strategic objective?"

Typically, she responded with a three-minute tutorial that articulated lucidly the whys and wherefores of our substantial military seaborne forces in the region.

Sandy felt herself snuggling closer to the young lawyer and husband of her friend, so clearly in harm's way a half-world distant, the two drawing mutual comfort from one another.

The drama in the White House played out, the next question totally unexpected. "Senator Montgomery, what is the basis for your alarming accusations concerning the death of Senator John Cassidy two years ago?" The briefing room became deathly quiet. The cameras zoomed to Montgomery, his face masking surprise at the question, his nimble brain cranking out the appropriate reply.

"Senator, would you answer the question, please?" said the President of the United States.

"Yes, Madame President," he responded, striding purposefully to the White House podium.

"My friends," said the still-youthful senator, "this is a time of great peril for our nation, indeed the world. It is inconceivable that we allow rogue powers to dictate by force the allocation of scarce energy assets to a needy world. Without reservation, I support — and will so urge my seven colleagues on our minority side of the aisle — to support the strategic and military decisions reached by President Stallingsworth. Accordingly, I will make no comments at this time regarding the untimely death of my friend and compatriot, John Cassidy."

Before he could leave the podium, another question. "Sir, you made some thinly-disguised statements regarding the source of the considerable wealth of a large number of politicians and arms-industry leaders. Would you elaborate, please?"

With his characteristic aplomb, the senator retraced his steps, glanced at the President and said confidently with the barest hint of a smile, "I promise you more information on this issue, rather than less, and sooner, rather than later. Pending a resolution of this crisis, I am hereby postponing the committee hearings into both of these matters."

With a wave and bright smile, the President put her arm around the Navy's CEO and left the room, scattered applause drifting after her.

As if on cue, the boom boxes in the Virginia Beach suburb came to life, the sensual swaying to and fro even more energetic, the resounding presidential recognition to the Barking Dogs, fodder for a wide-open relaxation of any latent inhibitions.

Rick was practically ambushed by a panting Suzette, who had just noticed him. "OK Sandy?" he asked as the two broke into an instant lock-step to the blasting beats.

"Hi, Sandy." It was her nemesis, the ex-Blue Angel turned airline pilot, sidling up behind her, his intentions overt. "Dance?"

"No. Please leave me alone."

"No way, gorgeous. Your husband is doing it. Why not you?" That he had clearly had too much to drink was of no solace to the confused young wife. Suddenly, he grabbed her, thrusting himself towards her supple body. She screamed above the cadence. "RICK!"

In a heartbeat, Rick had disengaged from the overloaded appetite of Suzette and had flung the former Navy fighter pilot aside, the shaken Sandy safe for the moment. "The lady said NO. NO MEANS NO," adding unnecessarily, "You worthless son of a bitch."

Rick Turner was no macho man, but at 5 feet 11 inches and 160 lean pounds, his spring was wound tight. He could have licked time-and-a-half his own weight. Opportunely, the host stood between the two would-be antagonists. "He meant no harm, Rick. Did you, Sam? Leave her alone," his ample fist clenched, the message clear and unequivocal. "Understood?"

"Come on Sandy, let's split," Rick's arm even more protectively around her. Quietly, they walked in the chilly night, hands held tight. Approaching her front door, he said guardedly, somewhat fearfully, "Sandy, the kids are all asleep. Yours might as well spend the night at my house rather than wake them. I'll take care of them, if that's OK with you."

"Sure. Sounds good." She opened her door slowly, the warm house uncharacteristically quiet, the remnants of the wine beckoning, the two glasses inviting, the fire in a low flicker. Hesitatingly, softly, her voice thin, she said, "Nightcap, Rick?"

"How about you and I relieving the babysitter first?" he said. "She has to be home no later than ten. Has a meeting or something in the morning."

"Hi, Mrs. Anderson, Mr. Turner. All's well here. The kids had a ball together. Never stopped 'til lights out about nine. Sounds like a good party down the street."

"Thanks, Regina. You were a jewel to come on such short notice. Don't you dare go near that bunch. In fact," Rick said, handing her a crisp twenty dollar bill, "I'll walk you home."

The four little ones were sprawled at all angles on the queen-sized bed of Rick and Becky, blissfully ignorant of the swirling sea of conflict, emotion and complications around them, secure in a home of love and stability.

The two moved nervously to the family room, the ornate wedding picture of Becky and Rick the centerpiece, neither daring to shatter the fragile emotional stand-off. Rick broke the silence.

"It felt good dancing with you. Did it for you?"

"Rick, without question, it felt better than good. It was wonderful. And thanks for coming to the rescue of a damsel in imminent distress. You're a good man," leaning her head once again lightly on his shoulder.

The next minute was a blur of desire, frantically starved hands and hungry lips, her blouse giving way to a higher calling. As if on a distant signal though, the two separated, the built-in moral compasses pointing in the same direction.

"Sorry, Sandy."

"No, Rick. I'm sorry as well. It's just as much my fault," said the woman, self-consciously rebuttoning her top. "We've got a lot to live for. Let's call it a night. I'll see you in the morning. And Rick. It's been a wonderful evening. Thank you," she said quietly, her arm on his. So, with her head erect, she returned to her home, her unseen tears of frustration and sadness reflected in the aching young facade of her neighbor three doors away.

No sooner had she locked her door, than the phone rang. Warily, Sandy answered, fearing it might be Rick with second thoughts. It was Beverly Demming Boone. "Where have you been? I've tried you several times. I was worried sick."

"Thanks, Beverly. I"m fine. Rick and I were out for a walk."

"Did you hear about the shoot down? And the President's speech?"

Without responding, Sandy recalled the conversation she and Beverly had had just two days ago regarding temptation and men. "Beverly, I need to talk. Can I come over now?"

"Sure, I'm wide awake. Come right over."

Her call to Rick was simply to let him know she was going to talk to the long-time wife of the skipper of the USS *Ronald Reagan* and not to worry. For a moment, though, when he first answered, the latent chemistry started its magical potion, the real reason for the call a relief to both.

"Sandy, you look like you've been in a knock-down, drag-out fight. What's going on?" queried Beverly Boone a few minutes later as Sandy entered the nearby, friendly Summerset Lane home.

The next hour was all female talk, Sandy recounting in graphic detail the events of the past four hours, focusing on her near disastrous loss of control. "Beverly, I know it's going to happen again. Just too damned much temptation. If both of us had not capitulated at the same time, the outcome would have been much different, I know."

Reluctantly, Beverly decided to confide in Sandy. "I've got problems of my own. It must be the next-door-neighbor syndrome."

She let her words sink in. Sandy asked. "Bill Montrose?"

"Same song, Sandy. Just different lyrics. Tonight he was picked up by Dolores Miller. You remember her — at the spouse gathering two nights ago? They swished off in a long, black limo and frankly, I'm embarrassed to admit, I felt a twinge of jealously. Can you believe it? What a world," glancing out the front window, "they're still not back."

Sandy laughed, the pressure off. "Well, so what? He's just a neighbor," she reasoned, realizing too late that what was good for the goose was good for the gander. Then, in a controlled voice, "Bev, are the men and women in our squadron having the same problems as we are? I mean, after all, we can shut the door and disappear for a few hours or days or weeks. They're trapped. Their next-door syndrome is only a thin steel wall."

"Tommy's talked to me about it — very privately. He's concerned, you bet. Has been for ten years. In his own way, he's spoken out, but adherence to the Navy's party line is job one, as you may or may not know. What I'm not so confident with though, is the degree to which the folks on the ship are in synch with our life here in Kings Grant." She added as an afterthought, "If they're not, they ought to be. You and Rick are a case in point."

Irreverently, Sandy Anderson broke in. "Well, they should be. My guess is that hanky-panky on the home front is a lot more prevalent than most folks in the high command would like to admit. You should have seen those bunch of wild left-behinds at the Barking Dogs. Not one connected husband and wife at the party. I think it's out of control. The longer the ship stays out, the worse it gets." She sighed. "I suppose the stress of being gone so long and the danger has taken a toll on redefining normal moral behavior."

Laughingly, the two started in on a growing litany of "Suzette" tales, her latest target, the husband of the Barking Dogs' exec. Beverly grimaced with the recollection of the husband-and-wife team on Reagan, he the skipper of the squadron and she, the ship's executive officer and right-hand person to her husband. "I'm not so sure how that's working out. From the little I've heard from Tommy, she spends literally all her time on ship stuff and he, of course, is fully occupied as the skipper of the squadron. Tommy's never seen them together and neither apparently speaks to the other. It makes me wonder how the 'studly' Rock Batori gets along with his exec whose shore-based husband's libido is in perpetual heat, the incorrigible Suzette, only the latest in a long string of easy conquests."

Sandy, shook her head. "Oh, my. It's too complicated for me. Think I'll turn in and do my best to avoid Rick for the rest of the weekend. Would you come with me when I pick up the kids in the morning at his house, please?"

Dousing the porch light, Beverly noted the long black limo parked in front, silent, the shaded windows obscuring whatever activity inside. She recalled the offer of the wife of the Reagan's weapons officer of extremely generous educational scholarships for the offspring of the ship's enlisted personnel. Almost as an aside, she remembered the off-hand comments of Sandy recounting the tale Rick had told her in confidence as an ". . . unbelievable amount."

For a few moments, she watched the limo from the security of her darkened bedroom windows until jerked back to reality by the strident headlines of the CNN late-night news:

- PRESIDENT ORDERS PUNISHMENT BY U.S. NAVY
- MONTGOMERY SUPPORTS PRESIDENT
- CASSIDY HEARINGS DELAYED

CHAPTER 21

With God's Help

"FLASH/TOP SECRET:
From: Combat Arms Directorate, Navy Staff, Pentagon
To: Commanding Officer, USS Reagan, CVN 76
Subject: Retaliatory Strikes
Classification: Top Secret for Captain Boone
1. The President has directed limited punitive strikes against the Iranian submarine piers at Bandar Abas and the Kleski Air Field. Objective: Destroy the NW 200 meters and adjacent support structures at Bandar and the SW hangar and aircraft parking apron at Kleski. Percent probability of kill to be 94% or higher. Minimize collateral damage. Use assets available within the battle group, including, but not limited to, sub-and surface-launched missiles, embarked stealth fighter assets and satellite-selected jamming as directed by the staff of Rear Admiral Nancy Chandler.
2. Report results via K5c satellite links ASAP.
3. Admiral Sweeney joins with me in wishing you good hunting. Vice Admiral Sarodsy sends with respect."

The unexpected early morning general quarters had sent a sobering message throughout the tense warship. Coming on top of the captain's clearly invasive anti-social dictates late the night before, the formidable aircraft carrier struggled to unshackle from years of permissive people and standards policies, guidelines that were more like a college campus than a front-line, killing combat machine.

"Men and women of the Reagan, this is your Captain speaking. Give me your undivided attention please." He paused, the quiet permeating the speeding warship. "Early this morning four Iranian fighters exhibited clear hostile intent. Two which did intrude into forbidden air space were quickly destroyed by our own VF-143 Barking Dogs. Just a few minutes ago, I have learned that the President has directed the Reagan battle group to strike selected targets ashore. My intention is to launch such attacks within two hours. Given that we may expect retaliatory responses, including submarine attack, I urge each of you to commit totally to the task at hand. Carry on."

Iron Lady Montrose was in total turmoil. When the general quarters alarm had unexpectedly sounded, she and Master Chief Randy McCormick had been engaged in conference behind the closed door of her stateroom, ostensibly for an in-depth discussion of squadron maintenance issues.

McCormick, a seasoned veteran of twenty-seven years of mostly shipboard service, was the quintessential team player. When his commanding officer had called, he was johnny-on-the-spot, the summons earlier in the evening not atypical.

Wendy Montrose, for the first time in almost nine months, did not have maintenance issues totally in mind. Her freshly-brushed hair and lavender fragrance had contrasted sharply with the sweat-stained and bearded persona of her hard-working maintenance chief. The stateroom's unusual ambience was duly noted by the stoic Red Ripper insignia — peering down from the barren bulkhead — the boar's nose almost quivering with disbelief.

Providently, after only a minute or so, the jarring clang of the ship's general quarters alarm had brought an instant and unexpected reality, McCormick and Montrose out the door in fifteen seconds, knowing that any hesitation could be fatal. The double thumps of the starboard bow catapult soon thereafter were tactile reminders that the two Ripper five-minute alert fighters were airborne. Except for those actually in the air, all flight crews were assembling in the squadron ready room, half already snoozing in

272

their traditional, leather-covered chairs.

In her tiny office adjacent to the ready room, Commander Wendy Montrose was deep in meditation, this time focused on the business of running a combat shipboard fighter squadron with a host of complications. She had 14 F-27C stealth jets, of which 13 were in a ready-for-action status. Her main concern was the flight crews. Normally personed with 15 pilots and an equal number of wizos, the past few months had taken a toll. She mentally ticked off her concerns:

- Lori Miller — Lots of problems. No fly with Anderson.
- Evelyn Swagger — Still recovering in sick bay.
- Studs Newman — Presumed dead.
- Susan Anthony — Grounded due to landing problems.
- Shorts Flanagan — Medically grounded.
- Three others — Not available.

A knock on the door. "Can I see you for a few minutes, Skipper?" said a respectful and somewhat contrite acting executive officer of the Red Rippers.

"Sure, Dave. Come in. I was just going over the list of which flight crews were available. We've got problems."

"I know. That's what I wanted to talk to you about," said Anderson.

"Skipper, Lori Miller is out of control. You know I had to switch the lead to Big Sister on the rescue mission because that worthless excuse for a naval officer sat in the back seat like a dormant lump. There is no way I'll fly with her again. Period. End of subject!" He added softly, respectfully, "How about me and Shorts teaming up again — please?"

"Dave, I understand. That's part of my problem. Got a call from the Doc an hour ago. Looks like your illustrious roommate may have boogied once too often. Doc grounded her. Says she's been having fainting spells and blacked-out a couple of times in the air."

"Shit," was the erudite comment by Anderson.

"Well, there's more, Skipper," he continued. "Big Sister has confided to me that her wizo, Scott Jacobs, and your Pete Dawkins are engaged in a manly contest over Patty Butts. Won't speak to one another. Becky said Scott hardly slept — tossed and turned all night."

"What a crock of baloney. Just what we don't need," sighed the squadron CO, feeling once again the pervasive pressures of her non-traditional job.

"There's more, ma'am. Don't ask me the sordid details, but Ensign Karen Randolph — you know, lives in paradise, one of the ship's OODs — is the target of Pete and Panky Pachino. Lots of interpersonal intrigue down there, for sure. More than we need," offered the fatigued pilot.

With that, Montrose raised her eyebrows. "Do you count yourself as one of the protagonists in paradise, Blues?"

Down below in paradise, shortly before the strident clangs of the ship's general alarm, Major Ying Tsunami had been in a fitful sleep in the stateroom of Lieutenant Evelyn Swagger, when he was startled to find the bathrobe-clad owner rummaging about in a set of drawers. Sensing the unknown, she flipped on the overhead lights to discover a chagrined Tsunami in Sam Newman's top bunk.

"Sorry to wake you, Major. Susan Anthony said you might be here. Temporarily, that is. I needed some underwear. I'll just be a moment." Ying was speechless, transfixed by the young aviator. She paused. "Susan says you saved my life. I am grateful, sir. Thank you."

Still covered, he muttered, somewhat formally, "I am Ying, Major Ying Tsunami. Sorry about your pilot. I hope to be back in my squadron before the day is out. You know you were very sick. You ought not to be up." The words came fast and confused from the Chinese pilot.

She smiled, a smile that despite her harrowing, near-fatal crash, was genuinely warm. "You speak excellent English. Well, sir, allow me to offer a belated welcome to paradise. Please, go back to sleep. Perhaps we could talk later," she said softly to the lean pilot, still horizontally uncomfortable in the top bunk. "If you don't mind, I'll catch a cat-nap in my bunk."

Above the constant sounds of an underway warship,

Ying could hear the muffled sobs of Evelyn Swagger as she futilely attempted to erase the trauma of the past forty-eight hours.

Lights out, the austere room was silent, the two burdened with mountains of competing emotions. "Evelyn," he said still on the top bunk, "you know we met before your crash?"

"Oh, really?"

"Yes. I was the pilot who flew alongside your jet three days ago. You took off your oxygen mask and smiled at me."

"Oh, my God. Ying, how embarrassing. Yes, I do recall." And with a girlish chuckle, "If you could have smelled my breath, you'd have had second thoughts."

Ying feared to move, the room once again hushed, the mood confused, the room's aroma permeating his every pore. I cannot believe that I am aboard the signature combat warship of the U.S. Navy only three feet above the most beautiful woman I have ever seen, he thought, eyes shut, brain askew.

The abrasive clang of the ship's general quarters alarm only minutes later, rousted the two, Ying practically landing on top of the still-frail Evelyn. "No need for us to move, Ying. Everyone here will go to our ready room to await further orders. We'd just be in the way, I'm afraid."

Ying broke the silence, standing awkwardly, his newfound roommate stunningly gorgeous despite no make-up, tousled hair and still-wane appearance. He said, "I understand you lost your baby in the ejection? You know you were close to a goner. I'm sorry. Why were you flying if you were expecting, may I ask?" the question more professional than personal.

"Ying, I was well along and had no business flying. We kept it a secret, Sam and I. We took all the precautions, but it happened. Not supposed to. Problem is that our squadron is short of aviators and I didn't want to be a part of the problem." To herself, she thought she felt pretty good. Maybe I can get back in the air in a day or so, and, out loud, "Sam would have been proud of me."

"Ying, are you dressed?" It was his escort officer, the recently grounded Susan Anthony knocking at the stateroom door. "Oh, Evelyn, I didn't know you were here. How are you feeling?

You're looking good. I'm Susan. Mike and I live next door — just got aboard three days ago. Got recalled from American Airlines, flown twice and nearly killed myself both times. Skipper has grounded me for a while 'til I get my act together." With a slight smile, she offered, "Sure is tougher than monitoring the automatic systems of a giant people-hauler."

The threesome stood for a few moments in the austere room, except them, paradise empty, the vibrant throbbing of the warship reminding them of the finality of their fragile environment. Ying, though, was having a hard time, the closeness of the two young women in the tiny stateroom, a distraction to his warrior-self. "Evelyn, you know Susan and I trained together in advanced flight training in Kingsville, Texas a few years back."

"Ha, no wonder you speak English better than me," she said with a wholesome chuckle.

Susan broke in. "If you would like, Ying, my skipper, through the carrier's Captain, has authorized me to admit you to our strike-planning process in combat operations."

"Wow, would I ever," he said, his war-fighting ethic once again in control, mundane personal issues seamlessly eased to the back-burner.

With another confident smile to Ying, Evelyn Swagger was off, "To see the Doc about getting back in the air."

"She's unbelievable, Susan. Forty-eight hours ago, she was at death's door."

"That she is, my old friend. Let's hit the strike-planning."

"Lead the way, MA," he countered with a newly discovered sense of energy and enthusiasm.

Lieutenant Becky Turner greeted them at the entrance to the highly-classified spaces. "Major, nice to meet you. Heard some good vibes about you," her eyes deep into his, her hand-shake firm. "Captain says you're cleared for everything. Good timing. We've just received a strike order. We launch in 1+45 hours. Here, let me introduce you to some of our strike team — Ensign Patty Butts, intelligence officer; my wizo, Scott Jacobs; our squadron exec and my boss, Lieutenant Commander Dave

Anderson; his wizo, Shorts Flanagan" — the latter, Ying recalled graphically, the winsome young woman who had squeezed by him in the paradise passageway only a few hours before and who, once again, offered him a firm handshake and gracious smile; "Pete Dawkins, our skipper's wizo; and, finally, Mike Anthony, Susan's better half."

The meeting chemistry would have baffled a resident psychologist. The group was homogeneous, no new-guy syndrome. It was warrior-to-warrior, aviator-to-aviator. Ying was impressed by this eclectic group, all of whom, of course, were naval aviators above all else, Ying included.

Becky provided an overview: "Pete Dawkins is standing in for the skipper, who will be the overall strike leader for the Red Rippers. She will lead one cadre of eight fighters designated 'Iron Strike;' Lieutenant Commander Dave Anderson will lead three more with the call sign 'Blue Cover.' Target for the Rippers is this hangar complex at Kleski Air Field, eighteen miles northeast of the port of Bandar Abas." The large satellite display zoomed to the airfield. "Within three hours, this real estate will be rubble, along with the twenty or so fighters nearby. Our objective, of course, is limited. We could easily destroy the entire air base if so ordered. This tract within the red hue is our responsibility. And don't forget, our orders dictate that collateral damage will be zero, thus all weapons must impact within this area," she emphasized, pointing her laser to the target confines.

Ying, the most combat experienced of the group, asked, "Are these attack options preplanned?"

"Yes, sir. They come from our carrier group planners in the Pentagon. We simply adapt them through interactive programming to our specific needs."

"How about air defenses?"

"See the amber circles, sir? These are specific targets covered by our submarine and surface ship-launched missiles."

"Jamming?" Tsunami snapped, his combat senses in a high, no-nonsense mode.

"Satellites mainly with our on-board assets catching any threats that slip through."

On the bridge of the speeding warship, Captain Tommy Boone was apoplectic, the target of his ire a call that a carrier-on-board-delivery aircraft was inbound to the ship. "Who in God's name sent a COD to us at this time? What stupidity!" From deep within, the nameless voice crackled through the old "bitch box" intercom system. "Says it's a high-priority potentate, priority two, sir."

"Karen," he said, turning to his diminutive officer of the deck, Ensign Karen Randolph, "we'll take the COD downwind. We've got to make our launch point for the strike. Can we do it?"

Punching an assortment of buttons on her bridge computer, the OOD gave a tired but sprightly, "Can do, sir."

Boone hit the direct line to his executive officer, Commander Angela Batori at her general quarters station far forward in the bow just beneath the flight deck. Traditionally called secondary conn, it was physically separated enough from the bridge, that should the captain be wiped out, the exec could fight the ship from the alternate site.

"Angela, how's it going?"

"OK, sir. We had the ship buttoned up in less than five minutes — a new record for us. I think your words last night took effect."

Angela Batori was uncomfortable for the first time with her captain. Her orderly, of course, had told her of the late night visit by the captain only hours earlier to her stateroom office complex. "Sorry I missed you last night, sir. I was with Stan Miller working out the details of the strike weapons loading."

"OK, Angela. No problem." And, on a spur, "How's Rock doing?" speaking of her husband, Commander Rock Batori, the skipper of the Barking Dogs. "They did themselves proud a few hours ago, for sure."

"Captain, I hate to say it, but I have not seen Rock for a few days. We're both up to our armpits, as you know."

"Sure, Angela. Understood. And XO?"

"Sir?"

"My guess is that we can expect retaliation within twenty-four hours after we launch our strikes. We need to ensure all hands are as fresh as possible. Max rest is paramount, insofar as you can manage."

Angela Batori thought back to the meeting she and the ship's weapons officer had had a few hours ago. The "conferences" had become more prevalent of late, the older, ex-enlisted Miller a font of strength and real deck-plate experience. Late last night, she had met with Miller in his stateroom down the passageway, ostensibly for business. Miller, she suspected, had been celibate for months. Fact be known, she and Rock had been husband and wife in name only. Lord only knows what he and that cutesy, next-door-neighbor squadron exec of his have been up to, she mused, a poor, last-ditch attempt at latent rationalization.

What had happened was a quickie, a one-time diversion. She tried to excuse her behavior by blaming other factors, a pattern replicated years earlier as one of the early female, carrier-based combat pilots. In the starkness of the ship's secondary conn, she could not blame her loss of self-control on the weather, the food or the noise. The only cause was herself.

On the flight deck of the speeding warship, hundreds of women and men were spotting airplanes, hauling weapons and fueling. The "Air Boss" announced over the booming topside PA system, "COD in the groove. MAKE A READY DECK."

With a solid crunch and whir of the expanding arresting cable, the svelte C-77 long-range cargo and passenger airplane slammed to a stop, its one passenger replaced by six obviously expectant young crew members waving a tearful goodbye to five confused young men.

Ernie Maltman stepped onto the flight deck, the familiar smells and sounds causing a finite increase in his heart rate, his juices flowing, the challenge and danger of combat carrier duty in contrast to his mundane civilian staff duties of the past few years.

"Mr. Maltman. Welcome aboard, sir. I'm the exec, Angela Batori. The Captain would like for you to meet with him and Admiral Demming in the flag quarters immediately. As you can see, we're busy. Launching strikes in an hour."

"Thanks, XO. Please lead the way."

"Admiral Demming, good to see you, sir," said the rumpled senatorial aide. "You're looking well. And Captain Boone. You, too, sir. I envy what you are doing," sensing the vibrancy of the pulsating warship.

"Admiral, Captain, Admiral Sarodsy asked that I brief you personally on the emerging political situation in and about Washington. What I will say is intended for your eyes and ears only and is, of course, extremely sensitive."

For the next fifteen minutes, Ernie Maltman provided an overview to the seasoned warriors regarding the enormous amounts of money revealed by the "Green Trees" findings, the astounding revelations of Cassidy's untimely death and the missing nuclear weapons under the rubric of "Missing Jewels." Boone was nonplussed, his sense of the political simplistic. Demming, though, gave cause to an outburst along the lines of ". . . it doesn't surprise me one bit" and ". . . damned politicians."

"The pragmatic reality of all this, gentlemen," the former Navy fighter-pilot-turned-congressional-aide continued, "is we need to convince China to move against the ISIs and to join us in so doing. Senator Montgomery, along with many others on all three sides of the aisle, is convinced that if we fail to draw a line in the sand in this instance, the world will beat itself into an energy-seeking frenzy never before experienced. And," he paused, collecting his fatigued thoughts, "Admiral Demming, you and I are to proceed to meet with General Wong of the Imperial Chinese Air Force in Chunking as soon as practicable," he smiled, "if not sooner."

Maltman continued. "Admiral, sir. Admiral Sarodsy asked you to call him on your personal phone to clarify the latest marching orders. He and Senator Montgomery are in synch with what needs to be done both militarily and politically. He wants, as does my boss, for you all to realize that the top objective of the Washington leadership is not to rock the boat, starting with the President. The existing system has been good for them."

Captain Boone broke in. "Ernie, I've only got a minute. You know we're launching a forty-jet strike in an hour. One question. "Any word on the missing nukes?"

"No, sir. As best I know, they're still unaccounted for."

"Thanks. Got to run."

"Admiral Demming," Ernie broke the silence in the confines of the comparatively ornate flag quarters, "you've had a rough few days since we were together in the Pentagon."

"Yeah. That said, however, it sure beats sitting in that over-stuffed chair of mine back in Virginia Beach. It's heady to be out here in the action. Gets my heart rate up. How about you?"

"Same with me. I really have missed all the challenge and excitement. Staff stuff doesn't hold a candle to this. Sir, do you suppose we could visit the Red Ripper ready room? Once a Ripper, always a Ripper."

"Well, I don't see why not. Perhaps Major Tsunami could join us as well. You'd relate to him. Captain said he had the run of the ship."

Entering the rear door to ready room one up forward just beneath the starboard bow catapult, the eyes of the old sea dog danced from the briefing conducted by Lieutenant Becky Turner to the twenty-two assembled aviators, to the worried facade of Ensign Karen Randolph and finally, in the rear of the room, to the squadron skipper and flight surgeon, deep in spirited conversation. No one noticed the old warrior and his younger civilian-clad compatriot as they slipped unobtrusively into a quiet corner.

Dr. Rose Johnson was shaking her head, "Skipper," she argued to Iron Lady, "no way on both counts. Only forty-eight hours ago, Evelyn Swagger was near death's door. She needs time to recuperate. And Shorts is most likely pregnant. I took a chance on Swagger. I'll not make the same mistake twice. They are grounded, period," said the assertive Doc to her senior.

Montrose walked to the front of the ready room, taking over the briefing details from Big Sister. Rose was melancholy, wrapped up in the complexities of the interpersonal relationships of the squadron. Her denial to allow Bikini and Shorts to fly, she knew, meant the squadron would field only eleven aircraft instead of the required twelve. She correctly surmised that the admiral in Washington would go totally bonkers when she discovered the reason. Her job, though, she correctly rationalized, was medical, not combat, notions reflected in her ever-thickening behavioral medical journal focusing on the interpersonal relationships within combat warships deployed for extended periods.

The most recent journal entry had been a vignette entered late the night before, the tearful entreaties of a distraught Lieutenant (junior grade) Nancy Flanagan, the catalyst. She had penned:

"LT(jg) Flanagan (call sign 'Shorts') asked if I could meet with her in sick bay at 2330, complaining of early-morning sickness and temporary black-outs while maneuvering in the air. When questioned about her periods, she admitted she had missed only one. Turns out, she is indeed pregnant. I therefore had no option but to ground her and report the fact to the Red Ripper CO. Much like the hundreds of others who have become pregnant on this almost nine months of deployment, Flanagan is in total denial and feels she has let the squadron down. She wants to keep flying, saying 'the Rippers need me.' The progenitor? 'Well, Doc, I'm not sure. How am I to know?' "

Noticing Ying Tsunami joining Admiral Demming and Ernie Maltman in the rear of the ready room, her medical self took over. "How are you two feeling? Looking good, except, Ying, you look a bit tired. Doing OK?"

"Sure, Doc. Didn't sleep too well. Evelyn seems to be doing much better though. Says she wants to aviate."

"Aviate, my rear end. She's got a good three days of rest and recuperation."

After a pause, the briefing details by the squadron CO continuing, Ying quietly asked the flight surgeon, "Doc, may I see you, please, in private, for a few moments?"

"Sure, Ying. How about we grab the skipper's office next door?"

"Doc, can this be in confidence?"

"Absolutely, no problem."

"It's Evelyn Swagger," he began. "You may not know this, but three days ago she and I met — in the air. She removed her mask and smiled at me. I have never seen anyone more beautiful. And, in the mountains, when I held her body close to mine, emotions I've never had roiled through me like a tornado. Then, an hour ago, in her stateroom, I felt like I was in a trance, floating on air." He paused, at a loss for the direction of his thoughts.

"I'll leave the ship in a few hours. I must return to my squadron. But," he added plaintively and softly, almost reluctantly, "I don't want to leave Evelyn. I think she needs me."

"Ying, trust me, please. I know how you're feeling. We've had literally hundreds of such confessions within our ship since leaving Norfolk. Medical fact is, the young men want to be protective and the women to lean. It's totally normal."

"Well, Doc," he took a deep breath searching for the right inflection, "how do you in the U.S. Navy manage to achieve the warrior ethic? In my squadron, there are no distractions — ever. My pilots live, eat and breathe the combat mission. In our spare time, we study. My area of concentration is, for example, your Navy's combat operational tactics and methodologies. I've got the next five chapters of my journal awaiting my attention."

Rose asked the rhetorical question. "I think I know the answer, but what is it in particular about the U.S. Navy that puzzles you the most?"

"No question, Doc. It all started at the Naval Academy and flight training. It's women. What's a huge enigma to me and many in our air force, General Wong included, is the drastic feminization of your combat units. Something has to give. Look, I've been aboard less than twenty-four hours and I myself have felt emotions long dormant. I sense there are a bundle of such feelings in constant random orbits around this ship. Doc," he knew he had to stop, "look at paradise. It's like happy hour after the Army/Navy game in Philadelphia. Except it never ends."

The remarkable *tête à tête* was abruptly interrupted by

the uncompromising order through the ancient squawkbox in the ready room demanding, "PILOTS, PERSON YOUR JETS."

Iron lady was first out the door, followed by twenty-one Red Ripper aviators, her parting words, "Let's get 'em, guys!"

Admiral Demming, Tsunami, Maltman and Susan Anthony made their way to the bridge to observe the launch of thirty-nine fighters. To the uninitiated, the flight deck was a scene of mad pandemonium. To Captain Tommy Boone, though, it was poetry in motion. Each of the jets had been fueled, moved to a predetermined deck spot, armed and readied for flight by a couple hundred young women and men in a mosaic of reds, yellows, browns, purples and greens, each signifying a combat specialty. Each of the Rippers poised about the two bow catapults were armed with four of the latest 2,000-pound, multi-seeker, air-to-ground weapons, along with a deadly mix of air-to-air missilery and internal cannon, the latter capable of firing a one-inch-in-diameter projectile at the rate of 143 rounds per second.

Arrayed behind the skipper were Dave Anderson's three jets with a double load of air-to-air missiles.

Although there were a dozen or more radios on the bridge, they were all silent. Thirty-nine aircraft would launch, rendezvous, head feet-dry, hit the assigned target, refuel, return to the ship, and land, with no electronic transmissions of any sort. Ying was charged by the quiet and total sense of professionalism. It was the way he had trained as a naval aviator ten years prior, the overwhelming sense of discipline setting the wings of gold apart from their lesser-demanding, shore-based kinfolk.

Vice Admiral Bruce Demming was in a quiet corner of the bridge, his arm around his tearful number-two daughter, Susan. "Daddy, I'm all torn up inside. I ought to be out there," her face visibly flinching at each firing of the four catapults as they methodically flung their charges skyward, only to be sucked up by the rotten weather, the angry sea but two heartbeats below each jet. "You know, I never worried about Mike, but I have a premonition," the tears welling more profoundly. "Damn it, he likes it. He's in his element. I should be with him."

The graying admiral wisely chose to say nothing.

Ying Tsunami stood beside the captain's elevated chair on the bridge, the timer ticking off the seconds to launch completion, four aircraft each minute the standard. The launch had been scheduled on the hour, the first two jets careening down the number-one bow catapult and number-four waist cat as the second hand hit twelve o'clock. Ten tumultuous minutes later, the flight deck was silent, the big warship heeling to a sharp ten degrees within moments of the last airplane's roar and catapult thump, the confident officer of the deck — whom Ying could not help but notice was one of the young women who had escorted him to the showers only hours before in paradise — maneuvered the 97,000 tons of warship as if an oversized sports car.

Susan, brightening, said to her brother-in-law, "Captain, see you later, sir. I'll take Daddy and Ying down to combat to watch the action."

"Susan, take Major Tsunami, please. Admiral, may I have a word with you and Ernie?" the captain said respectfully to his father-in-law.

"Sir, I just talked with Admiral Sarodsy in the Pentagon. We can expect a special courier COD with extended range tanks in three hours. You, Major Tsunami and Mr. Maltman, plus one other, if you choose, are to fly directly to Chunking, join with Rear Admiral Nancy Chandler and meet with General Wong at 2200 hours their time tonight." Captain Boone, mentally reviewed his remote satellite display, noted the progress of the attack groups, the absence of an airborne threat, the placement of his combat air patrol and the precise location of the four ISI Whiskey class subs, observing the close association to each of their clandestine "escorts." Some 1,400 nautical miles to the south, the lone symbol of the COD arced towards its assigned rendezvous with the Reagan.

Big Sister and her wizo, Twidget, hung close to the port wing of her squadron commander. The mission was really a case study in simplicity, just a matter of flying the pre-briefed profile, delivering the hyper-accurate weaponry, each programmed to a specific piece of the target complex and returning to base —

base, in this case, a heaving postage stamp in the Indian Ocean. Twidget was, uncharacteristically, barely paying attention, his focus on the skipper's back-seater, Pete Dawkins. Ever since the unspoken altercation in the darkened room of Ensign Patty Butts the night before, the two had hardly slept, manly chemistry in high gear. Pete looked back at his rival, only 23 feet away, and most methodically and slowly, gave him the finger. Twidget, in turn, removed his mask and mouthed a silent, up yours, you flaming asshole. The instant replay would have called it a draw.

"Twidget, what's happened to the HSI display? And what's Pete signaling?" referring to the non-standard middle finger she had noticed in her peripheral vision.

"Sorry, Big Sister," he said to his pilot and long-time roommate, "I forgot to align it on deck. I'll go to the override-alternate-satellite mode and see if I can get it back," his mind once again into the intricacies of the deadly mission, male anger on temporary hold. Fact was, he was tired. The familiar voice from his pilot gave no quarters.

"Twidget, you get that system up or your ass is toast. UNDERSTOOD?"

It was what he needed. His response, "I've got it. Not to worry."

The strike on the airfield was anti-climatic. The threat displays on all aircraft showed no hostile birds airborne, radars shut down and anti-air defenses quiet. Twenty-four miles out, at some fourteen-miles-per-minute and one hundred feet above the desert floor, Iron lady pitched her eight jets up to 5,000 feet, acquired the precise target coordinates, armed the weapons of selected destruction, noticed a dozen fireballs representing the former missile defenses taken out by the task force ship and sub-based missiles, and released a total of thirty-two, 2,000- pound weapons. Becky mentally figured the probability of kill would be greater than 94%.

Dave Anderson's three fighters were right behind, their job to counter any airborne threat. He noticed that the target area was obliterated excepting four bombs that hit a mile from the 200 meter square target area. Bad computer, he correctly surmised.

From time of the pitch-up to the supersonic, low-altitude dash outbound had been less than 44 seconds. Once feet-wet over the now friendly ocean, Anderson set up on a predetermined barrier patrol 300 miles north of the Reagan, the purpose to thwart any voyeurs seeking recompense at the expense of the U.S. Navy. Dave noted ruefully that the strike aircraft would have a ready deck upon return to the ship, while his jets would remain airborne for the next three hours. The carrier's defenses remained at maximum alert.

Tsunami was, once again, standing beside the Reagan's captain, the recovery of the thirty-six jet strike group under a gloomy and thick overcast taking just under twenty-two minutes, even without the automatic landing systems. As each stealth jet grabbed an arresting wire, it crunched to a stop, its awesome kinetic energy dissipated in 1.4 seconds.

Down below in the intelligence center, the air wing commander was in high warble, her voice demanding. "Good job on the Bandar targets, Rock and Sam," speaking to the squadron CO, Commander Rock Batori and his counterpart in the Jolly Rogers of VF-103. You all hit the nail on the head." All three of her squadron commanders were reviewing the imagery, a blending of infrared, radar and laser technology that readily permeated cloud cover. The designated rectangular pier area of the port was indeed close to 100% rubble with no adjacent collateral damage. "Well done, you guys," she said with meaning.

Shifting focus, she asked Patty Butts to zoom in on the target assigned the Red Rippers, the Kleski Air Field. "Montrose, what the hell happened? You all were assigned twelve jets, but only personed eleven," adding, without waiting for the response, "bullshit." Her pointer then lazed to four gaping holes some 2,000 yards from the target area and demanded, "And what may I ask, is this amateur hour? Admiral Chandler will go bonkers and the Captain's already had a piece of my fanny. Well?"

Iron Lady had been there and done that and was clearly on the fast track to becoming an air wing commander herself.

Although, it would most likely have been more politic for the CAG to have done the chain-jerking in private, the benefit would accrue to all, in this instance.

"I'm not going to make excuses, CAG. That said, I got hit with a double-grounding by the Doc. She wouldn't budge an inch."

With brow furrowed, the air wing commander asked, "Grounded for what?" steeling herself for the answer she knew was coming.

"Missed her period. Doc had no choice, influenced at least in part, by the poor call she made in the case of Lieutenant Swagger."

Losing her cool for a moment, the CAG let loose. "This promiscuity bullshit is totally off the scale — all three of you. I can't believe all this crap," knowing full well, having been a product of the Navy's combat socialization policies for the past sixteen years, that she could not only believe it, she related to it. "How about the other one?"

"That's Lieutenant Commander Lori Miller, my maintenance officer. She's totally retired on active duty. I would have gotten rid of her long ago if I could have. Fact was, though, that I needed the warm body. Put her with my best pilot and it was like mixing oil and water. No way. All she wants to do is fiddle with our younger enlisted under the guise of departmental counseling. All legal and accepted, of course. That best pilot flatly refused to fly with her."

"OK. Now, how about the four self-propelled bombs?"

"CAG, you're not going to like this answer any better. Turner said she forgot to align her system on the flight deck and noticed it only forty miles from the target. The emergency back-up was too late."

"But, that's the wizo's job, is it not?"

"Yes, ma'am. He's the best we have. Told Turner he wasn't able to sleep because he's been distracted of late."

"Distracted, my sweet ass. Where's any distraction on Dutch?" realizing too late that the double "no-no" reflected the extreme level of her frustration. "Female distraction?"

"Yes ma'am, I'm afraid so." Resignedly the skipper said, "I'll take care of it, CAG," her eyes wandering to the totally productive Patty Butts busy planning the next evolution, should that be an option.

The repartee had taken only minutes, but reflected volumes about the true combat readiness of the carrier. Further perturbations from the CAG would have only served to rub salt into the wound, the ramifications crystal clear to all three of her CO's. Quietly, the air wing commander made the solemn and thoughtful pilgrimage the eleven stories to her boss, Captain Tommy Boone. They all knew his jaws would pulsate, but deep inside, he would understand only too well the reality.

Back in ready one, the crews from the returning strike were somber, the mood tense, the aura of first blood short-lived. Iron Lady, still smarting from the embarrassing tongue-lashing by her boss, was off in a corner with Becky Turner and Scott Jacobs, the conversation private and one-way. Scott's face was crimson red. The duty officer interrupted with a flash message "Eyes only for the commanding officer, VF-11." Montrose read it, fearing the worst.

"To: Commanding Officer, Fighter Squadron Eleven
From: Diversity Directorate, Navy staff, Pentagon
1. I regret to inform you of the death of Lieutenant Samuel Newman. His remains were confirmed at the crash site of his jet in the mountains of eastern Iran by a Chinese recovery force.
2. Please arrange for appropriate memorial services aboard the Reagan.
3. Sent with condolences from a grateful nation. Lieutenant Newman was a true patriot. Vice Admiral Sharon McCluskey."

The memorial service, conducted with short notice in the Red Ripper ready room by virtue of operational necessity, was somber. Newman's squadron mates joined as one, petty differences laid at the altar of what might be. The captain had invited Admiral Demming to provide a short eulogy to the memory of Newman. Following the appropriate ablutions by the senior chaplain, Bruce Demming offered his thoughts, recollections carved by a lifetime of service, duty and honor:

"Captain, CAG, Skipper Montrose and fellow shipmates of Lieutenant Sam Newman. Sam's call sign was 'Studs.' To me, a stud is a tough guy, a guy willing to lay it on the line for what he believed in and was trained for. From all I have heard, Sam Newman was the quintessential warrior — anytime, anywhere. He was very highly respected in the cockpits and on the deck plates. He gave to his country and his Navy the ultimate — as have so many who have worn the naval aviation wings of gold before him."

Demming paused to collect his thoughts, his gaze dancing about the packed ready room, most eyes tearing or moist. The competitors, Panky, Pete and Scott, were shoulder-to-shoulder, united in a common cause, recent concerns far removed. Ying Tsunami had donned the gold wings of the naval aviator bestowed upon him by the sobbing Evelyn Swagger, wings borrowed for the occasion from the top drawer of Sam's diddy box, she standing close by the side of her savior. Rose Johnson, caught up in the emotion, wiped a tear from a still-youthful face unfettered with superfluous makeup. An assortment of the enlisted maintenance troops led by Master Chief Randy McCormick, squeezed in to take their places alongside the likes of Shorts, Twidget, Miller, Gumshoe, Big Sister and the dozens of others packed into the austere space of the pulsing warship.

The admiral reached into his back pocket, pulled out his wallet, looked over the sad assemblage and read from a well-worn plastic covered certificate:

"This is my designation as a naval aviator. Lieutenant Swagger provided me a copy of Sam's. Date of birth:

20 June, 1983. Date of appointment as a naval aviator: 9 March, 2005. On the back of mine are the words of the Navy Flyers Creed: It reads, in part: 'When the going gets fast and tough, I will not falter.' Sam did not hesitate, he did not falter. From that proud day in 2005, when he donned the wings of a naval aviator, he was on the first team, a team uncompromising in combat and humble in victory. Were he able to be with us today, he would be proud of his squadron mates standing here in the august company of a rich Red Ripper heritage of duty, honor and country. Sam Newman was tough. Sam Newman was a real naval aviator who was willing and able to take on the best — anytime and anywhere."

The admiral paused, studying, once again, the backside of his designation certificate, the final words of the "Creed" reading:

"I ask the help of God in making that effort great enough."

Wordlessly, he peeled off the frayed homily and handed it to Evelyn Swagger, along with Sam Newman's well-worn naval aviator certificate.

Wendy Montrose unceremoniously back-handed the free-falling tears, cleared her throat and offered, "One minute of silence for our fallen comrade-in-arms." The starboard catapult, inches above their heads, took the opportunity to blast its familiar crescendo of awesome power, reverberating vibrations and ear-splitting noise, reminding all that another fighter was airborne to face an uncertain foe. All of which, they knew, Sam would have loved had he had the opportunity to be present.

From the rear of the ready room a somewhat irreverent voice offered: "Three cheers for Studs: Hip, hip hooray; HIP, HIP HOORAY; **HIP, HIP HOORAY!**"

CHAPTER 22

Thirty-Seven Children

"ERRANT BOMBS KILL 37 CHILDREN"

"Washington, D. C. AP: The President's bold plan to punish Iran for hostile intrusion into international airspace claimed by the U.S. Navy, backfired with the death of thirty-seven Iranian school children near the Kleski Air Field, some twenty-two miles inland from the Persian Gulf port of Bandar Abas. The President is reported to be livid at the crass level of collateral damage, devastation she had been assured by the Navy's CEO, Admiral Carolyn Sweeney, would never happen.

In addition, some detractors have suggested she used the military action in order to divert attention in the matter of the increasingly clear suggestions of Senator Joe Montgomery, one of the minority leaders, that the death of the presidential hopeful, John Cassidy, two years ago, was 'deliberate and not accidental.' Connected, but apparently more opaque, were the allegations that the astounding wealth of at least some prominent politicians, was ill-gained, the sources subject to possible legal question. An increasing number of editorial positions are suggesting an inquiry may be in order.

The ordering of retaliatory strikes by U.S. Navy carrier-based aircraft and missiles from the Reagan battle group in the Indian Ocean, raised the specter that the decision was reached in order to divert attention from the Montgomery allegations. A similar situation occurred in the late '90s when the incumbent president ordered military action against terrorists, actions which later proved the connection with the fictional movie, 'Wag the Dog,' to have been real.

The White House has stated that the President has yet to decide when, or if, to address the American people, offering instead to extend her personal condolences to the Iranian people."

"Sweeney, where the hell is Nancy Chandler? She's the only one on that worthless staff of yours that knows what's going on!" screamed Virginia Roberts Stallingsworth to the Navy's CEO.

"As I said before, Madame President, she's on an extremely high-level mission for Vice Admiral Sarodsy of my staff and won't be available for three days. Among other issues on her agenda is a visit to the USS *Ronald Reagan*, one of the ships in her battle group. We felt it would be good for her to get out of the Pentagon for a while and mix with the troops."

Stallingsworth was steaming mad. "How the hell did you manage to toss four 2,000-pound bombs so far from the target area? Sounds like a grade-school exercise."

Sweeney wished Sarodsy had been with her, the warfighting vernacular foreign to her upbringing as a naval officer. Fact was, she had been on board an aircraft carrier only once and that for a change-of-command ceremony in Norfolk, Virginia and never in an operational combat fighter. She could hardly spell the type of weapons carried on the ill-fated mission, much less discuss them intelligently.

They had all reviewed the bomb damage assessment carefully, seeking to ascertain the veracity of the Iranian claim, to no avail. The destruction caused by the deadly bombs had been enormous. The full page, starkly-graphic, color photos of thirty-seven mangled young bodies though, had convinced a world

293

aching for peace, that the barbaric Americans had overreacted once again, the sentiment against the strikes overwhelmingly negative.

"Sweeney," she glared at the frightened naval officer, "I want that back-seater hung by his gonads! UNDERSTOOD?"

"Yes, Madame President. But . . . "

"But what?"

"How did you know it was a male in the back-seat of the jet? It could have been a woman, you know?"

"Madame Admiral," she articulated seethingly, wagging her finger inches from Sweeney's face, "there is no way a woman would have done such a stupid thing! Now — get me answers. You, in fact, will go on worldwide HDTV within the next five hours and explain concisely how such a monumental screw-up could have happened."

Admiral Carolyn Sweeney held back the tears only long enough to leave the Oval Office and pass the probing eyes of the presidential chief of staff, his stares pervasively obnoxious. Once in the staff car though, Sweeney and her aide erupted in a heaving symphony of sobs and free-flowing tears. Both understood that the President's ire was indeed justified, the full-page photos of the torn bodies only too graphic.

In the Oval Office, the President's ageless personal secretary entered and whispered a word to Virginia. "He says it's most important, ma'am. I told him you were busy."

"OK, send him in. Not your fault he's here, Martha."

The rotund figure of the old power broker waddled into the familiar room with a "Hi Virginia, how's it going? Tough times, eh?" guffaws of laughter rumbling about the ornate office.

"Get with it, Richard. Why are you here? I've got a few problems of my own. If you're here to help, OK. If you're here to gloat, go back to wherever. Fact is, I never should have authorized that strike."

"What goes around, comes around, I suppose. They tried the same thing back in '98. Backfired then, too. It's 'Wag the Dog' all over again."

Virginia, of course, was well-attuned to the enormous power and influence of Richard Redman and his "Redman Institute for Enlightened Awareness" and that his personal wealth most likely had accrued, at least partially, from the generosity of his longtime political friends. The untimely death of Cassidy, she knew, had been provident, the probability at the time high that he could have limited her presidency to one term and, more significantly, could have precipitated a domino-like free fall of the enormously popular ECATS party.

Abruptly, Redman changed demeanor in the quiet office, his voice muted, "I don't know what happened, but I may need your help on the Cassidy accident. Damned Montgomery is liable to make a mess. Fact is, aircraft accident investigations are privileged by hard law, no exceptions. If he has found anything, it has been done clearly outside of the legalities. An issue of this magnitude would surely elevate to your level. It would take a presidential finding to prohibit a violation of the accident board's determinations of fact."

Redman sat, his massive body hardly fitting the over-stuffed chair in the ornate office. "I know you did not want to strike back at the Iranians, but you must realize that the ISI situation could cascade into a full military commitment by the U.S."

The President piped in. "Look Richard, you know that if the Chinese don't get access to that oil, they'll go somewhere else. Fact one, when it comes to China, is that they still need our combat arms and technology. Without them, they are no longer a superpower. And," she paused, "fact two is that we ECATS owe our overwhelming political majority to the generosity of the Chinese government. We get the big bucks to keep us in power and they get the arms and technology to stay militarily dominant in Asia."

Redman offered a simplistic gratuitism. "Well, all I care about is keeping those big bucks flowing. I would not commit to further military action, no matter the provocation, particularly," he held up the full-color front page of *USA TODAY* showing the broken bodies of the children, "in view of this."

Meanwhile, Joe Montgomery and Stan Sarodsy had been hard at it, the latter mystified, not by the errant bombs, but the 37 dead school children. "You know, this could well be a set-up on the part of the Iranians. No way in hell to tell if those weapons actually hit the school bus. Just what we didn't need."

Sarodsy had just been briefed by his special intelligence unit, the issue having been the recent Iranian dollars destined for the Redman Institute concurrent with the arrival four days prior of the shipment of Super Pelican missiles to the port of Bandar Abas. There was no reasonable doubt that the *quid pro quo* was alive and well.

Montgomery, a constitutional lawyer by training, had been mulling a prudent course of action for some days. He reviewed the facts as best he could, placing his outline on the chalk board in the tiny conference room deep underground in Sarodsy's Pentagon command center:

1. ISI control of Caspian oil = disaster for economies of Japan, China, Asia. Price goes up dramatically.
2. Worldwide depression? Likely/maybe.
3. U.S. + China militarily, if necessary = Yes.
5. Big bucks to Redman and Miller re nukes — Yes.
4. $ to Redman re Super Pelican = Yes— no doubt.
6. U.S. arms industry in bed with Chinese — True.
7. Laws broken in U.S. — Maybe.
8. Cassidy's death no accident.
9. Status quo? World-wide depression + loss of confidence in U.S. + rise to superpower status by Iran, Saudi Arabia and Iraq.
10. Virginia will veto any further military action — True.

"Back to square one," he said resignedly to an equally somber Sarodsy. Not on the board, but real nonetheless, was the quietly-organized consortium of fifty-one lawmakers who had pledged to clean house, including a few ECATS of conspicuous honor. "Less than 10% of the congress — hardly a dent. Too many," he correctly added, "owe their livelihood and wealth to a continuation of the status quo."

Senator Joe Montgomery, above all else, was a realist. The nation's political system had become so pervasively corrupt at the altar of the almighty buck as to put the antics of some emergent third-world countries on a comparative mantle of decency. Impeachment of the president, he knew, was an exercise in total futility, lessons learned so long ago as one of the house leaders in the failed attempt to oust the then-president midway through his second term. Not that there had been insufficient cause. He recalled his research at the time, a portion of which were the legal opinions of a young lawyer in the impeachment preambles leading to the eventual resignation of Nixon — she at the time, a neophyte graduate of a prestigious law school. In part, she had determined that impeachment was justified if due to ". . . the misconduct of public men, or, in other words, from a violation or abuse of the public trust." The framers were, of course, in concert that criminal conduct by a sitting president was unthinkable — a non-issue. What was at issue was the more pervasive agenda of ". . . cheating the trust temporarily afforded a president by a willing citizenry," she had written.

Aloud, he argued to himself in the tiny room, "No, impeachment would only serve to win the battle and lose the war. We must convince Virginia to act responsibly. And," he continued, his brow furrowed, "what defines responsibly?"

"Joe," he was interrupted by Sarodsy. "Got Nancy Chandler on the red phone. She's about four hours out from Chunking now. Needs some direction. Let me hook you in."

Rear Admiral Nancy Chandler had spent the past six hours in the air studying the two, thick briefing books on China, the ISIs, the global economy and the broad subject of oil, all of which she could have written herself. Her one real enigma had been how the Chinese had managed to accumulate such a powerful military machine in so few years, a question a least partially explained by the "Green Trees" revelations. It was all coming together, she thought, recalling the mysterious Oval Office meetings with Virginia and Richard Redman. "Never did trust that devious slob," she muttered irreverently.

She wasn't sure how to approach the esteemed General Wong. All she could read was that he was one tough warrior of the old school and totally committed to a Chinese military second to none. The addition of Admiral Demming to the group, she was thankful, could well be the key to a successful dialogue.

"Nancy, how are you?" Montgomery said to the airborne naval officer.

"Just fine, Senator. Looking forward to meeting with the General. Help me out, sir. How should I approach him?"

Montgomery returned to the cozy conference space, the outline of the issues on the wall blackboard. "Here's what I'd suggest. Ready to copy?" followed by a recitation of items 1,2,3,9 and 10. "Your job is to make him understand the long-term consequences of doing nothing, both on the part of the Chinese and the U.S. Toss in a few groups on global stability and prosperity in general, if you get the chance."

"Roger that, sir. Makes sense," said the geo-politically astute rear admiral.

"There's more. I want General Wong to convince the Chinese leadership that what we're proposing is in the best interests of China and to go public with this new proactive strategy. Can do?"

"Wow — that's a tall order, Senator. I can sure try. One reality, though," she paused, staring out the window of the speeding jet at the muted glow of the pulsating-green starboard running light. "Virginia will go absolutely off-the-scale."

"Bingo, my sharp friend. Now, for the long-term objective. You ready?"

"Shoot, sir."

Sarodsy broke in. "Nancy, before the Senator gets too far, you should realize that I have reason to believe that Wong knows that we know of the nukes at his secret air field. You recall the mission by the Red Rippers overflying the base in northern Iran that had the nuclear sensors on board? Well, the Chinese got to the crash site, and aside from affirming the death of the pilot, I have no doubt that they have put two and two together. Don't bring up the subject; but if he does, simply indicate you are not prepared to discuss the information at this time. We don't want to slam the door too hard. OK?"

"Got it, boss."

"Nancy, here's the long-term objective," the senator said. "Pretty mushy, but here goes. Give it some thought and then get back to me, please."

"Go ahead, Senator."

"Long-range, we've got to convince the Chinese leadership to cease and desist in the art of the payoff. I am convinced in the decency of the American people, 99.9% of whom are not on the dole. We must somehow make the Chinese understand that when the Cassidy accident revelations hit the airways and front pages, and the massive dollar apportionments flowing through the Redman laundry machine are revealed, there will be a spontaneous backlash from the American people against the status quo. And, mind you, I'm talking decency, not politically."

She quickly added, "Makes sense to me, except you need to understand that this is the way business is conducted in China and has been for hundreds of years. Nothing new."

Sarodsy came on again. "By my reckoning, you'll have a chance for some shuteye prior to the 2200 meeting with the General. Admiral Demming and Ernie Maltman will be in Chunking at 1800 their time and will proceed directly to the American Embassy. Oh, by the way, a Major Ying Tsunami will be with them. He's an Annapolis graduate and went through Navy flight training before taking a commission in the Imperial Chinese Air Force. You can trust him. And, he is very close to Wong, his top up-and-comer, in fact. Also, I've just learned they will have with them an aide, so to speak, who can assist the Admiral and you. Her name is Lieutenant Evelyn Swagger. She was the back-seater in the crash in the mountains and is unable to fly for the time being. Use her as necessary. Any questions?" the conversation clearly terminated.

"No, sir. I'm all set. Good talking to you both. Say hi to Virginia, if you see her," she added, almost conspiratorially.

President Virginia Roberts Stallingsworth had gone directly

to the hideaway of her Georgetown house, safely out of reach and range to all but a chosen few. She needed some quiet time to sort out the covey of black balls coming her way, not the least of which was an upcoming lead editorial set to appear in the morning edition of the respected *New York Independent*. Through well-placed sources, she had managed to intercept a draft:

"DRAFT — DRAFT — DRAFT: There is a peppercorn's worth of credibility in the charges of Senator Joe Montgomery concerning the precipitous death of former Senator John Cassidy. Notwithstanding the current imbroglio in the Caspian, it is our belief that tripartisan hearings should not be placed on hold. Too much murky water has flowed over the dams of decency in the past decade. Let's review some of the fallout:
  • A political landscape overwhelmingly ECATS, an equilibrium out of reasonable balance.
  • A Supreme Court overly one-sided.
  • An arms industry that provides the world a bounty greater than that of England, Israel, France, Brazil and Russia combined, an industry that accounts for a whopping 17% of our nation's GDP.
  • An odor of ill-gotten wealth among the purveyors of power.
Had John Cassidy succeeded in his long-shot quest for the presidency, there could well have followed at least some minority wins to counter a political system grossly out of whack. Certainly, there is some credence to the truth of Montgomery's astounding accusations, charges that our well-placed sources have no doubt will be convincingly substantiated.

Just recently, the *Independent* has learned that the missiles fired in anger by the Iranians at the hapless Liberian-flagged tanker in the Indian Ocean that resulted in the unfortunate death of 24 seamen, the loss of the tanker and a massive area of crude-oil pollution, were the newly-developed Super Pelican. How the Iranians managed to acquire such advanced weaponry, our sources have confirmed, is under investigation. What is not at issue, but also readily confirmed, is that a major U.S. arms corporation and at least one other organization have profited rather handsomely from the alleged transaction.

The key issue, as we review the past fifteen years or so, is the influence of money on our body politic. Dollars may not necessarily reflect the root of all evil, but even a peppercorn's worth of impropriety could lead to a massive cascade of more fouled water over the saturated dam."

Montgomery too, had an advance copy of the piece, reading it with a subdued chuckle and twinkle in his eye. "Couldn't have done it better myself."

The art of the leak within the beltway of Washington was a highly-refined absolute of the daily routine, the sources for the proposed piece impossible to trace to either Montgomery or the underground alcoves of Sarodsy's command center. The streetwise politician decided to lay low and await the broadsides of presidential indignation.

Virginia had seen the draft and was in a high-temperature stew. "That damned Redman," she yelled as she hit his private access line.

The old lawyer was not privy to the editorial, but reacted much the same as a previous thousand crises with a, "Virginia, calm down. I'll take care of it. No problem."

"Richard, if you're involved in that Cassidy caper, your ass is grass."

"Trust me, Virginia. The release of FASA accident findings is extremely privileged, even to the most persistent congresspersons. Should Montgomery ever get to the hearings, it will be challenged within the first minute. And, if the lower courts screw with it, I've already got the Supreme Court in the bag. No way anything will come out of it!"

Virginia had heard the line so many times, she referred to

them as "Redmanisms."

"Tell you what," he said confidently, "I'll go you even better. I'll get that lead piece quashed now. Trust me. You'll never see that piece of crap in print."

The call to the publisher of the *New York Independent* was routine for Redman. On a first-name basis with most of the nation's leading publishers, he never bothered with the lowly opinion editor, preferring the heady arena of the front office.

"Sandra. How ya doing?" he said to his long-time friend, getting straight to the issue. "Got a problem with your lead editorial piece for tomorrow. You seen it?"

"Yes, Richard. I have seen it and the answer is no to your first question and not interested to your second."

A pause by the seasoned master manipulator of Washington influence, a moment's hesitation. "What's the second question, Sandra?"

The second question, of course, had to do with the newspaper's "Foundation for Journalistic Excellence," a scholarship source for aspiring student journalists and a funding reservoir for grants to those in the profession of particular stature. "Sandra, you know the Redman Institute is a firm believer in the FJE." He allowed his words to die, the implication clear.

"How much?" she countered, a pattern of actions not atypical when dealing with Redman.

The immediate response, "Ten million."

The publisher of the world's most influential newspaper audibly gathered her breath. "Ten million? All at once? My God, this must be important. Does the President know you're doing this?"

The flippant reply, the hook set, "No way, José."

Silence reigned. Her wits collected, the publisher finally responded. "No to the ten million, no to double the amount and no to any future payments to the foundation from you or the Institute." With a sudden jar, the line went dead.

Redman, his knees shaking, took an unmeasured belt from his office liquor cabinet. Money, he reasoned, had never before failed to grease the skids. Small folks would accept modest stipends; big ones demanded more. It had never before fizzled. The offer of ten million was, he knew, enormous, even in a world accustomed to obscene payoffs. That the publisher would not even consider the generous offer was troubling. For the first time in hundreds of tough situations, the old master of the deal had an uncomfortable premonition that the walls were crumbling. He punched the direct access line to the President of the United States and stoically awaited the tirade.

Not far distant, Montgomery and Sarodsy were having a rare moment of relaxation, enjoying a tasteful, albeit spartan meal of oriental stir-fry and a glass of mellow merlot. Joe had handed the draft piece to the old sailor. Sarodsy said, his eyebrows raised, "This is a bombshell. Where in hell did she get this information? My bet is that someone will torpedo this before we finish dinner," once again engaging the smiling eyes of Montgomery.

"Not to worry, Stan. There is no way that this information can be traced to me or this office."

"Well, how about the editor of the paper?" Sarodsy said, still not in the loop.

"Not the editor, my naive Navy friend, the publisher. I talked with her on her private line two hours ago. She's going with the opinion piece. Says it's long overdue."

The senator raised his glass and predicted to Sarodsy, "It's going to be an interesting twenty-four hours. Fasten your seat belt."

CHAPTER 23

"I Will Not Falter."

Halfway around the world and deep within the bowels of the USS *Ronald Reagan*, Master Chief Mitsi Moore was halfway listening to a young couple from the ship's second division. She: "Master Chief, I'm so scared. I just want to go home and live a normal life with Johnny," she mourned while lovingly gazing at her nineteen-year-old partner, presumably Johnny, who was in a deep study of the top of his shoes.

The senior enlisted person on board the Reagan was sticking to her avowed, self-imposed open-door policy that allowed any sailor to personally talk to her. So far this afternoon, she had seen sixteen individuals and twelve couples, all of whom played the same tune with slightly-altered lyrics. Almost universally, it was a repetitive litany of wanting to get off the ship. No psychologist, the master chief knew the troops were strung out, the stress levels off the scales. Early in the deployment, it had been *de rigeur* to simply assign a stress chit and send the person to the ship's Stress City, or, in severe cases, to the Navy's Central Diversity College in Memphis. The captain's recent edicts that sent many of the warship's accepted social agenda crumbling, had indeed been a wake-up call to many in the crew who felt that all was going to be peaches and cream, the reality being large dollops of turnips and sour vinegar.

"You," she countered to the young woman, "I want you to listen to me. This is a fighting ship, understood? The purpose of a warship is to go in harm's way if called upon to do so and inflict maximum death and destruction on any foe, no matter whether we agree or not. Am I clear? Now, what do you two people think you ought to do?"

The young man was contrite, his head still down, eyes averted. His companion though, was openly hostile. "Master Chief, I don't care. I didn't sign up to work twelve to fourteen hours per day, seven days a week forever. And I certainly don't agree with killing 37 school children on a bus. I can't be a normal person. Not only that, but I am scared to the bone." The male sailor reacted by putting his arm protectively around her body, the heaves and sobs erupting into a waterfall of tears. Meekly, she asked, "Can I get a stress chit, please, Master Chief?"

"No way. Captain's decided we need to pay max attention to fighting this ship and," she paused, glaring directly into the swollen eyes of the woman, "I agree totally with his call."

In a state of open rebellion, the sailor grabbed the hand of Johnny, slammed her chair against the bulkhead of the tiny office and, in a loud, angry voice said to Mitsi, " I hope you're satisfied. If I ever get off this bucket, we're going to sue the pants off you and the Captain for breach of promise. And," she stared down at the chief, "if we want to hold hands, we'll hold hands. Screw you, Master Chief."

"Young lady. You are on report for gross disrespect. Both of you. Stand by outside."

"Screw you again," this time in a shrill tone, almost a screech, the blasphemous reverberations echoing in the narrow passageway outside.

Randy McCormick sidled up unexpectedly, grabbing the dissident sailor by her upper arm, his tall frame towering over the woman. "I don't know who you are or what the issue is, but I can tell you right now, you'll be in the brig on bread and water within the hour. Now, pipe down," his face inches from the defiant sailor. He added, somewhat emotionally, "You're not only disrespectful to the Master Chief, you're a first-class cry-baby."

As predicted, within five minutes after the hour, the sailor was marched off, her division officer, Ensign Karen Randolph at her side, destination the ship's minute brig and three days, literally, on bread and water. It was a punishment that captains eternal reserved for the most blatant cases of disrespect or disobedience to a superior officer or petty officer, and was a centuries-old methodology to positively reorient the recalcitrant. A fact of life aboard any warship was the absolute of one set of rules and the total authority of the captain. Non-adherence normally resulted in swift retribution, no captain willing to look the other way in such cases, the bedrock of combat readiness reflecting an unconditional compliance to authority. Democracy on the deck plates had long been an anachronism. Within hours, the word of the grossly disrespectful sailor and her temporary home would have swept the ship.

The two master chiefs were finally alone in the compact office of Master Chief Mitsi Moore. Just as they had almost daily for the past nine months, the two openly commiserated, exchanging frank thoughts. Randy McCormick, their close relationship notwithstanding however, would never reveal to his friend the hurried — almost bizarre — meeting of the night before with his commanding officer. For him, it was an isolated incident with zero emotional implications. A knock on the thin door.

"Hi, Mitsi, Randy. Hope I'm not interrupting." It was Dr. Rose Johnson who, as one of the three medical physicians on board, cut a wide swath, her charter broad. "Got a problem. Need to talk. Have a few minutes?"

"Sure, Doc. Shoot," said the carrier's master chief.

"Let me show you a log I've been keeping — off the record. I've updated it since this morning's sick call, which, I might add, was a new record. The line stretched all the way to the forward mess decks — 175 people." She paused, checking her notes. "119 were females with complaints all over the sky — hips, ankles, periods, headaches and few of the inevitable," the latter word needing no embellishment to the two senior sailors.

She continued, "We left pier twelve at Norfolk 3 March, 2010. At the end of each month, I've noted the number of newly-pregnant females, both officer and enlisted. Here's the end of the month list as of today:

March	17
April	29

May	37	
June	42	
July	36	
August	62	
September	96	
October	102	
November	124	(as of 20 Nov)
Total	545	

It's clear to me that the little white rabbit is a ticket off the ship, along with the willing partner. My guess is that the pills work just fine to prevent conception, or at least, the vast majority. But they work only if taken or the guy wears a cover."

All three were well attuned to the Navy's amply-grooved pregnancy policies. A few here and there were to be expected, but it was clear that what the Reagan and the ship's of the battle group had experienced in the past few months was off the chart, the cases having gone exponential. Exacerbating the problem was the reality that, in the most recent three months, few cases were able to leave the ship. There were, in fact, more than a few obviously-expectant mothers emplaced randomly about the ship.

"Master Chief, I need to brief the exec on this. Would you come with me? She'll go ballistic. That said, however, she needs to swallow the whole pill — sorry, no pun intended — and take it up with the Captain."

Mitsi queried, "How far along are the most advanced cases, Doc?"

Rose checked her notes. "I've got three I'm watching closely that are right at the six-month mark. Like a few others, we've managed to get them on light duty. How about we meet at the XO's office at 1415?"

At the moment, the husband of the ship's executive officer, was deep in conference with his number two. Rock Batori was tired. He had just recovered in rotten weather from a four-hour combat air patrol, landing with minimum fuel. Ready for a short combat nap, the familiar knock at the door was that of his next-door neighbor, squadron executive officer and the wife of the lusty officer-in-charge of the Virginia Beach Barking Dogs contingent.

"Rock, got to talk," said the squared-away fellow commander and F-27C stealth wizo. The two, though CO and XO, were not only mutually respectful, they too, were friends. In close physical proximity for almost nine months, they conversed in private many times each day — and night. Discretion was indeed a hallmark of this close personal and professional rapport. Tongues could wag, but substance was only guesswork when it came to any suggestion of having crossed the sacrosanct Navy line-in-the-sand.

"Rock, did you hear about the party at my house in Kings Grant?"

"No. How could I? No e-mail. Have a seat," he replied, moving his junk off the bunk in his austere combination sleep, lounge and office stateroom.

"CNN. Can you believe it? After the shoot down yesterday, they sent a team to my house — heard there was a party — arrived at midnight. There was my asshole husband making out with some wench in tight leather pants and high heels."

"Did you tape it?" he replied.

"No chance. It was only a one-minute segment. That flaming asshole. That worthless sack of baloney! While we're out here busting ass, he's having fun, along with a few other boys and girls in our illustrious hometown team. Is there anyway I can send him a piece of my mind?"

"No way. You know the rules."

She calmed down. Never in their relationship had she been so demonstratively vocal. "You know, Rock, that the death of those 37 kids could have been you or me. The news has swept the ship. The feedback I'm getting is that most of our guys are really down, even though it was an obviously honest mistake." Quiet prevailed, the two senior combat aviators lost in a mélange of disparate thoughts, the specter of mangled bodies in a far-off land, laying heavily in the somber room.

"Skipper," she said, brushing her hair back and, for the moment, forgetting the specter of her wayward husband and the ubiquitous Suzette, "Doc told me we had two more 'medicals' this morning."

The sharp commanding officer of the VF-143 Barking Dogs laconically replied, "Doesn't surprise me. You?" She chose not to answer, slipping quietly instead to her private domain one-eighth-inch-fiberboard bulkhead removed from that of her skipper.

In the past few months, Commander Angela Batori had assiduously avoided her equally hard-charging husband, a feeling of mutual persuasion. Not that she particularly cared. She knew from her brief experience so long ago as a carrier fighter pilot in training, that pressures for the pilots and wizos flying the ship's fighters were enormous. The dalliance of the previous evening with the ship's weapons officer, she had rationalized, was a "one-timer" and would not recur. She inwardly kicked herself for her loss of control, knowing deep inside, she had only herself to blame — much the same as those traumatic days so long ago, she correctly thought to herself.

Her Marine orderly broke the seance, snapping her back to a grim reality. "It's the Master Chief and Doc Johnson. May I send them in, ma'am?"

"Yes, please, Corporal," she said, thankful for the change.

Fifteen minutes later, the briefing completed, she knew the captain needed to know the results of the Doc's survey. Clearly, the situation was reaching out-of-control proportion, the captain trusting his XO to handle such matters. Not that he was unaware, certainly. He simply had not focused on the total, but rather the dribs and drabs of the daily sick-call summaries. There was no doubt that his ability to effectively fight his ship was being steadily eroded by forces as old as the greening of the earth.

Batori's mind drifted back to her ensign days in flight training, recalling a long-ago spoofy article in the prestigious *Proceedings* wherein the author, among other mostly apolitical ruminations on the subject of women serving aboard combatant ships, offered the specter of the role of the ship's nursery in fighting the carrier. It had, of course, enraged segments of the population attuned to issues female, the vast majority of whom had not the tiniest notion of what combat entailed or the mix of chemistries in a warship.

The obvious issue on the table was, rightfully, what to do? What course of action? What program objectives and milestones? All three knew that Jaws Boone wanted solutions, not just open-ended problems. Pragmatically, they knew, as would Boone, that the solution was beyond their control, a manifestation of policies long flawed in a decade of feel-good socialization policies.

"XO, I need to brief the Captain on some other medical issues. I'll give him an overview if it's OK with you. Bottom line, from my perspective, is that you and he are doing all you can do. More rules and/or edicts will only serve to influence, rather than change, the crew's behavior. He's got to accept that what he has now is what he'll fight the ship with. The medically indisposed women are not a real problem. We just have to be smart enough to put them where there's minimal physical strain. Hefting chains twelve hours a night on the flight deck, for instance, is silly. It's manageable."

"Thanks, Doc. Appreciate all your extra effort," said the relieved XO.

Rose decided to stop by the combat operations center on the way to the bridge, finding Blues Anderson and Patty Butts closely examining the latest overhead satellite imagery, the subject, the area consumed by four deadly, but aimless, 2,000-pound bombs.

Rose had learned in confidence from the Ripper CO that the cause of the gross bombing miscue had been 100% error on the part of the fighter's back-seater, Lieutenant Scott Jacobs. The skipper's explanation was troubling. Iron Lady had told her that Jacobs blamed distractions caused, allegedly, by macho competition, the subject matter, the attractive, but business-like intelligence officer, Ensign Patty Butts.

Unobserved, she noted Anderson shoulder-to-shoulder with Butts, consumed in the details of the destruction before them. Rose, privy to most the carrier's swirling nuances, recalled the one-time embrace and brief kiss forty-eight hours prior in these same spaces by Anderson and Butts. With professional interest, she discreetly watched the two from a corner of the classified spaces, no hint of sidebars to the task at hand.

"Oh, hi Doc," Patty said, noticing the Doc. "Just checking out the supposed school bus hit. For the life of me, I cannot figure out where the 37 children came from. Best we can deduce," continued the wound-up Butts, "those bombs hit nothing but an empty road." Anderson nodded his head in general agreement. "I'm going to send our findings to the DNI in a few minutes and let her figure out how to counter the Iranian claims."

The DNI was none other than the Director of Naval Intelligence in Washington, Rear Admiral Sally Butts, Patty's mother, who would recognize the source of the info by the initials "GSB," Gumshoe Butts. The admiral and her sizable staff, along with other intelligence organizations, were working around the clock on the ISI situation, the errant bombs only adding fuel to the volatile fire. Unfortunately for the image of the U.S., the combined shore-based effort could find no plausible counter to the claims of the Iranians, the conclusions of her daughter notwithstanding.

"Doc, can I have a word with you, in private," asked the weary, acting executive officer of the Red Rippers.

"Sure, Dave. Have at it," convinced that the subject was the harmless tryst with the young Butts or the female findings of his roommate and former back-seater, Nancy "Shorts" Flanagan.

"It's Twidget. He's really down. Told me he wants to quit flying — now. He knows he messed up big time on the strike. Fact is, he's gone from totally pumped-up and dedicated wizo to one sorry young man." He gathered his thoughts. "That's only half of it. There's the other half," glancing at the backside of Patty Butts. "I think she's giving him the cold shoulder and it has everything to do with the skipper's wizo, Pete Dawkins. They had a little verbal exchange just before the raid. Fact is, all three of them have been so charged up for so long, I think the constant stress is getting to them."

"You're right, Dave. This is a CO problem, though, not medical. You need to brief your skipper. The loss of Twidget would be a blow to your combat readiness. He's one of the best you have, correct?"

"He is and more, Doc." responded an emphatic Anderson.

Patty Butts was intently reviewing the bomb damage assessment on the Kleski Air Field. "Hey Doc, want to see the BDA?"

"Sure, Patty. Keep it simple, though."

What she saw was the total destruction of the 200-meter square area assigned the Rippers, much akin to a powerful tornado cutting its swath of carnage through a rural hamlet. "Our guys really did a number. This is as good as it gets. Too bad about Twidget though. Fact is, they would only have chewed up more rubble," adding, "Mess with the bull and get the horn," a grim smile of professional well-being breaking her youthful facade. "Commander," Patty said suddenly to her boss, Anderson, "Skipper wants to see you ASAP."

The short walk aft on the starboard passageway on the ship's 03 level just beneath the flight deck of the fast-moving ship was surreal. Were it not for his vintage flight suit, he could well have been on a cruise ship bound for nowhere, a cold beer his destination.

"Hi, Skipper."

"Have a seat, Dave," said the grim-faced commanding officer. "I need to get your thoughts on a few subjects. Got a minute?"

"Sure, Skipper. I've got some input for you, too."

"Dave, looks as though Bikini, 'er Evelyn Swagger, will take a little sabbatical to China with Major Tsunami, the retired Admiral and Mr. Maltman. Captain said they were authorized someone to help out and she fit the bill. Sound OK to you? She won't be able to fly for at least a few days, anyway."

"Good idea. It'll take her mind off Studs and the baby, and," with his characteristic trademark grin, "I don't think the Major will mind one bit."

"Good. They plan to depart in 45 minutes. How about you bidding them farewell — kind of a 'following seas and a wind at their back' wish."

Dave had idly noted the stained work hat in a corner of the spartan room, the unmistakable emblem and twin stars of a master chief petty officer staring at him.

"Skipper, I've got an idea."

"Shoot."

"You know, the maintenance troops are doing an incredible job with our jets, including McCormick. How about you and me getting the day and night checks together and letting them know what a great job they're doing. I know I've been remiss in visiting the work shops."

"Me, too. Great idea. How about 1800? I've got the 2015 launch," responded the CO to her acting XO. "Nothing formal. Would you let Master Chief McCormick know, please?"

"Sure — and one more input, Skipper. Let's make sure Miller's not around. Even if she is the maintenance officer, she's a demotivator of the first order."

"I agree with you again, my number-one assistant. Now let me ask you a couple of questions."

What followed was a classic commanding officer and executive officer repartee, the intrigues of paradise, the top subject, Anderson's comments to her on Twidget's no-fly request, only a portion of the fast-moving and open dialogue. "You handle it, XO," she directed, her beeper breaking the flow of business. "CAG wants me. Got to go. Oh, and tell Bikini to get her bags packed."

"OK, Skipper. See you at 1800," and, noticing the cap in the corner, "You want me to take the Master Chief's cover to him?"

Montrose seemed confused for a moment, then said, a bit resignedly, "Sure. Thanks."

At the time, Master Chiefs Randy McCormick and Mitsi Moore were on an informal tour below decks, their unofficial destination, the second-division berthing spaces on the the third deck below the hangar deck and far forward.

The living spaces, normally home to some forty-four men and women, were about one-third full, the six-person cubicles randomly empty. Because the division operated around the clock standing underway watches on the bridge, as well as attending to a myriad of assigned spaces of the ship to maintain and clean, the lights were low, the mood quiet, many asleep even at 1530 in the afternoon. The pulsing power of the ship was more pronounced, the level of the unseen turbulent ocean just beyond, at foot level. Mitsi entered the first alcove, slowly pulling the curtain apart in the darkened space, eyes adjusting to the spartan ambiance.

"Master Chief! What are you doing here?" a young man exclaimed, covering himself as best he could, the young woman close beside him, doing her best to shield her partially exposed body. The two were, of course, well aware of the hurried captain's mast on the bridge hours before and of their shipmate's forced incarceration in the ship's brig. The woman burst out, "We were only talking, Master Chief."

The Reagan's second division was a microcosm of the 5,000 women and men of the crew. From all walks of life, far corners of the country, high school dropouts to Ph.D.'s, they reflected the socio-economic layering of the United States, one common denominator, an age of nineteen, plus or minus one or two years, and a predilection to single status. The ship's command master chief contemplated the ups and downs of the division as the months of the deployment ticked off. The two companions caught *en flagrant* in after steering not long ago were alumni of the division. Their division officer, Ensign Karen Randolph, was clearly a dynamite officer of the deck with a poise far beyond her years, but an inexperienced division officer, trusting, as she should, her divisional chief petty officer, a shore-based personage of dubious sea-going qualifications and lesser leadership competence.

"Looks to me like you guys were doing more than talking," the commanding figure of McCormick materializing out of the gloom at Mitsi's side. "What the hell is going on here? Didn't you hear the Captain just a few hours ago?"

"Yes, Master Chief, but . . ."

"But what?"

The young sailor, grasping for words, looked up at her

obviously intimate friend, "Tell them, Petie. Tell them what we've all been talking about for the past two or three months. Please," her voice cracking, the blanket pulled closer about her thinly-clad body.

"Master Chief," he began hesitantly, "we're both from the same state — Montana. We did not know one another until we met here in this berthing compartment. She was assigned to the adjacent privacy alcove. We sleep together — not that way — we eat together, we stand watches as a team, and, in the few times we've been in port, we've gone on the beach together. We love each other." He held her now with both arms, her tear-stained face hidden in the comforting crook of his bare shoulder.

She added, her girlish voice clearly stressed. "Fact is, we plan to get married. But, we never expected this. We thought it would be a great adventure — see the world and all that. For the first few months, we minded the rules, but," she collected her thoughts, "the work got harder, the cruise got longer and, I'm not ashamed to admit, we're both scared. The loss of the 37 kids is terrible. We didn't sign up for this." The woman looked up, the grief obvious in her youthful face.

"We were wrong, I know. When our bunkmates are on watch, we have some privacy. Fact is, we have many opportunities for creative privacy. Been that way for a long time. What are we supposed to do, play checkers?" the latter with an open honesty, disrespect far from the intent.

The master chief came at the couple with a vengeance, her words clear. "What do I expect from you two young people? The same as what Captain Boone expects, and that is simply that everyone in the Reagan's crew do her or his duty. You do what is ordained by the Captain and the rules by which he commands this warship. Does that make sense?"

Before she could continue the stilted dialogue, a cheery, manly voice penetrated the closed curtain, his giggling companion adding balance, "You two presentable?" Another giggle, another deep-throated laugh.

McCormick opened the the curtain, the two bathrobed and recently-cleansed members of the second division at an instantaneous loss for words, the man's arm quickly disengaging. "Sorry, Master Chiefs. Didn't know you were here."

Mitsi Moore spoke, raising her diminutive frame to full stature. "Did you two hear or see the Captain on TV?"

"Yes, but. . ."

"But, nothing. What did he say about male and female relationships?" Without waiting for an answer, the savvy master chief bitingly added, "And about shower hours? The XO specifically put out times for the women and times for the men. What the hell is this, a love boat?" Glaring at the hapless foursome, she ordered, "Write your names on this."

"Come on, Randy. I've seen enough candy-assed sailors to last me a lifetime in purgatory." The two older sailors departed the second-division spaces with an ambivalence honed by the knowledge that, at any moment, a death-dealing missile could penetrate the heart and soul of a warship struggling to maintain its purpose in life.

Concurrent with the mundane activities within the beehive known as the USS *Ronald Reagan*, Vice Admiral Demming, Major Tsunami and Ernie Maltman were preparing for the arrival of the carrier on board delivery aircraft that would transport them to the pivotal meeting with General Wong and the hoped-for entree into the intricacies of China. The three, bags in hand, were joined by a somewhat confused Lieutenant Evelyn Swagger.

"Evelyn, so good to have you on board. I'm Admiral Demming and this is Ernie Maltman. You know, of course, Major Ying Tsunami." The elder admiral put his arm around the recovering wizo, his fatherly hand a reassurance to the Red Ripper officer.

"Thank you, Admiral. I want to help out in any way I can. And," she added quickly, "to get back to my squadron as soon as possible. They need me," the latter with a self-assured confidence and maturity well past her twenty-four years.

Ying tried unsuccessfully to avert his eyes from her. He had been pinching himself repeatedly since the news that she would accompany the group. Hardly able to comprehend the multitude of events in the past few days, he somehow knew that his future would be unalterably connected with the young Navy lieutenant standing at his side.

The Marine orderly knocked on the door to the flag quarters and announced, "Sir, ma'am, the Captain requests your presence in flight deck control. The COD is three miles out on its final approach for landing. They'll refuel without shutting down and launch immediately."

"Thank you, Private. Would you please get me Commander Montrose of the Red Rippers on the phone?"

"Aye, aye, sir."

"Admiral," the skipper responded, "how good of you to call. And, lest I forget, thank you so much for the thoughtful words for Studs. He would have liked them."

"Skipper, I want you to know you all are doing a great job for our country and our Navy. I know it's tough. If you will, would you be so kind as to pass my compliments to all of the Red Rippers for the great job you all are doing. I would do it myself, but we are due to launch shortly."

"Yes, sir. In fact, I am meeting with a portion of my maintenance troops at 1800. I certainly will pass your comments to them. And Admiral, thank you for taking the time to call. It means a lot to all of us." She hesitated. "Things are kind of tough, sir. We'll make it, but it's tough. No tears, just tough." And, with a positive comeback, "Have a good trip, sir, and get Evelyn back to us soon. We need her."

"Good luck, Skipper," the meaningful response from the old salt.

"Captain's busy, Admiral. He wishes you all a good trip," said the ensign, hustling them into the still-turning and refueling long-range logistic transport.

Commander Angela Batori jumped on board the transport with a sprightly bounce. "Have a productive trip, sir," adding prophetically, "and get 'em on our side," the door closing behind her. As fueling hoses disconnected, the twin-jet slowly taxied to the number-one catapult. Destination: Chunking, China, 2,560 miles east northeast.

Watching the carrier on board delivery aircraft ease into the grips of the nose-tow catapult out of the corner of his eye, Captain Tommy Boone was preoccupied with his command display, the pulsing symbol of the the third Iranian Whiskey class submarine an urgent reminder that its locale was but an estimate, location unknown. Hitting the dialogue box revealed "Xray whiskey 3 contact lost as of 1347Z." Pressing the button for the combat direction center, the captain asked for the submarine liaison officer. "Sir," the young officer responded without being asked, "it looks like the Chicago has lost contact. The chances for reacquisition are low to nil. That's the bad news. Good news is that the Whiskey's a diesel and, without good targeting info, not a high threat to us, even with the Super Pelican missiles. If he uses his radar, we'll spot him in two seconds."

Boone knew all this. Nonetheless, he was concerned. Given the circumstances, he was convinced the Iranians were in a hostile mode — shoot first and ask questions later. The conventional U.S. intelligence findings were that the ISIs believed the U.S. would not act unilaterally, principally based upon the strident rhetoric of the American president not to respond to attack, the one-time retaliatory strike hours before notwithstanding. Should the submarine skipper detect a large radar target, he may well have standing orders to shoot and ask permission later.

He watched the transport aircraft inch its way onto the starboard forward catapult, a covey of F-27C's to follow. With a whine, the twin jets revved to full power, the yellow-clad catapult officer checked for a clear deck, one final glance at the steam pressure, and dropped his left hand to the steel deck. Within four seconds, the airplane and its human cargo were airborne, the first stealth fighter already creeping forward, its airborne destiny in fifty seconds.

"Captain," the gold-dolphined submarine lieutenant said, breaking the skipper's thoughts, "May I offer a few groups, sir?"

"Oh, hi, Annette. Sure. I was just going to ask you to come up."

"Sir, the Whiskey sub is, as you know, not nuclear powered and, as such, is severely limited in speed and range. Most importantly though, unlike our attack subs, he needs to have his search scopes up in order to launch his torpedoes or missiles. He has no external targeting information."

"Understood. What would you do in his situation?"

"No doubt, sir. I would have my scopes full-up unless I knew I was being tracked. Bottom line is, he must have a visual on us or an electronic line-of-bearing, at the least. Pretty crude, but that's the way it is. My guess is, he'll have his sensors out of the water a good bit of the time.

Boone, long a student of U.S. Navy sea-going combat operations, recalled the sad World War II saga of the sinking of the USS *Indianapolis* in the final days of the war. The cruiser, which had just delivered the ingredients for the war-ending atomic bombs in 1945, was steaming independently at high speed, when a chance encounter at night with a Japanese sub, resulted in the loss of the cruiser in short order, over 800 sailors losing their lives in the disaster and the shark-feeding frenzy in the days that followed. Clearly, back then, just as now, the submarine skipper had his scopes up, the range less than a half-mile when his spread of torpedoes sunk the complacent ship.

"Bingo," Boone offered, remembering his dad talking long ago regarding the insatiable appetite of the generic submariner to take a peek, underwater sensors only whetting the desire. "We need max lookouts. Correct, Annette?"

"Absolutely, Captain."

"OK. Now — get together with the XO and organize a maximum state of visual lookout, perhaps utilizing the large number of light-duty folks we have available. I'll give the exec a heads up. I want it done now. And Annette, thanks for the input. Good thinking."

In a defensive high-alert mode, Boone punched the button for the ship's weapons officer, concurrently activating his personal buzzer, his stateroom phone and his office deep within the ship. "Stan, how goes it?"

"Fine, Captain. We've doubled up on our alert status. All our defensive battery are up and ready."

"Thanks, Stan. Look, I want the Tomahawk offensive battery in instant readiness — five seconds or less. Can do? We've lost one of the Whiskeys. If they go active, I want to shoot immediately in either a home-on-jam mode or down a line-of-bearing and shove it down his throat. No need to ask permission to fire. Just do it."

Miller was in his element and clearly understood what the captain wanted and why. "Can do, Captain. Consider it done in four minutes."

"Thanks, Stan. And Stan, please give my best to your guys when you get the chance. I've been remiss of late in getting about the ship. I know you all are kind of out-of-sight and out-of-mind down there."

"Will do, sir," said the experienced sailor, his professional juices flowing.

Stan Miller had been deeply introspective the past few hours, the imminent danger a factor, but not the driver. His real concern focused on the late-night encounter with his boss, Angela Batori. He knew he could have nipped it in the bud and should have. The problem was, he rationalized, his latent desire had caught up with that of Angela's. Their chemistries had built to a point over the past few months, such that there was no way to defuse the mixture. What happened was ordained. Hers had been the predominant catalyst, but his had been unquestionably receptive, the two coming together like iron filings to a charged magnet. Stan Miller was no philosopher, but he knew hormones as well as the next person.

Miller, too, was increasingly remorseful over the missing nuclear weapons, even though the chances of his culpability were close to zero. He had often wondered where the weapons had gone, hoping the destination had not been the ISI consortium. Idly, he had dreamed of what to do with his substantial payoff — about $100 million — that was his share of the sale which, he surmised, would most likely have brought a cool one-billion-per weapon to the organization arranging the transfer. His part, he recalled vividly, had been easy, the payoff to his accomplices comparatively low. "Even so," he argued half-aloud, "what am I

320

going to do with all that wealth?" His had clearly been a monastic lifestyle, a life of duty, honor and service to his Navy. Remorsefully, he wished he could reincarnate the past. "When the ship gets back, I'll retire, and maybe Dolores and I can live a normal life together," he spoke to no one in particular, the monstrosity of his actions sinking even deeper. "The Tomahawks! Damn! I almost forgot!"

The meeting with the ship's executive officer, Master Chief Mitsi Moore and the submarine liaison officer regarding the around-the-clock visual watches reflected the stressed-out carrier's leadership. The submariner suggested two persons on each bow at the flight deck, two amidships on each side and two on each stern quarter. The XO reluctantly agreed to the use of the light-duty contingent, a plan to which Dr. Rose Johnson readily agreed, the XO having found her in the Red Ripper ready room attending to yet another quasi-medical problem.

Lieutenant Commander Lori Miller, the erstwhile maintenance officer of the Red Rippers, was put in charge of the lookout operation, reporting directly to the Captain. Miller, reluctantly acquiescing to the rather abrupt guidance, similarly enlisted the grounded Susan Anthony and Shorts Flanagan to act as her watch captains. Within an hour, the recalcitrant wizo had forty-eight persons from all over the ship assembled in the wardroom. The Reagan's XO observed, pleasantly surprised at the rapid and thorough organization, including foul-weather gear, binoculars, watch stations, and a briefing by the young submarine liaison officer on what to be alert for.

Paradise was quiet, a tranquil island in a sea of turbulent emotions and human needs. Patty and her roommate Karen had spent the past half-hour in low conversation, the tone reflecting a frustration and fear of exponential dimension. Central to the dialogue were issues male, specifically Twidget, Pistol Pete and Panky, spiced by sidebars concerning Bikini, Ying, macho Dave, Shorts' comeuppance, Miller's refusal to fly and the sad demise of their across-the-hall neighbor, Studs.

"What do you think we ought to do?" Patty said to her strung-out roommate.

"Beats me. I've got enough people problems in my second division to last a lifetime. Ship's XO is all over me." She told Patty of the surprise visit by the two master chiefs a few hours before to four of her finest men and women. "If we can't control ourselves as officers, how can we expect the troops to toe the line?"

The question was clearly rhetorical. Both women were superb naval officers and contributors to the mission of the ship. Patty offered: "It's not the job. I can handle that just fine. It's all the distraction. We don't have a life. How I would love to go off for a weekend in the mountains, with a glowing fire, and wine on a candlelit table overlooking a setting sun." After a few seconds of silence, the two laughed openly, the fantasy sparking a warmth far out-of-character to their present surroundings, the "with whom" aspect of the imagined escapade omitted for the time being.

The door next to their stateroom banged shut, the conversation one-way, loud. "Twidget, we've got to brief for a 2045 launch in thirty minutes. What's this bullshit about not wanting to fly? Let's have it, mister!"

The two eavesdropping ensigns next door were like mice, fearing to breathe. In almost nine months, neither had ever heard Big Sister raise her voice. Twidget was silent. His pilot continued. "When the going gets tough, the tough get going. Now, you listen to me and listen well. I'll be damned if I'm going to cry to Iron Lady about your problems. Those bombs were as much mine as yours. That happens. What doesn't happen in my jet is some half-assed, whining candy-ass. We've got a tough job. If I have to, I'll stuff your sorry ass in the back seat upside down and backwards. That said, you and I will be airborne at 2045. *Comprendez?*"

Twidget spoke, his voice low, his unseen neighbors noiselessly moving closer to the thin steel bulkhead separating the staterooms. "Big Sister, there's more. Please listen," his voice barely audible. "It's Patty. I really care for her. It's the first time for me. I think about her constantly. When Pete," his voice broke, "said he was interested in her too, something just snapped. I thought he was keen for Karen. That bothered me, too, because Panky and she were buds from way back in Norfolk."

The room next door was silent. Patty and Karen feared to move. The four young naval officers, thrust into harm's way, were seeking answers to a convoluted puzzle bent on resisting the final pieces.

Big Sister's voice was soft, but confident. "Look, Twidget, I know where you're coming from. Been there myself, except, thank God, not on this ship. I know it's hard. You think it's easy for me? I've got two kids I'm dreadfully worried about — constantly. And a husband I dearly love whom I haven't seen in forever. You've got to be tough. We've all got to be tough. We're not in some cushy, shore-based, staff-puke job. We're the tip of the spear. We *are* the spear. There are no points in our business for second place or runner-up. Sounds corny, but that's the way it is. Your job description is to be the best F-27C stealth back-seater in the Navy. Period!" She stood, her flight suit permeated by the unique aroma of a carrier pilot, her brows furrowed. "We've got a job to do. Are you with me, big guy?"

Twidget jumped up, put his burly arms around his pilot, gave her a crushing, brotherly hug, kissed her on the forehead and proclaimed, "Let's go get 'em, Big Sister. I'm with you!"

Paradise was quiet once again, witness to a remarkable display of raw human passion and naval aviation spirit. The seething eddies of interpersonal wants, jealousies, fears and intrigue were unpredictable, the one constant, a bedrock devotion to honor, duty and country.

The two non-flying ensigns, awash in confused thought, understood, words superfluous. Patty softly offered to her friend, "Now I understand why the Admiral's eulogy for Studs included the phrase, 'When the going is fast and rough, I will not falter,' " tearful sobs in a free fall from the two young naval officers.

323

CHAPTER 24

Chinese General Meets American Admiral

The *New York Independent's* lead editorial competed for attention with the newspaper's page-one headlines:

"ISIs DEMAND U.S. APOLOGY

Rashad Moheed, the spokesperson for the aggressive consortium of Iran, Saudi Arabia and Iraq, stood before the United Nations and emotionally demanded the immediate cessation of U.S. involvement in the region stating that, '. . . the Indian Ocean and its littorals were within a newly-proclaimed ISI sphere of influence and off-limits to Western powers.' Overcome by his own stridency, he was replaced by an assistant who argued for an unconditional apology for the double shoot-down by the American Navy pilots and the death of 37 schoolchildren, vowing to cutoff the flow of oil should the U.S. fleet not withdraw."

Rear Admiral Nancy Chandler received the editorial and ISI proclamation an hour out from Chunking, the Navy transport jet cruising leisurely at 52,000 feet and 1.1 indicated mach number, just past the speed of sound. The hand-written note at the end of both pieces from her boss, Vice Admiral Stan Sarodsy in his Pentagon command center, stated the obvious, "No points for second place, Nancy. Go for it."

Chandler, though a relatively youthful 38, was comfortable with the dynamics of the region comprising most of the Arabic world and the continent of Asia. The oil connection was, of course, second nature to her, the black gold transcending in import even that of religion. What troubled her, though, was the tone of the editorial, a fissure in the *quid pro quo* of global back-scratching. If, indeed, the political and industrial payoffs uncovered by Sarodsy's spooks were factual, nations would tremble and power structures crack.

The editorial piece needed little interpretation. It plainly stated the financial connection between the Chinese and the U.S. body politic and arms-related industries, an alliance, if true, of obscene proportion. The conclusion was inescapable: The Chinese leadership had bought the best technology and arms from the Americans. Chandler shuddered. Nuclear weapons were not mentioned.

Although a sophisticated student of the geo-strategic-political, she was a neophyte at the intrigue that wove seamlessly through the historical perspectives, the lessons of her politically-astute mother notwithstanding. Her notion of problem-solving implied that all cards were on the table, even, she reminded herself, when chief of staff to President Stallingsworth in her first term. She wished she could have been a fly on the wall to the dozens of locked-door meetings in her three-year White House tour, most often the participants being one or more of the Chinese officialdom, senior CEO ilk of the global arms industry and always, the ebullient wheeler and dealer, Richard Redman.

Snapped out of her reminiscences by the aircraft commander, the lieutenant gently nudged the only passenger of the functionally austere, twin-jet transport. "Admiral. We're starting our descent into Chunking's military airfield. Should be on deck in thirty-seven minutes. Notice our escort?"

Checking both wings, Nancy Chandler noted the muted silhouettes of the two fighters, seemingly locked together with the sleek American jet. On an impulse, Nancy waved at the fighter on the starboard wing, the only acknowledgement, a slight burble. "They've been with us for the last forty-five minutes, ma'am. Excellent formation pilots. They're on our frequency. Would you like to thank them for the escort?"

"No thanks, Sandra. I'll just keep my eyes closed. Don't distract them. OK?"

The transport jet broke out of the squalid overcast 1,500-feet above the ground, a gray pall of smog and smoke mixing with the somber vestiges of the late November afternoon. "Probably like Pittsburgh or Birmingham in the late twenties," she surmised, the stench of the sullen atmosphere adding credence to the dismal swamp of reduced horizontal visibility.

Once on deck, she went forward to the cockpit of the taxiing airplane, and thanked the two lieutenants, both of whom had been on the go for fifteen-plus hours. "Looks like a real paradise, ma'am," said the co-pilot adding, "Sure would like to fly one of those jets that escorted us in. Think I could?"

Sandra interrupted. "She's got more to worry about, big guy," playfully swiping the back of his head, her eyes unwavering from the "follow me" leading the way on the tarmac of the unfamiliar airport.

Chandler broke the after-landing repartee, adding, "You guys get max sleep. No telling when we'll be leaving or where. Maybe back to the Reagan."

"Aye, aye, ma'am," both replied in unison with a sparkle of enthusiasm that belied their obvious fatigue.

"Welcome to Chunking, Admiral. I am Major General Wu. General Wong asked that I extend to you and your pilots every courtesy. We are at your disposal."

"Thank you, General. Please lead the way."

Chandler knew, from her briefing book, that Wu was indeed Wong's top combat arms assistant, the same age as she, a graduate of the U.S. Air Force Academy Class of 1994 and Air Force pilot training one year later. Tall, articulate and immaculately attired, she suspected that he cut a wide professional swath.

He continued. "It is 1600 our time, two hours before our initial meeting with the General. You will be the guest of Mrs. Wong in the General's quarters. Admiral Demming and his group will arrive at 1730 and proceed directly to the conference."

The staff car eased to a stop in front of the rather modest house. Stepping out of the front door was a woman in her early forties, conservatively clad in a sarong of friendly hues, her soft eyes and pleasant smile a welcoming beacon to the tired naval officer. "Welcome, Admiral. Let me get your bag. Please come in to our home."

The old house was what Nancy would call cozy with a hint of old-style charm. Two stories, it fronted on a parade-like field framed by stately old oaks mostly bereft of leaves on the somber autumn day. The dark afternoon sky added to the sense of solemnity in the quarters. Nancy noted no house stewards or other help, the general's wife rolling the one bag of her guest to the spare bedroom on the ground floor. "Why don't you freshen up a bit and we can have some tea before the meeting?"

Over traditional green tea in the comfortable living room, Chandler paused at the portrait of a handsome young man attired in the regalia of a Chinese lieutenant, the wings of a pilot of the Imperial Chinese Air Force, prominent on his breast. "Our only son," lamented the hostess. "He was killed in an F-35 fighter shortly after he completed pilot training in your country — about five years ago. He was a fine son," she said softly, tears welling in the stoic facade, her gaze lingering. "He died doing what he loved the most. From the day he could ride a bicycle, he wanted to be a jet fighter pilot, just as his father."

"I'm sorry. He was indeed a handsome young man," and, though no tears, a moistness emanated in the eyes of the American naval officer.

For a few moments, the two women were silent, a respite of mutual understanding in the complex mysteries of the human spirit.

"I know you have been to China many times, Admiral."

Nancy interrupted her hostess. "Please call me Nancy."

"And me, Moonyeen, please," she said, the latter with a broad smile of immense warmth. "It means 'moonbeam' in Chinese, compliments to a full moon on the night of my birth and a father who had already settled on his son's name."

"Moonyeen. What a pretty name. Perhaps one day you

can visit America and we could spend some time together?"

"Oh, I would like that. We Chinese women though, are stay-at-home types. We seldom travel with our husbands."

Shifting subjects, Moonyeen Wong suggested a tour of the home. "These houses were all built in the early thirties." Pointing to a wall plaque, she offered, "This house was commissioned expressly for General Chang Kai Shek who was, at the time, a Colonel responsible for the early formation of our air force. He lived here, as you may know, until the start of World War II. To my husband, he is an original hero of the country whose core values linger deep within the warrior ethic of our pilots."

Her husband's study was an ordinary room converted to a spartan office, the only furnishings a desk and two upright chairs, several telephones and three photos displayed on the bare desk. Nancy said, "I would guess this is you and the General when he was a lieutenant," noting the smiling and confident young couple. "And this must be your son and husband, a major then, I think," the photo of a seasoned pilot and his four-year-old son held high as if to place the youngster into the jet's cockpit. Moonyeen added brightly, "Oh, those were happy days."

"And who is this?" said Nancy, peering at the montage of a handsome young aviator astride a sleek jet of unknown origin. Moonyeen laughed, her eyes sparkling. "That's our surrogate son, Major Ying Tsunami. He's a favorite of the General. Me, too. In fact, he'll be here for dinner. You'll like him. He's the commanding officer of one of our top, front-line fighter squadrons."

"Dinner?"

"Why, yes. When you finish your meeting, we'll meet here for dinner about nine or so, I would guess."

Nancy noted the simple place setting for eight. "Let's see," she smiled, her hostess antenna high in the air. "You, the General, Admiral Demming, Mr. Maltman and me. That leaves three to go?"

The older woman smiled, the creases of her still youthful face reflecting a matronly warmth to her guest. "Yes, but Major Tsunami and General Wu will attend as well, and, I think, a young Lieutenant who is assisting the Admiral. Should be fun. Want to see what we're having?" Moving to the functional kitchen, there was, prominent on the gas stove top, a large pot of a simmering stew-like concoction. "It's a specialty of mine — fish, shrimp, lobster and generous proportions of noodles, celery, onions, garlic, real Chinese hot sauces, and, with rice on the side. It's the quintessential one-dish meal. Good for the heart and not too heavy."

Noting Nancy's quizzical look, she continued. "I know what you're thinking. Where are all the house boys? Long story short, like much of our country in the past few years, the paradigms of the past have given way to a more enlightened — even westernized — era. We Chinese are much less formal now. I kind of like it," she added with a warm smile.

Major General Wu appeared at the door. "Greetings again, ladies. Looks as though you have had a productive visit," the chemistry between them obvious. "Smells good too, Mrs. Wong."

"You'll just have to wait, young man."

"Admiral," he said only slightly condescendingly and with a touch of formality, "Admiral Demming and his group have arrived. They're at the headquarters. You'll have a chance to chat before the meeting. Please come with me"

The gathering in General Wong's anteroom was like old home week. Nancy had become a fan of the warrior Demming, the retired Vice Admiral greeting her with a politically-shady bear hug and a slap on the back. "Nancy, good to see you. You've met Ernie Maltman, I presume?"

"Yes, sir. I knew him by reputation a few years back as the Navy's top fighter squadron commander," knowing full well that, had he stayed the course, he too would most likely have been a flag officer.

"And Major Ying Tsunami. Ying and I have known one another for many years and, more recently, we've added yet another notch to our friendship in the mountains of remote Iran." The young Chinese fighter pilot and the wary Navy rear admiral, shook hands, the eyes direct, the grips mutually firm.

"And Lieutenant Evelyn Swagger who was offered the opportunity to see another side of the U.S. Navy in spite of some rather traumatic events and personal loss less than a week ago."

329

Evelyn stood tall, her shipshape figure adorned only by a wash-khaki outfit, the parallel bars of a full Navy lieutenant astride her throat, the gold wings of a naval flight officer above her left breast pocket.

Nancy Chandler smiled warmly and extended her hand to Swagger. "Evelyn, I've heard of your ejection and the loss of your pilot. I am so sorry. Thank you for all you've done for our Navy."

"Thank you for remembering, Admiral."

The attentions and demeanor of Ying Tsunami during this briefest of interludes had not gone unnoticed by both admirals. The Chinese pilot was almost in a trance, his eyes hardly wavering from the Navy lieutenant, his attentions and adulations far from benign or transparent to the two senior naval officers. Nancy thought to herself — not in such a short time!

After a polite, albeit subdued, greeting by General Wong, the group retired to an adjacent conference room. Surprisingly, the only Chinese present were Wong, Wu and Tsunami. No aides, no projectionists and no coffee-servers. Wong got to the point.

"This meeting is off-the-record. The agenda and outcome are known only to our governing triumvirate. On your side, the only recipient is Vice Admiral Sarodsy, with whom I have been in personal contact on a number of issues over the past few days. My plan is to present an introductory briefing consisting of the ISI intelligence overview, our military force projection capability and offer a most general scenario that may appear to be in the best interests of our countries. Any questions?" His gaze circled the oval table, Chandler to his right, Demming on the left and Wu, Tsunami, Maltman and Evelyn Swagger equally seated around the periphery.

Surprisingly, Wong himself was the initial briefer. No legions of aides or junior officers, he called up the relevant information from a bank of computer controls. Much to the amazement of all, his compatriot Wu and protege Tsunami, the general projected a satellite image of a piece of northeastern Iranian desert as the first item for discussion.

"Bruce, my friend," he began, "here is a picture of you and Major Tsunami." The image, a nothingness of desert and low mountains, progressively zoomed to reveal the stark outline of a runway, then blurred images of an airplane and then finally to the awesomely clear picture of the latest in Chinese technology, a two-seat variant of the F-48 stealth Dynasty. "That, my flying Admiral, is you and Ying rolling out precisely fifty-three hours ago at our supposedly clandestine base in Iran." Evelyn Swagger was flabbergasted. It was indeed the same base she and her pilot had overflown only a few days ago.

The message was crystal clear to Chandler. The technology was first-rate. At least as good as that of the U.S. Irreverently, she spoke up. "Compliments of the Consolidated Company, no doubt?"

"Correct, Admiral," said the head of the Chinese Air Force, his eyes penetrating the psyche of the naval officer. "So, too is the fighter on the runway. Admiral Demming can attest to that. Right, Bruce?"

Wong continued. "Let me back off a bit, Admiral Chandler. I want you to see our Caspian pipeline. It's about 74% complete and will terminate at our northwestern province of Xian, near the old Silk Road," his laser pointer shifting to a large-scale map of the troubled region. "To put it without excessive embellishment, that pipeline represents the future of my country. Without it, we are hostage to whomever would seek to limit our incoming oil supply. We will never become free of coal until we get our fair share of the world's oil," he paused for effect, "at a fair price."

He let the latter sink in. Nancy's brain was in a fast-track mode, though nothing the general had said was news to her. Without asking, the general, in few short minutes, had clearly formed the conceptual framework for the ensuing discussions.

"Now, let me shift gears," Wong continued, all business. "I'll ask General Wu to provide an in-depth overview of the ISI military situation. And Admiral," he looked at Chandler, "I realize you are privy to all this, but I want to provide you with our best estimates. They may or may not track with your intelligence."

The Chinese major general, fighter pilot and military strategist proceeded to outline, in rapid-fire sequence, an analysis of the ISI consortium, the focus on the clear formation of the pincers about to envelope the Caspian Sea, the several tentacles of oil pipelines obviously at massive risk, excepting, of course, the line heading southeastward through northern Iran to the Persian Gulf. Chandler knew all this and could well have done the brief herself, blindfolded, the imperceptible arrogance of the young general noticeable only to the female antennae of the Navy flag officer. She wisely chose to keep her cool, the disdain for women in the Chinese military culture second nature to her. She was, in fact, Sarodsy had warned her, the first senior female officer to penetrate the interior of the male-dominated Chinese warrior ethic, the origins, right or wrong, the product of literally generations of a nation weaned on combat among themselves, the Mongolian hordes and, in later years, the Japanese.

Chandler was well-versed on what would come next, a two-pronged ISI strategy to capitalize on the Achilles heel of northern Iran: In order to control the Caspian region, the logistics lifelines through the mountains of northern Iran had to be preserved. The problem, though, was that the fragile link snaked through rugged terrain, a landscape at least as formidable as the Rocky Mountains of the western U.S. There were, in fact, Nancy recalled from her younger years as a top secret Pentagon strategic staffer, some twenty-seven viable choke-points in the lines of communication between Iran and Iraq and the Caspian. The neutralization of these barriers would result in an almost certain withering of the armed might of the ISI's mounting military presence in the oil-rich territory in and about the Caspian. Precise air power, was, of course, the pivotal key.

True to her mental prognosis, General Wu hit the exact points in the strategic briefing. Chandler resisted the temptation to simulate a demonstrable modicum of boredom and allowed the confident general officer to play his cards.

"General Wu, pardon me for interrupting, but may I ask a question, please?"

"Certainly, Admiral."

"What, and how many, weapons would you employ in

332

the most strategic choke-points and, would you clarify the highest priority," adding an after-the-fact, "sir?" her smile genuine.

Major General Wu, unaccustomed to interruptions, started a gentlemanly glare in the general direction of his guest of honor, only to be distracted by yet another gratuitism, this time from Demming. "Good question, Admiral. Wondered the same myself."

Without hesitation, Wu launched into a spring-loaded, diagrammatic, one-way brief, as if the intended audience were the assembled offensive power of the Imperial Chinese Air Force. The answer was tactically brilliant, crystal-clear and strategically appropriate, the five-minute tutorial emphasizing the combat-oriented thought processes of the Chinese. The choke-points could be neutralized largely by Chinese air power, provided they could be launched within 1,000 miles from the target objectives.

Chandler cut to the nub. "Could you effectively handle the targets unilaterally and," with a pronounced pause for effect, "keep them neutralized?"

The senior general broke in, the wisdom of years overriding the will to overly impress. "We could indeed cause severe stress to the Caspian invaders. But, our bases are limited." Wong walked to the large wall map. "It would be foolish of us to act alone, you know. That said, however, should this pipeline be threatened, we are prepared to act unilaterally. As you are aware, the string of defensive bases throughout the region have been structured to prevent damaging attacks on the ISI lines of communications. Just as the bases around Bandar Abas offer a buffer to the U.S. Navy fleet, so too, is the Teheran region a wall for attacks from the the west and east. General Wu was about to brief the second set of strategic imperatives, which, in general, must be dealt with before the choke-point targets." General Wong regained his seat at the table, adding, "Please continue, General Wu."

The concise briefing by Wu made it clear that unilateral military action by the Chinese was not a viable option. One-by-one, he pulled up overlays of the ISI perimeter defenses and, for each, it was apparent that the vaunted Chinese Air Force would have been hard-pressed to act alone.

Abruptly, Wong stood. "It is time for the meal Mrs. Wong has prepared for us. Please join me."

Upon arriving at the quarters, the older hostess took the visibly-fatigued Evelyn Swagger to the second-floor spare bedroom. "Perhaps you would like to rest, my dear?"

"Oh, no, ma'am. I'm fine. Who is this?" she asked, pointing to one of the two photos on the nightstand, the light subdued, the mood quiescent."

"That's our daughter, Yeen. She's twenty-two now. Just graduated from Stanford and will return here to join an aerospace technology firm as an engineer. And this is," she offered softly, "our son," holding the photo of the air force lieutenant astride his sleek jet, the smile contagiously friendly. "He died in a plane crash some years ago. He would have been just a few years older than you."

When the guests had arrived for dinner, Moonyeen Wong had hugged Ying Tsunami warmly, noting his waneness and a demeanor at odds to the usually energetic officer. Unmistakable, too, was a female premonition of hers that there was more than business between the major and his Navy lieutenant friend. When Mrs. Wong had mentioned her son's death, Evelyn had visibly flinched, her eyes locked onto the confident young pilot, her knees wobbly. Slowly she had sat on the single bed, tears flowing freely from a face struggling with what might have been.

"Mrs. Wong, three days ago I lost the love of my life and," she hesitated, opting to trust the kindly woman, "our baby. Our fighter went out of control in the Iranian mountains and crashed. If it weren't for Admiral Demming and Ying, I wouldn't have made it."

The two had held one another, soft sobs framed by tears that cleansed the souls of the two heroic beings.

Down below, General Wong asked Admiral Demming to join him in his study, leaving Wu and Chandler together and Ying in the kitchen stirring the Moonyeen concoction as his surrogate mother had wisely requested.

"Bruce," the general got right to the point, "sorry about

Wu. He's not used to dealing with women at such high levels."

"No problem, General. I guarantee that Nancy Chandler can handle him or anyone else for that matter. She's got her stuff together."

"My friend," the general began, "allow me to speak freely, please. Here's a copy of the lead editorial in the *New York Independent* that will appear soon in your country and throughout the world. Somehow, your Senator Montgomery is onto the pragmatics of our political and economic strategy of the past fifteen years. You, my dear compatriot, have been part and parcel of our efforts. We supply your industrial and political leaders with dollars and you, et al., present our country with the latest arms and technology. This is and has been, of course, all legal, indeed encouraged by your leaders." He paused, his fingers dancing about a large globe. "It is no secret that had Senator Cassidy toppled Stallingsworth as President of your country in 2008, the free flow of advanced weaponry to China would have essentially ceased. The facts are clear that we have treated business in the U.S. just as within our country. To get access to the right policy makers, means money under the table. You call it bribery, we call it access. Face it, access and bribery, in the context of influence, mean precisely the same."

Demming broke in. "We had our chances to reform the campaign morass long ago. You know what our politicians have known for generations. Money means power. It's the Golden Rule, trite though it may seem in these circumstances. He who has the gold, makes the rules. My sense though, is that fundamentally, the American people will not kowtow to outright bribery and that's what the campaign game has descended to. Our friend Montgomery, and, I'm sure, a covey of others, are in agreement that serious change must take place. Cassidy's death may just be the catalyst. You will be able to tap into our system, but most likely at a slower rate and with essentially no dollars under the table."

Wong continued. "Now, let me ask you, Admiral. How can we be confident that the U.S. will use military force against the ISI consortium? Your President has made it clear she will not authorize such action."

The admiral laughed. "Why not discuss it with Admiral Chandler? That's what she's here for, best I can figure."

"Well," the senior general said, his face to the garden windows, "I too, have a problem with the female admiral. Nothing personal, of course. It's just totally against the grain of our military culture." He smiled, turned and faced the older warrior. "Come, let's eat."

The atmosphere in the candle-lit living room was thick, the tensions obvious. Wu was avoiding Nancy Chandler and Ying was steering clear of both.

"Sorry for the delay, Admiral Chandler," said the host. "Admiral Demming and I have been friends for years and had some catching up to do. Have you two," nodding to his younger general and the American admiral, "been getting acquainted?"

Nancy Chandler was an impressive woman. Still in her thirties, she was dapper in her blue service uniform, the one broad stripe and a smaller one atop, framing a still-youthful figure. She could have worn flat shoes and indeed, had been so advised, but heels and her persona went hand-in-hand. There was no way she was going to be taken down a peg by the slightly overbearing General Wu. She had attempted a rapproachment of sorts while awaiting dinner by asking about his family. "None;" where was he from? "Beijing;" what he had flown the most, and so on. The answers had been only the minimum necessary for basic civility. Ying too, had noted the strain between the two senior officers, and wisely, made himself scarce in the kitchen.

Shifting gears, General Wong called upstairs to his wife. "Moonyeen, are you and the Lieutenant coming down? We're hungry."

The two women descended arm-in-arm down the stairs, Mrs. Wong noting the immediate change in Ying, his eyes alert. Too, the iciness between Wu and the younger admiral did not go unnoticed. "I am remiss. Please accept my apologies. Lieutenant Swagger and I found we had much in common."

The one-dish meal was superb, chopsticks *de rigeur,* the

steaming offering a saimin-like blend that fogged glasses and cleansed pallets. The host poured tiny glasses of a luke-warm local wine while the traditional green tea made its way around the table.

Nancy spoke up. "May I offer a toast, General Wong? This excellent meal deserves recognition."

"Why, yes, Admiral. Of course."

She raised her portion of wine, looked eyeball-to-eyeball in turn with Wu, Swagger, Ying, Demming, Wong and, finally, to Moonyeen Wong. "To our hostess, Mrs. Wong, with gracious thanks for your warm and cordial hospitality and the most delicious saimin I have ever tasted." With that, she held her cup high above her head, a beaming smile for all.

Demming smiled, Wu was confused, the senior general was stoic, Ying clinked her glass with his and Evelyn Swagger brightly proclaimed, "And with wishes for more to follow."

Following a brief pause, the senior general slowly stood and softly proclaimed, his cup at eye level, "Gambai." His eyes met those of his guests, a smile deep within. "For our distinguished guests, it means an empty cup, symbolic of a long life and lasting friendship."

Arising from the eclectic table, Evelyn gently caught the arm of Nancy Chandler. "Admiral, may I please be excused from the meeting? I don't care to admit it, but I'm terribly tired. I can help Mrs. Wong with the dishes."

"Absolutely. No problem. And," with her arm around the junior naval officer, "thanks for the follow-on toast." With a smile from ear-to-ear, she added sunnily, "Perfect!"

In the cloistered privacy of the general's conference room, the prominent red phone rang to life, the group just getting settled, the hour late for the Americans. Wu handed the phone to his boss, his face grim. Wong listened for a moment, then hit a few computer buttons, bringing the briefing screen to life. His laser pointer quivered, its target the termination of the Chinese pipeline just to the west of the Caspian Sea. Surrounding the strategic node, with clearly overwhelming force, was the advance contingent of the ISI ground forces. Punching another icon, the side-bar read simply: "ISI forces demand the withdrawal of U.S. warships in the contiguous waters of the Indian Ocean."

Off to the side of the conference room, was the ubiquitous CNN flat screen HDTV display, its omnipresent facade declaring to the world in English: "ISIs demand U.S. withdrawal," and just below, "ISI warning to other countries."

Nancy Chandler stood, her 5-foot-5-inch frame striking, her nimble brain collecting and focusing, her manifold mission clear. "Gentlemen," she began, shedding her blue service jacket, "we are obviously at a decision point. Allow me, please, to lay our cards on the table. Several points, if I may." She strode to the large map of the region, laser pointer borrowed from her host, the eyes of the warrior Wu trying to comprehend the assertiveness of the American naval officer.

"First — my Admiral, Vice Admiral Stan Sarodsy, has authorized me to suggest a policy that would offer a decisive, yet time-constrained, military set of actions." She paused, collected her thoughts and locked eyes with Wong. "These actions would involve joint military operations with your country and mine against the ISI forces, given, of course, that diplomatic efforts fail."

Wong interrupted. "But I was under the impression that your President would not condone such action. She has made it plain to the world that . . ." At this precise moment, the CNN screen took attention with breaking news, the smiling persona of President Virginia Roberts Stallingsworth filling the display, her hair coiffed in a becoming style. Her resonate voice came alive on the opposite side of the globe.

"Ladies and gentlemen of the United States and about the world. We are confronted by a situation 8,000 miles from our shores that is worrisome, but solvable by reasonable persons. The consortium of Iraq, Saudi Arabia and Iran, as you are no doubt aware, has been engaged in overt military action, the purpose of which is to gain control of a substantial portion of the world's oil supply." Her smile faded, her face taking on the specter of a pouting young girl. "I ask, in the name of decency, for the ISIs to back off. There has been enough blood shed over oil. We want no more. The thought of our young women and men coming home in body bags is terrifying. PLEASE — you leaders of the aggressors — PLEASE return to your homeland and let those in the Caspian region live in peace. I do not appeal to you from a military perspective. I plead with you to act in the name of decency." Uncharacteristically, her eyes were moist, her brow glistened. "PLEASE — — I IMPLORE YOU — — — **PLEASE!**"

Abruptly, she turned, her back to the camera, and disappeared behind a welcome curtain and the minions of presidential power.

Clicking on mute, the group around the the conference table were silent, unbelieving. Nancy was concurrently stunned and ashamed. Virginia, she knew, was not only scared, she was petrified and it showed. The room was silent, mute blanking the attempts of gratuitous pundits to explain the President's sad performance to a world struggling for leadership.

"General, I know what you are thinking," Nancy said, standing to address the group, realizing the frailty of the duly-elected leader of the civilized world and her former mentor. "The facts are that there are those in our civilian political leadership who firmly believe a laissez-faire appeasement of the ISI attacks on free countries will throw the world into a dangerously destabilizing imbalance. I want to outline a conceptual framework for discussion, all of course, once again, contingent on the failure of diplomatic efforts."

"First, is military action; second, is the generic subject of China's 'access' into the U.S. body politic and industry; and the third, and toughest of all, I'll outline in a moment." General Wong was reflective, but realistic, while his younger compatriot, Wu, was openly disdainful, the notion of a woman dictating military strategy to him, outright heresy.

Rear Admiral Nancy Chandler, walked to the giant electronic display. "First, here's what we would propose, militarily." She proceeded to articulate a concise, rational series of decisive strikes, the common denominator being a forty-eight hour, five air-craft carrier and three Chinese air force wings' worth of deadly air power. The combined combat forces would effectively seal the northern Iranian mountainous choke-points and result in an almost immediate diminution of ISI combat capability in the Caspian, the loss of ammunition, food and supplies devastating to the ground and air forces. "The key, gentlemen, is a total, around-the-clock, precise and targeted destruction of the targets highlighted on the screen. The considerable ISI forces in the Caspian will start to shrivel from a lack of basic logistics within days, their military ef-fectiveness but a shadow of what it is today."

The ten-minute strategic dissertation was brilliant, even to the employment of Chinese air power. Wu's only comment was a gratuitous, "Makes sense, Admiral."

Wong just nodded, knowing the harder part was yet to come. "And second, Admiral?"

Nancy shifted gears, from the military to the political. "Let me cut to the bottom line, sir, without mincing words." She looked squarely at her host. "The considerable monies your country provides for 'access' into our country must cease. Our senior offi-cials, both political and industrial, have become acquiescent to a degree never before experienced in our country. It is totally out of control. For what it's worth, the details will eventually be subject to the light of day. When that happens, the backlash from an en-lightened populace will be enormous. We must have assurances that the payoffs — we call them bribes — will cease."

Wong let this latter point sink in. Long a routine way of business in Asian countries, the notion of business competing solely on the merits was alien to the culture. He knew the issue would eventually surface, as did the Chinese ruling triumvirate that had met the day before, the recognition that times were changing, finally sinking in. Quite simply, matter-of-factly, he said, "That can be arranged, Admiral." And, with a sigh, his voice still commanding, "Perhaps we can take a short break."

Wu moved to Chandler's side, his handsome demeanor a

sliver softer. Peering down at the assured naval officer, he offered, "That was an excellent strategic and tactical briefing, Admiral."

"Why, thank you, kind sir. I'm happy you approved." Looking up at his hardened face, she smiled and said, "Would it be asking too much for you to call me Nancy? It's an old American custom."

Wu, in turn, sensing a spirit of halting rapproachment, said gruffly, "And perhaps you could call me Ching. It's an historic family name going back nine generations."

"Happy to, Ching. It's a nice name. I like it. And thank you for the compliment. It does make sense, provided," her eyes locked upwards with his, "the strikes are perfectly coordinated and precisely executed."

"Perhaps," he responded, his eyes on hers, shifting the subject only slightly, "I could provide you a tour of the base following our meeting?"

Her laughing response, "Don't you ever sleep? This is as bad as our Pentagon."

"Well, *mon Amiral*, it's not often we have the opportunity to host one so strategically and tactically aware," the hint of a smile cracking the tough exterior.

Reassembling in the quiet headquarters, General Wong got right to the point. "And the third point, Admiral?"

"Yes, sir." She stood and walked deliberately around the conference table, all eyes expectant. "We want your country to request the assistance of the U.S. Navy in executing a military strategy to neutralize the ISI dominance of the Caspian and allow China its fair share of the region's oil."

Wong responded. "I am not surprised by your request. It must be understood, of course, that the objectives are extremely finite, focused and time-constrained. Also, in concert with your President's fears, you must acknowledge, that while militarily feasible, these actions will result in severe ISI retaliation against your naval forces. You — and your leaders in Washington — must be willing to accept substantial casualties."

Following the meeting, Nancy got on her secure phone with a direct, covered line to Admiral Sarodsy's Pentagon command center. His only response was a pragmatic, "Good job, Nancy. We'll stand by on the request. Senator Montgomery is with me now and is prepared to handle the political aspects. He's got quite a tripartisan group in tow," adding a fatherly, "You get some sleep."

The meeting broke up with Wong explaining, "Got some work to attend to," the midnight hour no hindrance. Wu asked if Nancy was up for a tour of the base.

"Sure, Ching, but I must admit my motor's winding down. Make it short."

"Short" for Wu, was not in his vernacular, the first stop for the duo an immense hangar housing a formidable wing of F-48 stealth Dynasty fighters, a quartet about to take flight.

"Where are they going at this hour?"

"Just a training mission. We operate twenty-four hours per day and every day of the week. Come, let's visit one of the ready rooms."

Snapping to rigid attention, the dozen or so young fighter pilots responded to the general's dictum to "Provide the American Navy Admiral an overview of your missions for the night."

Nancy Chandler, though fatigued, was most admiral-like, her blue service uniform and high-heeled shoes still the uniform of the day. To the annoyance of her host, she walked up to each pilot, looked him in the eyes and shook hands, a warm smile for the young warriors, an unaccustomed bonus.

En route to the quarters, Wu cautioned Nancy. "In our military, we do not shake hands with those our junior."

Chandler's matter-of-fact, friendly response? "We do."

Despite the hour, Mrs. Wong opened the door. Warmly, she asked, "How did you two get along?"

Nancy laughed, her sense of achievement nurtured by a genuine likeness for the Chinese general officer. "He's a nice man, though a bit old-fashioned, I'd say." With a twinkle in her eyes, she said, "You didn't have to stay up for me."

The older woman smiled. "Oh, I'm used to it. We keep rather random hours in this house. Actually, Evelyn just turned in. We had some wonderful girl talk. She told me all about her Sam and I about our son. I don't often have the opportunity, you know."

Nancy Chandler drifted off to a restless sleep, her thoughts on the forthcoming Chinese communiqué to the world and a captivating general who would not go away.

CHAPTER 25

Potpourri

Deep within his Pentagon command center, Vice Admiral Stan Sarodsy hit the red-phone button for his combat arms assistant, who, at the moment, was two hours into a well-deserved sleep deep within the interior of China.

Groggily, the confused dream drifting off to a vapid nothingness, Rear Admiral Nancy Chandler shook off the cobwebs, reached for her tiny phone, punched in her PIN and answered gruffly, "Chandler."

"Nancy, I hate to wake you. Are you awake?"

"I am now, sir. What a twenty-four hours!"

Sarodsy, giving her a chance to regain her composure, said, "You did a great job with General Wong. I just finished talking with him and he was most complimentary of you. I might add, it was my impression that his top sidekick was, too."

Nancy smiled. "We ended up with a good rapport, Admiral. I wouldn't call it bonding, but at least we managed a level playing field."

"Roger that. Got some marching orders for you. Ready to copy?"

"Yes, sir. Shoot," responded the now wide-awake naval officer.

"Well, the proverbial stuff is about to hit the fan. Wong read me his proposed statement to the world. It's perfect. He'll present it personally on behalf of President Jiang, in about two hours. The gist is simple: 'We request the military support of the U.S. naval fleet in pursuit of limited combat operations against the ISIs. Objective? Quit the Caspian. Two phases —first will be a forty-eight hour precision series of strikes against the ISI lines of communication in northern Iran. Second will be concurrent, pre-emptive-defensive strikes to neutralize the ISI's ability to counter our choke-points strategy.' "

Nancy, her strategic antenna in full spread interrupted. "Sir, if I may?"

"Go ahead."

"How's Virginia? We saw her embarrassing spectacle on CNN."

"Nancy," he paused, "our sources indicate she's an emotional basket case. Senator Montgomery has the entire town running scared. There's no telling how she will react when Wong goes public. Probably best to tighten your seat belt."

Sarodsy continued. "Here's the immediate game plan. First, you are to proceed directly to the Reagan in the Indian Ocean along with the young Lieutenant. I want you to take charge of our battle groups. Fact is, I need your candid input as the situation unfolds. The specific strike plans, weapons, targets and timing are being worked out now for the Chinese and our forces. Got it?"

"Yes, sir."

"Second. Please relay to Admiral Demming that I want him to stay in Chunking to act as our liaison with Wong. He and the admiral are on the same frequency for sure."

"Lastly, Ernie Maltman is to return to Washington ASAP. The Senator needs him to help orchestrate the political scene in this town." A slight pause. "Any questions?"

"No, sir. You may expect both airplanes to be airborne in a bit over an hour."

A soft knock on her ground floor bedroom broke the silence following the call. "Come in." It was Mrs. Wong.

"Oh, Moonyeen, I hope I didn't wake you."

"No problem, my dear. I sensed that events were brewing. The General is still not home. I'm used to it. Come, I'll fix you some breakfast and wake Evelyn, if that's a part of the plan."

"Yes, please, and thank you. We will depart in less than an hour, I'm afraid. May I use the General's command phone?"

345

Nancy gave the requisite instructions to be relayed to Maltman, the four pilots, Demming and to ". . . please let the General know of our intentions."

Evelyn Swagger appeared at the table, her work khaki uniform showing the effects of the past twenty-four hours, her face reflecting the blessing of a few hours sleep. "We're headed back to the Reagan, Evelyn. You'll get a chance for some sleep en route. I'll brief you once we're airborne. So far, so good."

General Wong, as usual, had not slept. He was mentally preparing himself for the live telecast to the world. His three-minute pronouncement must be clear, unambiguous, and leave no opportunity for misinterpretation.

He had an additional concern. Two days before, in the cold and barren reaches of the Iranian mountains bordering Pakistan, the wreckage of the U.S. Navy F-27C stealth Phantom III had been discovered, along with the unrecognizable remains of the pilot. Almost intact though, had been a cigarette-sized gadget on the port wingtip, that, he had recently learned, was a miniature device to detect weapons-grade plutonium. The readings were conspicuous, the meanings unmistakable. There had been, of course, two airplanes on the flyover of the remote and formerly clandestine base. He thought that surely the Americans would put two and two together.

Wong's ruminations were suddenly broken by General Wu. "General, I will bid farewell to the Americans, if you like."

"Yes, please do. I trust Major Tsunami is about to land at his base?"

"Yes, sir. He should be on deck in about 27 minutes. He's got a full plate facing him." He paused. "General, I have a request."

"Go ahead," the general responded tersely, his mind in full afterburner.

"Our coordinated strike-planning with the Americans is about 87% complete. It is my intention to personally lead the first strike groups."

With barely a moment's hesitation, General Wong retorted

with a matter-of-fact, "Of course."

The diverse group at the two waiting U.S. transport jets stood shivering in the frigid, early-morning darkness, Nancy reflecting on the emotional goodbye with Moonyeen Wong. The two had hugged as had Evelyn and the older woman, embraces that symbolized a common bond of valiant warriors and their mothers since the dawn of written history. "We will meet again, Moonyeen," Nancy had said, climbing into the staff car driven by the flight-suited Major General Ching Wu.

Hesitantly, Evelyn Swagger asked from the rear seat, "Will Major Tsunami see us off, sir?"

"No, Lieutenant. He was airborne at 0215 this morning to return to command of his squadron. Should be landing about the time you get airborne." The general, unaccustomed to such trivia, added an uncomfortable, "He asked me to say goodbye to you."

Nancy Chandler met off to the side with Demming and Maltman. "Admiral Demming and Ernie, Admiral Sarodsy directed that I proceed direct to the Reagan battle group, for you Admiral Demming, to stay in Chunking, and for Ernie to return as soon as possible to Washington."

"I know," responded the former Tomcat pilot. "I just talked with my boss. Washington will soon experience the biggest blockbuster to hit it since the Civil War. So far, the Senator has about 142 members of Congress lined up, including 106 ECATS, ready to seize the day and bring some semblance of sanity back to a governing font of power that has gone, with few exceptions, totally corrupt." He smiled at Nancy and the Navy lieutenant. "Personally, I would give my eyeteeth to join with you on the Reagan." They all shook hands, the old admiral offering a vintage, politically-incorrect hug and slap on the backsides of the two naval officers.

Purposefully, slowly, Chandler walked to the tall, handsome Chinese general officer about to turn fighter pilot, the cold wind biting her bare legs, the blue service uniform jacket scant protection. For a moment, he thought to put his arms around her, a natural human reaction in most such occasions. Her hair blow-

347

ing, she took his hand in hers, brought her gaze to his and said in a voice barely audible above the whine of the idling nearby jet transport, "Until we meet again, Ching Wu."

The handshake lingering, his response, eyes penetrating, "*A bien tôt, mon Amiral.*"

Relinquishing the handhold, he brought his right hand to a crisp salute. Without a pause, she did the same.

With that, she ushered Evelyn Swagger into the jet, stood at the top step and waved to her host, a confident smile topping her high-heeled shoes .

The flight of Major Ying Tsunami from Chunking to his secret base in Iran had been routine, the eight F-48 Dynasty stealth jets moving supersonically as one through the skies of China's forbidden wastelands to the north and west. The precision of the recovery, he thought, would almost rival that of a U.S. Navy aircraft carrier. One by one, the pattern was repeated. In six minutes, all fighters were on deck and swallowed by the giant hangar.

Ying received a short update on his squadron, checked the security of the curtained enclave within, noted the rapid loading of precision munitions being hoisted onto his 24 jets and retired to his austere office and sleeping quarters.

Throughout the hour-and-twenty-minute milk-run flight, he had attempted to erase the visions of the Navy lieutenant from a brain attempting to focus on a highly-complex tactical action plan for sustained combat. Repeatedly, his mind drifted to the specter of her limp body seeking the warmth of life from his, the unbelievable meeting in her stateroom in paradise on the Navy carrier and her candidly refreshing assertiveness at the dinner only hours before. How he wished he could have bid her farewell! To himself, what will the future bring? A troubled sleep, his head on the desk.

Halfway around the world, Beverly Demming Boone was, at the moment, watching the ritual 10:00 p.m. CNN news, her brood of two girls and the little ones of her sister Susan, tucked away for the night. The sleek newscaster indicated breaking news was to be aired shortly having relevance to the ISI situation.

A soft knock at her door. It was Bill Montrose, her worried next-door neighbor. "Didn't want to wake the girls with a phone call. I saw your light on and wanted to make sure you knew about the upcoming news. Sounds ominous!"

"Come in, Bill. We'll watch it together. Good therapy. I sense all hell is going to break loose. My dad is still over there. Last I heard, he was on board the USS *Reagan* somewhere in the Indian Ocean. Can you believe it? Mom is worried sick. How about some slightly-tepid coffee?"

"Sounds good. Thanks."

The announcer came onto the HDTV giant flat-screen display in the homey family room, indicating that due to technical difficulties, the breaking news would be delayed fifteen minutes.

"Bill, I noticed the long black limo of Dolores Miller outside last night. You two getting along? She does seem to be a generous person. You heard about the scholarship fund, no doubt?"

The rush of words gave Bill's flushing cheeks a chance to normalize, a glow only a female would have caught. Sipping his lukewarm coffee, he said, "She's a nice lady. Kind of lonesome is my guess. No kids and a phantom husband. Wants to set up some sort of advanced school for Navy dependents. Apparently expense is not an issue. Asked if I would be interested in heading up the business side."

"Why, Bill, how marvelous. What an opportunity." With a swallow of her coffee, the mood cautious, she said, "Are you lonesome, Bill?" immediately wishing she had stuck with the school subject.

He grinned. "I guess so, but with school, the kids, you next door, I keep my mind on the ball. My life is so simple compared to you and Tommy and," his gaze on the dying fire, "all the troops out on the front line, including Wendy. My guess is her plate is overflowing." Permeating the cozy family room, the aroma of freshly-brewed coffee filtered into the quiet brain waves of the two. He asked, "You doing OK, Beverly?"

"I guess I do have a pot of problems. Don't we all? My dad, Sandy Anderson, Suzette, the kids, Susan — in particular. I could go on and on. I must admit, I'm pretty strung-out. It's nice to be able to talk to someone other than my mother or Sandy. I hope you don't mind. As Tommy would say, you're kind of like an anchor to windward." A tear eased out of each eye, her head harboring a blob of competing personal demands, the closeness of her neighbor both distracting and comforting.

The television came to life, the newscaster proclaiming breaking news from the Chinese, but that the subject was unknown. Flashing to a lone, uniformed figure seated at a bare table, the room's only adornment was a poster-sized map of the Middle East, Indian Ocean and western China.

"Good evening. I am General Wong of the Imperial Chinese Air Force. I am speaking for the Chinese governing leadership and our President Jiang with a most important announcement which will be brief and concise: Unless the ISI forces cease hostile combat operations in the Caspian region, my country will take military action to preserve our fair access to the oil reserves in the area. It is our judgment that such action on our part is risky and our losses would be severe. That said, however, we are prepared to accept such risk simply because the very survival of our country is at stake. Control of the Caspian reserves by a consortium bent on holding our nation hostage, is unacceptable."

Wong had proceeded, as was his style, with no notes or prompts. Slowly, he turned in his chair to frame the large map, his laser pointer highlighting the snaking outline of the critical pipeline and the presence of five U.S. Navy carrier battle groups spread throughout the Indian Ocean, Mediterranean Sea and Red Sea. His eyes returned to the inanimate camera.

"In order to provide the clearest message possible to the ISIs, our leadership is hereby requesting that the

350

U.S. join with my country in joint military action to cause an expeditious withdrawal of hostile forces from the Caspian. Specifically, we propose an around-the-clock series of focused, massive air and missile strikes against the ISI lines of communication in the mountains of Iran in concert with the preemptive neutralization of strategically-significant ISI air defenses. We therefore request that American naval forces in the region join with us in such actions. These strikes will commence no earlier than thirty six-hours from now. Thank you. We await the responses of the U.S. government and the consortium of Iraq, Saudi Arabia and Iran."

As the embers in the fireplace struggled to stay alive, Beverly broke the tense silence. "I hope the Reagan is up to it. I've heard so much via the grapevine that scares me."

"Well, I know Wendy. She's as tough as they come. I'll guarantee you the Red Rippers will be ready. She'll have them whipped into shape for sure."

The television scene shifted to a group of reporters standing in the blowing cold of the November night, the illuminated outline of the White House at stark contrast to the leafless trees.

Concurrent with Wong's short, but convincing discourse, the diplomatic channels between the U.S. and China had been frantic. Somewhat mysteriously, one such Chinese communiqué had offered the prospect of "No further political contributions or payments to either American officialdom or industry top-brass." The statement, received some two hours prior to Wong's public request, was read in the cloistered alcoves of the Washington and arms-industry boardrooms with a sense of profound disbelief, a crumbling of the past two-decade's worth of status quo, a finite probability. On top of the Montgomery allegations, the simple message from the Chinese portended real trouble to the incumbent body politic, party affiliation a non-issue.

In the upstairs living quarters of the White House, the hour close to 11:00 p.m., the expensive oriental vase, a long ago gratuity from a willing Asian accomplice, crescendoed against an un-yielding wall. "Those miserable, ungrateful sons of bitches! After all we've done for them." The intended recipient was none other than the omnipresent Richard Redman, who, at the moment, had some reason to believe that he could well be a victim of the next airborne *"objet d'art."*

Ever since President Stallingsworth's abominably embar-rassing spectacle on TV imploring the ISIs to ". . . PLEASE be reasonable," her emotional barometer had been in a tumbling free-fall.

"If those presumptuous assholes think I'll authorize the use of U.S. military forces, they are sadly mistaken. Mark my words, if those uniformed ignoramuses go against my express wishes, I'll fire every last one of them." As an afterthought: "That worthless Montgomery. He's behind all this."

The tentative knock at the door to the sacrosanct living quarters brought forth a harried national security advisor and press spokeswomen. "Madame President, the press wants you to make a statement. Specifically, they are asking what the 'cease payments' business is all about and does it have any-thing to do with the recent initiatives of Montgomery. Also, they want to know if you intend to consult the Congress before taking military action."

"NO MILITARY ACTION. Read my lips. What's it take for those simplistic morons to understand?" Her voice was a barely controlled, high-frequency screech, a frazzled hairdo re-flecting the turmoil deep within a severely-distressed psyche.

The CNN reporter held her microphone to a dignified Senator Joe Montgomery. "Senator, would you please comment on the request by General Wong and the Chinese government relative to their request for joint military operations and the promise to cease and desist in future under-the-table payments?"

"I think the General's request was quite articulate. Clearly, if the free world were to appease the ISIs, oil blackmail will become an everyday fact of global business. That said, how-ever, I must accede to the judgment of our duly-elected President. She is most conversant with the facts. Hopefully, we will hear from her sooner rather than later. Thank you."

"But, Senator. Would you explain what is meant by the cessation of payments communique?" Grimly, Joe Montgomery walked back to the camera and the expectant reporter. "The only point I would make in this moment of crisis — and truth — is to ask that you review my statements over the past week and the numerous opinions expressed in the op-ed pieces of the nation's leading news journals. The lead editorial of the *New York Independent* two days ago is particularly germane. Thank you, again."

For once, Richard Redman was penitent. His closest cronies, were, for once, frangible, the protective walls crumbling. For many lucrative years, he and his ilk had managed to slip the noose and avoid what seemed, to most, the inevitable. The cloakroom murmurings of late, though, had reached a pinnacle of concern and divisiveness, the bounty of decades of greed, collusion and obscene wealth about to wither as a climbing vine severed at the ground.

"SHIT! SHIT! **SHIT!**" Virginia screamed at no one in particular.

Pragmatics and reason won the day for the battle-scarred, political warriors, the aides sent scurrying to placate a hungry press corps. One by one they phoned the party faithful seeking support for what they sensed was yet another in the constant blackball affront to the adoring and compliant "people of America."

At four in the morning, they were halfway through the dog-eared crisis list. Contrasted to the uncountable such dilemmas in years past, the tone and tenor of the sleeping responses were glum. Most were hesitant to commit to the President until more facts were on the table.

The harried press secretary suggested to the President that she must appear before the American people. Noon the same day was suggested and reluctantly agreed to. In a controlled voice, she asked the security advisor and the spokesperson to prepare a short statement for her, the gist of which was, "NO military action. Under _any_ circumstances."

In the very early morning hours, oblivious to the glaring

lights and forlorn platoon of reporters outside, the top floor of the nation's First Home became silent, the lights off one by one.

As the early morning sun struggled to pierce the night sky of the capital city, it was also grasping for a last glimmer above the overcast and stormy stomping grounds of the USS *Ronald Reagan* and her far-flung battle group, the carrier, as usual, maneuvering randomly and at a high rate-of-speed. Captain Tommy Boone contemplated the JP9 fuel tanker symbol some 47 miles to the southeast. His ship desperately needed to top-off its dwindling supply of fuel for its stable of thirsty jets. Prominent by its red-blinking, triangular icon, the missing Whiskey class diesel submarine cast a nervous web about the dispassionate, flat-screen electronic display.

Amidships on the 03 level, just below the flight deck of the speeding, blacked-out warship, Dave Anderson knocked on the door of his skipper, Iron Lady Montrose. "Got a moment, Skipper?"

"Sure, XO. Come in," his sweat-soaked flight suit blending within the tiny stateroom with hers.

"Had some problems in paradise an hour ago. OK now. Bottom line is Pistol Pete and Twidget had at it. Nobody seriously hurt, except one sprained wrist, one swollen eye and two hurt feelings. I ordered both of them restricted to their staterooms until further notice."

The Ripper skipper hung her head, the room silent. "And what, may I ask, precipitated such ridiculous unofficer-like conduct?"

Her acting executive officer gave a respectful two-word answer, further embellishment redundant. "Patty Butts."

"And the catalyst?"

"Apparently the three were in the shower stalls and one thing led to another. Oh, by the way, your back-seater, Pete, is the one grounded with a severely sprained right hand. Can't fly."

"Oh, God," lamented the CO. "We have a combat air patrol launch in two hours. No Pete, no fly. CAG'll have a stroke. Maybe we can get the Doc to back off on Shorts and put her

354

back in the cockpit? Oh, and good news for a change. I just got word that Bikini will return from China in about two hours. Maybe she can get an up-chit from the Doc. How about you lay some words on Rose Johnson. OK?" said the weary and harried CO to her exec.

On an impulse, her eyes frigid, she picked up the phone and barked to the squadron duty officer, "SDO, I want every pilot and wizo to assemble in the ready room at 1900. No buts. Just DO IT," slamming the black phone back into its unyielding cradle. "Dave, I've got to take a stand. The guys and gals have got to realize the fat lady's about to sing."

Dr. Rose Johnson and Dave Anderson had been in heavy discussion in a quiet corner of the ready room, the former shaking her head sideways more than once. Dave tried one more time.

"Look, Doc. If Shorts can't fly with the Skipper tonight, we'll miss the launch and the ship will have one less combat air patrol than is required. All hell will break loose. Better to take a chance on her precious health than get our home base sunk," the latter with a vehemence that was new to Rose.

"Dave, I know where you're coming from, but the answer is an unconditional no. Period. For what it's worth, the Barking Dogs have the same problem."

The ready room filled with a dispirited assemblage of the squadron aviators. Surprise visitors, both slipping unobtrusively into the rear via the back door, were the ship's executive officer, Commander Angela Batori and the Command Master Chief, Mitsi Moore, both taking seats next to the Doc.

At precisely 1900, Iron Lady strode at full-tilt into the ready room, banging the front door open in the process, her face contorted, lips thin and demeanor hostile. "Attention on deck" yelled the duty officer. The twenty-seven aviators eased to a ragged, standing posture.

Her voice was controlled, measured. One-by-one she locked eyeballs with her charges, most of whom quickly averted their gaze to a study of their flight boots or the backside of the person in front. "Please be seated, ladies and gentlemen." The swollen eye and cheek of Scott Jacobs and the Ace-bandaged right hand of Pete Dawkins caused only a few milliseconds of additional attention on the part of the skipper. Rose Johnson pulled out her notebook, pen at the ready.

"In about ten minutes, I expect to get a summons to the bridge, stand at attention in front of a torqued-off aircraft carrier captain and explain to him why the 87-year proud legacy of the VF-11 Red Rippers can't handle the assigned missions. Would any of you like to come with me?"

After another round of eyeball contact, the CO continued. "Commander Anderson just informed me of the most incredibly absurd and juvenile conduct I have ever heard of. Totally unbelievable! Between commissioned officers of the United States Navy, no less. What a crock of unmitigated crap! As far as I'm concerned, this abhorrent behavior is totally uncalled for. My job is to person fourteen jets with pilots and wizos who are completely combat ready. NO EXCEPTIONS! Recently, we've had four bombs land in the boondocks and presumably kill 37 children, a back-seater who thinks the U.S. Navy owes her a livelihood, two female-related medical groundings and now this ridiculous spectacle."

Hands-on-hips, Iron Lady continued. "Just yesterday the Captain listed a drastic series of leadership adjustments he felt necessary to fight the ship. You all saw it and, I presume, understood his directions. Yet, less than twenty-four hours later, three of my trusted officers disregard the simplistic shower hours of the the ship's executive officer, a direct and clear disobedience of a lawful order."

The room was silent, some thirty folks wondering what would come next, the ship's XO glad she was not on the firing line. Above the electronic situation board, the impassive Red Ripper logo glared at them all, reflecting the mood of most.

"Up until a few weeks ago, you all had it easy. Problems? Just get a stress chit. Home port to look forward to. Routine full-automatic landings. Simple missions. Pregnant? Back to

356

Memphis. I could go on and on. But, my cohorts, it's now out of control. The promiscuity quotient has gone off the scale. I want all you boys to keep your zippers zipped and you girls to keep your legs crossed. This isn't a college dorm . . ."

At once, she regretted what she knew was a mistake. She should have kept it on a higher plane, not stooped to the gutter. In the subdued aviator briefing room in that far-off, rotten and stormy ocean, a lone voice of indeterminate origin, almost girlish, said, "Why not, Skipper? You do it."

If one had looked closely, the snout of the Ripper boar's head did, in fact, quiver, a reaction to the most blasphemous statement of a junior aviator to a commanding officer in the eight-decade pedigree of the squadron. Rose's pen stopped, afraid to commit the utterance to paper. Mitsi Moore and the ship's exec exchanged worried, albeit hesitant, glances.

"Would the squeaky voice care to elaborate?" the non-plussed Ripper skipper retorted. "Perhaps, whomever you are, you would enlighten us?"

No eyes connected with the naysayer, the embarrassment amongst the collected warriors pervasive to all. Hesitantly, the young pilot stood from the rear of the room, her CO staring hard at her.

"Skipper, I was out of line and apologize for my disrespectful comment." Thankful for little things, the room relaxed. Much to the surprise of all, however, the pilot remained standing. "May I continue, ma'am?" The curt nod from the occupant of the ready room's podium said volumes.

"Ma'am, this is my first deployment. Like you said, at first it was rather routine. Then it got boring. But then the weather turned terrible and it was more of a challenge. Finally, the hardest of all . . .," she looked about her squadron mates seeking some manifestation of support, a fruitless effort, and continued, "is the constant grind. Up until two days ago, we had an escape via the stress chit. No more. It's just not fair. My best friend is in the Barking Dogs, but now I am effectively cut off from his strength as well." She paused, the room silent.

She continued, the ready room hushed. "My ill-timed comments to you were wrong. But, Skipper, you know, I know, the Doc knows and each person in this squadron knows that this ship is a beehive of creative social-interaction or whatever one chooses to call it. It's normal and natural. Trying to artificially suppress these instinctive urges is an exercise in total futility," adding a hesitant, "ma'am."

Before Iron Lady could retort, the squawk box on the duty officer's desk barked a curt order from the air wing commander for all commanding officers to report to her office immediately, "if not sooner."

The squadron commanding officer's concluding comments hearkened back to the comments of Vice Admiral Demming at the solemn eulogy for Sam Newman and the simplistic words of the Navy Flyer's Creed. "Commander Anderson. Please take charge. I would ask that you personally read the Creed to our fellow squadron mates. For those of you who may feel the need to disregard the rich traditions of the U.S. Navy in exchange for personal gratification, private or not, I want you to know that my long-standing belief is that when the going gets tough, the sons of bitches come out of the woodwork. Times will get tougher. Carry on, please."

Oblivious to the mini-leadership crisis within the Red Rippers, Captain Tommy Boone was focusing on the upcoming refueling, the blacked-out tanker only a few miles ahead. His officer of the deck, Ensign Karen Randolph, had attended to the requisite ablutions such as the course to steer, speed, relative wind and a polite, but redundant advisement to the tanker captain for "maximum visual lookout." All of the above, of course, was done in total electronic silence, the infrared pulses of the flashing light transmitting the information, just as so many decades long past. Alongside evolutions, such as refueling and taking on ammunition and supplies, had long been the Achilles heel of the carrier because it meant remaining on essentially a constant course and at a relatively slow speed for two or more hours. "Three miles to go, Captain. All replenishment stations report ready-to-go and check-list complete."

"Thank you, Karen. I have the conn."

The Reagan's XO and command master chief made their way to the bridge, pausing en route to check out the plethora of visual lookouts strategically placed about the edges of the flight deck. Lieutenant Commander Lori Miller, the self-grounded maintenance officer of the Rippers, was near the number-one starboard bow catapult, huddled behind the giant jet-blast deflector, the night dark, the wind howling. With her were the medically grounded, Susan Anthony, and the expectant Shorts Flanagan. At the direction of the captain, the visual lookouts had been doubled for the refueling evolution, a precaution in spades for the elusive missing Whiskey class Iranian submarine.

On the bridge, the exec and master chief watched the calm competence of the captain as he deftly maneuvered the 97,000-ton warship to 145 feet alongside the plodding, fuel-laden tanker, the minions below orchestrating the flow of essential JP9 through multiple nine-inch black hoses at 180 pounds-per-square inch. Every minute or so, he would order a one-half degree course adjustment or alter a few RPMs from the four spinning screws, the result a precise positioning abeam the port side of the tanker. Finally, he handed the conn over to his officer of the deck.

"Good evening, Angela, Mitsi. I hope it's good news that brings you topside?"

"Always, Captain. That was a nice approach," said the ship's energized XO.

What followed was an easy banter, the captain keeping an eagle eye on his conning officer, the ship's master compass and the dimly-lighted distance markers from the behemoth a stone's throw away. His XO briefed him on the lookout augmentation, the latest disciplinary status, including the two hapless couples in the ship's second division and, somewhat reluctantly, the recent embarrassing spectacle in the Ripper ready room.

The captain, unexcitable as usual, told Angela and Mitsi Moore abut the missing Whiskey class sub and the pending arrival of Admiral Chandler in an hour. "Angela, please greet the Admiral and take her to flag quarters. Work up a schedule for her to include all the ready rooms, the engineering spaces, representative berthing, both officer and enlisted and," with a short pause, "the weapons spaces, including the sanctum. Add anything you think would help her acclimate to this warship. No sugar coating. Master Chief, you go with her, please. I want her to see as much as possible. Oh, and ask Rose Johnson to give her a few groups, too."

The junior officer of the deck appeared. "Forty-seven minutes to top-off, Captain. And, sir, the number-four CIWS appears to be unpersoned," the blinking icon on the computer status screen screaming for rightful attention.

"XO. Get hold of Miller. Find out what's going on. I told you I wanted a max state of defensive weapons readiness. Have him call me," the tone uncharacteristically sharp. The close-in-weapons system, a battery of eight rapid-fire cannons firing one-hundred, one-inch-in-diameter, depleted-uranium rounds per second each, were the final defense against an incoming missile and, though fully automatic, required two persons at each weapon.

Two minutes later, the executive officer said to her captain, "Stan Miller says it's supposed to be personed by Baker and Donowitz and he can't find them."

The ship's captain was about to nod a grudging acquiescence to another readiness-degrading blip, but suddenly exclaimed, "Those were the two I met holding hands and acting like teenagers last night when I was headed for your cabin." Fortunate for Angela, the blacked-out bridge provided cover for the flush of crimson, the remembrance of events only twenty-one hours prior, sending shivers pulsating deep within her.

Despite the inner thoughts of the Reagan's commanding officer, there had been good news from the tanker in the form of a ton of mail, the first in over a week. Lieutenant Becky Turner had retreated behind closed doors in paradise to savor the letters from her Rick and the scrawlings from her two little ones back in Virginia Beach. The letters were triply welcome because of the recent cut-off of the traditional e-mail, the embarrassing all-officers meeting and the unbelievable fisticuffs between her wizo and Pistol

Pete Dawkins only hours before.

The asinine comments of the young Ripper pilot to her commanding officer spoke volumes to Becky. It was no secret that she and a male-pilot compatriot in the Barking Dogs had become very close, her flushed cheeks upon returning to paradise clearly not the results of a hot shower.

The one letter was different, the return address simply, "Big Guy" in capital letters. Curiously, she opened it, the simplistic message a one-liner needing no embellishment. "Big Sister: Hope you're having a good time on the love-boat because Rick sure is here in Virginia Beach with Sandy." It was signed, "Big Guy." Becky stared at the words. "Not my Rick. No way," tears of frustration, fatigue, fear and reality oozed forth. "Oh, God. I hope it's not true."

Impulsively, she went into the corridor of paradise and knocked softly on the nearby stateroom door of Dave Anderson. "Dave, I need to talk — now." Thankfully, Shorts Flanagan, his roommate, was absent, presumably attending to her supervisory lookout duties on the flight deck.

"Come in, Becky. Have a seat." Reluctantly, the pilot handed the letter to her acting executive officer.

"That worthless son of a bitch. I'll skin his ass alive when we get back. It's baloney, Becky. I know him. He's an ex-Blue Angel turned people-hauler with the airlines. Horny as the day is long. Don't believe it."

Along with their skipper, Anderson and Turner were the undisputed top pilots in the squadron, highly respected in the stealth community for their professional competence and leadership in the air. In the nine months since leaving Norfolk, Dave had never seen the pilot so down and, for the first time, openly sobbing. "It'll be OK, Becky," he said, putting his arms around her heaving body, his strength ebbing into his shaken squadron mate, her head relaxed on his sweat-stained shoulder.

Suddenly, the door opened and Shorts Flanagan entered, then stepped quickly back into the corridor. "Sorry, Dave," she blurted. "I'll come back later."

"It's OK, Shorts, we were just talking," said the younger

pilot, her eyes red.

The lieutenant commander, the lieutenant and the lieutenant (junior grade) stood awkwardly, emotions off the scale. Big Sister cautioned her junior of a couple of years. "It's not what you think, Shorts," she said resignedly while returning the few feet to the comparative comfort of her tiny alcove within the huge ship.

Anderson's phone brought him back to reality. "Yes, ma'am. Be up in a moment."

Wendy Montrose had been on an emotional barrel roll of her own in the past twenty-four hours. The poorly-aimed bombs, the open display of disrespect in the all-officers meeting, the per-soning problems fostered by a shortage of crews and the open hostility in paradise, all presaged a crumbling of her natural lead-ership qualities. Not the least of her worries, by any measure, had been her abbreviated liaison with the squadron's main-tenance chief, Master Chief Randy McCormick.

To herself, she muttered, "How incredibly stupid of me. There's no way that pip-squeak pilot could have found out. I go 263 days without a dalliance, and wham, it almost happens." Leaning back in her straight-backed chair, she thought how thank-ful had been the unexpected general quarters alarm. Gazing at the Ripper logo on the wall, and almost smiling, she said to the snout of the boars' head, "If that pip-squeak pilot only knew."

"Dave, the reason for the meeting with CAG just now, was to give us a heads-up. It appears as if we may go into full-scale combat operations before long. Aside from the defensive combat air patrols, we'll be assigned four mountain-choke-point targets to attack repeatedly over a forty-eight hour period. Patty Butts," referring to the squadron intelligence officer, "is hard at it with the computer, putting all the square pegs into round holes."

"Last I heard," said the former Blue Angel, "the President was dead-set against the use of further military force."

"Beats me, Blues. Oh, the CAG indicated an admiral would be arriving shortly by transport. Party line is to keep no secrets from her. She's an inside-the-beltway type, but very knowledgeable and influential. Captain wants her to be exposed to everything."

Dave smiled. "Perhaps, Skipper, he could put her down in paradise for a few hours."

"Not amusing, my friend. Oh, Bikini'll be coming with her. I've already talked to the Doc about getting her an up chit. If so, she'll fly with you. OK?"

"Yes, ma'am. She's a good kid. Been through a lot." Anderson thought it best not to add to the CO's problems by mentioning his latest parley with Big Sister.

Rear Admiral Nancy Chandler was in a pensive mood. The dictate to proceed to the Reagan battle group from her boss had come as a surprise. There was nothing that could be done from the ship that could not be replicated ashore at her Pentagon command center. Though not comfortable in the unfamiliar environment of a warship at sea, she had always been a high achiever. She sensed a logic in the motives behind Sarodsy's direction.

But, truth be known, she had spent the better part of the four-hour flight commiserating to herself on the tall, handsome, articulate warrior, known also as Major General Ching Wu. "What is happening? I've never felt this way about anyone."

Her reverie was broken by the aircraft commander. "Admiral, we're starting our letdown for the Reagan. They're alongside a tanker now," adding brightly, "Hope you had a good snooze."

The e-mail message on her personal computer during the descent had been cryptic. It relayed, verbatim, the gist of the Chinese request for U.S. military assistance and the predictable, "No way," response of a frightened President of the United States.

The two passengers tightened their seat belts, the younger yelling above the din with a giggle, "Never landed backwards before."

Approaching the blacked-out carrier, the duo peered out the tiny portholes of the speeding transport, the slight turbulence and reflection of the aircraft's dimmed exterior lights on the frothing wake, just a few feet below.

With a bone-jarring crunch, the big transport grabbed the number-three arresting wire stretched across the six-inch steel deck of the formidable aircraft carrier and came to an abrupt stop. Stepping onto the windy, rain-swept deck, the admiral gripped the hands of the grim ship's exec and master chief, only dimly reacting to the strident clangs of the ship's general quarters alarm and the determined voice of the ship's captain, ordering an **"EMERGENCY BREAKAWAY"** from the tanker close aboard to starboard.

CHAPTER 26

The Tightening Noose

Despite only a few hours of troubled sleep, the President bounded sprightly onto the stage in front of a packed press gallery in the east wing of the White House, her smile radiant, not a hair askew. Spontaneously, the crowd erupted into a resounding applause, her pleasing persona reflecting poll numbers at record approval levels.

"My fellow Americans and friends about the world." She paused, her eyes making millisecond connects with at least several dozen of her minions. "Just a few hours ago, I received word that the Chinese government has requested the assistance of the U.S. government in combat operations against the ISIs. I want you all to know," her eyes once again dancing from the throng of reporters to the dozens of HDTV cameras fringing the majestic room, "that I find the notion of committing our country's military women and men to potential danger, anathema — utterly obscene. In the past hours, I have tried repeatedly to contact President Jiang, but to no avail. My response to him and his government is an unambiguous NO! I will not put our youth in harm's way. Period. I have taken the precaution of directing Admiral Carolyn Sweeney, the CEO of the Navy, not to use military force — even if provoked."

President Virginia Roberts Stallingsworth stepped back from the podium, the smile even more engaging. "I have two further comments, please. First, as you are well aware, our nation's airlines have had to cancel numerous flights due to the congressionally-mandated call up of certain reserve pilots, particularly stealth fighter pilots of the U.S. Navy. At the personal urgings of the leading airline CEOs, I am hereby overriding the Congress and ordering that all reserve pilots recalled to active duty as a consequence of this so-called emergency, be returned home ASAP. NO EXCEPTIONS!" In the periphery of the ornate chamber, scattered applause broke out, the assemblage awaiting the third presidential edict.

"And finally, my friends, I have asked our Vice President to use his good offices in a personal attempt to bring reason to the ISI leadership. Shortly, he will be airborne in Air Force Two. His mission? To use his ample powers of persuasion to call for an immediate cessation of all hostile activity on the part of the ISIs in and about the Caspian Sea region. This was, I want you to know, his idea, a concept that we think prudent under the circumstances." The trademark smile had lost a micro-percentage of its luster, the enthusiasm quotient down a notch.

"Madame President," an unseen voice within the gathering asked, "there seems to be a great deal of confusion as to why the Chinese presented the world a statement to the effect that payments would cease, but then was followed by the passionate speech on worldwide TV by General Wong requesting American military assistance. Is there indeed a connection, ma'am?"

Before the question was complete, the stately smile returned. Her head high, the President said in a measured, diplomatic tone, "There certainly is no connection that I am aware of. In fact, I plead ignorance as to what the Chinese are talking about regarding payments. I do know there has been a great deal of rhetoric on the subject, especially by Montgomery, er, Senator Montgomery. But I want you, the American people, to know," her gaze zeroed in on the CNN and Fox news cameras, "such allegations have as their genesis, the frustration of a severely-reduced minority party presence in our political arena."

With that, she leaned forward, erased the smile and wagged her finger into the stoic lens of the numerous cameras. "I know of no such payments from the Chinese government to any political entity in this country." The words were uttered slowly, almost defiantly, the articulation crisp, the meaning inescapable, vague reminders to some, of such presidential finger-pointing some twelve years before.

Awaiting her in the imposing trappings of the Oval Office were the press secretary, the national security advisor and the unctuous Richard Redman. Virginia banged into the room, her smile long since history. "Who was that asshole reporter? Cut her off, you hear," the statement directed at the frazzled press secretary. "I thought you had the questions greased?"

"Sorry, Madame President. She's a new one. Won't happen again."

"Richard, we need to talk. Would you all excuse us, please," she said, with a strained civility in her voice.

"What's this crap about the Super Pelican missile in the hands of the ISIs? Sweeney showed me the overhead photos which supported the limited strikes by the Reagan. I gave specific orders that they were releasable only to China, along with the usual gratuities on the side. Richard, the jury's still out on the Cassidy fiasco, but this is total bullshit. What's the action? I want answers!"

The old purveyor of influence and intrigue had been through all this countless times, all the while admitting that the presidential diatribes had become more venomous of late.

"Look here, Virginia," he offered, his sizable girth seeking comfort in the latest hot seat, "the Chinese offered the ISIs six-dozen missiles in exchange for a locked-in supply of oil — one year's worth. They asked me and I okayed it along with . . ."

"Along with what?" interrupted the clearly irate President. Redman studied the floor, his antenna on the lookout for errant presidential-launched artifacts, the awkwardness of the impasse interrupted by the arrival of the Veep.

Virginia stood, her disciplined demeanor at contrast to the two men. "Gentlemen — and I use the word advisedly — the three of us, and, indeed, the ECATS power base, are at a crossroads. We've taken some heavy hits of late. The Super Pelican debacle is only the latest. We pull together or the shit will fly. Do I make myself clear?"

"Paul," she glared at her Vice President, "you get your ass on that airplane fast. It's waiting at Andrews. You figure out what to say to the press and that worthless bunch of ISIs. If we can get them to back off the Caspian, we'll be in the driver's seat again."

Her gaze shifted to the troubled Redman, his eyes still in direct contact with the deep-blue, presidential carpet. "Richard, I don't know what the latest machinations on your part are, but let me make myself absolutely clear. You get your miserable self in gear and mend the fences." She added pensively, unnecessarily, "The noose is tightening, my compatriot."

Resignedly, the two departed, Virginia belatedly recalling Redman. Softly, she put her arm part-way around his fat waist, asked him to be seated, inserted her face six inches from his and whispered, "I don't know what's going on, but handle whatever it is. Understood?"

Redman's matter-of-fact response, in a low conspiratorial voice, "It's all on track. Not to worry."

With a bright smile, the American President patted the old conniver on the backside and announced gruffly to her secretary, "Get Sweeney."

The CEO of the Navy was not available, having been well-ensconced in the deep underground of the Navy command center in the Pentagon for the past two hours attending to military matters.

The conversation had been heavy, the premonition of an impending unknown permeating the solemn conference room. She, Vice Admirals Stan Sarodsy and Sharon McCluskey and the Director of Naval Intelligence, Rear Admiral Sally Butts, were huddled about the vertical situation board, the blinking icon of the missing Iranian Whiskey class submarine the immediate focus of attention and concern. The fading rhetoric of the president was reflected in the red "mute" icon on the HDTV display.

The DNI had just completed a thorough recapitulation of the tactical scenario, including the evolving strike plans. They had, though, taken the time to watch the press conference of the

President, her second in less than twelve hours, with some modicum of collective dismay. The no-strike edict was astoundingly
negligent. To lie back, look the other way and capitulate to a
greedy oil consortium was an exercise in grade-school appeasement.

Though it had only taken a fast-moving ten minutes, the
update to the trio by the DNI, Sally Butts, on the three hyper-
classified intelligence programs, had taken the resting pulse rates
up a few notches. Only three slides, each had a series of bullets
that told an inescapable tale of greed gone sour:

GREEN TREES
- Special team intra-Navy/FBI — computer results
- Enormous wealth over 15 years. Major names
- Many politicians' increase in wealth
- Industry payoffs & wealth accumulation
- Sources mainly intra China
- Redman's fingerprints

FIND CAUSE
- Cassidy's death no accident
- FASA payoffs = yes
- Wreckage in former Minuteman silo
- Major dollars to ECATS ++
- Redman's fingerprints

MISSING JEWELS
- Four nukes — USS Reagan
- Dolores Miller/ Carrier's weapons officer
- Chinese air base in Iran
- Big dollars to Miller, et al.
- Redman's fingerprints

The four naval officers had been silent, the implications of
the potential combat intertwined with the unbelievable information
extant in the short DNI briefing. McCluskey broke the silence
with a few arcane comments regarding the President's edict to

cease the call-up of all Navy reserves and return those deployed to home. "Damn, boss. We can't even get our most advanced medical cases off the ships now. How in hell will we get the airline pilots back? Facts are that most every squadron in the five battle groups is down about 15% now. This will kill us."

Realizing the futility of a response, the DNI countered with a verbal update of the missing submarine. Sarodsy interrupted. "The Reagan is in extreme danger! Steaming on a steady course at 20 knots is a killer. And, he's only half-done with taking on jet fuel." Sarodsy had taken the precaution of communicating with the chagrined skipper of the technically-advanced Seawolf sub, directing her to take a position more in line with the Reagan. To the group, he added gratuitously, "The Reagan needs to take on max jet fuel in order to execute the forty-eight-hour strike plan."

"Ma'am, sir. I know you asked not to be disturbed, but it's the President and she's in high warble," said the crisp aide, the reference to the president's state-of-agitation as in a missile about ready to strike its target.

Sweeney took the secure phone and, in a cheerful voice, answered, "Good morning, Madame President. May I help you?"

"Help, my sweet ass. Where's Nancy?" responded the furious leader of the free world.

"Why, Madame President," she glanced at the situation board, found the icon of the transport airplane carrying Rear Admiral Nancy Chandler and offered a pleasant, "She'll be landing on the USS *Ronald Reagan* in about ten minutes. I felt it would be good for her to observe her battle forces first-hand for a change. May I pass your regards on to her?" adding a stilted, "ma'am."

"What an absolute waste of talent. What the hell can she do on that damned ship?"

"It'll be good for her, ma'am," the Navy CEO responded politely. "And, oh, your edict about the airline reserves has caught us short-handed. I hope we can have some leeway. Perhaps two weeks?"

"Two weeks, my ass! Get them off now."

The conversation was bizarre, surreal, recorded, the Navy's CEO gritting her teeth and doing what she considered right, not necessarily correct in the context of an inside-the-belt-way mentality gone berserk. "Madame President," she articulated, "do you want the reserve pilots to take priority over the most advanced medical cases?" Without waiting for an answer, adding, "If so, I would respectfully request you put it in the form of a written order."

"Sweeney, what an abjectly stupid statement. Of course. Do you want the nation's airline schedules disrupted just because you're short of pilots?"

Continuing, the President said caustically to the Navy CEO. "Is Sarodsy there?"

"Yes, ma'am. Would you care to speak to him?"

The President, of course, remembered the repartee of two days prior in the same briefing room, the incorrectness of Sarodsy at the time, absolutely unbelievable. "No. Just tell that asshole I send my best."

Abruptly, the President shifted gears on the secure phone. "Anything going on with the nukes?"

The question took Sweeney by surprise. She had been read into the "Missing Jewels" findings by Sarodsy only the day prior, along with the suspected huge payouts to the chosen few. Gaining her composure, she answered, "Why no, Madame President." And, smoothly shifting the subject, "May I tell Nancy you said hello when she lands?"

The silence on the dead line spoke volumes, a reminder of a commander in chief who had lost her way.

Unbeknownst to the uniformed quartet, Joe Montgomery had entered the room and listened to the Presidential/Navy CEO conversation. The senator shook his head in disbelief and embarrassment.

"Hi Stan, folks. Guess I came at the wrong time, eh?" Getting no answer, he sat down at the oval table, poured a cup of lukewarm coffee and said, "Would you all like an update on the political front?"

Sarodsy took the lead. "Sorry, Senator. Didn't mean to ignore you. It's been an unreal couple of hours what with the Reagan refueling, ridiculous press conferences, one stupid phone call just past and a game plan that is more complex by the hour. What gives with the politicos? And, oh, all four of us have been read in to 'Find Cause,' 'Missing Jewels' and 'Green Trees.'"

"Roger that," said the senator. "I've briefed over two hundred of my colleagues, both on the Senate and House sides, and I think the pendulum is swinging towards some semblance of sanity. Would you all be interested in a summary of the action inside the beltway?"

Sarodsy spoke for the group. "Absolutely," his eye on the nervous carrier icon some 8,000 miles away.

"Point number one, and common knowledge, is that over the past fifteen years our congress of 100 senators and 435 representatives has gone from a rough two-party parity to overwhelmingly ECATS. In the house, less than 10% are Republicans or Democrats and in the senate, only thirteen of one hundred. The impact over the past few years on the courts and political appointees reflects the imbalance. This is, of course, no news, but it represents a good starting point for the next perspective."

Methodically, the senator unfolded a well-worn one-page document, a simple graph. "You'll notice that on the horizontal axis are calendar years starting in 2000 and going to the present. The vertical axis has two measurements: In green, are dollars and in blue, the percentage of the 535 person congress who are ECATS." He smiled, knowing, as did most who saw this graphic relationship, the astounding impact of raw money and resultant political gain.

"Stan, the dollar figures come from your spook group, a related program off the 'Green Trees' findings. Was not hard to do. Note that we are not talking of specific amounts. That said, however, the aggregate contributed so far over the years to political coffers has been in the neighborhood of $47 billion."

He stood, laying the graph on the table. "Even my most non-analytical colleagues understand the correlation of one, between money, getting elected and staying an incumbent. For once, though — through the efforts of you and your clandestine group, Stan — the relationships are clear."

Stan Sarodsy spoke up. "So what's the bottom line, Joe? The President has made it clear that we are to take no military action. If that's the case, the Chinese will act unilaterally in my opinion, and," he paused, his strategic mind in high gear, "if that happens, they clearly will not prevail, the ISIs will gain control of the Caspian and world oil prices will sky rocket."

Four star Carolyn Sweeney stepped to the wall display of the troubled region, her pointer on the Caspian. "Gentlemen, you may be overlooking one salient variable." Slowly, purposefully, she moved four feet to her right in front of the giant display, the pointer moving to a tiny dot in the northeastern Iranian desert, a speck contiguous to the long, snaking outline of the Chinese oil pipeline.

"We are all convinced that at least one of the missing nuclear weapons from the Reagan is at this Chinese air base. My intuitive sense is, that should the Chinese find themselves backed into a corner, they will employ this weapon or others. How and where, I have no idea. But to me, it's a logical strategic progression."

The three women and two men were quiet, five brains struggling to make sense of a maze that had but two exits. One was marked "appease" and the other, "action." The problem was how to get there, given the intransigence of an unhappy and presumably weak president, a political body reluctant to alter a lucrative status quo and a potential ally in China that could make the necessary outcomes viable.

Sarodsy cut in. "Good point, boss." After a short pause, he shifted his gaze to the senator. "Joe, militarily we're covered. Our joint planning with the Chinese Air Force is 95% complete. We could begin our initial campaign now if necessary. The unknowns, though, are in your court, sir."

Resignedly, the senior senator spoke, the stress and creeping fatigue eating at the crust of his tough exterior. "I know, Stan. I've got forty-three senators on board now. They realize the system of payola has gone out of control and must be rationally addressed. In my judgment, at least a dozen more will come over. I just need the time to get to them."

Sarodsy countered. "How about the House?"

"Different story, Stan. They are much closer to the people and the people are totally taken in by the Virginia personality. Most Americans would not believe what we now know to be a massively broken system of governance and a defense and technology industry for sale to the highest bidder. That said, however, about forty percent of the house is with us and recognize that the system needs a good enema." After a ten-second pause, he asked, "When will Ernie land? I sure could use him."

Sarodsy hit two buttons, the screen shifted to the continental U.S., the flashing icon over Canada headed for Andrews Air Force Base. "Should be on deck in one hour, Joe."

Vice Admiral Sharon McCluskey spoke. "Senator, how do you propose countering the express orders of the commander in chief? I'm a political science junkie and it seems as if the office of the president has become more than the equal of our other branches. In the military arena, for example, she managed to get rid of the civilian secretary of defense, the service secretaries and the entire joint staff. She's now defacto far more powerful than any president in our history."

Montgomery smiled. "Bingo. Good thinking. Answer is, I'm not sure. However, we have had a special group — much akin to your spook group, Stan — that has been researching the constitutional prerogatives for avenues in which the Congress can override the President. When it comes to military action, you know, this is an entirely convoluted ball of soggy wax. Bottom line? We think that if a majority of the House and Senate opt for rational and limited military action as an alternative to total appeasement, we can prevail."

Concurrent with the highly-classified underground Pentagon gathering and only six-tenths of a mile distant, there were gathered in the opulent top-floor digs of Killington Associates, a shadowy group of five men — referred to as the "Board." The subject on the table? What else? Money.

"Gentlemen," the self-anointed czar of the influence firm pronounced, "We are faced with a financial crisis not experienced

374

in fifteen years." The quintet nodded sagely in unison, the bodies all dark-blue suited, tops of graying and thinning hair, all white, all male and all, excepting one, in varying stages of well-fed corpulence.

"Mr. Chairman, it appears that the bulk of our income from Chinese sources will evaporate. What do you propose we do? My clients are extremely concerned." The speaker was the sleek leader of a consortium of arms-related denizens that stood to forgo enormous sums should the lucrative Chinese arms and technology bounty wither, and whose collective representation contributed substantial sums to Killington for the express purpose of preserving the status quo.

The double-breasted head of the table responded. "I am well aware of your concerns, believe me. As I understand it, one of our best consultants is now in China and reported to be a confidant of General Wong. I have repeatedly tried to contact him, but to no avail. If there's anyone who can get the Chinese on track, Admiral Demming can do it."

The opulent meeting rooms in the top two floors of the twelve-story office building overlooking the capital city and the Pentagon were reserved only for the "Board," the private elevator and separate garage, defenses against the inquisitive.

"General, may we have the benefit of your wisdom as to what options you would suggest?" The retired general was on the board for the most pragmatic of motives. His good offices were a conduit to the extreme inner sanctums of the U.S. military and access on a first-name basis with those once subordinate to him, a few of whom would one day ease seamlessly into the same arena.

The general stood, his athletic persona reflecting thirty-six years of tough, mostly altruistic, duty. "Gentlemen, in my opinion, the onset of the crack-in-the-dam has everything to do with the allegations of Senator Montgomery regarding the non-accidental death of John Cassidy. In my apolitical mind-set, Cassidy would have been President now had it not been for his untimely demise. Clearly Senator Montgomery has access to financial information on a scale never before imagined. Somehow, someway, there may be a kernel of credibility to his charges. He may indeed," he paused, stepping to the east windows overlooking the Pentagon, "have us fingered."

The mention of Cassidy's death brought a slight blush to the fat face of the fifth member. The Redman Institute had been the major conduit through which the pragmatics of influence and personal wealth had flowed, both in and out. Richard Redman shifted his girth in the oversized chair constructed especially for him.

"Gentlemen, let me assure you there is no way the cause of Cassidy's accident will ever be known. As you are aware, an extremely competent investigation was conducted by Dr. Sam Armstrong of the Federal Aviation Safety Authority and his hand-picked people. The cause of the crash was indisputably, an accident."

The four studied Redman. His salacious reputation was, of course, a matter of record. Fundamentally, he was a crook, albeit a canny one. Though all in the room were obscenely wealthy, Redman's was an order of magnitude greater. Without Redman's influence and organization, the effectiveness and resultant profitability of Killington Associates was moot.

The politician spoke up, an aging, former U.S. senator from the Midwest, his voice plastic. "From my perspective, it's all a big smokescreen. I don't think Montgomery has any more knowledge than the next guy. I side with Richard. In my judgment, we should ride this out, give the Chinese anything they want, hope they prevail, and then work out the future. This is only a temporary downturn." He regained his seat, the room quiet.

The elder leader took the floor, and asked in a deep, practiced voice. "Is there any way we can get to Montgomery? Clearly, he's the fly in the ointment. If not for him, we wouldn't be here today."

"We've been working for a year to get some dirt on him. Nothing. He's cleaner than anyone in this town. We've checked out bank accounts, campaign finance records, former friends and his business dealings. Nothing." The voice was that of a former

White House legal counsel, on the board for obvious reasons.

In a clipped tone, the resonance still commanding, the old man at the head of the table rose, faced the group and said. "Gentlemen, here's what we'll do." He ticked off a series of actions, the upshot of which were to lay low on the home front and put a full-court press on the Chinese leadership to provide them any and all arms and technology they desired with payments "in the future."

To the casual observer, the two meetings — one in the basement of the Pentagon and the other high on the twelfth floor of the Killington offices — were an astounding moral contrast. One painted a case history of greed and lost principals and the other, a "full-speed-ahead, damn-the-torpedoes." Bad guys and good guys. Personal gain contrasted with doing what's right.

The five men wordlessly peered toward the underground Pentagon command centers and then to the White House several miles distant. Knowing the facts, a sideline philosopher would be inclined to color the grandiose house a muted black, reflecting an occupancy on the dark side of Camelot. Quietly, the four insiders were swept to a walled, inside garage and then to a covey of black cars driven by black-uniformed chauffeurs while tucked securely behind blacked-out windows. All, naturally, fitted well with the Killington logo of a black-suited knight of old astride a jet-black steed.

The formidable deliberations within Admiral Sarodsy's command center were shattered with the simultaneous arrival of a breathless aide and a situation board blinking an urgent missile alert in the vicinity of the Reagan. Almost immediately, the carrier's icon indicated the ship had sounded general quarters.

To the side of the display appeared a simple flashing box — "SS-46 X 4" — an acronym for the firing of four Super Pelican missiles some sixty-four nautical miles north of the carrier. Only seventeen miles to the east of the elusive Whiskey class sub, the icon for the U.S. Seawolf submarine also came alive, indicating the stalkers had finally regained contact on her prey, herself a stalker. Too late, though. The four deadly Super Pelican missiles were airborne, headed directly for the refueling aircraft carrier.

Sarodsy calmly suggested to the Navy CEO that she call the President immediately, knowing full well that if the missiles found their intended target and the alongside oiler with her volatile cargo of several million gallons of JP9 jet fuel, a fireball the size of a miniature nuclear explosion would likely result.

"I need to talk to the President. It's a matter of immediate emergency," the voice of Admiral Sweeney commanding diligence from the party on the other end only six-miles away.

The missile icons streaked toward the hapless carrier and tanker just as the Seawolf's missiles were seeking the hostile submarine, the remaining life of which was now measured in seconds.

CHAPTER 27

Broken Bodies — Staunch Spirits

Stepping onto the windswept, steel flight deck of the blacked-out USS *Ronald Reagan* far out in a lonely ocean, the scene was surreal, a dream gone unbelievably sour. The noise was deafening, the F-27C stealth Phantom III at full power on the number-two bow catapult, the whine of the idling jet transport's engines and the unmistakable beats of the ship's general alarm, orchestrating a discord beyond the threshold of pain.

A strong arm grabbed Rear Admiral Nancy Chandler, propelling her to the interior of the ship's island structure accompanied with the strident crescendo of:

"CLANG, CLANG, CLANG, CLANG, CLANG — ALL HANDS PERSON YOUR BATTLE STATIONS — CLANG, CLANG, CLANG, CLANG, CLANG — ALL HANDS PERSON YOUR BATTLE STATIONS — **THIS IS NOT A DRILL!**"

The muted flight deck announcing system added to the ballet of sound, the stern voice of the captain calling for an "emergency breakaway" from the alongside oiler while concurrently ordering modest left rudder and ringing up flank speed to the four giant propellers.

"Admiral Chandler, I'm the XO, Angela Batori. Please follow me — quickly." Mitsi Moore led the way to the seldom-used flag quarters amidships under the flight deck of the accelerating warship, Lieutenant Evelyn Swagger bringing up the rear.

On the bridge, Captain Tommy Boone was all business. The opening between the thousand-foot aircraft carrier and its jet-fuel supplier had widened to 240 feet, two of the massive JP9 fuel hoses still connected. The blinking status board clamored for attention, the highlighted "SS-46 X 4" irrefutably indicating the on-coming nature of the four incoming missiles. Barking into the deck side PA system, he ordered, "All crews personing the refueling stations, CLEAR THE DECKS!"

Grabbing the toggle to the command squawk box, he growled, "Weapons, bridge."

"Weapons, aye," responded the harried voice of Lieutenant Commander Stan Miller deep below the waterline in the defensive missile control spaces of the warship. "Got two covered, Captain. No joy on the other two. They'll be in range in fifteen seconds."

"OK. I'm coming hard port to put them fine on our port bow," he said, concurrently commanding to the helmsman, "Hard left rudder."

"Hard left, aye, aye, sir," responded the young boat-swain's mate, twirling the tiny wheel counter-clockwise to the stops.

"All ahead emergency flank," the captain ordered. Almost instantly, the two nuclear reactors commenced generating maximum heat to the four steam turbines far below the waterline of the formidable warship.

Both commands, he knew, were exercises in futility, but worth a try. Once again, he barked into the flight deck PA system, "All hands topside, take immediate cover. Incoming missiles on the port bow." Suddenly, with a characteristic whine, three of the four portside, close-in-weapons systems activated, each projecting one-hundred rounds of one-inch-in-diameter, depleted-uranium shells per second towards a precise piece of sky that, hopefully, would be coincident with the trajectory of the unseen missiles.

With a massive double "crack," the two remaining fuel hoses and carrying wires from the alongside tanker, exploded into a spaghetti-like mass of writhing, oily froth, the design tensions of the rigs having been ultimately exceeded.

With its two ribbons of after-burning fuel, the second stealth fighter lit up the forward port side of the flight deck. External lights on, the pilot's signal to the catapult officer to launch the jet, the big fighter broke the thin holdback temporarily attaching it to the ship, and lurched forward. Halfway down the track, the first missile struck near the waterline seventy-feet below, the flaming explosion enveloping the accelerating fighter, now minus most of its port wing.

Seconds before, Tommy Boone had peered into the black gloom off the port bow, the dim glow of two fireballs indicating the defensive systems had been partially effective.

In a few moments, the rumble of the first missile explosion subsiding, flames billowing up from the wounded warship, the second missile hit aft on the port side about thirty feet up from the waterline with a crescendo of eardrum-crushing noise and blinding light.

Almost like a dream, Boone picked up the old-fashioned mike and matter-of-factly intoned throughout the ship, "Missile hits forward and aft port side." And, almost as an afterthought, "OK, guys, we've taken some hard hits. Let's get this ship buttoned up fast. I ask each of you to do your best."

The corkscrew of the Barking Dog's jet as it attempted to fly without one wing, was short-lived, one futile ejection at a 100-degree angle and the other inverted — directly into the unforgiving sea.

The four women en route to the flag quarters were knocked en masse off their feet by the first hit. "Admiral, I've go to get to my GQ station," said the disciplined exec. "Lieutenant Swagger, you stay with the Admiral. Mitsi, come with me, please." With that, the two were off, headed forward to the ship's secondary conn, the lingering intrusion of acrid smoke already piercing the darkened passageways.

Dr. Rose Johnson had been in the Red Ripper ready room awaiting the arrival of Evelyn Swagger when the general quarters alarm had penetrated the relative silence of the ship.

The first explosion had knocked her across the ready room. In a heap, she noted the dispassionate internal TV recording the stealth fighter just above her as it began its ill-fated quest for flight, the departure of the wing almost in slow motion, the airplane and its crew no longer animate.

When general quarters had sounded, Lieutenant Susan Anthony had been attending to her temporary duties as coordinator of the ship's port-side visual lookouts. The first deadly missile had struck just below her exposed catwalk vantage point. Within milliseconds, the American Airlines jumbo-jet first officer, stealth fighter pilot, wife of Mike Anthony, and mother of two, was vaporized, her being immersed in a rising fireball of fuel, explosives and rubble. Not a hair remained for mortals to touch.

Rose Johnson made her way directly down and forward into the teeth of the maelstrom below. Suddenly, it was pitch dark, the screams of anguish, pain and fear permeating from hundreds of sources. She stumbled upon a young man clutching his hapless shipmate, a shipmate now a remembrance only, her raggedly-limp body enveloped in a bear hug of denial. The two fell before Rose, who, with her flashlight, tended to the bulging entrails of the young man, a triage she knew to be pointless. Quickly, thankful for her longstanding ritual of having with her a black bag of medicinal necessities, she reached for a needle and punched a sizable dose of morphine into the thigh of the writhing, frightened young sailor.

"Doc. How's it going?" hollered the ship's executive officer, the master chief at her side.

"Not good, I'm afraid, XO." The Doc was already tending to several broken men and women, the heat searing, fuel-fed flames only sixty-feet away, the smoke limiting visibility to a few feet, lungs seeking a rapidly-diminishing supply of life-sustaining oxygen.

"Captain, XO," the exec spoke into her command phone, seeking the attention of the ship's captain high above on the bridge and, as yet, unscathed.

"Go ahead, Angela."

"Captain, it's bad. Can't make it to secondary conn. I'm

on the third deck forward, just above the second division berthing spaces. The damage control team is pissing upwind, I'm afraid. Looks like the missile exploded dead center in the division's berthing compartment. Only a few got out. We're setting fire boundaries now, sir."

Out of the gloom and horrible human torment appeared the apparition of four, naked second-division sailors, blackened, eyes hollow, no hair, the same quartet, Mitsi Moore recalled, caught *en flagrant* by her and Randy McCormick not long before. Mitsi sucked in her breath. The four exhibited a woeful collection of one limp arm hanging uselessly, one nose totally gone, an obliterated face, blood flowing freely from a gaping chest wound and total incoherency times four. "Doc, Doc," she yelled fruitlessly to the physician bent over two prostrate forms not thirty feet away in a gathering crescendo of heat, bedlam and thickening smoke. Resignedly, like lost sheep, she shepherded the foursome to the relative comfort of the ship's starboard side.

About two hundred feet from the chaos below decks, the Red Ripper officer staterooms in paradise came alive at the first clang of the GQ alarm. The accepted protocol for all aviators, Red Rippers included, was instant movement to the nearby ready room just under the flight deck between the two bow catapults.

Ensign Karen Randolph, at the time, had been engaged in a long and emotional session with Panky Pachino — for the first time. The privacy of her shared stateroom had been assured by the hardworking Patty Butts, who was diligently grinding away on the pragmatics of the Ripper-assigned strike plans in the event the forty-eight hour campaign was implemented. The two young officers, far from home, in imminent danger and constant stress, had sought the comfort of one another, a behavioral scenario so very logical and reasonable under the circumstances — naval regulations notwithstanding. The unbelievable first rasping clang of the alarm brought initial denial, then frustration and finally, only seconds later, reality and fright.

Karen's general quarters station was on the bridge as the

officer of the deck. In five minutes, naval standards required she be on the bridge at her duty station. Hurriedly, reluctantly, she and Panky disengaged. Slipping hurriedly into a well-worn khaki uniform, boots and fire-retardant headgear, she was just at the entrance to paradise when the first missile exploded not far away. The world went black for Ensign Karen Randolph, a young warrior who was now a lifeless heap two decks below the flight deck of the USS *Reagan*.

The initial explosion was accompanied by a deafening, ear-splitting blast, the pungent odor of caustic smoke almost immediate, the darkness not unexpected, the beams from a dozen battle lanterns only enough light for Panky to see his love crumpled by the door to paradise. Sobbing, Panky held her, blood pooling from her lifeless body. Without hesitation, he gathered her into his arms and headed for the ready room amidst the growing, below-decks conflagration and carnage.

"Ripper one, be advised home base is under attack. Repeat, under attack. We have incoming missiles from 020 degrees, range unknown. Your vector is 167 degrees, buster, angels zero." The dialogue was the cryptic language of a fighter and its shipboard controller ordering the Ripper flight of four F-27C stealth Phantom III's to head 167 degrees magnetic, at max speed for a target that was presumably at sea level.

Iron Lady Montrose stroked the afterburners, honked her jet into a 6.8G turn, armed her missiles and twin 20MM Gatling guns, and replied nonchalantly, "Ripper one, roger that. Say distance."

"No distance available, Ripper one. The firing vessel appears to be the missing Whiskey class submarine. For info, that sub has been taken under attack by our trailing Seawolf submarine."

Iron Lady responded. "Roger all that. Say tanker position. We'll be ready for fueling in ten minutes." No response. Headed inbound to the unseen target, she let a full minute pass and radioed, "Dutch, this is Ripper one, over." No answer. "Try the backup frequencies, Pistol," she said to her wizo.

"Already have, Skipper. No joy. It's like they're totally off the air. And, Skipper, I've started an infrared search for any ship targets and am trying the satellite guys for backup info."

On the bridge of the severely wounded carrier, Captain Tommy Boone was reflective, a short time-out to organize and calm his overloaded brain. For a moment, his thoughts went back in years to the memorably catastrophic scenes of out-of-control fires aboard the old super-carrier Forrestal off the coast of Vietnam, his father then a lieutenant commander in one of the fighter squadrons. The hell of the flight deck and compartments below, back in 1967, was enormous. Explosions of nine, one-thousand-pound bombs on the flight deck had scythed down heroic sailors like a dispassionate bush hog leveling the tall weeds of a farmer's field. Below decks, those who tarried for only seconds, succumbed to suffocating deaths, sixty-seven of whom back then, had been sleeping in one Red Ripper berthing compartment just below the flight deck aft.

Compared to carrier days of past decades, the Reagan was a masterpiece of damage control automation, the concept originating with methods employed by the mega-ship cruise industry. With one switch, the ship's master could remotely close all the watertight doors on the ship, or, with another, secure all smoke-distributing ventilation systems, and with yet another, activate one or more remote fire-fighting apparatus.

The damage control board on the Reagan's bridge was identical to one deep below decks under the tutelage of the damage control officer and chief engineer. Several thousand heat, smoke and flooding sensors throughout the vessel could literally paint a picture of trouble spots. Clearly visible were red and orange blips showing compartments with high heat levels. One by one, Boone noted watertight doors being shut, as fire and flooding boundaries were remotely set, followed by selective activation of foam, water or Halon V fire extinguishers.

The damage, both forward and aft, was extensive. Searing-hot fires prompted a spread laterally to adjacent spaces and vertically to those above and below, red-hot steel decks a perfect conduit for expanding heat. Boone noted that the sacrosanct conventional and nuclear weapons storage complexes far below, were safe for the time being.

While his crew flung themselves at the task of controlling the carnage below, Boone had other worries. His speeding ship was now at a comfortable 36 knots, changing course randomly. "Fortunately," he muttered, "the recovery of fourteen jets and one transport had been complete when the first missile buried itself within the ship's innards far below." Momentarily, he marveled at the resilience of the incoming missiles in thwarting the most intensive countermeasures U.S. technology could muster. Back in control, he said to his temporary officer of the deck, "We've got a ship to fight and job to do. Let's get with it."

Amazingly, despite the massive damage and trauma, the ability of the aircraft carrier to conduct offensive combat operations was about 90%, the only real diminution being several fueling stations on the starboard side and a bent number-two catapult, reducing the launch capability to the remaining three. Annoying, but less critical, was the loss of the primary command and control satellite linkage. Presently, a backup link was offering about a 50% capability. Keeping his eye on the ball, Boone knew, his *raison d'être* was to ensure the Reagan's ability to execute its part of the forty-eight-hour strike plan — should that become a reality.

"Attention on deck," screamed the high-pitched voice of the boatswain's mate of the watch, followed by, "Admiral on the bridge."

"Tommy, good to see you," she said, resisting the temptation to hug the wizened warrior. God, he had aged, she thought.

"Admiral. Sorry, I forgot all about you. What a time for a protocol visit. We're kind of busy now." His words were spoken hastily, his mind a blur of war-fighting options. "I think we have the two damaged areas under control. The next hour will tell."

Rear Admiral Nancy Chandler, though standing tall in her shipboard attire, was a first-class mess, the pair of twin stars at her collar, reminders of a kinder, gentler, shore-based Pentagon

Navy. "Tommy, does Admiral Sarodsy know what's happened?"

"No ma'am, not yet. We've lost our direct communications. We're on a backup link now."

On an impulse, Nancy, thinking quickly, reached into her back pocket for the diminutive red phone. "Tommy, you can give him a try on this gadget," she said, glad to be of use in a time of high trauma on the big ship.

Sarodsy spoke up immediately, 8,000 miles distant. "Tommy, what's the action? Are you hit?"

"Yes sir, badly, I'm afraid." Boone proceeded to transmit for a full minute in clipped, warrior lingo, a factual summary of the Reagan's havoc and ability to sustain air operations, both defensive and offensive.

"Casualties?"

"Don't know now, sir, but they will be extensive. Most likely in the hundreds. It's still too early to assess."

"Roger that. Let me speak to the Admiral, please. And Tommy, I don't need to remind you to do what you think to be right at the time and worry about asking permission later."

"Roger that, Admiral. Here's Admiral Chandler."

"Nancy, I'm getting a press release out now as we speak. Admiral Sweeney will be interviewed within five minutes. This attack will no doubt change the Washington dynamic. My guess is that the President will have no choice but to order implementation of the forty-eight-hour contingency plan. Oh, and we're working to get your command and control back in battery. Bottom line is you have five carrier battle groups ready to go along with the three Chinese tactical wings." Sarodsy's sizable hulk settled deeper into the conforms of the hot seat. "For what it's worth, the Whiskey sub was hit by our Seawolf. Presently, he's on the surface. We've got a backup link with your fighters — Ripper flight, I believe — and ordered them to administer the *coup de grâce*. Keep me posted, please. Got to go."

"Stan, was anyone hurt on the Reagan?" It was the breathless and ashen-faced Navy CEO, Admiral Sweeney.

"Yes, ma'am, perhaps in the hundreds. It will be several

hours before we have a head count. Right now they're trying to control the two sets of fires and flooding and avoid anything else that may be coming their way. And," he stood, looking down at the despondent executive, "Captain Boone is convinced that the missiles were indeed the Super Pelican, the same missiles at the Bandar Abas dockside with the fingerprints of the Redman Institute. Need I say more, boss?"

Fifteen minutes following the first hit forward, the slightly-singed Master Chief Randy McCormick of the Red Rippers, was hard at it organizing a fire-fighting and rescue effort in the after part of the carrier where he had been attending to a Ripper fighter that was in need of intense maintenance. The second missile had struck on the ship's port side, exploding on contact, its residual fuel and explosives penetrating and spilling onto the warplane-packed hangar deck. Nearby, absorbing the brunt of the impact, was the berthing compartment in which sixty-three Red Ripper day-check maintenance men and women had been sleeping.

McCormick shook his head. Sadly, from the first clang of the alarm to the second missile hit had been only a shade over three minutes. Most of his troops were still in the doomed space and met their maker in a searing flash of micro-seconds, the resultant inferno taking others less fortunate, a bit longer.

In the darkness and smoke-limited visibility, McCormick, oxygen-breathing apparatus on his ample back, had, by feel and instinct, pulled several young men and women to safety. Within two minutes, though, the automatic doors and hatches started their inexorable closing sequence, the fire-consumed spaces flooded in a chemistry of clinging foam and Halon V extinguishing agent.

The hangar deck of the big carrier was packed with air-planes, mostly in one state of repair or another. McCormick, though, had been warned by his skipper just before she launched, that the squadron would be required to field thirteen of fourteen jets if the proposed strike plan was executed. "No way for this bird," he proclaimed.

The scene was ghastly. In one corner, darkened bodies

were being neatly stacked, instantaneous burn victims. Randy knew, from an earlier inferno, that a human being exposed to extremely high temperatures for even a few seconds, was literally seared beyond recognition and, more grotesque, the result was an almost instant shrinkage of all limbs by some finite amount, adult bodies taking on the physical proportions of a ten-year-old.

While refilling his air bottle, the master chief had difficulty staying focused. Screams of despair and pain echoed from side bulkheads to high overhead in the tangled space. The stench of burned human flesh mingled with a steel deck slippery with the blood of his shipmates, missing limbs and crushed remains grim reminders of the reality of combat on the deck plates.

Spying the ship's XO and his compatriot, Mitsi Moore, he asked the disheveled duo, "How's it going up forward?"

"Bad, real bad," said the XO keying her mike for another on-scene report to her captain.

Angela Batori, tears in her eyes, looked about her at the carnage. Kneeling, she crept close to a young couple and covered their nakedness with her jacket as best she could. The youthful woman's leg was at right angles to her hip, the flesh gouged as if by a giant scythe followed by the coarsest of sandpaper. Her companion lay beside her, his eyes open, staring at the unseen overhead forty feet above, blood seeping freely from punctured ears and a half-open mouth. His body had a hundred punctures as if from a hand grenade detonated nearby.

The woman screamed, a prolonged and deep guttural sound, adding to the cries for comfort and solace from the one hundred or so poor souls strewn about the unyielding deck. She had seen the near lifeless form of her division mate so close, but yet so far away. "How's Richard, ma'am," she exclaimed, her eyes wide with fright. "Oh, God, my leg hurts. Will he be OK?" The sharp thunk of the morphine needle into her thigh would bring peace for an hour or so.

Batori keyed the bridge on her handheld. "Captain, XO, over."

"Go ahead, Angela."

"I'm back aft on the hangar deck with the command Master

Chief. It's tough. Real tough, sir. Looks like the Red Ripper maintenance berthing compartment took a direct hit. The surrounding bulkheads are red hot, all hatches are closed and the wounded, about a hundred, are being attended to. I see about twenty-seven bodies stacked in the center of the hangar deck aft. No telling what the count is inside the damage control boundaries." Heaving a submissive sigh, she simply said, "Over."

"Thanks, Angela. I think we're holding our own so far. I assume that one of the Docs is on scene?"

"Yes, sir. Talk to you in a few minutes. I'm headed for weapons control. And, sir, how's the Admiral doing? I kind of dumped her trying to get to secondary conn."

"Roger that. Remember I wanted her to see everything? Well, she's getting her Ph.D. in advanced carrier combat operations. A bit disheveled, but none the worse for wear."

The ship's executive officer and her Marine orderly disengaged from the ship's master chief, who opted to remain with Randy McCormick, and wound their way down in the the geographic center of the ship towards weapons control, the working offices of Lieutenant Commander Stan Miller.

Apathetically, he said while rising slowly, "Hi, XO."

"Stan, I'm making the rounds. It's tough topside. How are your weapons spaces holding up?" The weapons officer gave her a quick sketch of his piece of the action. "Bad news is all four of the close-in-weapons systems on the port side are gone. Good news is we are ready for the strike loads. All systems are go."

"Stan, the Captain says one of the CIWS was not personed. What happened?"

"I'm afraid to admit it. As it turns out, we found the crew in an intimate powwow in one of the bomb armories shortly after the GQ alarm went off," adding an irreverent head-shaking, "Shit."

Commander Angela Batori headed for the door, hesitant to leave the calmly pristine preserve of the control room for the bedlam and hell above. Opening the watertight hatch, she heard Miller say softly, "Angela, please be careful."

The vestiges of smoke in the Red Ripper ready room forward beneath the number-one bow catapult were just enough to cause eyes to tear, but not debilitating. Dave Anderson, just landed before the first missile hit, had taken charge, his skipper airborne with four Ripper jets. He walked with a pronounced limp, the result of being blown from the side of his jet's cockpit parked in the extreme forward corner of the flight deck. The fall to the deck had been fortuitous for it could easily have been a seventy-foot free-fall to a cold ocean below, a fate at least three or four brave souls attending to his airplane had suffered, the probability of survival nil.

Just as he was attempting a head count of the squadron's aviators, the front door of the ready room burst open, the frail, but still beautiful Lieutenant Evelyn Swagger, framing the entrance, head high, blouse askew, hair frazzled and unkempt.

"Bikini!" screamed the usually stoic Big Sister. As one, the aviators surrounded the young officer, hugging, touching, commiserating. Tears gushed freely.

The appearance of Swagger was electric for she symbolized the essence of the sacrifice implicit in tough carrier duty. For a few moments the ready room escaped from the realities of the carnage surrounding them and the specter of more to come.

"Welcome home, Evelyn," said the beaming squadron executive officer, "We've missed you." His words were spoken softly, uncharacteristic of the brash pilot.

Swagger stood, shedding tears of humility, joy and sadness. Softly, she spoke, the tattered room quiet, expectant. "You guys remember the words of Iron Lady in this very spot not long ago?" She paused again, seeking the warmth of understanding from her squadron mates. "She said, 'When the going gets tough, the tough get moving and the sons-of-bitches come out of the woodwork.' Well, XO," she said, standing tall, "this is one SOB that intends to get back in the air. Who will I fly with and when, sir?"

Without a missing a heartbeat, Anderson looked down at her, then to his squadron mates and said, "Me, Bikini. We launch in an hour. Get suited up!"

The Rippers erupted in a frenzy of clapping, cheers and a few sustained hugs, disparate flight suits blending as one.

Airborne, Iron Lady and her wizo, Pistol Pete Dawkins, were hot on the trail of the wounded Whiskey class Iranian sub, some seventy-five miles north of the carrier.

"Got a lock-on," he said dispassionately to his pilot.

"Roger that," she responded to her back-seater, then radioed, "Ripper 3 and 4 proceed to high cover. Out."

Some thirty-miles ahead, the infrared seeker had found the surfaced sub, the orders from the far-away satellite link, "Seek and destroy." Iron Lady had decided to make one strafing run at a shallow angle, the fighter's twin-20MM Gatling guns, the weapons of choice.

"Ripper two, spread out, stay above me, use guns, minimum altitude two hundred feet, aim for the waterline forward." The stark, cryptic transmission was the death sentence for seventy sailors, a game plan remarkable for its lack of emotion and direct clarity to the crew of Ripper two. The laconic reply? Two equally impersonal clicks of the mike, universally understood in the clipped vernacular of fighter pilots, as an "I understand and will comply."

The two rapid-fire cannons in the nose of the F-27C stealth Phantom III would project a combined 280 rounds of one-inch-in-diameter shells each second with an awesomely high muzzle velocity. The skipper had decided on a three-second burst commencing at 2,500 feet slant range, her target area concentrated on the sub's conning tower from the waterline up.

Grimly, casually, she flicked the master arm knob to "arm," the weapons suite of the jet now energized. The FLIR display turned a black night into day, tiny dots of human heat scurrying about the topside deck of the wounded warship. Of 750 rounds hurled forward by her fighter, 600 most likely struck the hapless craft, followed eerily in the empty night by another 700 fired by her wing person.

On the return run, there was no target. Like a desert barrel riddled with a hundred holes, the once-proud warship and her valiant crew of seagoing warriors was en route to share an Indian Ocean grave with others equally as unfortunate.

"Skipper, we just got word over the back-up circuits to max conserve." Max conserve meant just what it said and, to generations of Navy carrier aviators, was an ominous order, for it indicated trouble at the only landing field within hundreds of miles. In this case, their home base was struggling to keep the below-deck infernos under control. The pragmatics of the moment, though, was a landing area still littered with debris and unknown damage from the second missile hit.

In carrier-based aviation, ashore landing fields as a safe haven, had been a long-standing oxymoron. Because carriers were more vulnerable the closer they were to shore, they preferred the open-ocean, blue-water environment, where stealth and speed would be the tactical advantage. In this case, though, mutual support from another carrier battle group several hundred miles distant, could be available to provide needed airborne fuel and a ready deck, should one be required.

In the tactical nerve center of the ship, Ensign Patty Butts was hard at it for the nineteenth-consecutive hour, tweaking her computer to optimize weapons loads, far-off mountain targets, in-flight refueling parameters and a host of related tactical impera-tives. She had not been impervious to the stark events swirling about her station, nor was she overly concerned. She had her job to do and was totally focused.

The Ripper piece of the proposed strike plan involved the launch of thirteen fighters in the initial wave; six attacking specific targets at the Bandar Abas port; four the nearby Kleski Air Field; and three, for defensive high cover. The Barking Dogs would fol-low seventeen minutes later with the same scenario, but slightly different target objectives. The Diamond Backs of VF-102, would provide a defensive combat air patrol for the Reagan's battle group in the initial twenty-four hours.

The strike plan was analogous to a five-hundred piece jig-saw puzzle involving five carriers, a host of ship-launched mis-silery and the integration of the Chinese Air Force assets. At the end of a forty-eight-hour, around-the-clock period, the objectives would result in the complete neutralization of all ISI air defenses and, more significantly, the entire blockage of all supply and logistics lines of communications to the Caspian through the Elburtz mountains of northern Iran.

The plan, Butts knew, was ambitious, but doable. The Rippers would be required to have thirteen of their fourteen aircraft available to start and at least ten up and ready at the termination of the first phase, a tall order. She hoped the crews were up to it, numbers-wise and motivation-wise, professing privately to her roommate not long ago, as not understanding all the paradigms of the fighter-pilot mystique. She had no idea what the hits on the carrier would foretell. Her piece of the action was covered. For the first time in many hours, she wondered about her friends and compatriots in and about her Red Ripper family.

The temporary euphoria of the ready room fostered by the dramatic appearance of Evelyn Swagger, had regressed to a somber status quo. Dave Anderson surveyed the unkempt pilot's briefing area — still infused with the acrid odor of things burning — and, with a sad heart, saw the pale face of young Karen Randolph held tightly in the unyielding arms of Panky Pachino.

Looking up at the acting executive officer of the Red Rippers, Panky, his face a grim mask of denial, said, "XO, I don't mean any disrespect, but I will not leave Karen. PERIOD. Please understand, sir." And quietly, "I just can't." The recently-arrived wizo buried his face in the lifeless form of his love, tears of frustration and enormous sadness, unseen.

Macho Dave Anderson faced the lifeless officer, brushed a hair from the eyes of the young woman and said softly, "Oh, Panky. Oh, Karen," and collapsed onto the two, fatigue and a despair fraught with fear, finally unleashing an emotion long held in stoic abeyance.

Regaining his composure, he said to Panky in a subdued tone, "Panky, help me take Karen down below. She can't stay here."

The newly-arrived wizo and the weary, sorrowful

Anderson then carried the body of Ensign Karen Randolph three decks below to a temporary morgue set up in a corner of the hangar deck, her body laid gently among several dozen of her lifeless shipmates. Panky removed his squadron neckerchief and movingly placed it over her peaceful face, but only after a gentle and final kiss. Unnoticed, of course, was the hard lump in Dave's throat.

Returning to the ready room, Anderson took charge. "Big Sister," he yelled with a renewed energy, "let's see if we can get this organized. We've got a job to do and it seems we'll be short of crews. Will you help?"

"Yes, sir." Her brain got to work.

"First," she said assertively, "we'll put Susan Anthony back in the air. I'll pair her with Twidget. And," before Anderson could remind her of Anthony's grounded status, she added, "Shorts Flanagan may be with child, but as far as I'm concerned, she's back-seat material. I'll put her with Mike Anthony. What the Doc doesn't know won't hurt her. We've got to be realistic."

Incredulously, Dave Anderson studied the young pilot. "Big Sister, by damn. If we ever get out of this mess, I'm going to put you in for the Blue Angels."

She smiled and said lightly, "By the way, I haven't seen Shorts or Susan . . ." wishing for an instant that she could recant the words. "Oh, my God. Both of them were topside lookouts when the missiles hit!" her face instantly reflecting a montage of fearful premonition.

CHAPTER 28

For Those In Peril

Shortly after ten a.m., the news of the Reagan catastrophe broke upon the quiet, suburban domain of Kings Grant in Virginia Beach, word spreading like a sudden tornado. Sandy Anderson, tending to her brood of twenty-three third-graders in the local elementary school, was interrupted by a white-faced teacher next-door, himself the spouse of a squadron mate on the carrier. Almost as characters morphed by agile technicians, the schoolhouse was transformed into a fearful arena of denial and premonition, the teachers hurriedly assembling in front of the grim CNN reporter.

"CNN breaking news has just learned that the U.S. Navy aircraft carrier, USS *Ronald Reagan*, has been seriously damaged by at least two sub-surface-to-surface missiles. There is no definitive word on casualties, but informed sources state they could be in the hundreds. We hope the President will enlighten us soon."

The schoolroom was still, fearful sobs breaking the veneer of a fragile stoicism while the TV announcer reviewed the salient statistics of the big carrier — number in crew, length, tonnage, aircraft, time out of Norfolk and so on.

Sandy's next door neighbor, Rick Turner, burst into the room, having hurried over from his nearby law office. "Come on Sandy, let's get the kids and head for home," he said, his arm about the younger woman, both on an emotional roller coaster headed ever steeper to an uncertain bottom.

Within minutes, the largely Navy community was energized, the word sweeping faster than a speeding jet fighter, thousands glued to TV sets, grasping for an elusive glimmer of hope. Many of the Reagan's spouses gathered at the bustling home of Beverly Demming Boone.

The dapper CNN reporter, standing in the frigid November morning outside the south lawn of the White House, exclaimed breathlessly, "Ladies and gentlemen, I have just been informed that the Navy CEO, Admiral Carolyn Sweeney, will be making a brief statement from the Pentagon in one minute. Please stand by."

The Navy's top officer strode somewhat unsteadily to the podium, Vice Admirals Stan Sarodsy and Sharon McCluskey on either side. The glare of lights, flash of cameras and hastily assembled press corps, added to a sense of immense foreboding.

"Ladies and gentlemen," she began, her swollen eyes seeking a ray of understanding or comfort in the austere room, "it is my sad duty to inform you that we have just learned that the gallant aircraft carrier, the USS *Ronald Reagan*, has been struck by at least two sub-surface-to-surface missiles somewhere in the Indian Ocean. I just spoke with the commanding officer, Captain Tommy Boone, on a backup communications circuit, and the news is not good. Please understand that what I am about to say is most preliminary. Because the missiles penetrated deep within the ship before exploding, it may be that hundreds of casualties could result. I regret that I cannot be more specific. The Captain informs me that damage-control efforts are in place to contain the spreading, below-decks fires and flooding and will report within the hour as to how successful his crew has been. Given that the damage is contained, he has indicated that he could be at least 90% capable of sustained combat operations within twelve hours. I regret that I will not take any questions at this time, but will brief you on the hour, each hour, as the situation unfolds. Thank you. And," as an afterthought, "I trust that you and the American people will join with me in prayers for our brave women and men aboard the heroic warship Reagan."

In only fifteen minutes, Boone's Kings Grant home had

become a mecca for those spouses assigned to the ship and its embarked squadrons, eyes and ears engrossed with the news. Coffee and a bit of California merlot spiced the strained dialogue.

One hour later, precisely at noon, the camera zoomed in on Sweeney again, the press room silent, expectant. "I have learned from Captain Boone that the forward fires and flooding have been contained and that the after damage is under control, but with a great deal of dense smoke. The ship had sixteen aircraft airborne and are being refueled by contract Air Force tankers. We still have no definite word on casualties. I know there are many questions. I'll do my best to answer them, given that they will not compromise our tactical situation."

"Ma'am, will the President order retaliatory strikes against the ISIs?"

"I have no idea. I'm sure she will speak to the nation in due course."

"Admiral. Do you know the source of the missiles?"

"Yes. It appears they were fired from an Iranian Whiskey class submarine which has since been sunk, compliments of our trailing Seawolf sub and four fighters from the Reagan's Red Ripper fighter squadron."

"What will you recommend to the President, ma'am?"

"That we execute the joint strike operations now in a final planning stage — at the earliest."

"We understand there were pregnant women on the ship. Is this the case?"

"Of course. They are no different from any other U.S. Navy sailor."

"Admiral, one of our sources indicated that the missiles in question may have been the newly-developed Super Pelican. They state we recently sold several dozen to China. Can you confirm this story?"

"No."

Abruptly, she turned and walked briskly into the inner sanctum of the Pentagon, the husky Sarodsy close aboard. "How in hell did they get that information already? The President will have a conniption!" Sarodsy wisely chose not to answer.

At the moment, the President of the United States was in a high-pitched, animated and one-way dialogue with her chief of staff and the ubiquitous Richard Redman. Her longtime personal secretary, Martha, knocked softly and reported, "Ma'am, it's Senator Montgomery. Says it's urgent."

"Urgent, my ass. Handle him. Understood?"

With a practiced exit, she muttered a respectful, "Yes, ma'am."

"And get me Sweeney!"

Another contrite, "Yes, ma'am."

Senator Joe Montgomery was watching the convoluted news broadcasts, his aide, Ernie Maltman, having just returned from his whirlwind trip to the interior of China.

"Virginia won't talk to me. She's putting off the inevitable, I'm afraid. What happened to the Reagan was a direct act of war." The senator stood, facing the window overlooking the Washington Monument, Arlington Cemetery and the distant Pentagon, a gray, cold sky adding to the increasingly somber realities. "Any hostile action against a U.S. warship on the high seas is, has, and always will be, a direct act of aggression, just as if it took place on our soil. We must act!"

"Ernie," he continued, glad to have the wisdom of the former naval officer and combat fighter pilot once again at his side, "my sense is that the President will stonewall any actions by the U.S. She's petrified. I'll bet you a cold one she'll be on the air within two hours bemoaning the loss of life and ordering our naval forces to back off."

"Boss," Ernie countered, "perhaps it would clear your mind if you could review where we are — what options we have on the political front. It would do me good, I know."

Montgomery produced his dog-eared, one-page graph of dollars versus ECATS numbers in the Senate and House of Representatives, a case history of a self-flagellating system gone astoundingly corrupt. Following that were the simplistic briefing graphs summarizing the findings of "Green Trees," the innocuous

399

bullets citing a fifteen-year pattern of corporate greed and governmental excess.

Ernie asked the obvious. "What's been the reaction, boss?"

"Good question, Ernie. Most all of the one-on-ones I've had, resulted in furrowed eyebrows and shaking heads. But, the reality is, the overwhelming majority of the payoffs and policy dictums have been legal. Most all of the senior industry consortium and political benefactors have operated within generally-accepted legal boundaries, even the Redman Institute. Most of those I've reached agree that the system is in dire need of an enema. It's just that no one has had the guts to take on a system that has egregiously contributed to a ruling class so enormously insulated from the just plain wealthy."

His trademark smile generated to full bloom. "So far that's been the easy part. Aside from a few thousand of the privileged elite, not too many folks have been inconvenienced. Times have been good — minimal inflation, taxes tolerable and an all-time low-level of unemployment. That said, though, we need to face the harsh realities of the Cassidy issue. 'Find Cause' appears to be a case of overt criminality, and you know where the finger points, as do a lot of nervous folks. This has been the real catalyst. In a sea of cesspools, Cassidy's non-accidental death rises to a pinnacle of political greed hearkening to the days a century ago when tommygun-toting gangsters made policy and openly gunned down dissent."

"How about the nukes?" Ernie questioned, referring, of course, to the missing nuclear weapons off the Reagan.

"As far as I know, no one outside our small group is aware of this. Stan Sarodsy is convinced the Chinese know we know they do have at least one of them, and," he once again surveyed the bleak autumn landscape, a lone jogger braving the chill north wind, "the finger in the 'Missing Jewels' case, points increasingly to the Redman Institute for Enlightened Awareness and the kindly Richard Redman."

Montgomery's private, secure phone jangled the duo back to the present. "Hi, Stan." The senator listened intently for a few moments, and said, "OK, how about thirty minutes? Your place?"

"Sarodsy wants to brief us on the military angle. Bottom line is the forty-eight-hour plan is 96% ready for execution, even without all the Reagan assets."

Ernie, part politico, part military and totally constitutional, asked his boss. "Senator, given that the President is the commander in chief and refuses to take military action, no matter the circumstances, how can our system not comply and obey her edicts?"

The senator buzzed for his legal aide, a young woman of about thirty, with straight hair, plain face and a demeanor that suggested an intellect off-the-scale. "Ernie, I'd like you to meet Penelope Pinson. She's headed up a small group of constitutional scholars for the past few days, addressing the legality of overriding a presidential military order."

She moved right at Ernie, looked him in the eye, gripped his extended hand, and said, "I've heard a great deal about you, Mr. Maltman. It's a pleasure."

Preambles dispensed, she got to the point, all business. "We have come to a unanimous agreement that the Constitution does, in fact, expressly provide for the Congress to order military action given two conditions: First, there must be clear and convincing evidence that the President, as the commander in chief, is derelict in not taking reasonable and prudent military action to protect the global interests of the American people. Second, should such a finding be determined by the Congress, there must be a 75% plurality in both chambers to sustain it. Because such an action has never been taken, there is no case law to argue. The statutes are clear."

Ernie looked directly at the obviously hyper-intelligent woman and asked, "What is your opinion, Ms. Pinson?"

"In what regard, sir?"

"Should the Congress take such action in this case?"

"Without reservation," she said. "The President has clearly abdicated her responsibility. The consequences of allowing the ISI consortium to go unchecked will have overwhelming adverse ramifications on the global economy and world stability.

401

It's a no-brainer, sir."

"Your colleagues agree with your logic?"

With a noticeable frown and only a hint of annoyance, she replied with a curt, "Certainly."

On the short drive to the Pentagon, Montgomery and Maltman were comfortably quiet, the muted TV display of CNN twenty-four-hour news, flashing its trademark breaking-news icon.

"Ladies and gentlemen. We have been informed that the President will speak to the nation in one minute." The screen switched frames to a White House briefing room, a smiling president striding to the podium on cue.

"My fellow Americans. I am saddened by the death and destruction foisted upon our young women and men so very far away in the Indian Ocean. I know no more than you, and trust that Admiral Sweeney will keep us posted. As the Admiral has so eloquently requested, I join with all Americans in prayer for those in peril on the seas who have so gallantly sacrificed for all of us." Having mastered the knack of knowing just when to toss her head aside, thrust away an errant hair and dab at an invisible tear in one eye or another, she paused for effect.

The scene within the privacy of the Oval Office in the preceding hour, though, had not been so amiable, one more over-priced artifact meeting its demise against an oft-patched south wall in the stately chamber. The subject of her flamboyant ire? The "incompetent" captain of the Reagan in allowing his ship to be hit, the "stupidity" of the Seawolf submarine captain for losing contact with the Whiskey class submarine and a U.S. Navy "that couldn't fight its way out of a wet paper sack." Richard Redman, a veteran of a thousand such "blame-the-other-guy" tirades, sat impassively, albeit guardedly, in his special chair.

Virginia had hesitated at the podium, the collected minions expectantly waiting for their heroine's next utterance, the words startling. "The commanding officer of the Reagan has clearly been negligent in his duties. He alone is responsible for this national tragedy. As of this moment, I am ordering Admiral Sweeney to

402

have him relieved immediately and be replaced by his executive officer. I shall not condone mediocrity in our military forces."

The interval this time was longer, more profound, lingering, her eyes seeking a friendly face in a sea of usually compliant reporters, her smile like that of an oriental mask.

"Body bags and the Stallingsworth administration are mutually exclusive. There will be no more body bags, no more deaths and no more combat. I am herewith ordering the removal of all U.S. naval forces from the region and to cease and desist from all combat operations — no matter the provocation."

The room was silent, a quiet reflected in the limo transporting Montgomery and Maltman. Nearing the underground entrance to the Pentagon, the senator directed his driver to, "Pull over, Mac. Ernie, this is unbelievable. I must be dreaming."

"Time to act, if you ask me," said the laconic aide, who, truth be known, never understood the psyche of politicians.

The questions came at the President fast and furious: "Where did the missiles come from?" "Who is the executive officer?" "Why were expectant women on board?" "Is this not appeasement?" "What will happen to global oil prices?" "Have you talked with Redman?" "Is any of this connected to the death of Cassidy?"

Inconceivably, the questions were openly hostile, almost frantic. The answers were clipped, defensive, short and ungarnished with the usual glib presidential hyperbole. Montgomery noted that her normally ebullient exterior was strained, almost afraid. None of her answers made sense nor was there a kernel of truth in her dialogue. Suddenly, she pivoted, walking stiffly to the comfort of a darkened nearby door. Ernie thought to himself for a moment that she might turn, face the belligerent questioners, and offer the gratuitous symbol of a middle-fingered goodbye, a fitting finale to a bizarre ten minutes.

In the home of Beverly Boone, some 150 miles to the south of the nation's turbulent capital, a crowd of about forty kids, spouses and active duty watched the President of the United States make absolutely no sense, an impression reflected across a nation seeking solace and understanding from their president.

Rick Turner, broke the awkward hiatus. "Wow! I can't believe what I just saw and heard. Can you believe it?"

The mood in the home of the Reagan's commanding officer was ambivalent. On the one hand, most were grateful for the presidential proclamation of no combat and the slim hint that maybe, just maybe, their loved ones would soon return. On the other, though, was the reality that one of the casualties could be their own. The presidential firing of the ship's captain was a subject too close to home, any mention discreetly avoided.

A few miles away, at the giant Oceana Naval Air Station, shore-based home to the Reagan's brood of fighter squadrons, the pragmatics of the far-off tragedy sprung into a disciplined mode known euphemistically as CAP or casualty assistance program. The shore-based next-of-kin for each person on board the hapless carrier killed in action or severely wounded would be assigned an active-duty person skilled in assisting the homebound. The temporary headquarters were the shore-based administrative spaces assigned to the Red Rippers and the Barking Dogs. Busy briefing the hastily-assembled team was an eclectic mix of a dozen or so all-faith persons of the cloth. All would await the sterile listing of names of those no longer with us.

At precisely 1:00 p.m., Admiral Sweeney stepped up to the Pentagon podium, accompanied, once again, by the resolute warrior Sarodsy and the diminutive McCluskey. "I am pleased to announce that the damage control efforts of the Reagan's crew appear to have been successful. The ship, as I speak, is recovering its aircraft. The Captain considers his command to be ready for sustained combat operations. He is, of course, devoting maximum efforts towards ensuring the defensive posture of his ship, as well as attending to the myriad of actions necessary to fight the remaining fires and minister to his sick, wounded and dying shipmates. This will be my final meeting with the press. And," she gritted her teeth, glanced at Sarodsy and said, "I will take a few questions now."

"Admiral, what is your response to the President's order to immediately relieve the Captain of the Reagan?"

"I have received no such order. Further," she hesitated, seeking the questioner in the harsh glare of lights, "the authority to relieve a commanding officer reposes with his immediate superior in the chain of command, Rear Admiral Nancy Chandler, who is currently attending to her battle force command responsibilities aboard her flag ship, the USS *Ronald Reagan*. Next question, please."

"Admiral Sweeney. Have you commenced withdrawing your fleet from the region per the commander in chief's orders?"

"I have received no such orders nor have I had occasion to speak with the President. If she has issued such direction, I feel confident she will communicate them directly to me, as is the norm."

"What will happen if the ISIs continue to solidify control of the Caspian Sea oil?"

"Ask the State Department."

"Admiral, one well-placed source indicated the missiles fired at the Reagan were the U.S.-produced Super Pelican and that they were provided to the ISIs by way of China. Is this the case?"

"No comment. Next question."

"How many women were casualties, Admiral?"

"I have no idea. You know the crew, as in all our warships, was gender equal, so make your own assumptions. We are working to obtain the names of those lost so that we may start the notification process to the next-of-kin," adding in a low voice, "It is a sad day for our nation."

"Did you see the President on TV just a while ago?"

"No. Next question."

"Have you or your staff been in communication with Senator Montgomery recently?"

"Why do you ask, if I may? I am the CEO of the U.S. Navy, not a political operative. I have enough on my plate."

"But, ma'am, the Senator has been seen entering and leaving the Pentagon on several occasions. Why would he do so?"

She quickly responded to the question. "The Senator is

405

one of the minority leaders of the senate and a member of the Senate Armed Services Committee and, as such, has a need to know many aspects of our military operations, present circumstances included."

Sarodsy whispered into her ear. "Boss, time to go."

"Ladies and gentlemen. I have matters to attend to. Good afternoon."

The three naval officers retreated to the command elevator, headed six stories below to Sarodsy's secret war room.

"Good job, Admiral," said an energized Montgomery.

The senator broke in. "Ernie, give the Admirals a thumbnail sketch of your China visit, please."

After a five-minute quickie, Ernie concluded. "Bottom line is that Admiral Chandler did an extraordinarily competent job with General Wong and his top war-fighting assistant, and that the Chinese Air Forces are fully capable of sustained and extremely credible offensive combat air operations."

Sweeney spoke up. "Any talk of the missing nukes, Ernie?"

"No ma'am, at least not at my level. I don't think the subject came up. However, there is no doubt in my mind that the Chinese know that we know they have at least one weapon."

The ramifications of the "Missing Jewels" program were increasingly clear to the group. The sudden flow of four-billion dollars into the Redman Institute from Chinese sources was undeniable as was the convoluted outflow to many nefarious recipients. The funds had been distributed to several of the highest officials of the U.S. government, a few underlings, such as Dolores Miller, and the ubiquitous political parties under the rubric of several hundred, thinly-disguised, money-laundering shells.

Joe Montgomery spoke up. "For the time being, the missing nukes are close-hold. It's just too sensitive. If we need to access the Chinese ruling body, though, we can do so through the good offices of Admiral Demming and General Wong."

"How bad is it aboard the Reagan, Stan?" asked the senator.

"Tough, I'm afraid. Just talked with Captain Boone.

They've counted 267 bodies so far, with a lot more still trapped in the smoke-filled inner compartments and many who have simply vanished in the initial explosions or who were blown overboard. It'll be a tough pill. Good news is that the ship can still conduct defensive and offensive operations notwithstanding the massive internal damage and the loss of the port-bow catapult and one-half of its battery of eight, rapid-fire, close-in-weapons systems."

The senator continued. "Admiral Sweeny, you know the President has ordered you to remove your forces from the region, correct?"

"Yes, sir. Let me explain. Fact is I have not spoken to the President. When and if she does call, I'll ask to have the orders in writing. That's reasonable. And the reality is that the 'region' is literally thousands of miles in any direction. One just does not go home instantly. If she does so order our forces to depart, I'll translate that to a strategic withdrawal. Sound good, Stan?" she added, turning to her combat arms honcho.

"Could not have stated it better," said the hardened warrior with a nonchalant thumbs-up.

"Facts are, folks," the senator continued, his lanky frame striding to the giant wall display, "Ernie and I plan to meet later this afternoon with an emergency steering group. I can't predict the outcome, but it looks as if it's all coming to a steaming head. And," he faced the two admirals, "you all be ready for anything by about 1800 this evening. It may well be," his trademark smile in full bloom, "a 'damn-the-torpedoes, flank-speed ahead.' "

The clandestine meeting an hour later in Montgomery's Watergate condominium was astounding. In addition to the senator, Maltman and Penelope Pinson, there were eight house members and five senators spread amongst the three political parties, the ECATS, as usual, in the majority.

"Gentlemen and gentleladies," Montgomery commenced, a stack of sandwiches on the table, the group expectant, "I have no set agenda. You are all aware of what's occurred in the past fifteen years, and, more to the point, the past seventy-two hours. I'll not add my personal thoughts at this juncture, but would prefer, if you agree, to spend a few minutes reviewing what we do know, provide a short constitutional brief, an overview of the military plan of attack — should that be an option — and at the end, a summary of disturbing revelations regarding nuclear weapons." The room was still, quiescent, the sandwiches unwrapped.

For an hour, the group of fifteen briefed, questioned and offered individual, mostly apolitical, perspectives. Given the synergy of the information in the chamber, the cryptic news of the missing nuclear weapons from the Reagan, came as no great surprise.

All agreed that to back away from military action was clearly overt appeasement with dire, near-term consequences for the world, including the U.S. The clean-up of a money-compromised political body and global arms industry was another imperative. The operative question on the table though, was how to convince the President to modify her "no combat" edict and, if she was unwilling, the pragmatics of how to override her decision. Montgomery reminded the group that he, and others, had tried to get to her all day, with no success. "She has made it abundantly clear that she has no use for anyone who disagrees with her," the senator offered.

The CEO of the Navy had no such access problems with the President. In Sarodsy's command center, she was holding the phone at arm's length listening to a screeching tirade from her mentor, Virginia Roberts Stallingsworth. "Damn it, Sweeney, I want Nancy! NOW! Can you get that through your thick head?"

"Madame President," she responded in a calm, assertive voice inured in only a few days to the irrational rantings, "I have explained to you that she is aboard the Reagan and cannot return for several days. As you know," she said somewhat sweeter than necessary, "she is in command of our naval battle forces in the Indian Ocean and adjacent waters."

The response? "Bullshit," followed by a "Get your worthless ass over here now. Understood?"

"Yes, ma'am. Admiral Sarodsy and I will be there within the hour."

"No Sarodsy. That fat ass is out to lunch."

"Madame President, I regret I will be unable to meet with you without my chief assistant for combat arms. In fact, when we do meet, I would also like to bring along my diversity chief, Vice Admiral Sharon McCluskey, as well."

The embarrassing one-way outburst lasted for a full minute, Sweeney hardly listening. Fortunately, as with all secure, top-secret voice communications within the command center, the conversations were taped, the recent dialogues with the President grist for future presidential historians.

As the somber, gray skies over Virginia Beach turned to an ominous darkness, then a black nothingness, the throng in the Boone household had spilled over into the home of Beverly's neighbor, Bill Montrose. Sadly, as the names of those lost in the action so far away trickled in, the protocol in each case was that of a young naval officer delivering the lamentable tidings in person. By nightfall, some fifteen next-of-kin in the immediate area had received the grim news, the rest waiting expectantly, minds made up one way or the other. The spectacle of an obviously distraught President did little to salve the grief or worry, many asking silently, where was the leadership?

Since days of old, the Navy hometown of those left behind had gathered in time of need, a kind of modern-day circling of the wagons. Kings Grant, and many neighborhoods like it throughout the Tidewater area, were meccas of relative comfort for so many seeking a meaning to the madness of the far away conflict. Wives and husbands, friends and lovers, bundled arm-in-arm, shoulder-to-shoulder, an occasional sprinkling of a mom or dad adding balance to the troubled waters. Senior officers and those of the cloth motored from group to group. In some cases, loved ones from far away had flown to be near the font of emergent news about their loved ones. Hope ran strong. Rumors were rampant.

Senator Joe Montgomery had finally arranged a late-night meeting with the President, accompanied by the majority leader of the senate and speaker of the house, the latter two, members of the majority ECATS party. Virginia, alone, failed to smile, greet, stand or acknowledge the presence of the congressional leaders, only mouthing a curt, "Get with it."

The Speaker of the House, third in line for the presidency, spoke for the trio. "Madame President, events of the past few days portend a series of grave emergencies for our country. . ."

"Cut the gratuitous crap, Sam. I want the bottom line of this meeting."

"Yes, ma'am," said the old politico, "Of course. First is the issue of military action; second are the ominous implications of Cassidy's death; and third, the out-of-control flow of political and industry under-the-table monies of the past fifteen years."

"So, what's new? I've told you dunderheads many times that I will not commit our troops to battle halfway around the globe. PERIOD! End of subject."

"Madame President, " the elder politician, himself a veteran of four decades of changing Washington intrigue and guile, said with authority, "there is near-unanimous consent throughout our chambers that to appease the ISIs now and overlook the attack on our warship, would result in a global recession and loss of confidence in the U.S. of incalculable proportion." He paused, allowing the words to sink in. Surprisingly, the President was quiet, warily watching the seasoned leader form his next words, a watchful eye on his compatriots for reaction. The Speaker's next words were articulated slowly, clearly, unambiguously. "Madame President, it is our strong belief that our nation should join with the Chinese in executing a finite, limited-military strategy to relieve pressure on the Caspian Sea oil and do so at the earliest. We are prepared, in both houses, to vote a resolution calling for immediate action. In effect, Madame President, we are prepared to override your 'no retaliation policy' as commander in chief."

With that, the benign Virginia sprang to an instant attack mode, grabbing a handsome desk clock of ancient lineage from an end table and hurling it directly at the Speaker. "You override me? No way! It's not constitutional!"

"No, ma'am," the speaker regained his composure tempor-

410

arily lost in a defensive instinct, "it's not unconstitutional. We can do so with a plurality of 75% of the votes in both houses. At this point, we have substantially more votes than necessary and are prepared to act in a joint session of the Congress at ten tomorrow morning."

The color drained from the parched face of the unflappable chief executive. Heavily, she sat and said softly, yet with great conviction, staring all the while at the composed Senator Joe Montgomery, "You assholes. YOU FLAMING ASSHOLES!"

"Madame President," the ECATS majority leader of the senate, herself a street-wise politician of great comparative repute and relative honesty, took the floor for the first time and said formally, "there is more, I fear. We have accumulated quite a list of specific information regarding the accumulation of considerable wealth by the body politic and others over many years. There is a groundswell of revulsion amongst our members on all sides of the aisle that the system has gone far beyond what is reasonable and prudent. In some cases, there may indeed be persuasive illegalities associated with the flow of funds into our country. Without being more specific, we have gathered a dossier of extremely credible facts, not allegations, concerning you, your close advisors and Richard Redman. Madame President, it doesn't look good. I am not accusing or threatening, just advising." She paused, her eyes on the President. "This includes the Cassidy accident as well."

"Well, you have been busy little beavers, haven't you? All this is interesting, but you know the American people won't buy it. My approval ratings are higher than any President in history. No way. They trust me." This time, the smile reappeared, the Stallingsworth persona invigorated. "Go ahead and have your resolution. Won't do any good. The military answers to me, not the Congress. In fact, that worthless Sweeney is en route over here now. I tell her what to do, not you bunch of armchair quarterbacks. Fortunately, I know nothing of the Cassidy issue other than the findings of the accident board."

"Madame President," Senator Joe Montgomery stood, speaking in the strained enclave for the first time, "I'm afraid there is more. Admiral Sweeney is prepared to brief you on a highly sensitive subject regarding nuclear weapons." Montgomery purposefully looked away from the President, allowing his words to resonate within the Oval Office. "The money trail leads to the highest officials of the U.S. government. I'll leave it at that, ma'am."

The President stood, the worry lines about her tough eyes more pronounced, lips drawn. "Well, I must say gentlewomen and gentlemen," she said commandingly, her demeanor once again under control, "you all have presented quite a plateful of innuendo, allegations and obvious hearsay. It's all supposition and generalized baloney. The American people will never buy it. Why don't you nice folks go home, have a drink and we'll discuss it in the morning?" her classic smile once again radiating confidence.

The Speaker of the House responded, his voice low, almost conspiratorial. "I'm afraid, Madame President, that it's not quite so simple." Choosing his words carefully, he continued. "The House is prepared, following its resolution to approve limited combat operations, and, in conjunction with the ongoing Cassidy deliberations, to vote on approving hearings incident to your impeachment as President of the United States."

Without missing a beat, Virginia Roberts Stallingsworth continued the dialogue, almost as if a participant in a mundane college debating contest, her infectious smile obscuring her inner turmoil. "You all seem to overlook that I am an expert in matters of impeachment. Bottom line, boys and girls," she continued, rising from her chair, a rakish, furrowed eyebrow for the majority leader, "is that without the approval of the American people, you are pissing upwind in a hurricane. Now, you good people, go home and think it over. GO!"

Pensively, the hour late, the threesome departed for the waiting limo. Just seated, Montgomery noted the Navy CEO, her hefty combat arms cohort and the diversity chief striding towards the east entrance to the White House. Catching their attention, the senator whispered a few words, gathered his briefcase and closed the car door. In the limo's rear view mirror, he saw the trio re-enter the Navy staff car, do a reversal and exit the grounds just behind them.

Stan Sarodsy, upon arrival at the command center deep underground, had another tough call to make, this time to Beverly Demming Boone, in Virginia Beach. "Beverly, I talked to Tommy an hour ago. He's OK, but I fear I have bad news. He asked me to call you personally and let you know that Susan Anthony is missing and it doesn't look good. I'm sorry. He asked me to give you a heads-up."

The strained voice on the other end simply muttered, "Oh, no. Not Susan. Not my little sister."

The following morning, at precisely 10:00 a.m., 535 troubled lawmakers and a few disparate members of the high court and cabinet gathered in the imposing chambers of the nation's capitol, a standing-room-only press assemblage observing from above. Notable by her absence was the President of the United States; in her stead, the Speaker of the House calling the special meeting to order and asking for a prayer from the congressional chaplain:

"Eternal Father, strong to save
    Whose arm hath bound the restless wave
Who bade the mighty ocean deep
    Its own appointed place to keep
O hear us when we cry to Thee
    For those in peril on the sea."

CHAPTER 29

Save A Fighter Pilot's Ass

At 0405 in the morning on board the wounded aircraft carrier USS *Ronald Reagan*, the naval message caused hardly a ripple:

Precedence: FLASH
Classification: Top Secret Eyes Only
Personal for RADM Nancy Chandler from Sarodsy
Subject: Strike Plan Standby
1. This is a heads-up on combined strike plan 67-10. Stand by for an execute order within the next four hours on phases I, II, IV and VII of Strike Plan 67-10. Plan will run concurrent with your five carrier battle groups and elements of the Imperial Chinese Air Force for no longer than 48 hours. Targets and weaponry are at appendix M.
2. I regret assets are unavailable to off-load the dead and wounded from Reagan. In this regard, please expedite the names of those KIA.
3. The execute order will come from the national command authority now vested in the Congress of the United States which has just recently overridden the dictates of the President and is, for now, the commander in chief.
4. Admiral Sweeny and I wish Godspeed to you and your gallant warriors on the front lines. Vice Admiral Stan Sarodsy sends with respect and admiration.

Within minutes, Chandler had attended to the transmission of the message to her far-flung captains, the fifth delivered personally to a strung-out Captain Tommy Boone seeking a catnap in his austere sea cabin, the red light outside futilely signaling, a "Do not disturb."

As befits an admiral's prerogative, she knocked and entered. "Sorry to awaken you, Tommy. Please read this."

In ten seconds, Boone had grasped the essence of the anticipated directive with a sleepy grumble, "That means we start in daylight. Not a good move. That said, Admiral, we'll be ready. You know, one of our catapults is hard down for the duration, as well as one arresting engine. Even so, we should be able to handle our assigned share. Admiral, please have a seat, if you like. I want to get the ball rolling."

On this sad, cold and dreary night, so far from home, the routine was no different than any other hour on the big warship, like an anthill, never asleep. Phase one alpha of the operation plan called for the simultaneous time on target from the air wings of five carriers and three Chinese fighter wings, all focused on a massively destructive attack on the command and control assets of the ISIs, as well as all air bases and attendant defensive missile systems. Phase one bravo would be a similar follow-up eight-hours later in the early evening. In all, Reagan's air wing of six stealth fighter squadrons would launch an initial wave of 64 attack missions, with one squadron held for internal ship defensive combat air patrol, followed by a 60-sortie mission in the follow-up phase. Given the traumatic condition of the carrier, it was a tall order, indeed.

Boone, of course, was no stranger to carrier tactics. The "launch everything you have," philosophy, à la World War II, was the pragmatic result of being able to finally rid the carrier deck of all support aircraft excepting a trio of small, off-the-shelf civilian helicopters for minor logistics, rescue and utility. No early warning aircraft, no electronic jammers, no dedicated tankers and no search and rescue. Just all business, thanks, in part, to versatile satellite technology and the embedding into each tactical jet of an equally flexible array of avionics and defensive armaments.

The captain peered into a darkness shrouding the lingering vestiges of smoke from still-smoldering fires. In only seven hours, the ship had gone from routine refueling, to massively wounded, to 90% combat-ready, the valiant crew attending to duty with honor and several hundred individual acts of heroism. "Could have been worse," he muttered positively.

The catacombs of Stan Miller, deep within the ship, as yet unaffected by the two blasting missiles, came alive, the deadly stable of 2,000-pound high-tech bombs and associated missilery responding to a computer-generated weapons load-out for the most part untouched by human hands until on the flight and hangar decks, a destructive destiny for each measured in milliseconds.

The weary ship had been at general quarters since the detection of the incoming Super Pelican missiles, sleep to most, an elusive luxury. Boone, having set in motion the requisite myriad of complex inter-related steps explicit in the strike plan, stepped to his well-worn chair on the port, forward part of the bridge, picked up the public address system mike and spoke to his crew, his voice positive, the message anxiously awaited.

"Men and women of the Reagan, this is your Captain speaking. I want you to know that your damage control efforts have been successful and that most all fires are out and flooding contained. To each one of you, I offer a tip of the hat and pat on the back for a job exceptionally well done." He paused, his gaze taking in the functional bridge of the carrier, his thoughts going to the replacement officer of the deck for the fallen Ensign Karen Randolph.

"It's been a demanding and tragic few hours. We have lost many shipmates, shipmates who died in the line of duty, with the greatest of honor and ultimate sacrifice. My prayers are with them and those of you suffering from all forms of injury."

The ship was silent, the crew listening intently to the captain, in whose hands rested their fate. "I have a grave announcement which will further test your abilities and duty to the core. Rear Admiral Nancy Chandler, who arrived on board just as the

416

first missile struck, has just handed me a message from the Navy's Pentagon command center advising her to ready her five carrier battle groups for immediate action against the ISIs, most likely within the next four hours. The role of our fighter squadrons in the initial phases will be to totally eliminate two Iranian air bases and supporting defensive forces. As I speak, weapons are being up-loaded for the initial strike of sixty-four aircraft. May God be with us all."

Down below, in the Ripper ready room, Dr. Rose Johnson was taking a hurried break from the grim trauma of torn bodies, broken limbs and shattered hopes. At dawn, the cadre of three medical doctors on the Reagan were to be buttressed by the addition of several surgeons from other carriers, along with some needed medicines. She had managed to establish a temporary sick bay in the officer's wardroom, the most serious cases going directly to the small hospital complex in the center of the ship. To herself, she thought, it had actually gone comparatively smoothly, thankful for the Navy policy of holding periodic mass casualty drills.

The Ripper ready room had taken no lasting damage, the briefing boards and pilots' chairs restored to some semblance of normality. Spying Lieutenant Commander Dave Anderson, Rose motioned for him.

"How goes it, Doc?" he said with a slight limp, his flight suit torn and tattered. "We sure took some hits. Skipper's airborne now. Due to recover in a few minutes." His demeanor was subdued, eyes betraying an inner sadness at events clearly beyond his control.

"How many have you lost in the Rippers, Blues?" asked Rose. "I was working mainly back aft on the hangar deck. Seemed like your berthing compartment may have taken the brunt of the second missile hit."

"Correct," replied the executive officer of the squadron. "We're trying to get a head count now. Problem is, as you know, getting a reliable ID on those burned to death. It'll take a while. So far, we've accounted for 147 of our maintenance troops out of

217 assigned, so worst case is yes, we've taken some heavy losses. The ship's XO is collating all those missing now and sending the names to the Pentagon."

The Doc continued. "I've only got a few minutes. How about the flight crews?"

"Right now, we can't account for Shorts Flanagan, Lori Miller or Susan Randolph. They were topside lookouts. No telling. Oh, and Bikini just returned with the Admiral. She'll be flying with me once we get the execute order for phase one," the latter without embellishment or emotion. "Got to do it, Doc. We're really short of flight crews. Skipper will lead six jets, I'll take four and Big Sister will take three in a defensive support role on the first go. Then we brief again and go for the follow-up attacks. We need every warm body we can muster."

Off in a darkened corner of the disheveled ready room, the two noted the forlorn figures of Panky Pachino and Mike Anthony, both of whom had arrived on the Reagan less than a week prior and the sad recipients of lost loved ones. Rose knelt before the duo. "I am so sorry, Panky. What happened to Karen?"

His eyes glazed over from tears since dried, he put his head on the Doc's shoulder and heaved a dry sob. "When GQ went off, Karen headed for the entrance to paradise en route to the bridge. The first blast knocked her sideways — I think her head hit something — she was bleeding badly — so I carried her up to the ready room. She wasn't breathing." The young wizo pulled Rose to him and held her tight, tears once again in a free-fall.

The Doc pulled a pill from her bag saying, "Here, take this. It'll help you," and managed to disengage.

Moving to the next chair, she put her arm around the Fed-Ex pilot and husband of Susan Anthony. "I've scoured every nook and cranny I could find, Doc. I think she was in the port cat-walk when the forward missile hit. SHIT!" said the macho pilot, putting his head in her arms, Rose Johnson holding tight. "She had no business being out here. Damn it, she's the mother of our two kids. It's just not fair," and plaintively, sadly, his voice low and strained, "I want my Susan, Doc."

Rose, her flight surgeon persona in high gear, wondered how the two hapless young men would be able to function on two arduous, back-to-back, two-and-three-hour combat missions, launching in only a few hours. Wisely, she had resisted entering the arena of the grounded Evelyn Swagger, thinking to herself in the darkened ready room, all bets are off. The old rules are out. We do what we've got to do. If Bikini wants to go, so be it. The acrid tendrils of smoke remaining in the air were tactile reminders of human suffering run amok.

A small voice nearby jolted her to reality. "Doctor, may I have a minute, please?" It was the dirty, soot-stained apparition of Lieutenant (junior grade) Nancy Flanagan, whom, Rose recalled, had been grounded due to her pregnancy and subsequently assigned by the captain to topside lookout duties. "What's the problem, Nancy?"

"Doc, I'm bleeding — you know?" the voice tentative, pleading.

"You room with Commander Anderson, correct?"

"Yes, ma'am."

Anderson had noticed the bedraggled figure of Shorts tentatively enter the rear of the ready room. "Shorts, good to see you," he almost yelled, his eyes misting. "You had us worried."

Rose Johnson took charge. "Dave, I'm taking her down to your stateroom for a few minutes. Please don't bother us."

"Sure, Doc," said the sometimes naive pilot.

Paradise, though not a disaster, was close to it. Doors were ajar, blood stained the entrance and several light fixtures and wires hung loosely from the overhead. Not a soul appeared, the odor of smoke overwhelming, a sense of abject human misery prevailing.

Flanagan spoke up once the door to the tiny room closed. "Doc, I was supervising the starboard lookouts, like the Captain wanted, when the missile hit. I have no idea what happened — I just woke up in a corner of one of the topside foul-weather lockers."

"OK, young lady, let's take a peek," the blood-smeared jacket covering her midsection exposing the obvious trauma of a pregnancy no more.

"You'll be all right, Shorts. I'd like to pump you some blood as you've lost quite a bit, but don't have the time now. You'll live, if you stay horizontal, drink plenty of liquids and rest. I'll check on you in few hours. Got to run." With that, she grabbed her trademark black bag and beat a hasty retreat to the triage, cries and misery of her temporary work place in the officer's wardroom several decks below.

A knock on the door a few minutes later. "Shorts, it's Dave. OK to come in?"

"Sure. Door's open."

"Thought you were a goner. We've already put you in as missing in action." Dave noticed the stack of towels about her middle and guessed the cause. "Sorry, Shorts, but glad to have you back and reasonably well." What ensued, for the first time in the almost nine months of their close relationship as roommates, was a soul-bearing dialogue, the crusty, manly former Blue Angel, almost breaking down with emotion, not only for the gutsy young woman, but for the many others in the Red Rippers and through-out the ship.

"Dave," she said weakly, lying on the bottom bunk, a smile almost breaking her dull facade, "are you short of flight crews?"

"Way short, I'm afraid. And we have a near max all-up jets launch in a few hours."

The junior officer took a deep breath and spoke, the words a surprise to the weary pilot. "I know I've been kind of a goof-off and really haven't pulled my weight. I thought it was all a lark. Lots of guys, too many liaisons and more attention than I ever deserved." She paused, forcing back tears of frustration and said simply to Anderson, "I have a request."

"Go ahead," said her roommate.

"I want to be on that strike. I'll fly with anyone. Please, Dave," she whimpered, her voice thin, "I can hack it and the Doc won't care — her plate's full now."

Anderson stared at the brave young woman, a human being he had never known until this moment, a newfound respect clamoring for attention. "We'll see, Shorts. You need to get your strength back first," resisting his protective instinct to hold her close, to comfort, to nurture.

Becky Turner hit the paradise passageway just as an almost tearful Blues Anderson was departing. "It's Shorts, Big Sister. She just came to off in some topside-storage room. Lost some blood, but Doc says she'll be OK in a few days."

Turner piped up. "Well, now. A bit of good news. Hey, I hear we may launch soon. How about we get ourselves organized? McCormick says we have a chance for thirteen jets, if he can dig 103 out of hangar-bay three."

Despite all the action and forced trauma of the past nine hours, Becky was upbeat. A truly remarkable naval officer, thought the squadron's acting executive officer. "Let's go," he exclaimed, as the duo trooped off to the intelligence spaces some 400 feet aft.

The intelligence war room was a haven of antiseptic calm, not unlike the pristine weapons control complex deep below in the speeding warship. Status boards blinked, decks still shined with newly-laid wax and banks of computer displays quietly and impersonally cranked out the data needed to fight the complex weapons system known as the nuclear-powered aircraft carrier USS *Ronald Reagan*. Huddled over one such modem was the indefatigable Ensign Patty Butts.

"Hi, XO, Becky. How's it going up forward?" referring to the Red Ripper ready room a football-field length away, adding warily, "Have we lost anyone?" The question hit the two like another bombshell. Becky asked her "Have you not been to your stateroom or the ready room?"

"No. Been too busy here. You all like an update? I'll be ready to brief our part in about ten minutes."

Becky took the lead. "Patty," she said, guiding the obviously unknowing officer to a quiet corner of the secret war-planning space, "please sit down. I'm afraid I've some bad news."

In a heartbeat, Patty blurted, "Not Twidget?" tears already forming.

Becky put her arms about the trembling young officer. "No, Patty. It's Karen. She was lost when the first missile hit — didn't know what hit her. She was heading for the bridge." She held the young officer closer, and said mournfully, "I'm so sorry."

"Oh, not Karen. Does Panky know?"

"Yes, he was holding her when she died. He's in the ready room now. Perhaps you could take a few minutes and talk to him. He's really down."

It took only a moment before the ensign gritted her teeth, denial competing with the stark reality of combat on the deck plates and said forcefully, "No, Becky. We have a job to do." Standing with her shoulders square, head high, she returned to her console, all business, tears dripping onto the complex strike plan. "I would appreciate your thoughts on how phase one will go. Still needs a bit of refinement."

Clearly, the strike plan was ambitious, but doable. Timing and the concentration of massive force were the keys. Once the complex of ISI defensives was neutralized, the following phases of mountainous choke point destruction were comparative milk runs. Turner spoke up. "At least this is being done right. None of the piecemeal approach, like the politicians have done in the past. We give it a full broadside and hope for the best."

The threesome sensed another close behind them. It was the imposing figure of a two star admiral, her uniform at stark contrast to the sweaty and smoke-permeated flight suits of the two Ripper pilots. "I'm Admiral Chandler," she said, and noticing the ungainly boar's head apparition on their right breast pockets, offered, "You must be Red Rippers. I'm sorry for your losses."

"Thank you, Admiral. I'm Dave Anderson, acting exec; this is Becky Turner, our operations officer; and Patty Butts, our intelligence officer."

"Oh, you must be Sally Butts's daughter?"

"Yes, ma'am," the gutsy young officer responded, her eyes red and puffy. "I was just going to brief Commander Anderson on the Ripper attack specifics for phase one. Would you care to sit in, ma'am?"

"I would indeed, Patty. Please proceed."

The Ripper computer-generated attack plan was not all that complex. How it fit into the overall forty-eight-hour plan, however, was. Chandler watched as Butts outlined the scenario, the target, the Iranian air field near the Persian Gulf port of Bandar Abas, the same one partially struck some four days prior and the home to some 47 aircraft and support facilities. The thirteen Red Ripper fighters would follow by five minutes the precise placement of fourteen surface-to-surface missiles launched from submarines far out in the Indian Ocean, each assigned a final destiny of a solitary piece of strategic real estate in the Iranian desert. The Ripper stealth jets would carry a standard load of four, 2,000-pound, GPS-guided, Mark 84 (mod 2) stand-off bombs as well as a mix of missilery and cannon. Time on target was critical, the allowed tolerance plus or minus fifteen seconds. Following the first wave, the probability of kill on the assigned targets would be in excess of 90%.

"Most impressive," said the admiral catching the eye of Anderson. "Any problems, Commander?"

"No, ma'am. If we had our druthers, though, we'd do it at night. Really, it's six of one, half dozen of another. We'll be in and out so fast, they won't have time to tie their shoelaces."

Patty then offered an overview of the first two phases. Essentially, given the total U.S. and Chinese assets of about thirty and twelve squadrons, respectively, the plan called for an almost simultaneous confluence of over 500 attack sorties on a multiple of targets, followed by phase one bravo eight hours later from some 450 attackers. By any reasonable measure, the ability of the ISIs to mount any effective defense would be practically nil, thus opening the door to the potent mountainous choke-point strategy.

The foursome was interrupted by the appearance of the ship's executive officer, Commander Angela Batori and the command master chief, Mitsi Moore. "Captain said I would find you here, ma'am. Would you care to take a look at the damage forward and aft?"

"Sure. Thanks. Not much I can do here." To the Ripper officers, she offered her hand and an honest smile of gratitude.

"Good meeting you all. Thank you."

The scene below matched the sullen, sooty London street scenes of a Charles Dickens novel. The troops moved like zombies, faces filthy, uniforms soiled, stepping gingerly around the still-smoldering zones of devastation. Just aft of the forward mess decks, the XO led the admiral to a large walk-in freezer, mountains of frozen foods replaced by a grotesque assemblage of blackened bodies burned beyond recognition. "We don't have the wherewithal to do positive identification at this time, so this is a temporary morgue." The ghostly apparitions, in most cases, were not covered nor in body bags, the XO's laconic reasoning, "Ran out of body bags, Admiral."

Mitsi Moore led the way down three decks to what was once the second division's berthing compartment. "Looks like the first missile penetrated the skin of the ship and exploded here. Most of the remains were unrecognizable as humans, The only ones who got out were those that moved at the first clang of the GQ alarm. Pretty much the same in the Ripper berthing spaces back aft."

The stench, a mixture of burnt flesh and spent explosives, mingled with the odor of lingering smoke, the retreat to the medical spaces amidships, a welcome respite.

The small sick bay, designed for twenty-five patients, was bulging with about fifty, some on cots in the passageway. These poor souls were the most severe, attended to by two MDs, triage having separated the most life-threatening from those just plain damaged. The lead physician, the ship's senior medical officer, noticing the exec, said wearily, "Hi, XO. Not doing too good. Be glad when we get another surgeon. I hear they'll be landing shortly." The screams of agony from a young sailor nearby pierced the busy noise level of the temporary trauma center, her leg at a grotesque angle to her bare hip, a quick shot of morphine, the fix. "We've got to amputate, I'm afraid," the Doc stated matter-of-factly, "let's get her ready."

Heading aft near the ship's executive officer's stateroom and office complex, they stopped at the temporary workplace of

Dr. Rose Johnson and some 250 of the injured, wounded and broken of the Reagan's crew, many with oozing burns, blistering pink from the raw flesh. Horror ran deep, the grit tough.

Rose greeted the three women, briefly described the grim medical status, rough loss of life and asked the XO, "Any chance of off loading our most critical? Some of these folks need more than we can provide, you know," the latter with a pique unusual for the Doc.

The admiral broke in. "We may be able to get a couple of CODs in to take them to Diego Garcia. Problem is," she thought out loud, "we have a major strike involving most of the air wing." Chandler knew at that instant, as the battle force commander, she had three options, none of which was easy. She took the toughest.

"Sorry, Doc. We have a job to do — takes every carrier and max strike aircraft, even if it means further loss of life. We'll have to hang tough."

Rose's thoughts were to herself as she studied the mayhem that was once the formal dining area for the ship's officers — as if they haven't hung tough for the past nine months.

"Admiral," the XO said, "would you like to take a break? My stateroom is close by."

"Sure. Lead the way," the command master chief taking the opportunity to disengage.

In the relative comfort of the XO's digs, the Marine orderly at parade rest just outside, Chandler took stock. "Understand your husband is the skipper of the Barking Dogs?" It was more a question than a statement.

"Yes, ma'am. Rock's had his hands full," wishing privately that she could one day elucidate more fully on the precise meaning of what his hands had been full of. "Fact is, we might as well be on different ships for how much we are together," wishing, once again to herself, she could say what she felt.

"Mind if I use your head?" said the shore-based senior naval officer to the XO.

"Help yourself, ma'am."

As if on cue, the door burst open, the harried face of Lieutenant Commander Stan Miller thrust forward, a look of despair never before seen by Batori. "Angela, got to talk. You OK?"

"Sure. A bit stressed-out, though," she responded, suddenly feeling a decade older.

"I've been in this man's Navy for thirty-seven years and I've never seen anything like it."

"Like what, Stan? I hope the weapons' load-out is on track."

"You won't believe this. First, it was the cute couple who failed to person the topside close-in-weapons system that could well have made the difference in the missile attack. Now I've got a platoon of sobbing sisters and wimpy boyfriends who refuse to handle our 2,000-pound bombs. It's crazy!"

Angela Batori foresaw another black ball coming her way, her attention diverted from her two star Washington visitor. The agitated weapons officer continued. "They're having a damned sit-down, all intertwined with one another like the flower children of the late '60s." Plaintively, he asked, just as Chandler reappeared from her constitutional, "How about coming down and getting these sorry malcontents pointed in the right direction. We've only got 40% of the weapons load-out complete as it stands now. Oh, Admiral. Sorry — I didn't see you."

The subject of insubordination on a warship, any ship, was foreign to the naval profession, the kinder and gentler Navy of recent years notwithstanding. "What's the problem, Commander?" Chandler questioned, somewhat peevishly.

Miller snapped to attention, his blue-and-gold quotient at the ready. "Admiral, ma'am. Sorry . . ."

Batori broke the ice. "Oh, Stan. This is Admiral Chandler. Admiral, Lieutenant Commander Miller, our weapons officer."

Miller, admittedly more comfortable in his below-decks fiefdom, hesitantly spoke up. "Admiral, I have a group of about twenty-three who are adamantly protesting our use of force against the ISIs. They said we should spend more time talking. I think the catalyst was the dozens of big bombs streaming to the flight deck, the obvious implication to our precious flock, death and destruction for untold thousands. What am I supposed to argue?

Oh no, they won't hurt anybody?"

The XO's phone buzzed concurrent with the bleatings of the crusty, up-through-the-ranks weapons officer. "Admiral, we've got the execute for phase one. Launch seventy jets at 1007. I'll have my orderly escort you to the war room. Stan, let's go below and find out what these bunch of grade-school candy-asses have on their love-struck minds." To her orderly. "Corporal, once you've taken the Admiral topside, get the command Master Chief and have her meet us in the weapons control spaces, stat."

The old mustang, a veteran of uncountable around-the-clock weeks and months of shipboard duties, followed the ship's executive officer into the leadership imbroglio far below.

"Attention on deck," hollered a futile voice to the motley assemblage of non-uniformed sailors crowding the weapons control room. Not a soul moved, the preplanned response predictable. Surly eyes glared at Miller and Batori.

The ship's exec spoke softly, slowly. "Who's the the leader of this group?" No response. She icily surveyed the two-dozen malcontents, huddled tightly, arms about one another. One young man, his eyes downcast, caught her attention. "Your name is Watson, correct?"

"Yes, ma'am."

"Please tell me what the problem is." Without awaiting an answer, she snapped, "You know we have a seventy-jet strike launch coming up?" Eyes lifted, locked onto the XO, he stood slowly, his compatriots silently urging him to sit.

"Ma'am, it's nothing against you or Mr. Miller or the Captain. It's just," he paused, seeking comfort from the rebellious group, "it's just that those bombs were the final straw. So much has happened in the past few months. It just seems to get worse. No telling how many of our shipmates have been killed or maimed. It's just too much. We are all scared beyond words." The room was silent, all eyes of the group searching for solace among the cracks in the tile deck.

A young woman spoke up, her arms tightly about her muscular friend. "Mr. Miller, it was the bombs. Except for one

427

time, those bombs lay in their pristine, climate-controlled storage. Every day we saw them on our inspection tours. It's no secret that the spaces were comfort zones. We could always get an hour or two of privacy." She continued, holding her protector and obvious lover. "Now the same weapons will be used to kill people. We don't think it's right."

Her friend interrupted, his voice harsh. "And, we will not be a party to the death of innocent bystanders. The obscene death of thirty-seven school kids just a few days ago was the final straw."

Master Chief Mitsi Moore entered the troubled space, her persona in a spring-loaded-to-the-attack mode, her eyes glaring, the bedraggled group an insult to her ilk. "XO, may I say something, please?"

"Of course, Master Chief," thankful for the distraction.

"I'm not going to mince words," she said, her tone challenging. "You know very well what you are doing. In simple terms, it's called mutiny. You may think you are doing the right thing, but, my shipmates," her demeanor stiffened, eyes tight, "this is a ship of war of the United States Navy. You get your miserable asses off the deck and start handling weapons or . . .," she was interrupted by the captain on the squawk box, asking, in no uncertain terms, for the weapons officer.

"Stan, this is the Captain. We launch in just under two hours and only half the weapons load is complete. What's the action?"

Miller wisely switched to a private phone and spoke quietly. "Captain, we have a problem down here. The XO and Master Chief are trying to sort it out." The remainder of the conversation was unintelligible, the veteran weapons officer finally speaking quietly to the two women, three heads nodding in the affirmative.

"Ten seconds, you bunch of wimps," barked the diminutive master chief. "Ten seconds to get off your asses, on your feet and back to work." Not a soul moved.

Miller simply said to the motley group, "OK, have it your way. Follow me."

Within two minutes, the recalcitrant twenty-three were herded into a now-vacant 2,000-pound bomb-storage vault only a few feet from the weapons control center, the ship's exec intoning, "By order of Captain Boone, this space is hereby designated a temporary brig. You will be allowed head calls in groups of two every three hours. Your meals will be dry sandwiches and water, when we have the time."

At that, the heavy steel door slammed shut. For the first time in twenty-four hours, Mitsi Moore felt good, Miller was contrite over the preceding sacrilege and the XO scurried off to check on the status of damage aft on the hangar deck.

High above, just below the number-one catapult, the Red Ripper ready room had come alive, flight gear and warm bodies replacing the gloom and despair of lost shipmates. Iron Lady, Blues and Big Sister were deep in conference, the operative overriding issue, how to get thirteen pilots and an equal number of wizos for the back seats. "That is, given we have thirteen jets," the skipper offered.

"We're short one pilot and back-seater, Skipper," said Turner, not aware of the wane arrival of Shorts Flanagan, fully-dressed for flight.

"Make that one pilot short, Big Sister," said Anderson. "Shorts will go. Talk to her, Becky. See if she's up to it. Doc said she'd lost a lot of blood."

The two women, joined by Evelyn Swagger, spoke quietly for a few moments, culminating in a three-way high five, smiles surfacing for the first time in many hours. Turner said simply, "She'll hack it," and an equally matter-of-fact, "I'll check with the Barking Dogs and see if they have an extra pilot who wouldn't mind a respite with a class outfit."

Panky Pachino and Mike Randolph, haggard and drawn, joined the briefing, resigned to a destiny in a far-off desert, avenging warriors in search of prey.

The attack plan, replicated on five carriers and twenty-four fighter squadrons, was strike tactics 101 — nothing unusual or profound. While not exactly routine, neither was the plan overly complex. The Rippers were assigned one-half of the air field at Kleski, some one hundred miles from the entrance to the Strait of Hormuz. A total of forty 2,000-pound, extremely accurate, stand-off weapons would hit forty separate and distinct targets, from bunkers, to barracks to runways. The Ripper flights were divided into three flights of six, four and three, led by the skipper, Dave Anderson and Becky Turner, respectively, the latter with a covey of electronic homing air-to-surface missiles and an extra load of air-to-air missilery, should any airborne threats appear. The complex plan included the arrival of a dozen sea-launched missiles three to five minutes prior to the Rippers' designated time-on-target. And, finally, each carrier had in reserve, one squadron of twelve to fourteen fighters for self defense, both airborne and in an on-deck alert status ready for instant launch. Each carrier was assigned two giant fuel-laden contract airborne tankers overhead for emergency and mission tanking.

The weary crews noted the target coordinates, assigned aircraft, defenses, rendezvous points, ingress routes and the myriad of tasks so necessary for a successful attack. Slowly, methodically, the twenty-six aviators straggled to their assigned aircraft on a cold, windswept and misty flight deck.

"Shit," proclaimed Blues Anderson when he arrived at his assigned F-27C stealth Phantom III, chained securely to the steel deck with sixteen unyielding tie-downs, the pig's head on the vertical tail uncaring, "we've only got two bombs. What's going on?" His back-seater, Bikini, meanwhile, was busy acclimating to the jet's cockpit while her pilot preflighted the fighter. The jet next to him piloted by Mike Anthony and the recovering — and still weak — Shorts Flanagan, likewise had only two bombs instead of the assigned four two-thousand pounders. Stoically, realistically, Anderson told the red-shirted ordnance persons, "We'll go with what we have. So be it," an admittedly ominous start to the mission.

Master Chief Randy McCormick was all over his Ripper jets like bees to a honeycomb. The last jet, Ripper 103, he personally orchestrated out of the aft hangar deck and onto the number-three elevator as the ordnance crews frantically loaded the fighter assigned to Big Sister, with its mix of cannon, radar homers and launch-and-leave air-to-air missiles. Her words to him, as she and Twidget personed the machine, were a simple, "Thanks, Master Chief," words worth more to the old sailor than a ten-thousand-dollar cash bonus, an ethic understood by few external to the arena of warships and fighter aircraft.

McCormick had managed to round up a few stragglers from about the ship to replace those no longer able, including about a dozen sailors, formerly on light duty, and set them to work cleaning wind screens, hauling chains, lugging assorted ordnance and providing sterile sandwiches and drink to the tired and hungry workers. The mood, in the close-to-hurricane-force winds, as the captain drove the ship hard towards a closer-in launch point at flank speed, was somber, hundreds of young souls and bodies reacting as greyhounds chasing the elusive rabbit. Only in this case, there was no reward at the end of the tunnel, only more tunnel.

On the bridge, Captain Tommy Boone set his ample jaws, glanced at his digital Timex and thought to himself, feet propped on the standby gyro repeater. The shortage of Mark 84, 2,000-pound bombs had not gone unnoticed. To his credit, one of his more positive traits, evolved over many years in the hot seat, was not to run in circles and scream and shout when the going got tough or plans went awry. As long as the leadership and troops were doing their best, it did little good to rant and rave. Nonetheless, it was high-school combat U.S. Navy protocol to never launch strike aircraft absent the assigned load of ordnance. What had happened in the weapons spaces, in fact, had been perilously close to a classic mutiny. He almost smiled between gritted teeth, the specter of the Navy's high command, shore-based do-gooders getting wind of this, was almost too juicy to contemplate.

The first of the jets was making its way cautiously to the three operational catapults, the minutes and seconds ticking down to launch time, the stinging rain, like horizontal sleet to the multi-colored minions on the flight deck of the USS *Ronald Reagan*. The deadly blows absorbed by the tough warship only a few hours before were almost invisible to the untrained observer, the human screams deep within masked by the collective vibrancy of the birds of prey about to take flight.

A tear came to the eyes of the seasoned sailor, the sad call to his longtime wife, Beverly, having been completed several hours ago. His sister-in-law and Red Ripper pilot had only been aboard a few days, jerked from her comfortable airline perch and growing family and suddenly thrust directly into harm's way with little fanfare and no promises. He wondered, peering down at the crowded flight deck with its stable of Phantom IIIs coming to life, which one was piloted by Susan's husband, Mike. God, what a system, he mused, the tears no more.

As the first two jets were blasted skyward by the number-one bow catapult and the number-three waist cat, the planes swallowed in seconds by a low scud layer, he was joined by a weary Rear Admiral Nancy Chandler, escorted by the ship's command master chief. Respectfully, he stood, annoyed only for a fraction that she had not been properly announced. "Admiral, Master Chief, good to see you. Looks like we go with only sixty-four jets — lack of crews, I'm told by the air wing commander. She was the first in the air. Keep our fingers crossed for an RTB of 64 in 1 plus 57," cryptic lingo for all to return home safely at the completion of the mission.

The three stood in the time-honored vantage point on the port side of the bridge, just abaft the captain's chair, the complex sequence of events within each aircraft and about the deck like the coherent blending of the symphony's many instruments to the learned conductor.

Boone broke the silence as the final stealth skimmed the urgent waves and eased into the cloud deck, 64 angry jets crewed by 128 of the best the country could produce. "Out of sight, but not out of mind, you brave souls," whispered the captain, wishing he could be in the vanguard, as he had in years past.

"What happens now, Tommy?" asked the admiral.

He responded, pleased for questions with easy answers. "Each of the five squadrons has rendezvous sectors generally north and west. They'll be on top of the weather about 17,000 feet. Then, it's on to two target complexes, as you know. Let's hope our civilian tankers can hack this weather. We may need them. I've cut the landing interval down to forty-five seconds to reduce the total recovery time. It'll be get aboard on the first pass or go find the tanker."

"Tommy," she said, the question sincere, almost rhetorical, "this is tough, is it not? I mean, *really* tough?"

"Yes, Admiral. We have three hours to refuel, rearm, brief the crews and launch again for phase one bravo. Same targets, with a few less strike assets. With the trauma of the past ten hours, no sleep, loss of buddies — I could go on and on. Yes, ma'am. It's real tough — tougher than I've ever seen or heard of. The problem is, as you know, all the pieces are interrelated. If one ship or squadron screws up, the plan could well fail. The key to this is massively concentrated and coordinated destructive power over many targets. And, for what it's worth, the weather is an impediment, even if all the shore-based staff experts think otherwise."

"XO on the bridge," screamed the young boatswain's mate on watch, still smarting from her failure to notice the admiral in time.

"Morning Admiral, Captain, Master Chief," she said respectfully, the responses perfunctory.

"Captain, got a moment?" asked the XO. "Master Chief, you too," the leadership moving to the starboard side of the bridge, the admiral left contemplating an empty flight deck. "Sir, we've got several dozen crewmembers who are badly hurt and in need of better medical attention than we can muster up on board. Rose Johnson will be on her way up here shortly to plead for an off-load of any kind. The Admiral has already indicated she is unwilling to pull back or change the strike planning," adding, "Just a heads-up, sir. And, Captain, Stan Miller is totally distraught at the weapons load-out. He's taking it as a personal failure on his part. I guess it took a double-missile hit and real combat to bring out the worst in that bunch of weenies. At any rate, they're safe and sound for the duration."

433

"Thanks, Angela. Maybe, for once, the Washington eggheads will learn a few lessons about the reality of sustained combat operations!"

"Captain, for what it's worth, I'll be at your side flipping slides when you give the brief."

With a face lined by grief, stress off the scale and years of understanding, her boss said, "And we'll end up as officers in charge of the daily Norfolk sludge barge."

Ensign Patty Butts and Dr. Rose Johnson were taking a well-deserved break in the empty Ripper ready room. Even the duty officer was in the air. Gripped with emotions in the stratosphere, Rose, her medical brain in maximum overload, hardly noticed the names of the twenty-six flight crews, Shorts and Bikini included, just blips on the mantra of necessity. Patty, too, drifted from target ingress routes and weapons load, to Jacobs, six letters on a grease board, Twidget and Big Sister off to battle with no points for second place.

Hesitantly, the front door to the shrouded ready room opened, the lanky frame of the Red Ripper maintenance officer looming into focus. Patty froze, her muddled brain seeking rationality in her roommate Karen's tearful revelations not so many days ago, of events in the shower, Miller's hands caressing the back of her dead roommate.

Rose, of course, was privy to the brief encounter several days ago, a one-way liaison indelibly inscribed for the record in a medical journal growing thicker by the day.

"Oh, I didn't see you all," said the maintenance officer, starting to back out the door. Patty struggled to rise, her face contorted, muscles forming two small fists, adrenalin at max flow. The Doc forced the young woman back into her seat.

"Miller," the Doc said forcefully and with nary a twinge of regret, "the next time I see your cowardly ass, I'm going to personally pound you to a pulp and then turn you over to the rest of the Red Rippers." She stood. "Get out of here! NOW!" Miller quickly retreated to destinations unknown.

Alone again, Patty said, "You know, Doc, not long ago, I

heard Twidget and the rest of the Red Rippers singing an old fighter pilot song down in paradise, 'Throw a nickel on the grass, save a fighter pilot's ass.' Now I know why."

CHAPTER 30

Four Years Later

Four years later, in 2014, there assembled at the Naval Academy in Annapolis, a few of the notable players of that tumultuous November week in 2010. Hosted by Vice President Stan Sarodsy, formerly of the U.S. Navy, the purpose of the gathering was to preserve for posterity the many lessons learned, both militarily and politically.

Organized as a quasi-retreat, the setting was as gorgeous as the tabled issues were auspicious. Clear Annapolis skies were framed by sharp, idealistic midshipmen marching to daily lessons of war, conflict, science and leadership. Honor, duty and country remained indelibly woven into the fabric of the everyday regimen. The ritual Wednesday afternoon full-dress parade, resurrected two years before, was reviewed by America's Vice President and the entourage of the official party, the roaring arrival of a Blue Angel foursome in a missing-man formation overriding the strident commands of the brigade commander to "PASS IN REVIEW." The number-two jet, piloted by Lieutenant Commander Becky Turner, pulled up sharply into the crisp, sunlit sky, as her leader, Commander Dave Anderson, winged his remaining brood towards the entry point for nearby Andrews Air Force Base. As if on cue, the midshipmen stepped out smartly to the patriotic drums and fifes of the "Stars and Stripes Forever."

In attendance, along with copious media, were legions of historians from all ideological corners and a smattering of family and loved ones. The gathering the next morning in the giant field house was filled by the 4,200 blue-service-uniformed brigade of midshipmen, the focal point, as a lazy Susan atop a huge dining spread, a series of tables forming a circle atop a raised dais, the participants randomly arranged. Room-sized HDTV screens projecting the dialogue and animation of each of the thirty-one participants gave those in the audience a feeling of individual attention. The objective was to remember the many events of four years prior, including combat operations, social issues, revolving doors of the influential, crime and punishment and the lot of the hometown folks left behind. The concept of the conference had its roots in the desires of President Joe Montgomery to host a substantive reunion of those instrumental in the incredibly far-reaching outcomes of that week so long ago.

First on the agenda was a discussion of the lessons learned from Strike Plan 67-10. Moderated by four star Admiral Nancy Chandler, the Navy CEO, she was ably assisted by Lieutenant Patty Butts and Lieutenant Commander Evelyn Swagger Tsunami, both assigned to her immediate Pentagon staff. The audience was hushed, expectant — most on the edge of their seats.

In macro terms, five U.S. Navy carrier air wings accomplished adequately their portion of the plan, launching 87% of the required sorties, delivering 84% of assigned ordnance and accomplishing an overall probability-of-target-kill of 86% while incurring losses of twenty-one downed aircraft, all F-27C stealth Phantom IIIs. At rather stark contrast was the performance of the three Chinese air wings which flew 106% of the planned sorties and weapons loads with a target kill probability of 97%. One aircraft was lost.

Following the first two phases intended to neutralize ISI defenses, U.S. carrier forces were hard-pressed to generate the required strike sorties. The stress factor in each air wing and ship was far greater than ever before experienced, particularly with those carriers deployed constantly for four months or greater. All five aircraft carriers and their battle group ships had personnel problems somewhat similar to those experienced aboard the USS *Ronald Reagan*.

The choke-point strategy was successful, the combined

concentration of force onto twenty-seven target complexes prudent and reasonable. Predictably, ISI ground forces in and about the Caspian Sea rapidly withered to a militarily insignificant factor, the world's oil supplies once again in a tenuous balance. Overwhelmingly, all strategists, pundits included, agreed with the centuries-old notion of employing massive and concentrated military force in order to seize an objective, eschewing the more politically acceptable notion of incrementalism and limited losses.

Following a lively discussion of tactics and strategy, the focus shifted to the aircraft carrier USS *Ronald Reagan* (CVN-76). Moderating the panel, as expected, was the ship's captain at the time, Captain Tommy Boone. Assisting was his former executive officer, Commander Angela Batori and the sprightly Master Chief Mitsi Moore. As befitted their retired status, all were attired in appropriate civilian dress.

The damage sustained by the carrier from two Super Pelican missiles failed to slow the mammoth warship or her stable of deadly fighter aircraft. In all, 327 men and women were killed and 417 wounded and injured. Despite the traumatic damage, the Reagan managed a contribution to the strike plan only slightly less than her fellow aircraft carriers.

Angela Batori offered an eye-watering description of the carrier's triumphant return to Norfolk just before Christmas of 2010, after having been deployed for nine-and-one-half months. Three-hundred-and-fifty loved ones were flown to the carrier the day before arrival to stand in solemn tribute at the memorial service conducted near the Chesapeake Light House, twenty-one miles offshore. Among the gathering were the parents of Ensign Karen Randolph, Lieutenant Sam Newman, Lieutenant (junior grade) Nancy Flanagan and the two small children of Lieutenants Susan and Mike Anthony. The eulogy, offered by Admiral Carolyn Sweeney and Captain Tommy Boone on the piercingly-cold, wind-swept flight deck, focused on the notions of duty, honor and country under an umbrella of past sacrifice by untold thousands who had preceded them. A four-jet Red Ripper missing-person flyover, led by Commander Wendy Montrose, concluded the simple ceremony. A lone wreath, cast jointly by the Anthony offspring, joined the frigid waters of commingled oceans.

Captain Tommy Boone, whom many thought was clearly destined for flag rank, opted to retire from active duty, his reasoning irrefutable. With the addition to his family of Susan's and Mike's two little ones, he felt it time to "get my priorities straight" and tend to his brood of one sacrificing wife of eighteen years and four girls. He resisted the lucrative offers of those diehards in the profitable arms industry and chose instead to concentrate his energies as the headmaster of the newly-formed National Academy of Virginia Beach, a learning center focusing on Navy dependents and disadvantaged youth. The creed, prominently displayed over the impressive entrance read, "Duty, Honor, Country."

The dynamo known as Master Chief Mitsi Moore continued as the Reagan's top enlisted person and advisor to the captain, serving as a low-key purveyor of integrity and no-nonsense work ethic. Retiring from active duty, she and her husband went to work as role models and instructors at the National Academy, teaching the repetitive message of character, honor and service.

Commander Angela Batori retired from active service after divorcing her Barking Dog husband, and now stands by the side of her Reagan intimate, former Lieutenant Commander Stan Miller, their discourse of necessity behind inch-thick plate glass at the federal penitentiary in Fort Leavenworth, Kansas. True to form, she blamed others for the demise of Miller.

With a grim smile, Captain Boone reminded the packed gathering of the near-mutiny far below in the ship's weapons' spaces. The twenty-three cowardly malcontents spent the final three weeks of the 2010 voyage in the temporary brig deep within the ship, were transferred to the naval stockade at Norfolk and were awarded individual general court-martials. All received eight years of confinement at hard labor, said incarceration in equal, but separate facilities. The audience broke into an unceremonious applause.

The next discussion had no moderator and no panel. The

dais offered tidbits of perspective on the sordid political machinations within the nation's power elite.

The impeachment of Virginia Roberts Stallingsworth had commenced with the seating of the 119th Congress of the United States early in January of 2011. Presided over by the Chief Justice of the United States, the charges were dispatched in short order by a tripartisan majority of 87% of the Senate

The three articles of impeachment included an abuse of power arising from the accumulation of $3.4 billion in personal wealth, principally the result of nefarious, though legal, monies emanating mainly from Chinese sources. Added by a unanimous voice-vote, was dereliction of duty, the result of a failure to take reasonable and prudent actions incident to substantial violations of international law arising from overt aggression by the Iranian, Saudi Arabian and Iraqi consortium's attempts to gain control of the Caspian Sea oil riches. And finally, considered by most to have been the most egregious, was failing to react militarily to overt hostilities on a U.S. warship on the high seas.

Richard Redman, the master wheeler and dealer to the high and mighty of influence and power, and his immediate lieutenants were finally ensnared, the criminal charges stemming from his involvement in the death of Cassidy, the sale of nuclear weapons to China, bribery in a host of instances and his authorization for the delivery of the Super Pelican missiles to Iran. Providently, before his trial commenced, he suffered a massive heart attack, the ravages of corpulence overcoming the finest medicine unlimited money could buy. Sadly, to some, the funeral was attended by only a few.

Following her removal from office, Stallingsworth was tried in federal court and found criminally guilty of all charges and sentenced to prison for eleven years with no opportunity for parole. Insofar as was reasonably possible, her enormous Swiss bank accounts were emptied and the collective amounts distributed to charitable causes.

Subsequent to the near-unanimous impeachment, the Congress voted overwhelmingly to drastically curtail the bounty of campaign financing, a twenty-year notion that had willingly evolved into a special-interest fact of business known as "personal enrichment," or, in the rhetoric of the 119th congress, "bribery." Tough new laws dramatically pared donations to politicians, abolished PACs as a conduit for unlimited-access dollars and detailed finite limits on the expenditure of personal or family wealth for political office, all within the constraints of the sacrosanct intents of the first amendment to the nation's Constitution.

The financial information extant in the top-secret program deep within the Pentagon known as "Green Trees," turned out to be close to 100% correct, the windfall to thousands in the political, technology and arms-industry arenas over many years, enormous. Though not entirely altruistic, overwhelming national sentiment was to grandfather those recipients by leaving the monies in place. It was recognized that the alternative task of separating the ill-gotten from the earned, would have been a process of long-lingering acrimony and not worth the effort. Those excepted, most all agreed, were the ring leaders of the greed factory in and about the "Redman Institute for Enlightened Awareness," including those involved in the Cassidy "accident" and sale of nuclear weapons.

By unanimous consent, clear-cut laws were enacted early in 2012 severely restricting the established concept of the well-greased revolving door of those involved in the political process, political appointees and senior officials. These learned folks, though, would be encouraged to offer their wisdom and accumulated expertise to the nation et al., *pro bono*.

Partially as a result of the justifiable bonding and personal associations that occurred during the upheavals that fall of 2010, a few folks continued their altruistic public service. Foremost among these was former Senator Joe Montgomery, who ran for president in 2012 against the incumbent ECATS, winning in a landslide, capturing a modern-day record plurality of 63% of the popular vote. The plank was a thoughtful return to the fundamental concepts of honor, character and what's best for the country.

Ernie Maltman, the now-graying former Navy fighter pilot, followed his boss to the White House as his chief of staff, a cleansing long overdue, the results positive.

Admiral Stan Sarodsy was promoted to full admiral in command of all military forces in the Pacific following the ISI confrontation. He, in turn, requested that Rear Admiral Nancy Chandler be assigned as the defense attaché to China with a promotion to the rank of Vice Admiral. In 2012, however, he was tapped by rising star Joe Montgomery to be his vice-presidential candidate, the straight-shooting, no-nonsense talk of the old warrior an agreeable ray of sunshine to an American people in search of a glimmer of political grace.

Given the emergence of China as a true superpower, the next agenda discussions were awaited with great anticipation by the brigade of midshipmen, the ovation resonating throughout the field house. The moderator was no less than the bemedaled Deputy Chief of Staff of the Imperial Chinese Air Force, Lieutenant General Ching Wu, assisted by the equally sharp Colonel Ying Tsunami. They had no notes, spoke without excessive verbiage and totally captivated the midshipmen. The astounding outcome of the combined strike plans spoke for themselves, the Chinese Imperial Air Force having performed brilliantly.

Moonyeen Wong and Vice Admiral Nancy Chandler became fast friends, the former's desires to visit the U.S. attended to personally by her benefactor, the dutiful objections of her traditional husband overridden by common sense and a partially-liberated wife.

With great pride, Wu reminded all that the Chinese-Caspian pipeline had been completed in 2012, China's insatiable quest for oil satisfied for the present, her economy jump-started to a new vibrancy. The cutting-edge, technological and arms capabilities of Chinese industry, both military and industrial, had expanded exponentially and were increasingly sold to the U.S.

China's agreement to honor "no further payments to American political and arms-industry officials" withstood the original trauma, business practiced as in days of old, but not in America.

In the short biography provided to the audience, all knew of Lieutenant General Ching Wu's promotion. Not in the bio, but well-accepted scuttlebutt, was Wu's close relationship with the striking Navy admiral. That the admiral outranked him seemed to have made not a scintilla of difference to the chemistry.

Lieutenant Evelyn Swagger became Rear Admiral Nancy Chandler's personal aide shortly following the hostilities of Strike Plan 67-10, and was awarded the Silver Star medal for heroism under hostile fire as the wizo for Lieutenant Commander Dave Anderson on six back-to-back combat missions in that traumatic fall of 2010. As admirals sometimes do, when Chandler was promoted and assigned as the defense attaché to China, Swagger followed, her promotion to lieutenant commander ahead of her contemporaries. Professional duties aside, Evelyn Swagger succumbed to the torrid advances of her savior and suitor, Lieutenant Colonel Ying Tsunami. Predictably, the two were married in 2012, a bonding of some interest in the two countries. The honeymoon was a hiking trip to the rugged mountains abutting the southern regions of Pakistan and Iran, and a few days and nights to themselves, pieces of scattered aircraft wreckage reminders of emotions past. When Chandler's tour of duty was completed in 2013, the new Mrs. Ying Tsunami was assigned to the Navy Pentagon staff, while her husband continued his studies as a student at the prestigious National War College and lectured on the imperatives of combat readiness to his alma mater on the banks of the nearby Severn River.

As the subject of nuclear weapons came to the fore, the audience was quiet, the subject almost too hot to handle in an open forum. The President, however, called the shots and felt the lessons learned outweighed the downsides. Taking the podium for the short discussion, was the grizzled Captain Sam Banaro. He reminded all that it was the incredible breakthrough by the "Missing Jewels" group within the Pentagon that cleared the logjam of the missing nuclear weapons. Without embellishment, the snare of delusion and deceit at the highest levels of government was impassively recalled, the complex web within the Redman Institute laid bare.

The proud sailor, Lieutenant Commander Stan Miller,

though contrite, was led away from his final ship in leg-irons and handcuffs to face a general court-martial and life in the federal penitentiary without parole. Fortuitously, his considerable ill-gotten wealth migrated to those in need. At his trial following the divorce from his long-neglected and unknowing wife, Dolores, he was attended to by his lady-in-waiting, Angela Batori, who, true to her character, blamed factors other than greed as the cause of her lover's demise.

The four weapons of hyper-mass-destruction nesting in the still-secret confines of the Chinese Air Force base in the Iranian desert astride the meandering pipe line, were quietly destroyed in accordance with a covert agreement. Captain Sam Banaro and Colonel Ying Tsunami were the witnesses for posterity.

Following each set of briefings in the vast Naval Academy field house, a dialogue ensued by those who had a role in the outcomes, the audience engrossed and attentive. Finally, it was the turn of the Red Rippers in the saga of unfolding intrigue and real-life drama, led, of course, by the squadron's former commanding officer during those traumatic days, Captain Wendy Montrose. Those in the know, could hear an irreverent chant from the corners of the vast gathering, along the lines of "Iron lady — Iron lady — Iron Lady." Montrose smiled.

After the brief ready room drama witnessed only by Dr. Rose Johnson and Ensign Patty Butts, Lieutenant Commander Lori Miller, the onetime maintenance officer of the Red Rippers, was never seen again, her mysterious disappearance at sea presumed to have been linked with cowardice in the face of the enemy. The mood of the audience was reflected in a scattering of applause from those present, a few not understanding the connection.

Lieutenant (junior grade) Nancy "Shorts" Flanagan perished in the back seat of Lieutenant Mike Anthony's jet en route back to the ship from her fourth combat flight in thirty-six hours, the cause of death attributed to a massive loss of blood incident to an earlier medical problem. Her grieving parents were proud to have received the Distinguished Flying Cross, presented posthumously by a grateful nation.

On his final combat flight, his fifth in forty-three hours, Lieutenant Mike Anthony, the proud FedEx pilot, husband of his vaporized wife and father of two youngsters, hit the ramp of the Reagan upon a landing approach in his F-27C stealth Phantom III at night, in low-visibility conditions, and with little fuel. The flaming ball of fire and flesh, though but a speck among the swirling plethora of events, reminded some of the sacrifices expected of the citizen soldier.

Captain Montrose paused, turned her back to the dais, and wiped a tear from her face. The lump in her throat, though, stuck for the remainder of her presentation.

Lieutenant Patty Butts was known more appropriately these days as Mrs. Patty Butts Jacobs, having tied the knot with her former next-door neighbor in paradise, Lieutenant Scott "Twidget" Jacobs. The best man was Lieutenant Panky Pachino and Lieutenant Becky "Big Sister" Turner, the maid of honor. Few eyes were dry, the symbology deep.

Regaining her demeanor and smile, and without embellishment, Montrose recalled that the real maintenance officer of the Red Rippers, Master Chief Randy McCormick, was summoned more and more on the long voyage home to her office and stateroom. Appropriately, shortly after arrival in Norfolk, McCormick successfully annulled his marriage to the specious Suzette and focused his latent drive first on the hard-driving former Red Ripper commanding officer and then, following his retirement from active duty, as a leadership instructor in the National Academy, his boss, the Reagan's former skipper.

Wendy "Iron Lady" Montrose left the Rippers on schedule, her tour of duty complete, was promoted early to captain, married Randy McCormick, became a proactive opponent of women in combat and was seldom known as Iron Lady. Maid of honor at the well-attended wedding was Master Chief Mitsi Moore, the best man, Commander Dave Anderson.

At the wreath-laying ceremony on board the Reagan off the Virginia Capes late in December of 2010, Lieutenant Panky

Pachino was assigned escort duties to the parents and sister of his lost love, Ensign Karen Randolph. Within months, the older sister, a clone of her sibling, became Mrs. Panky Pachino.

Lieutenant Commander Dave Anderson remained with the Red Rippers, one of only a handful in the entire forty-eight-hour campaign to receive the nation's second highest award for valor in combat, the Navy Cross, and went directly to command of the squadron, relieving his former skipper in the process. He and his wife renewed their vows of marriage, the transgressions of past years, forgiven. Unbeknown to anyone, he had met with his old Blue Angel friend, the tenacious suitor of his wife and author of foul letters to his squadron mate, Becky Turner, and proceeded to quietly and permanently rearrange the facial features of the former naval aviator and airline pilot. Following his squadron command tour, he, Sandy and their two little ones returned to Pensacola, friendly locals welcoming the new leader of the Blue Angels and his hometown wife.

Lieutenant Becky "Big Sister" Turner performed gallantly in strike plan 67-10, flying six combat sorties in the forty-eight-hour period and was a deserving recipient of the Silver Star award for heroism above and beyond the call of duty. Promoted early to lieutenant commander, she became an instructor pilot in the shore-based stealth training squadron, only to be relocated a year later as only the third female pilot to become a member of the prestigious U.S. Navy Flight Demonstration Squadron, the Blue Angels. In 2014, she was starting her second year with the team, living with her family next door to the Andersons in the Marcus Point neighborhood of Pensacola, the regimen of duty away from home unrelenting.

Noticeable by his absence was Turner's back-seater, Lieutenant Commander Scott "Twidget" Jacobs, also the recipient of the Silver Star, who was, at the moment, serving in the familiar waters of the Indian Ocean as the Operations Officer of the VF-143 Barking Dogs, flying the latest stealth variant aboard the USS *Ronald Reagan* (CVN-76).

The former Red Ripper skipper took the occasion to flash on the giant screens the Red Ripper logo, a few in the vast field house standing in respect. As most were aware, the boar's head insignia of the Red Rippers survived another four years despite the continued attempts of former skipper Montrose to cast it overboard. The toast, at the squadron's 87th year reunion continued to be, "Here's to the Red Rippers, a bunch of pig-headed, gin-drinking, baloney-slinging, two-balled, he-men bastards," clear testimony to warriors, the will to win and meaningful tradition. Her glass held high, the toast was led with gusto by Montrose.

A highlight of the conference, the photo on enormous screens for all to see, was the close-up image of the smiling, confidant and unshaven face of Major Ying Tsunami surrounded by his F-48 Dynasty stealth fighter, staring in wonder at his photographer. Not to be outdone, Tsunami produced an equally revealing photo, never before seen, of the beautiful, helmeted face of his wife, ensconced securely in the back seat of her F-27C stealth Phantom III, her look sultry and provocative. The repartee, of course, had taken place in a forlorn piece of Indian Ocean sky four years earlier, the reminisces by the Chinese fighter pilot of the happy hour that followed bringing howls of laughter from the midshipmen, a fake frown from his new wife, a smile from Captain Montrose, a knowing grin from Big Sister and a nod of approval from the old sea dog, Bruce Demming. Colonel Tsunami had then, deliberately, circled the table, the audience hushed, gently pulled his bride from her seat and, in a most un-officer-like manner, kissed her soundly. His unexpected actions and her willing response brought forth a crescendo of approval, the rafters of the field house raised to new limits. Even John Paul Jones took heed from his nearby grave beneath the Academy Chapel.

Some thought that the subject of the hometown folks left behind would have been somewhat mundane compared with the imposing issues preceding. But, when Beverly Demming Boone took to the podium, along with Sandy Anderson, the entire brigade of midshipmen stood spontaneously, the applause deafening.

Smiling, Beverly started with her dad, the indestructible, retired Vice Admiral Bruce Demming. Having done his duty for his friend, now the nation's vice president, he regained his well-worn leather chair in the comfortable Virginia Beach home. In the interim, he had managed to contribute yet again to his nation as the leader of a presidential commission with the objective of bringing some semblance of balance to the exportation of arms and technology. His real *cause célèbre* though, had to do with the loss of his younger daughter Susan to the deadly Super Pelican missile attack four years ago. This had reignited his moral indignation at the absurdity of women, particularly young mothers, being placed in the line of hostile fire. On a lighter note, he had, in his "last" speech at the 87th Red Ripper reunion, regaled the younger warriors with tales of helicopter crashes in far-off mountains, front-seat flights in the latest Chinese stealth variant, a surprise visit to an aircraft carrier named Reagan and ending, appropriately, with a rousing toast to the Red Rippers, past and present, even Iron Lady raising her glass to that of her new husband. One eye of the pig's head randomly checked for compliance.

Beverly took pains to note that her life style had changed little. Her sister's kids joined the Somerset Lane home, hardly skipping a beat, too young to grasp the meaning of no mother or father. Her husband's sudden retirement from the Navy the day he completed his three-year command tour of the Reagan came as no surprise to the blue-and-gold wife of eighteen years. Symbolic of her lot, she was selected for the prestigious Flatley Award as the Navy spouse of the year, having contributed so much to her family, shipmates and community. As the wife of the headmaster of the avant-guarde and well-endowed National Academy nearby, her role of nurturing, tending and providing hardly skipped a beat.

The Boone's next-door neighbor, Bill Montrose, married the enormously wealthy Dolores Miller, cleared in her own right of wrongdoing in the case of her former husband's misdeeds. Part of the stipulation to relieve her of blame had been her guarantee to return all but the seed money for her academy and divest herself of the Whitewater mansion. Her husband became the business administrator of the school at a modest level of compensation. Best man at the simple wedding in the nearby Congressional

448

church was Bill's new civilian boss, Tommy Boone, the maid of honor, Beverly Boone.

Not understanding the hoopla, Beverly and Sandy regained their places at the dais, the brigade once again erupting into a foot-stomping, sustained applause, the importance of stability on the home front being an imperative understood by most in the profession of arms.

Dr. Rose Johnson then stood, pleasing in her reserve Lieutenant Commander uniform, at her side a bulging journal, the contents not for public discourse or dissemination. It had, of course, created a sensation at the congressional hearings in 2011 under the leadership of then-Senator Joe Montgomery. The hearings had been open, fair, probing and balanced, the agenda seeking only to ascertain the impact on combat readiness of past gender policies. Most of the conferees had agreed that the 1994 laws allowing women into combat positions had experienced a rocky genesis and that the results had been spotty. The dam had broken, though, in 2004 with the passage of laws, supported by the high court, that all combat units were required to be personed with an equal number of men and women, the so-called "Gender Parity Law."

The realities and experiences of fifteen years worth of women in the traditionally-male bastions of deck plates, foxholes and cockpits had exploded onto the sensibilities of the American people following the horror of the Super Pelican attack on the Reagan and the significant losses of strike plan 67-10. Intuitively, most middle-of-the-road folks knew that the feelings of young men and women pressed shoulder-to-shoulder for long periods at sea, react predictably. The results, documented in several hundred cases within Rose's imposing medical volume, were a reduction in the ability of the ship or squadron to fight and win the war at sea.

Among some one-hundred witnesses called to the stand then was Dr. Rose Johnson, her thick medical journal — "The Confluence of Young Men and Women Within the Confines of a Warship Deployed for Extended Periods" — at her side. Chock full of well-documented case studies, it graphically portrayed the

449

face of life aboard a warship and the complex interactions of the mostly young crew under stressful conditions. Her well-publicized bottom lines, derived from hundreds of situations within and about the Reagan battle group over almost ten months, lent credence to the conclusions that men and women cannot objectively handle the around-the-clock, seven-day-per week, months-on-end regimen of a warship constantly at sea, exceptional leadership notwithstanding.

Surprisingly, though she had distinguished herself in tough combat and was herself the recipient of the Navy Cross for extreme valor, had been the arguments of the former Red Ripper skipper, Captain Wendy Montrose. Speaking from a measure of personal experience, she had argued that temptation on the deckplates was incontrovertible. Her amplifying comments in the context of the Naval Academy setting seemed superfluous as she traded affectionate looks across the table with her retired master chief husband, the implications crystal-clear to most.

In spite of those sideline pundits arguing that pregnancy was a non-issue, those who had experience in the foxholes and deck plates persuasively countered with thousands of examples to the contrary. Rose Johnson wisely chose not to embellish, but simply let the facts speak for themselves.

Several psychologists of great repute and moderation had buttressed the consistent findings of Dr. Johnson, that stress and fear were catalysts in the attraction for both men and women, the men seeking to protect, the women willingly acquiescing to the comfort and nurturing in the process.

Consistent throughout the 2011 congressional hearings, and reaffirmed at the conference, was the notion that heroism and contributions to combat readiness were mutually exclusive of gender, Becky Turner, Karen Randolph, Nancy Flanagan, Patty Butts, Wendy Montrose, Susan Anthony and Rose Johnson — along with hundreds of others — obvious by their bravery and extraordinary contributions.

Related issues on the home front, though not as overt and not the subject of a medical journal, were articulated by Beverly Boone, Sandy Anderson reluctantly at her side. The two women adequately summarized the social issues from the Virginia Beach perspective, the raucous party of the Barking Dogs adding grist to the mix, next-door neighbors left unsaid.

Though not to the liking of all, the law of the land was changed at the near-unanimous agreement of a broad slice of the American psyche to prohibit women from clear combat roles, including any warship of the U.S. Navy. Hastily brought to a legal head by a consortium of strident women's groups, including the indefatigable DACOWITS organization, the Supreme Court had dismissed the suit with a one-line, unanimous decision reading simply, "Dismissed with prejudice." Interestingly, the star witnesses before the high court included Admiral Carolyn Sweeney, Admiral Stan Sarodsy, Captain Wendy Montrose, Dr. Rose Johnson, retired Commander Angela Batori, Vice Admiral Nancy Chandler, Lieutenant Commander Evelyn Swagger Tsunami, retired Master Chief Mitsi Moore, Vice Admiral Sharon McCluskey and Lieutenant Patty Butts.

The conference closed on a breezy, ice-cold Annapolis Sunday in the Chapel of the United States Naval Academy, the towering stained-glass windows orchestrating a two-century litany of honor, duty and sacrifice on the deck plates and cockpits. The message was delivered to an audience throughout the land by President Joe Montgomery, flanked by a few of those who found themselves at the confluence of momentous events back in that troubled November of 2010. As was his style, the President's remarks were focused, without notes and devoid of extraneous embellishment:

"Admiral Chandler, midshipmen of the Naval Academy, ladies and gentlemen, my friends across our great land. Thank you for the opportunity to lend my personal thoughts to the stormy events of recent years in our body politic and sense of national decency.

Four years ago, our nation came to a crossroads of a national destiny. The well-worn path ahead led to more of the same greed and self-indulgence, notions of character which had, sadly, in many quarters, become the norm. There were, thankfully, many notable exceptions, a few of whom are with us today. Those who cannot be with us, paid the ultimate price, a sacrifice that no person can overturn.

Political allegiances aside, the American people opted for a drastic course-correction, the road to honor, duty and country a clear and convincing choice. Service over greed; honor over wealth. Wisely, those in the collective leadership opted for a mandate of decency, strength of character and fundamental moral values."

The President smiled and paused, taking a full minute to catch the eyes of a few random Americans seated in the towering chapel and the HDTV cameras beaming the message to world-wide millions, and began the end to his simple message:

"I commend to you, here in this impressive Chapel, the thoughts so long ago of one of my predecessors during the heyday of the Cold War, 'Ask not what your country can do for you, but rather, what you can do for your country.' "